REFLEXIVE
ACTION

A novel by
D. R. Evans

Author's Introduction

Reflexive Action, my first full-length novel, was written and set in 1990. Re-reading it now, sixteen years later, it is quite astonishing to see the extent to which technology has impacted our lives in the intervening years. In these pages you will see no mention of mobile phones (which existed in 1990, but were unwieldy, expensive and of strictly limited use) or the World Wide Web (whose birth occurred in 1990, although at the time no one could have predicted its impact) — technological advances that would doubtless have had considerable impact on the plot of *Reflexive Action*.

Conversely, the novel's descriptions of computer technology, which were necessary at the time, now seem hopelessly antiquated. The wiretapping technologies mentioned in the chapters on the National Security Agency and the Government Communications Headquarters are similarly outdated — advances in eavesdropping capability have more than matched the greatly expanded communications that now pervade our lives.

While technological advances may have relegated the details of the plot to historical rather than current interest, they have made possible something for which every author longs: control over the design of even the minutiæ of the finished product. Few authors are able to exert more than token influence on the look of the book they have written. Too often, publishers have committed any number of sins in the interest of pushing a book out the door as quickly as possible, regardless of howls of protest from the author. And while there have been many good publishers, there have also been far too many willing to plaster an irrelevant cover on a book, to provide barely-recognizable back-cover blurb, or to typeset a novel so poorly that the presentation detracts from the story (a sin usually compounded by the use of an awful ligature-free typeface that sacrifices beauty and readability for *soi-disant* modernity).

So here for the first time is an edition of *Reflexive Action* that closely approximates the look that I always intended. For those, like me, with a love of beautiful typography, the details can be found in a colophon at the end of the book. And for those who don't care, I will waste no more of your time, except to say that I hope you enjoy the book.

D. R. Evans,
Boulder, Colorado,
June, 2006.

Contact information for the author can be found at:
   http://www.sff.net/people/N7DR.
The same site contains any number of tedious details about the process of producing the book you are now reading.

Chapter 1
Friday, August 17
Denver, Colorado

George Harris killed people for a living, and he was in Denver on business.

He halted on the sidewalk in front of the skyscraper and studied it for a full half minute, rubbing his chin thoughtfully. The building was set apart from the city's other tall buildings: the banks, the downtown lawyers' offices, the savings and loans; and stood in splendid superiority in a neighborhood of three- and four-storey structures, like an adult surrounded by a gaggle of children.

Above the paired revolving doors, the words "The Denver Cotterell Building" and the insignia of Cotterell Industries left no room for doubt about the building's owner.

Starting at ground level, Harris's eyes followed the lines of the building, up, past the dark glass and silvery steel until, his head craned back, he was looking at the thirtieth floor and, beyond that, at the cloudless sky of the Colorado summer day. The temperature was already uncomfortably warm despite the early hour, the forecast for another day in the nineties.

Harris wore a well cut, lightweight business suit. In his right hand he carried a leather attaché case; his left hand gently stroked his chin. Around him scurried lawyers and

1

bureaucrats, receptionists and businessmen, middle managers and accountants, the small people who were the life blood of the city.

Somewhere up there, on the thirtieth floor, was Vincent Cotterell, one of the richest men in America and the reason Harris was in Denver. Momentarily oblivious to the crowd around him, Harris's mind skipped forward to their meeting, wondering how it would end.

Someone jostled him.

"Sorry," a heavyset man apologized over his shoulder as he hurried toward the revolving door and disappeared into the building.

His train of thought interrupted, Harris walked forward, blending with the crowd, one more businessman about to start the last workday of the week. As he entered the building he glanced at his wristwatch. 8:26. The appointment was for 8:30.

A crowd of workers stood in the elevator bay, waiting for the next car. Harris attached himself unobtrusively to them. Around him the talk was of the Denver Broncos and their chances in the upcoming season. No one paid him any attention.

An elevator car arrived, the doors opened, and the crowd heaved forward. He was swept inside, the last person in. He stood facing the rear of the car, unable to turn around in the squeeze of bodies. Buttons were pressed, and the elevator began to rise fitfully up the building, disgorging its passengers in ones and twos.

The highest number on the buttons was 29. Harris waited until the last remaining person in the car, a petite blonde who ignored him with studied unconcern, got out with a coy smile at the 25th floor. As the doors closed, he pressed the button for the 29th floor.

Stepping out of the elevator, he found himself in a boxy, blocked-off corridor, about thirty feet by ten. A window ran the entire width of the corridor at one end, flooding it with daylight. At the opposite end there was nothing but a blank wall. Along the third wall, behind him, were arrayed the five elevators that serviced the building. The middle set of doors, out of which he had just stepped, were already closing. In the fourth wall, immediately in front of him, was a single pair of double doors and, to their right, a button marked "CALL." From a corner of the ceiling near the window, a video camera looked down on the corridor.

A speaker next to the camera squawked, "State your name and business." The voice was male and authoritative, used to giving orders.

"George Harris. Here to see Mr. Cotterell."

There was a moment's pause, then the voice commanded, "Call the elevator and come up, Mr. Harris."

He pressed the button, and the elevator doors opened.

This car was luxuriously carpeted on floor and walls. A limited edition print hung on one wall. The light from a panel in the ceiling was pearly and diffuse. From one corner of the car, in the angle between walls and ceiling, the lens of a video camera looked down. Beside the elevator doors was a single button, marked "29/30." He pressed it, the doors soundlessly closed, and the elevator rose smoothly to the highest floor in the building. The time was 8:29.

The doors opened, and Harris stepped out.

There were three burly men in security uniforms: two stood in front of him, blocking his way, the third sat at a table nearby. In the last man's hand was a gun, pointing directly at Harris.

"Your attaché case, please, Mr. Harris," one of them said.

Harris wordlessly handed over the case.

"And if you would lean against the wall and spread your legs."

Harris shrugged, then did as he had been told.

Hands rested heavily against his shoulders, then moved quickly down his body. The search, for all the importance that was placed on it, was perfunctory. The men would have found a gun, had Harris been carrying one, but the garrote wrapped around his right ankle under his sock went undetected. The men might be big, but they weren't very smart.

The hands retreated and he was free to turn around.

He was standing in a small hallway similar to the one on the floor below, except that here the window was smaller and there was no wall blocking off the corridor.

Harris held out his hand for his case.

"Open it," said the guard who was holding it. "Slowly."

Harris looked at the man, evaluating him. He lowered his hand without taking the case.

"No."

"Then the case stays here. Nothing gets taken into Mr. Cotterell's presence unless we've made sure it's safe."

"Fine. Keep it until I come out." He glanced at his wrist. "Now, I have an appointment, and you've made me late. I suggest you take me to Mr. Cotterell without delay."

The guard with the gun holstered the weapon and smiled not-too-convincingly.

"Sorry about that, sir. I hope you understand it's nothing personal. Mr. Cotterell is concerned about his security." Hardly waiting for Harris's non-committal grunt, he continued, "If you'll follow me, sir, I'll take you to Mr. Cotterell now."

The guard led the way down the corridor with Harris following close behind.

They walked quickly down a wide, luxuriously carpeted corridor, passing several offices, many of whose doors were open, permitting Harris brief glimpses inside. They were spacious and opulent, more like living rooms than offices, with deep piled carpets on the floor and what looked like original oil paintings on the walls. All had occupants, most with a telephone at their ear. The latest estimates put Vincent Cotterell's personal wealth at well over a billion dollars, and the people in these offices were hard at work trying to increase it even further.

They halted at the end of a corridor, in front of an unmarked, closed door. A large reception desk stood at their right, almost filling a wide bay. A youngish woman, less than thirty, and sporting a tan that left Harris with the impression that she must have recently returned from the Caribbean, looked up from the desk.

"Mr. Harris to see Mr. Cotterell," said the guard.

The woman flashed them a white, perfect smile and said, "Go ahead," before returning her attention to the paperwork on her desk.

The guard knocked quietly on the door and a muffled voice invited them to enter. The guard opened the door.

"Mr. Harris, sir."

Harris walked through the open doorway and, despite himself, was momentarily awed at the sight that met his eyes.

It was not the room itself, nor even its occupant, that demanded immediate attention, although in another setting either would have given justifiable pause. It was, rather, the view behind the figure rising from the desk.

For a moment, all that Harris registered was a long line of white-capped, jaggedly profiled mountains over which hung a sky of unsullied blue. The grandeur, the sheer majesty of the sight, took his breath away and it was several moments before he could wrench his attention from the vast window that comprised the entirety of the far wall and concentrate instead on his immediate vicinity, on the man now standing and offering his hand over the enormous mahogany desk.

As Harris moved forward to greet Vincent Cotterell, he heard the door close quietly behind him as the guard left the room. George Harris, professional assassin, was alone with one of the wealthiest men in America.

Vincent Cotterell was unnervingly like his photographs: fiftyish, dignified, a full head of gray hair, his face broken by a wide smile of greeting; he looked disarmingly like an actor chosen to portray a successful businessman in a Hollywood movie.

Cotterell's greeting was cordial, with no indication that the man he was welcoming was anything other than a successful business colleague.

"Mr. Harris, good of you to come. I have been looking forward to this meeting for some time."

Cotterell leaned across the desk, grasped Harris's hand, and pumped it vigorously.

So this was Vincent Cotterell. He did not look remarkable; but maybe that was the most remarkable thing about him. The gray hair, the firm eyes, the expensive suit, all bespoke the successful American business man at the height of his powers, but none gave any real intimation of the dizzying success that this particular specimen of that breed had attained.

Why would such a man want to engage the services of George Harris? It was a puzzle, and Harris was no nearer knowing the answer than he had been nearly six months earlier, when the first electronic message from Cotterell had appeared in his computer mailbox. But the answer would surely not be long in coming now.

"Good morning, Mr. Cotterell. I'm pleased to meet you at last. And I hope we'll be able to do business together."

"Not much doubt of that, I think. You come highly recommended by a mutual acquaintance."

Harris smiled politely. Behind the smile, he wondered from whom the reference had come. Apparently, Vincent Cotterell, for all his wealth, had friends in low places.

Cotterell gestured towards a chair, and Harris sat. Harris felt the comfortable, familiar constriction of the garotte, and the thought crossed his mind that Cotterell was fortunate that he was in Denver simply to talk to him, not to kill him.

"Before we get started, would you like a coffee or something?"

"If it wouldn't be too much trouble. With caffeine if possible. It's still a little early."

"Certainly. No problem. Stay here and I'll get it myself. Feel free to look around." Cotterell swept his arm around to encompass the room, and then moved towards the door by which Harris had entered. He turned and added, "Leave the desk and the folder alone."

Leaving no time for a response, he left the room, closing the door behind him.

Harris sat motionless for several seconds. His gaze wandered over the room, looking for the cameras. He found them, four in all, one in each corner, nestled in the orthogonal shadowed crooks between walls and ceiling. He stood and began casually to stroll around the room, his hands in his pockets, his eyes moving every few seconds to Cotterell's desk, in the center of which was a closed manila folder.

He craned his neck to try to read the handwritten label on the tab of the folder. "Catherine Kent," he read. That was all. He wondered who Ms. Kent was, and whether he would shortly be taking a professional interest in her.

He refrained from touching the folder. A man in Cotterell's position did not personally fetch another man's coffee for no reason; Harris had little doubt that at this moment Cotterell was standing in front of a bank of television monitors, watching his every move.

As he turned away from the desk, he had to will himself to concentrate on the room instead of the view. He noticed that the desk was so placed that anyone using it would have his back to the distraction represented by the enormous window that ran along the western side of the room.

He moved around the room slowly, acquiring mental pictures for later transcription into the notebook that was locked inside his attaché case. The carpet had a luxurious deep beige pile that yielded softly beneath the weight of his feet. The decorations seemed Spartan at first, but then he realized that the sheer size of the office would make them seem so whatever furnishings were present.

One third of the office was cozy and almost intimate, made over in a passable imitation of a comfortable suburban living room, with a pair of coffee tables, easy chairs and a couch, even a mock fireplace that seemed both incongruous because of the heat of the day outside and pointless because of the controlled climate of the building. In the wall at the end of the office there was a door, which led, presumably, to a private bathroom and possibly to other rooms beyond.

The remaining two thirds of the office was almost bare. Apart from the massive mahogany desk, which had one chair behind it and two in front, there was only a single large table in one corner. On the table was a personal photocopier, a small fax machine and a personal computer.

The walls held four small paintings that looked as if they might be the work of Picasso in one of his more accessible periods. The room had no windows except for the one vast expanse of glass facing the mountains. The remainder of the walls were finished in light oak panels that, along with the beige carpet and wide open window to the west, gave the room a feeling of even greater spaciousness than it might otherwise have had.

Satisfying himself that there was nothing further to hold his interest except the forbidden desk and folder, Harris turned, finally, to look out the window.

The western horizon was formed by the jagged, fractal pattern of the mountains of the continental divide. Harris's view was uninterrupted for perhaps forty miles to the north and ten miles to the south, where mesas hid the more distant mountains. Even though it was August and the temperature in the city would exceed ninety degrees today, there was snow on many of the peaks. Harris found it oddly disconcerting that such extremes of temperature could occur in such proximity.

He found his thoughts wandering as he looked at the mountains, wondering how the early settlers could possibly have found paths through the immense physical barrier as they made their pilgrimages to the promised land of California.

His reverie was broken by the sound of the door opening behind him. Harris turned as Cotterell re-entered the room bearing a tray that supported two elegant china cups and saucers and a coffee pot.

Cotterell apologized: "Sorry to keep you, Mr. Harris. Nice view, isn't it?"

"Magnificent."

Cotterell placed the tray on the desk and poured himself a cup of steaming black coffee. "Help yourself," he said, lifting his cup and saucer and walking around behind the desk, "and have a seat."

Both men settled themselves. As soon as Harris had poured himself a cup of coffee, Cotterell spoke again. "So, to business?"

Harris nodded.

Cotterell looked at Harris for several seconds, apparently weighing what he saw with interest. "So you're a professional killer," he eventually said.

"Not if this is on tape."

Cotterell laughed — a loud, honest laugh of genuine pleasure.

"Quite so. But if we aren't going to trust one another, we aren't going to get very far, are we?"

Without waiting for an answer, he continued, "But of course you're quite right. A tape is being made of this conversation. But you have my word that its contents will be at least as incriminating to me as they will be to you, and its purpose is simply to serve as an internal record of any agreement we might reach.

"Let me put it bluntly: I propose, Mr. Harris, to engage your professional services. By that I mean that I will offer you a sum of money, a substantial sum of money, in return for the deaths of two people whose lives I would very much like to see ended. So, Mr. Harris, how much do you usually charge for your services?"

Harris answered with a question of his own. "You're a very wealthy man, Mr. Cotterell, and you have many men working for you. Why exactly do you need me to perform this service? I'm sure there are many perfectly competent men on your own staff."

Cotterell smiled broadly. "Yes, perhaps so. But then, if anything were to go wrong, there would be an obvious connection between myself and my employee. Besides which, as you will shortly discover, there is — how shall I put it? — a rather delicate aspect to my request. I doubt it will offend your sensibilities. You are, after all, a professional. But I'm afraid that men in my employ might object to the job that I have in mind."

Harris pondered this, wondering what Cotterell had in mind. He returned Cotterell's gaze evenly.

"And so, your charges?" Cotterell repeated. "To save time, I will tell you now that I'll pay anything within reason. I understand that you are worth whatever you cost."

Harris arched his eyebrow at Cotterell's offer of a blank check.

"My terms depend on the nature of the contract," he replied, dropping his eyes to the bright caustic on the surface of his coffee. "After all, I could hardly charge the same for some hobo on the street down there" — he gestured vaguely down towards the street three hundred feet below — "as for the president of the United States, could I?"

He looked up and knew that he had made his point: if he was sufficiently well paid, he was willing to consider any target, no matter how visible or well protected — even the president.

Harris continued, maintaining eye contact with Cotterell as he spoke.

"Typically, my fee would be about one and a half million dollars, but it varies widely depending on circumstances. The fee for any particular job includes my estimated expenses. I don't charge extra if my costs are greater than anticipated. As for my terms, they are very simple: all up front, in cash."

There were several seconds of studied silence. Harris's eyes slipped away from Cotterell's face and he sipped his coffee in silence, then refilled his cup from the pot.

"That's asking a lot, isn't it? It's not the fee, you understand, but what am I supposed to do if you don't fulfill your part of the agreement? I didn't get where I am by making bad investments, you know."

"My terms are non-negotiable, Mr. Cotterell. You may take them or leave them, but they won't change. If you want easier terms, you're talking to the wrong man."

Cotterell laughed and held up his hand. "No, no. I didn't get where I am by accepting second best either. I'm reliably informed that since Kelton retired you have adequately filled his shoes. I have no doubt you're the best man on the planet for the job I have in mind. So, no more quibbling."

He pushed the folder across the desk towards Harris. "There she is, and her daughter too. I think five million should be more than adequate for the two of them, don't you?"

Harris nearly dropped his coffee. His mind began to race, trying to fathom a possible reason for the ridiculous sum Cotterell was offering. Five million dollars would have bought Cotterell the British prime minister or the American vice president. What could possibly justify Cotterell's willingness to part with such a sum in return for the death of two unknowns?

Recovering himself as best he could, although he was aware that his surprise must have been all too visible, he picked up the folder. It was thinner than he would have liked, little more than quarter of an inch thick. He flicked through the papers quickly, more interested in trying to understand why Ms. Kent's demise might be worth so much to Cotterell than in trying to learn very much about the intended target.

There were a couple of photographs clipped to the first sheet of paper. They showed the same smiling face, separated by a period of perhaps a few years. It was not an unattractive face, especially in its more youthful configuration.

The first photograph was black and white, posed, the kind of picture that might accompany a passport application. There was a date penciled on the reverse: March, eight years ago. The second picture was a snapshot, the face slightly

11

blurred, as if the picture had been overenlarged from the negative. It was in color, and taken from the left side. From her expression and the angle of her eyes, the subject evidently did not realize that the photograph was being taken. There was a date on the back of this one too: January, this year.

The woman in the photographs looked pleasant enough, her hair strawberry blonde, her face unblemished, her nose perhaps a little crooked, her teeth not quite straight. She looked guileless. Nice, but nothing special.

Harris skimmed the papers. The first two sheets were filled with biographical data. The only facts that struck Harris on this first, superficial reading were that Mrs. Kent lived in England, she was married to a Mr. Paul Kent, whose name signified no more to Harris than did his wife's, and the daughter that Cotterell had mentioned, Elizabeth Mary Kent by name, was now a few months past her fourth birthday.

There was a photograph of Elizabeth attached to the second page. It was also dated January of the current year, and showed a blurred, nondescript female child. The only other items in the file were a series of about five pages of typescript that provided an assortment of facts about Mrs. Kent, her likes and dislikes, regular movements and suchlike, that Harris did not bother to study on this first reading.

"It's the daughter that's the delicate matter," volunteered Cotterell. "You have to guarantee that both of them will be killed, daughter as well as mother."

"And you thought you might not be able to persuade one of your employees to...." Harris let his voice trail off, leaving the rest of the sentence unsaid.

"Exactly. She is four years old, and has done nothing to deserve her death other than to make a poor choice of parents. Can you accept the contract knowing that?"

Harris closed the file and placed it on the desk. He looked Cotterell directly in the eye.

"Mr. Cotterell, I am neither judge nor jury. I am simply the executioner. I can accept the contract."

He paused for a moment, then asked, "Who is Mrs. Kent? I've never heard of her." He felt like adding, "And why are you willing to pay so much?" but left that question unasked. One thing at a time.

Cotterell replied, "You said yourself that a typical target would cost about a million and a half. So for these two targets, that is, Mrs. Kent and her daughter, maybe two or two and a quarter would be a fair price. The remainder of the money is to buy a couple of other items.

"Firstly, you should understand that the information in that folder is all you're going to get. You are not to go snooping into Mrs. Kent's background. Who she is and why I want the two of them dead are my concerns, not yours.

"I can tell you a little about her, but not much. Mrs. Kent and I were, how shall I say it? ...involved several years ago, not long before she was married, and she has extorted a considerable amount of money from me since then. I am willing to put up with a little blackmail for the sake of a peaceful life, Mr. Harris, but recently the woman has begun to push her luck a little too far, and I'm afraid I can no longer tolerate her threats. You need know no more than that.

"The second reason I'm willing to pay such a high price is that I'm going to dictate, in a small way, the manner in which you will accomplish your assignment." He paused and thought for a moment before continuing. "But before we go into any of that, I must know that you can accept the assignment with these conditions attached."

Harris considered the proposal before him.

He had an uncomfortable, nagging feeling at the back of his mind that he had somehow become engaged in the early stages of an unlooked-for chess game; an instinct was warning him that perhaps it would be a good idea to resign right now rather than risk deeper entanglement.

He submerged the thought as mere fancy and straightened himself in his chair. "Basically, it sounds fine. But before I can give you a definite answer, I need to know *all* the conditions. After all, *I* didn't get where *I* am by having my methods dictated to me."

Cotterell nodded. "OK. That seems fair enough. I don't think you'll find the restrictions I have in mind are too burdensome.

"My first condition is that Mrs. Kent's husband, Paul Kent, is not to be harmed in any way. The second is that the demise of his family members is to appear to everybody, including and especially Mr. Kent, to be accidental. That's all. Apart from those conditions, you're free to go about fulfilling the contract however you wish."

"Then I have some questions."

"Go ahead. If I can answer them, I will."

Harris gathered his thoughts. "The fact that you don't want her husband to be hurt in any way suggests that maybe he's in on this somehow. Is that correct?"

It was an obvious inference, but Harris knew immediately that it was wrong. Cotterell's face flushed and he leaned forward and barked vehemently, "No! No, Kent knows nothing and is to know nothing about any of this. That is one thing you absolutely must understand. You are not to contact Kent. He is to be kept completely in the dark. Understand?"

Harris guessed that he had momentarily glimpsed the real man behind the mask of the successful businessman. He inclined his head and said, "OK. Sounds fine to me. Another question: when you say that Mrs. Kent and her daughter are to meet with an accident, do you mean a natural accident, or merely that their deaths are not to be suspicious in any way?"

"I'm not sure I understand what you mean."

"Let me give you an example. Suppose they were to be killed in a traffic accident. That would ordinarily be taken to be a fairly natural death, and wouldn't warrant detailed investigation by the police or other authorities. But if someone was of a suspicious nature, they might start digging and discover that the accident was not as accidental, so to speak, as it had appeared. So such an arranged mishap has a small but not inconsequential degree of associated risk.

"On the other hand, if, for example, Mrs. Kent and her daughter were to die while shopping in London's West End, by being unfortunately close to an IRA or ILF bomb when it happened to explode, well, that would be quite a different matter. The authorities would vigorously pursue the putative bombers, but no one would think much about the bad luck of the people who happened to have been killed in the blast."

Cotterell nodded thoughtfully as Harris continued.

"You see, the ultimate misdirection in arranged killings is often to ensure that nobody realizes who the intended victim is; and the best way to hide that is to hide one death among several."

Cotterell nodded again. "Yes, I see what you mean."

Harris watched him carefully. It was plain that Cotterell was unmoved by the possibility that other, innocent, parties might be killed along with the intended targets. Harris found himself revising his opinion of Cotterell yet again.

Cotterell continued nodding, his eyes far away, a trace of a smile on his face. "Yes, something along the lines of a bomb would be good, very good indeed."

He refocused on Harris. "That kind of misdirection would be perfect if it could be managed. If there's even a hint that Catherine and Elizabeth Kent met their death by a premeditated act, then things might get very messy indeed."

Harris wondered for whom things might get messy. There were too many gaps and unanswered questions for him to feel comfortable about the job that was on offer. If it weren't for the prospect of five million easy dollars, he would have told Vincent Cotterell exactly what he could do with his contract. Perhaps there would be some clues in the folder; but even if there weren't, with five million dollars in cash up front he could afford to throw some money around trying to dig to the bottom of all this if he had to, Cotterell's warning not to snoop notwithstanding.

"And the final questions," Harris said. "You said that Mrs. Kent has been blackmailing you for some time. Does she have any idea that you're no longer willing to pay? And if so, have you told her what's likely to happen to her now that she's gone too far?"

Harris watched Cotterell closely, trying to catch him out in a lie. When Cotterell's reply came, it was delivered smoothly. The question had obviously been anticipated and the answer, whether a lie or otherwise, slid easily from his lips.

"No. I'm still paying her off, and I'll continue doing so until she has been eliminated."

"OK," Harris nodded, "I understand. Well, perhaps 'understand' is too strong, but I think I know enough, along with what's in this folder, to carry out the job. If you are agreeable, then so am I."

He extended his hand across the desk.

Cotterell accepted with what appeared to be a genuine smile, a grin almost, of delight. They closed the deal with a handshake.

"Fine. Glad to have done business." Cotterell started to rise.

Harris remained seated. There were still some matters to attend to. "A couple of minor logistical details before I leave," he said. "A pen and paper?"

Cotterell supplied them and Harris tore the paper in half across its width. On one half he wrote a thirteen digit number. He passed both halves and the pen across the desk to Cotterell. "That's my account number at the *Banque de Genève*. I will notify them to expect a transfer of five million US dollars into my account within the next seven days."

"OK. Fine."

"And that other piece of paper is for you to write a phone number on. It doesn't have to reach you personally, but I want to know that if I dial that number at any time, day or night, I will be speaking to you in person within sixty minutes."

Cotterell frowned, unsettled at the thought of linking himself so closely to Harris. "That's a little unusual, you know," he temporized. "I'm a man who values his privacy."

"You needn't worry about your privacy. I've never yet had to call a client. But if something unforeseen happens, I may need to contact you quickly."

"I suppose you're right, something might come up. I'll set up a number and get it to you in the next few days; but you can be sure the connection will be dissolved as soon as you've done your job."

"That's fine. I won't need it then. Just send the number to my computer mailbox. Oh, and one last thing: what sort of time frame are we talking about for the job?"

Cotterell thought for a moment. "Let's see, it's mid August now. Let's say by the end of the year. Is that reasonable?"

"Sure, fine by me." Harris smiled. He had been half afraid that an impossible timetable was going to be forced on him. On the contrary, four and a half months was almost an eternity.

Both men stood. On an impulse, Harris asked, "Do you have a rest room around here somewhere? Too much coffee, I'm afraid."

"Certainly, be my guest. Through that door there." Cotterell indicated the door Harris had noted earlier.

"Back in a moment."

Closing the door behind him, Harris found himself in a bathroom suite worthy of a luxury mansion.

A vague fragrance of expensive air freshener hung in the air; the floor was carpeted thickly, the fittings marble and gold; the room contained an oversized combination bath and shower, a toilet and a large sink, above which was affixed an oak medicine cabinet. He opened the cabinet, exposing a meager selection of common pharmaceuticals: NyQuil, a small bottle of Extra Strength Tylenol, Pepto-Bismol, Preparation H. All but the last were unopened. He silently closed the cabinet.

There was a door in the far wall. Opening it, he poked his head into the room beyond. Yet another luxurious room, this time a bedroom. Canvases hung on the walls, oil paintings of warm scenes: a forest; a couple of European landscapes; a lonely beach on a desert island. The faint odor of freshener hung in the air here, too.

A large table hugged the wall to his left, its surface empty. An unmade double bed to his right indicated that only one person had slept here last night, presumably Vincent Cotterell himself. A glass, half filled with what looked like orange juice, stood on the bedside table, along with a lamp and a paperback book, the title on the spine too small to be read.

The room had one other obvious feature, an incongruity: a metal door in the far left corner of the opposite wall. The door had a push-bar at waist height, from which Harris inferred that the door led to the fire escape. Harris retreated back into the bathroom, walked over to the toilet bowl, and flushed it. After washing and drying his hands, he made his way back into Vincent Cotterell's office.

Cotterell handed Harris the folder, and together they walked in silence to the elevator.

The three guards were still there, all seated now, but at the sight of Cotterell they rose hurriedly to their feet, looking suitably subservient.

One of the guards handed Harris his case. Cotterell and Harris shook hands one last time, then Cotterell turned and strode away while a guard called the elevator for Harris.

A minute later on the twenty ninth floor, Harris slipped the Kent folder into his attaché case while he waited for one of the main building elevators to arrive. He glanced at his watch. Nine o'clock. Five million dollars in half an hour. Not a bad start to the day. Now, where might he be able to dig up something about Mrs. Kent?

Arriving on the first floor, he stopped at the information desk to ask directions to the public library. Perhaps Mrs. Kent had once made the papers.

Harris settled into the plush comfort of the plane's first class seat. The business suit of the day before was gone. In its place he was wearing a short-sleeved shirt, jeans and inexpensive sneakers. His attire had earned him disapproving frowns from several of the businessmen who shared the first class compartment. He studiously ignored them. He was worth a lot more than they would ever be.

"Newspaper, sir?"

Harris accepted a copy of the day's *Washington Post*, and unfolded it to look at the front page. The twin headlines were inconsequential foreign stories, but in the lower right corner of the page was a small box headlined: *Cotterell makes bid for PlanetAir*. While Harris had been wasting yesterday at the library, Vincent Cotterell had been making overtures to expand his empire in a new direction.

The thought of the wasted day caused his brow to wrinkle in annoyance. After skimming the article about Cotterell, he put the paper down and extracted from his attaché case the Catherine Kent folder, a pencil, and a writing pad.

He had spent yesterday in the library, reading articles and columns about Vincent Cotterell and his dead brother, Carl.

It was Carl who had originated the empire that had become Cotterell Industries. But whereas no one seemed to doubt that Vincent Cotterell was an entirely legitimate businessman, the name of his older brother had been linked countless times to dealings that were at best suspect and at worse illegal. Twice, Carl Cotterell had been arrested and tried before a jury for racketeering. Twice, Carl Cotterell had walked away a free man. But he had not been able to walk away from the bullet that had ended his life five years ago, thrusting his younger brother into control of the empire he had created.

All of which was interesting background on his client, but was not what Harris had been looking for. After five hours of

19

fruitless searching, Harris had given up. The name of Catherine Warner (as she was before she became Mrs. Kent, according to the file) had never appeared in association with either of the Cotterell brothers.

Neither had either of them ever visited England, where Catherine Kent had lived her entire life.

He jotted in the notebook in an angular, vertical script: "Find out about VC and Kent. *Who is Kent?*" He glanced up at the ceiling for a moment, then added a third note: "WSJ — VC — PlanetAir" to remind him to pick up a copy of the *Wall Street Journal* on Monday to see what that paper had to say about Cotterell's attempted acquisition.

As he placed the notebook on the empty seat beside him, he closed his eyes in thought and pondered for some time the enigma that was Vincent Cotterell. Once he had been little more than a playboy. Now he was one of the most successful businessmen in America. And all because of an assassin's bullet.

The plane taxied to the end of the runway while Harris was thinking. Now the motors roared and the plane raced down the runway and took off. Harris opened his eyes and looked vacantly at the distant mountainous horizon.

After a while, he picked up the folder and opened it. Placing his pencil in his mouth, he furrowed his brow, and began to read yet again what the file had to say about Mrs. Catherine Kent.

Chapter 2
Saturday, September 29
New York

On the fifty-second floor of Cotterell Tower, Vincent Cotterell was in conference with half a dozen attorneys, going over the paperwork for his latest acquisition. In the basement of the same building, in a large, untidy office with an unmarked door, a massive man leaned far back in his chair, his feet planted firmly on the paper strewn surface of his desk while he read *Soldier of Fortune*. Victor Brezhnerov, head of personal security to Vincent Cotterell, was on the job.

The telephone rang.

Marking his place with a six-week-old internal memorandum that he had never bothered to read, Brezhnerov placed the magazine on the desk, dropped his feet to the ground, leaned his bulky frame forward, and lifted the telephone.

"Hello," he snapped.

"Ah, yes," said a hesitant voice. "I'd like to speak to Mr. Williams, please."

Brezhnerov was instantly alert, connecting two apparently disparate facts: the man who was calling had a strong English accent, and George Harris had flown to England two days earlier. The coincidence was too great. He glanced down to make sure the tape was turning.

"This is Mr. Williams," Brezhnerov said.

Five minutes later, Victor Brezhnerov knocked and walked into the conference room on the fifty-second floor without waiting for a reply. Cotterell looked up irritably from the paperwork in front of him. The attorneys looked at Brezhnerov speculatively, wondering who he was to have the gall to interrupt their meeting.

"This had better be important," Cotterell said to Brezhnerov, clearly annoyed.

"I have to see you privately, Boss. About the English matter."

"Now?"

"Now, Boss."

"All right, you lot. Out!" He waved the lawyers away.

Scurrying to obey the billionaire's command, they rose as one and left the room.

"Now, Victor, what is it?" Cotterell snapped.

"I just got a phone call from one of my informants in England. Would you like to hear the tape? I brought it up with me."

Cotterell indicated his agreement with a gesture, and Brezhnerov fished in his pocket and withdrew a small dictation machine. Placing it on the table, he rewound the tape, turned up the volume, and set the machine to play.

"Hello," the tape began: Brezhnerov answering the phone.

"Ah, yes. I'd like to speak to Mr. Williams, please."

"This is Mr. Williams."

"Good. This is Henry Halton here."

"I see, Mr. Halton. PC Halton, actually, isn't it?"

"PC stands for Police Constable, Boss," Brezhnerov interpolated. "Basically a beat officer." Cotterell raised an eyebrow but said nothing.

"Yes, sir, that's right. Calling from England."

"Do you have something for me, constable?"

"Yes, sir, I think I do. You said I was to call you if ever anyone came around asking about the Kents. That's right, isn't it, sir?"

22

"That's right."

"Well, sir, I sort of spread the word around here quietly, like you suggested and, well, I got a phone call about an hour ago from the landlord down at *The Surrey*, that's one of the pubs a couple of miles away. He said there was an American sitting in the bar waiting for his dinner. Seems this American is staying the night at the pub — they run a sort of part time bed and breakfast affair on the side — anyway, this American had been asking about the Kents. Said he was interested in buying their house and did anyone know if the Kents might be interested in selling?

"I went over to the pub as fast as I could. I'm not on duty tonight, you see, so that made it nice and easy. Well, sir, the American was still there. I managed to have a little chat with him. Didn't say anything about the Kents of course, didn't want to tip the chap off; but he's certainly an American, and he said that he was over for a day or so, interested in buying some property for his firm so that executives could use it like a sort of home from home while they're over here."

"I see. He didn't happen to tell you what firm he was with, I don't suppose?"

"Matter of fact, he did, sir. Thought you might ask that." The note of pride was evident in PC Halton's voice. "Merrill Lynch, he said."

"Pity it's a real company," interjected Cotterell.

On the tape, Brezhnerov said, "I see. All right, you've done very well, constable. You'll be paid according to our arrangements."

"Thank you, sir. Do I try to keep tabs on him for you?"

"No, I think not. By the way, what's the name of this landlord?"

"George Matthews, sir. The pub's called *The Surrey*; it's down the Kenley Road maybe a couple of miles from Darnley Drive, where the Kents live."

"Phone number?"

"Hang on a minute. Yes, here it is. 0171-685-4327."

"Did you get the name of the American?"

"He'd given it to the landlord's wife. Had to when he signed for his room. 'George Harris' was what it said on the charge slip."

Cotterell's eyebrow lifted again.

"Good. Thank you. Tell me, what did this American look like?"

"Oh, tallish. Mid to late thirties. Wore glasses, quite expensive looking. Dressed casually, but quality clothes. More Harrods than Marks & Spencer if you know what I mean, sir. Seemed like a nice enough sort of bloke, if a bit uncommunicative."

"Thank you, constable. You'll be receiving a check from me shortly as we arranged. Let me know if it doesn't arrive in a couple of weeks."

Brezhnerov switched off the machine. "I've already started enquiries. It shouldn't take long to find out if he's for real."

The intercom beeped, and Cotterell's secretary said, "Telephone call for Mr. Brezhnerov, sir. Says his name is Mr. Merrill Lynch." Her voice was steady, as if she did not recognize the name as an improbable pseudonym.

"Put it through, Glenda."

Brezhnerov lifted the telephone. "Brezhnerov here, Mr. Lynch."

He nodded a couple of times, said "I see" and "yes, thank you," then put the phone down.

He said grimly, "That was a hacker, Boss. He tells me Merrill Lynch has no employee by the name of George Harris anywhere in the world."

"Is the man reliable?"

"He's the best, Boss."

"Right, Victor. I want you on a plane to London within the hour." Cotterell stabbed his finger at the intercom. "Glenda, find out where we have a plane that can reach London nonstop. Check La Guardia first."

"Yes, sir."

"I want a plane to take Mr. Brezhnerov to London as quickly as possible. If we don't have one available that can make the trip without stopping, rent me one or pull one from the PlanetAir fleet. Whatever it takes. I want him there as quickly as possible."

He released the intercom button. Victor Brezhnerov was already on his feet.

Cotterell continued, "I'll have you met at whatever airport you arrive at. You'll be supplied with the necessaries then. Travel clean; we don't want any trouble with immigration or customs."

"All right, Boss. Any specific orders?"

"Yes. Try to scare Harris but don't go out of your way to harm him. I'd still prefer to have him do the job. He's the best man for it, even if he is too curious."

"Don't worry, Boss, I'll handle him with kid gloves."

"Let me know how it turns out. And of course, I don't really need to tell you this, but if Kent so much as dreams there's anything wrong, you're a dead man."

"Yes, Boss. You're absolutely right. You don't need to tell me that."

Ninety minutes later, Brezhnerov was airborne, destination London.

Chapter 3
Sunday, September 30
Surrey

A light drizzle hid most of Surrey in gray fog. From the road, the large house at number 5, Darnley Drive, was visible only as an indistinct, brooding shadow. Inside the house, Paul Kent looked out across the green front lawn as he waited for his wife and daughter to get ready for church.

Kent was approaching his forty-first birthday, but as yet there were no permanent lines on his face except for the hairline scar high on his brow that he habitually hid behind his forward-combed hair. He wore a neatly trimmed beard that, like the hair on his head, showed no trace of gray. He turned as his wife entered the room.

"Aren't you ready yet?" he asked when he saw that she was still coatless and carried Elizabeth's favorite teddy bear in one hand.

There was an uncharacteristic shortness in his voice, and he regretted his abruptness as soon as the words were out of his mouth. Before Catherine had time to reply, he apologized.

"I'm sorry. I know Elizabeth makes it difficult to be on time. Is there anything I can do to help?"

"You can go and start the car. We're almost ready. Now where did I put my handbag?"

Kent crossed the room to his wife and gently took her in his arms, arresting her search for the errant handbag. He kissed her, first on the cheek and then on the lips. "I love you," he said.

Catherine smiled, and then turned as a four-year-old voice called loudly from the hallway, "Mummy, I can't find Mr. Bear."

"I have him, darling. Have you seen my... Oh! Never mind. Here it is." To her husband she said, "You go start the car and we'll be there in a couple of minutes. There won't be much traffic on a day like this. We won't be late."

She hurried from the room, followed by her husband.

A couple of minutes later, Paul Kent backed the blue Mercedes out the garage, and his wife and child got inside. The car turned in the turning space halfway down the drive, and then they were gone.

For a full minute, nothing moved. The only sound was the gentle *drip-drip-drip* of accumulated drizzle falling from the branches of the tall evergreens around the edge of the property. Then a head appeared around the back of the garage.

George Harris began to search for the spare key. There weren't many places to hide it, especially if the kid was supposed to be able to use it.

He found it in eighty seconds flat, under what looked like a forgotten shard of old flowerpot.

The key fitted and turned easily in the lock of the back door.

Harris hesitated for a moment, wondering about the possibility of a burglar alarm. But there was no red warning box on the house's exterior, and Catherine had left the house with the girl instead of staying behind to set an alarm. He decided he was worrying unnecessarily.

He removed the key from the lock, placed it in his pocket, and cautiously entered the house and closed the door behind him.

He was in a kind of utilitarian anteroom with coats hanging on hooks and shoes and wellington boots clustered on the floor. A narrow door stood ajar, leading into the kitchen.

Drying his feet on a doormat, he pushed open the door and went inside.

He made a slow circuit of the house, pausing in every room to take stock of what he saw. There were two storeys. On the lower floor were several good-sized rooms: the kitchen, hallway, dining room and living room, as well as a play room for Elizabeth, a medium-sized study strewn with papers, and two small bathrooms.

Upstairs were two full bathrooms, one obviously used by the parents and one by Elizabeth, bedrooms for the parents and child, two spare bedrooms, and a large box room-cum-library with hundreds of books lining the walls and several piles of boxes filled with miscellaneous junk cluttered in the middle of the floor.

The house was furnished expensively throughout; it was obvious that the Kents were wealthy people. The chairs were deeply upholstered; the drapes next to the windows were heavy and moved silently and easily along their valence rails. The pile on the carpet was deep. The kitchen was modern, with a dishwasher, a garbage disposal and a trash compactor.

George Harris began wonder if he was on a wild goose chase. Perhaps Vincent Cotterell was telling the truth after all. Maybe everything was just as his client had claimed; perhaps it was indeed Cotterell himself who was the unwilling source of the Kents' wealth.

He saw no photographs, except a recent pair on the sideboard in the dining room: one of Elizabeth smiling cherubically, pink cheeks dimpled in a wide smile; and one of the child with her mother, holding hands in a shot that was obviously unposed, the two enjoying a walk together on a beach somewhere on what appeared to be a cool, blustery day, but both smiling at the camera — a mother and daughter at peace with one another and the world. There were no pictures of Mr. Kent.

28

Harris went back downstairs and stood thoughtfully at the foot of the stairs, wondering if he should simply leave. But having come this far, he had to try to find some evidence that would either corroborate or disprove Cotterell's story.

The obvious place to look was the study. He stood in the doorway and looked dubiously at the piles of papers, then set the timer on his watch for thirty minutes. If he found nothing by the end of half an hour, he would move to the Kents' bedroom, give that ten minutes, then ten minutes more in the living room, where an escritoire looked like it might repay inspection. After that it would be time to leave.

The only furniture in the study was an oversized flat-topped desk in the center of the room, a pair of chairs — one drawn up to the desk, one hiding in a corner — two filing cabinets — one green, one gray — a personal photocopier on the floor in one corner plugged into an electric socket, and piles of paper and books scattered around the floor and over the surface of the desk.

He walked to the desk and picked up an open book: volume three of Winston Churchill's *A History of the English Speaking Peoples*. He glanced at the other books. They were all about the Second World War — its causes, the activities of the secret services, detailed histories of actions in the European, North African and Far Eastern theaters; there were biographies of Churchill, Neville Chamberlain, Attlee; colorful picture books of Blenheim Palace.

On the desk stood a typewriter with a sheet of paper in it. It was headed: "Churchill: The Last Years / P. M. Kent." There was a paragraph of prose, something to do with India and partition. Paul Kent was writing a book.

Stepping gingerly around the piles on the floor, Harris moved to the filing cabinets. Both had locks, but neither lock was in use. He pulled open the topmost drawer on the green cabinet, revealing a drawer full of folders.

He flicked through them, reading the tabs: Charterhouse, War Room, Chamberlain, Boer War. Most of the folders were

29

quite thick. They were arranged in no discernible order. He lifted one out at random, the one headed "Boer War." It was filled with photocopies of pages from other books, with red handwritten annotations in the margins.

He replaced the folder in the drawer.

"Ahem."

The intrusion was so quiet, so completely unexpected, that George Harris's mouth dropped slackly as he spun around looking for the source of the sound.

It was not hard to find.

Framed by the doorway was a bulky, muscular man, roughly Harris's own age, who was looking at him with an expression of insolent superiority. In the man's hand was a silenced pistol which was aimed at a point high in Harris's chest.

"Kent!" Harris blurted.

"Mr. Harris, I'm disappointed. Not surprised, I suppose; but still disappointed." After half a week in Britain, the man's American accent came as a surprise to Harris's ears.

A doubt began to form in his mind. How could this be Paul Kent? Kent could not possibly have known his name.

"Who are you? You aren't Paul Kent, are you?" Harris's mind was racing. If this wasn't Kent, then there was no reason why he could not use the cloth-covered length of wire wrapped around his right ankle. No reason, that is, except for the fact that the man's gun had not wavered from his chest.

The man ignored the question.

"Mr. Harris, I'm here to deliver a message from Mr. Cotterell. Mr. Cotterell is concerned that you have broken your side of the agreement. I admit there was never anything on paper, but there was a handshake, and a high quality video tape exists of the entire meeting. I know. I've seen it."

Harris remembered the cameras in the crooks of Cotterell's Denver office. The man continued.

"And as I remember it, that tape shows the two of you agreeing that in anticipation of certain services being performed and certain conditions being met, a considerable sum of money was to be paid into a Swiss numbered account. Tell me, Mr. Harris, has there been some problem? Did the money not arrive?"

"No, the money arrived OK."

The man shook his head in exaggerated puzzlement. "Then I guess I'm confused. The assignment was clear enough, and so were the conditions attached to it. Yet here I find you, making yourself at home in the Kents' house while they are at church, in direct violation of your agreement."

Harris had had enough. It was time to go on the offensive. "Who the hell *is* Catherine Kent, anyway? And for that matter, who the hell are you?"

"Catherine Kent is a nobody whom it is your job to kill. As for me, my name is Victor Brezhnerov and I am in charge of personal security for Mr. Cotterell, who personally sent me here to remind you of your agreement. Now, what am I to tell him? That you've decided to return the money? That your handshake is worthless? That you're sorry and you'll be a good boy and you won't do it again?"

Brezhnerov shook his head as if shocked at the perfidy of the man before him.

"Come on now, what's it to be?"

But before Harris could answer, Brezhnerov glanced at his watch and said abruptly. "We've been here long enough. Time to get moving. Back the way you came; into the kitchen and back to the place where the key was hidden. Don't try anything. I assure you that at this range I won't miss."

They went outside without speaking. Brezhnerov's pistol never wavered from Harris. Five seconds was all it would take for Harris to unwrap the garotte from his ankle and have it ready for use; but it was five seconds that Brezhnerov did not give him. Sullenly, Harris handed over the key and Brezhnerov locked the door and replaced the key under the shard of flowerpot.

Harris turned to look speculatively at his captor. What would happen now? A look of resignation crossed Brezhnerov's face.

"Mr. Harris, much as it would give me great pleasure simply to shoot you, Mr. Cotterell has directed that first I must ask you one question. What I do next depends entirely on your answer."

Brezhnerov paused, drawing out the tension. Harris swallowed.

"If you give your solemn promise that from now on you will simply get on with the job for which you have been paid, Mr. Cotterell has instructed me to inform you that he will forget that this incident ever took place. Personally, I wouldn't give you a second chance, but then, I'm not as kind-hearted as my employer. What do you say, Harris?"

"If I agree to keep away from the Kents, this incident will be forgotten?"

"That's what I said."

"And what if I don't agree?"

Brezhnerov smiled. "In that case Mr. Cotterell says he has no further interest in you. And after I've finished with you, the only person who would have any conceivable interest in you is a coroner."

"Then I don't really have any choice, do I?"

"Not if you want to be alive twenty seconds from now."

"Then you have my word. I will not investigate the Kents any more. I will fulfill my half of the contract as we originally agreed."

Brezhnerov dug in his pocket with his unencumbered hand and held up a small tape recorder. "I will inform Mr. Cotterell of your words. If I were you, I'd stick to them this time. Now, get out of here. I never want to see you again."

George Harris turned and strode quickly away down the driveway, fury on his face. He was more sure than ever that there was something, something important, that Cotterell was not telling him about Catherine Kent. But he would be true to his word. He would kill the Kents — he was not such a fool as to risk five million dollars. But afterwards... afterwards he would embark on a small, unpaid, but particularly gratifying job of his own: he would kill Victor Brezhnerov.

Chapter 4
Thursday, November 15
Surrey

Catherine Kent walked into the living room. Her husband picked up the remote control and turned off the news. The picture died with a barely-audible *pttt*.

He smiled at her and asked solicitously, "All finished, darling?"

"Just a few minutes more. Elizabeth's finally asleep and I thought I'd take a break for a moment before I go back upstairs to finish. Anything on the news?"

"No. Mostly it's about the Irish Liberation Front and *Saoirse Eireann*. Nothing very interesting. Just the usual threats of violence because the government is dragging its feet and the IRA aren't being militant enough."

Catherine shook her head and tut-tutted. "You'd think after all the years of bloodshed they'd be willing to be a bit more patient."

"You might, except that patience isn't usually the hallmark of a liberation army. And I suspect they aren't particularly pleased that the IRA and *Sinn Fein* are hogging all the glory now that peace seems a real possibility. Anyway, we can forget about all the depressing British news. That's one thing about Florida: it helps put Britain and its problems in perspective. It's hard to be glum for long with Disney World just down the road."

"You know, I think Elizabeth's even more excited about the trip this year than she was last year. One more suitcase, then I'll be done."

"I keep telling Elizabeth that since I won't be there, she's going to have to look after you."

"I know. She told me half a dozen times not to worry because she'll be there to look after me. And she says that I'm not to worry about her because Mr. Bear will look after her. Now what are you looking at?"

Kent was in his favorite armchair, his stockinged feet stretched out before him. By his side was a small table on which was the book he had been reading before the late-evening news had diverted him. Next to the book was a glass half filled with white wine. He was regarding his wife with a vaguely benevolent smile.

"Did I ever tell you're beautiful?"

Catherine flushed the way she always did when he paid her a compliment. It had happened the very first time they had met, and she supposed it would happen until she finally became too physically decrepit for there to be any possible truth to his words.

"Every day," she replied.

"If I ever stop saying it, you have my permission to get a new husband."

"Never," she said firmly. She crossed the room and bent to kiss him.

He beat her to it, wrapping his arm around her head and pulling her to him. What she had intended as a simple kiss threatened to turn itself into a passionate embrace. Laughing, she extricated herself. "One more suitcase," she said firmly. "Give me fifteen minutes."

"A drink?" he asked.

"Just one, otherwise I won't sleep."

"Remember when we didn't sleep? And not because of the drink."

"We were young then."

"We're young now."

"You're incorrigible."

"And you're beautiful."

She turned from him, feigning annoyance, and flounced to the door.

"Catherine?" Something in his tone of voice caused her to halt in the doorway. She turned to look at him. "Thank you for saving me," he said.

She frowned.

"I mean it," he said. "Thank you."

"What did I save you from? A life of freedom?"

For a moment he looked much more serious than he usually did when they were bantering. Then he laughed. "No. A life of empty wealth. If I'd never met you, by now I would be fabulously wealthy and incredibly lonely. Thank you for saving me from that."

Catherine shook her head. Sometimes Paul was a mystery, even to her. She turned and left the room, leaving her husband staring at the vacant doorway. He listened to her climbing the stairs and then moving around in their bedroom overhead.

He'd almost told her. He'd almost broken the vow he'd made that very first evening, more than five years ago. He'd promised himself that he'd never tell her, that he must never give her that pain. But wasn't that what love was all about? he asked himself. Sharing pain as well as joy?

He had known it straight away. One look across the dance floor at Ambassador Warner's homecoming ball was enough. He had known in that instant that his life would never be the same again.

He had been holding a drink, chatting amiably with the Egyptian ambassador about the Iranian situation. The dance floor was empty; at one end of the varnished surface the band was tuning up for the evening's entertainment. Finishing the drink, he idly looked up to find a waiter to replenish it and his eyes strayed to the other side of the room.

Ambassador Hussein said something, but Kent didn't hear. "I... I'm sorry," Kent stammered. "I didn't catch that. Would you say it again, please?"

"Ah, you have noticed our host's daughter. She not infrequently has that effect on people."

"She's Ambassador Warner's daughter?" Kent asked incredulously, not taking his eyes off the vision on the far side of the room. She was a large-eyed strawberry blonde, wearing a white dress that curved by just the right amount in exactly the right places. She was laughing at something one of the men gathered around her had just said, and the sound of her laughter carried across the floor to Kent. Kent had never seen anyone so beautiful, nor so free of artifice.

"Yes. One reason for the ball is to introduce her to London society," said the Egyptian ambassador.

"I'm going to marry her," declared Kent, still not taking his eyes off her. As he spoke she chanced to look up, and her eyes met his.

"You're beautiful," he mouthed, and even though they were separated by half the width of the enormous room, he saw her blush with embarrassment.

"Excuse me," he said to his companion without looking. Clutching his empty glass, he headed off across the dance floor.

They spent most of the evening together, and most of the evenings of the week that followed. The following Saturday, they became engaged to be married.

He fabricated a simple and thoroughly believable story to explain his wealth: he'd inherited a small fortune from a father who had owned a small building company in a provincial city. Through astute investments, he had amassed enough money that he need never work again. He was mildly wealthy, if not exactly rich.

Part of the story, at least, was true. Once he'd finished the contract on which he was currently engaged, he'd never work again. Once they were married, he'd never leave her. They would be together forever.

He explained earnestly to her father that his wealth would give him the freedom to be a good husband to Catherine and father for their family. He loved her madly, just as madly as she loved him. Their marriage would be strong and last the rest of their lives....

"Where's that drink?"

He looked up, startled. "Sorry. I was just thinking."

"Don't get up. I'll get it myself now. You want one? Oh, you haven't finished the last one. What were you thinking about?"

"That you changed my life. That I don't deserve you. That I love you very much."

She poured a splash of gin into the bottom a glass, and filled it from a bottle of bitter lemon. "Do you want to drink these here, or shall we go upstairs?"

He picked up his glass and pulled himself out of the chair. "Upstairs sounds nice."

He slid his arm through hers and led her from the room.

Friday, November 16
Surrey

Excitement was in the air. Four-year-old Elizabeth was talking non-stop. Her mother had twice told her to be quiet and eat her Marmite on toast, but Elizabeth simply ignored her and kept on talking and asking questions about the day ahead.

"When do we leave for the airport, Mummy?"

"As soon as you've finished breakfast Daddy will bring the suitcases down."

"Is Daddy taking us to the airport?"

"No, darling; we'll take a cab. Daddy has to go to London this morning. That's why he's not coming with us. Now eat some of that toast."

"I'm not hungry. What's a cab, Mummy?"

Catherine did her best to explain, but before she had finished, her daughter interrupted her. "Daddy will be coming to America soon though, won't he, Mummy? Then he'll be able to look after you, won't he?"

"Yes, dear. He just has to stay for a couple of days. He's flying out to be with us on Sunday."

"Then can we go to Disney World like last year, Mummy? Mr. Bear says he wants to come too. He'll be able to come with us, won't he, Mummy?"

"Yes, dear. Now, please, just one slice. It will be a long time before we eat lunch on the plane."

Fifteen miles to the northeast, the alarm clock went off in George Harris's hotel room.

The clock did not wake Harris, for he was already awake. For the past hour he had been mentally rehearsing the day ahead, trying to spot any mistakes, trying to anticipate and allow for everything that could go wrong. If there was a flaw in his preparations, he could not find it.

Glad that the day had at last begun, he silenced the alarm and headed for the shower.

Ten minutes later, he returned and began to dress, studying himself carefully in the mirror as his assumed persona began to take shape.

He dressed slowly and methodically. When he had finished, he was wearing a pair of faded jeans that sported several dirty streaks, nondescript brown socks, scuffed tennis shoes, a shirt, its collar limp and curling, all topped by a thick, dark sweater.

In the past six weeks he had let his hair grow slightly longer than was completely respectable, and now he carefully mussed the result in the mirror. He wore a simple, inexpensive, wire-framed pair of glasses. Although he had showered, he remained unshaven, and the overhead light cast his chin into a suitably scrubby shadow. He examined his reflection critically, rearranged his hair slightly, then turned away with a nod of satisfaction.

From a suitcase he removed a laptop computer, a couple of lengths of wire, and a set of tools. Unhurriedly, he dismantled the telephone on the bedside table and clipped the wires to the innards of the disemboweled instrument. He turned on the computer.

Five minutes later he turned the computer off with a satisfied grunt and reassembled the telephone. The electronic mail message had confirmed that the reservations for PlanetAir flight 11 from Gatwick to Orlando remained unchanged. Seats 3A and 3B were still reserved in the names of Mrs. C. and Miss E. Kent.

Harris methodically emptied the room of all signs of his presence, dispensing items into one of two cases: the medium sized, teal, hard sided suitcase from which he had withdrawn the computer and to which he now returned it; and a largish, soft sided, canvas carryall. A third bag was on the bed: a blue, zippered, roughly cylindrical sports bag displaying prominently the name and logo of a manufacturer of sports shoes. This bag he did not touch.

When he had finished, he glanced around for stray items, grunted with satisfaction, then hefted the three bags and left the room.

Paul Kent looked first at the pile of suitcases in the hallway, and then at his wife. He smiled encouragingly. Then, deciding that she deserved more than a smile, he bent towards her and they kissed.

"Thank you for last night," he said in a whisper.

"Nice to know we're not too old. But I wish we'd gone to sleep earlier."

"Never mind. You'll manage."

They separated, and Kent glanced up at the wall clock. "I'd better be going," he said. The auction was scheduled to begin at ten, and he wanted to arrive early to be sure of getting a good seat.

"I suppose it is time. You'll give us a call, though, won't you, when you get back this evening?"

"Of course. It won't be until pretty late, though. I thought I might as well make the most of a trip into town and do some Christmas shopping and maybe catch a show this evening."

"OK. Well, I'll switch the answering machine on if I can't stay awake."

Elizabeth entered the room carrying Mr. Bear by one ear. "Mummy, is it time to go yet?"

"Not for a few minutes. Say goodbye to Daddy. As soon as he's gone, I'll ring for a cab."

"Goodbye, Daddy."

Paul Kent knelt on one knee and hugged his daughter. "Now, you look after Mummy for me, won't you?" he asked in a serious tone of voice.

"I will. And Mr. Bear promises to look after me."

"I'm sure he'll be a big help, Elizabeth. And remember that you and Mr. Bear have to do what Mummy tells you."

"Yes, Daddy."

"I'll be with you in a couple of days. Maybe we can go to Disney World early next week."

"Do you think we'll see Mickey again like last year?"

"Yes, dear, I'm sure he'll be there. Bye-bye, darling."

Kent stood up and exchanged a last kiss with his wife. "See you on Sunday."

"Yes, dear. And don't pay too much for that desk."

"It shouldn't cost more than £150,000, even if Henry Parminter is there. Which, of course, he will be. It's the biggest collection to come on the market in the past three years. Henry would leave his death bed if he had to."

"And you would leave your wife," she said, feigning petulance.

Kent looked hurt. Then a smile twitched around the corners of his mouth.

"What's so funny?" Catherine demanded. They both knew that she wasn't angry, not really, but it was bending the rules of the game for her husband to laugh at her simulated anger.

"I was going to say that actually it's my wife who's leaving me. But I thought better of it."

"Good thing too, you brute. It would serve you right if I did leave you after a comment like that. And watch yourself. If you don't ring me tonight I might begin to get suspicious about what you're up to."

He kissed her a really, truly last kiss. And then one more. For the millionth time, he wondered what obscure providence had led him to a wife like Catherine.

"Goodbye, darling," he said. "I'll see you on Sunday."

Two minutes later, Kent eased the Mercedes out the garage and down the drive. With one final wave and a mouthed "You're beautiful and I love you," he pulled out into the road and headed in the direction of the railway station.

Carrying a beige overcoat that had seen better days, George Harris entered the International Departures Lounge of the South Terminal at Gatwick airport. The time was nine thirty.

He carried two pieces of luggage: the canvas carryall and the blue sports bag. The hard sided suitcase had disappeared into the Thames, its rapid disappearance abetted by the two holes that he had drilled in the case.

He looked around, surveying the lounge.

It was large, airy, strangely quiet and sparsely populated, amazingly so for the international departure lounge of a major airport. There was a quiet, calm dignity to the place; no one seemed in a hurry and people moved around with the minimum of fuss. There was a public address system, but it was used only for paging; boarding calls went unannounced, and were displayed instead on banks of television screens hanging from the ceiling.

Scattered around the carpeted floor were blocks of seats, perhaps a quarter of them empty. To Harris's left was the duty free shop; far away to his right was a restaurant. Between where he stood and the restaurant, stairs led down to the rest rooms on the floor below.

He made his way to the men's rest room, where he stepped into a stall and locked the door. Seating himself on the toilet, he opened the two bags.

One, the blue sports bag, was almost completely filled by a single large block of a solid blue-white foam, around which was packed a cushion of towels. In the folds of the towels was hidden a variety of ordinary household objects, designed to give the bag a completely ordinary appearance to the X-ray machines through which it had passed.

From the other bag he extracted an apparently unused canister of film.

Prising the lid off the canister, he revealed a small electronic circuit wedged firmly in place next to the short length of film that was glued to the inner surface of the canister and passed through the slit to the outside.

He fitted the canister to a small terminal attached to the block of foam in the sports bag. A high-pitched tone sounded, then, after three seconds, ceased: the connection was good.

He closed the bags, flushed the toilet and left the stall.

Upstairs, he selected a seat close to the point where passengers entered the room after passing through passport control.

With every appearance of weariness, he dropped heavily on to the seat, stuffing the sports bag under the chair and clutching the carryall to his chest. He leaned back and gazed vacantly toward passport control. Crossing his legs in front of him, he assumed a bored attitude of tired indifference.

He watched, and he waited.

Around him people passed by, taking no notice of the tired, disheveled traveler. He heard snatches of conversation in half a dozen languages, but tuned them all out. Nearly half an hour passed before he felt a sudden surge of adrenaline.

Momentarily, his eyes narrowed, but he gave no other outward sign that he recognized the mother and daughter as they entered the lounge. He glanced at his watch. It was just after ten o'clock. There was about an hour before boarding would begin for PlanetAir 11.

Mrs. Kent carried a large handbag over her left shoulder, and was holding the hand of her four year old daughter, who had a child's backpack strapped to her back.

In the flesh, Mrs. Kent looked younger and much prettier than Harris had expected. She paused only a few steps away, looking around for a pair of empty seats.

She found what she was looking for and began moving towards them. Harris watched the pair carefully, moving in his seat to keep them in view.

They reached the empty seats and sat down. Mrs. Kent opened her daughter's backpack, scrabbled around inside for a few seconds, then withdrew a large teddy bear and a coloring book and crayons, and gave them all to her daughter.

Harris gathered his things and ambled in the general direction of the Kents.

There were no empty seats near them. Harris stopped and leant nonchalantly against one of the columns that supported the ceiling, looking at the pair.

Elizabeth was absorbed in her coloring, the teddy bear on the seat beside her. Mrs. Kent was reading a paperback, oblivious to her surroundings.

Harris's eyes drifted on: a tired, bored traveler passing the time until his flight was called.

Several minutes passed in this manner, until the occupant of the seat immediately behind Elizabeth glanced up at a television screen, made a face that clearly communicated relief, then collected his belongings hurriedly, and strode away from his seat.

Harris made for the empty seat. He sat down and shoved the blue sports bag under the chair, keeping a hold on the carryall. With his feet he pushed the sports bag backwards, farther and farther, until it straddled the space between his seat and young Elizabeth Kent's.

Next to him, a pair of Australian businessmen were discussing cricket loudly. A burnous-clad Arab strode majestically past, a wife two steps behind, and, behind her, a quartet of swarthy boys in school uniform.

Harris's gaze wandered desultorily around the lounge.

His eyes met those of a man seated perhaps ten feet away, in a seat on the opposite side of a wide aisle. For a moment the two stared at each other.

The man was perhaps in his early fifties, possibly older, an academic-looking gentleman wearing an outdated sports jacket and cuffed trousers. He had a long, lean face, etched with lines that in ten years would become crevasses. His hair was thin and white; the scalp showed pinkly through its sparse covering. Bushy gray eyebrows sat atop heavily framed spectacles. His face was red, with broken capillaries dotting the hollow cheeks. But despite the air of vague decrepitude, the man's eyes were clear and steady; his expression held an intimation of unease, as if something about Harris disturbed him profoundly.

Harris looked away and counted to ten under his breath. Then he looked back at the man. There was a tightening in Harris's stomach. Their eyes met again.

For a moment, Harris wondered if perhaps he had met the man somewhere, but he quickly rejected that idea. The frown on the man's brow was one not of possible recognition, but rather one of ill-defined anxiety, as if he was puzzled and concerned about something he had seen Harris do.

Harris swallowed once, his mind racing, wondering if the man had watched him push the sports bag purposefully backward, almost underneath Elizabeth Kent's seat.

He made an instant decision: there was nothing to be gained by waiting. Glancing at the closest television screen, he feigned an expression of harried relief, as if his flight had been called.

He arose quickly from his seat, clutching the carryall, and, without pausing, strode across the lounge towards a gate in the far corner. As he walked, his hand dipped into the right pocket of his overcoat. Inside was a small plastic box, wrapped entirely within a handkerchief. With his thumb he located the button in the middle of one surface. But he did not push it. Not yet.

Harris walked purposefully past several blocks of seats and then ducked behind a column. Edging around the curvature of the pillar, he looked back toward the seat he had vacated.

The man who had been watching him was only now turning his head back to face forwards; he must have been watching Harris until he had ducked behind the column.

For several seconds Harris watched, trying to convince himself that it was simply a false alarm, just a man whose eyes had settled on his own for no good reason and whose mind had been far away, considering other matters entirely. But no; after a few seconds, the man stood up and crossed the aisle. He leaned over the vacant chair behind the Kents and tapped Mrs. Kent on the shoulder. She turned, and the man spoke to her. Harris saw the man point to the chair that Harris had vacated, under which still rested the blue sports bag.

The man made an obvious motion for the Kents to leave their chairs. Harris was not too far away to see the sudden look of horror cross Mrs. Kent's face. She grabbed her daughter and pulled her out of the chair, spilling the crayons and the book in which she had been coloring to the floor.

Harris ducked back behind the column. Taking a deep breath, he braced himself with his back against the pillar. He closed his eyes, then firmly pressed the button.

Sixty feet away, inside the blue sports bag that was tucked partway underneath the seat on which four-year-old Elizabeth Kent had been sitting, a relay moved a millimeter, closing a microswitch. A current began to flow.

The room seemed to heave with an enormous *whump* that was felt more than heard.

It was more a spasm than an explosion. The sudden over-pressure was not enough to cause major structural damage, but it was certain to kill anyone unfortunate enough to be within a dozen feet of the sports bag.

Harris opened his eyes, exhaled and peered around the pillar. The Foamtex explosive had produced only a pale haze of smoke, already thinning into nothingness.

For perhaps another second there was a stunned silence. And then the screams began.

In the place where the Kents had been seated little was recognizable. Twisted metal and shards of plastic were strewn around the area, the closest about nine feet from the source of the blast. Within that radius there was nothing at all. Harris could see part of Mrs. Kent's body, recognizable only by its clothes, thrown several feet to one side. It was several moments before he saw Elizabeth Kent, spread-eagled on the floor, either dead or unconscious, drenched in blood, her right leg severed above the knee.

Several people who had been near the blast were kneeling or crouching in pain, spouting blood. One of the Australian businessmen was standing, holding a severed arm. His companion was laid out, bloody and unmoving, on the floor.

For perhaps five more seconds, almost no one moved. Then everyone started running. Some ran straight towards where the explosion had been, others directly away from it. Everyone was either shouting or screaming.

Harris located a convenient trash can and gingerly lifted the plastic box, still wrapped in its handkerchief, out of his pocket. Holding the handkerchief over the receptacle, he let it open and the box fell out into the trash. It was the only evidence he intended to leave for the authorities.

He glanced at his watch. 10:31.

People were milling everywhere; the first men wearing uniforms ran into the lounge. A passenger pointed to where the blast had been, directing the men to the source of the explosion. Cries and screams still filled the air.

Harris walked toward a row of telephones located on the far side of the lounge, near the restaurant. Soon there would be long lines waiting to use the phones, but at the moment only one booth was occupied, by a young man excitedly gesticulating while he spoke in to the telephone. Harris entered the booth farthest away from the young man, lifted the receiver, and dialed 999.

"Emergency, which service do you want?" a neutral female voice asked almost before the phone had begun to ring.

"My name is Shamus O'Riley. I'm with the Irish Liberation Front. We just blew up part of Gatwick Airport."

Harris left no time for comment or questions. He put the phone down and stepped back into the lounge. People were gathering at the far side of the lounge, clustering around the point where the explosion had been. Authoritative shouts demanding calm emanated from the crowd and were clearly audible even from this distance.

Already the first of the injured were being taken away. Two men were carrying the diminutive body of Elizabeth Kent between them, a uniformed man moving ahead of them, calling, "Make way! Make way!" The Australian who had been injured was being led away in the same direction. He kept looking back at his companion on the ground. Harris could see from the unnatural angle of the man's head that he must have broken his neck. "John! John!" the Australian was shouting as he was led away, either unaware or unwilling to believe that his companion was dead.

Harris joined the knot of now-silent people clustering around the scene of the explosion, in the center of which a uniformed man was telling everyone to be calm and to remain where they were.

For a while, it seemed that everyone was going to be detained and forced to undergo interrogation by the police. But word reached the authorities that the ILF had admitted responsibility, and someone realized that the bomb could have been planted earlier in the day, maybe hours ago. The bomber might be on another continent by now. After an hour or so, the authorities decided there was no point in detaining anyone unnecessarily.

In the meantime George Harris descended to the men's room, where he shaved, rearranged his hair, and exchanged the clothes he was wearing for the clean, casual and entirely respectable business clothes that had been in the carryall. No one gave him a second glance as he returned to the lounge and joined the throng of people milling at the end of the room awaiting the authorities' decision.

Two hours after the explosion, PlanetAir flight 11, bound for Orlando, lifted off the runway. In seat 4A, George Harris closed his eyes and sighed deeply at the moment the airplane left the ground. In front of him, seats 3A and 3B, still reserved in the names of Mrs. C. and Miss E. Kent, were unoccupied.

Chapter 5
Friday, November 16
Redhill, Surrey

Dr. Patricia Worthington smiled at the young woman perched on the stool at the checkout till. The young woman, surely barely old enough to have left school, briefly returned the smile before casting her eyes wearily over the line of half a dozen customers stretched out behind Dr. Worthington. She began to ring up the groceries, picking them up and hesitating over the scanner just long enough for each item to ring up with a beep before thrusting it away and grabbing the next one.

Dr. Worthington produced her check book and begin to write the check so that the girl would not be unnecessarily delayed when it was time to pay. As the last few items were being rung up, Dr. Worthington felt the pager attached to her waistband begin to vibrate.

For a fraction of a second she was annoyed at the intrusion into her day off, but she quickly pushed the thought aside. Patricia Worthington took her vocation seriously; if she was being paged, it was because someone needed her services. She had given up any right to days off when she had graduated at the top of her class from medical school. In the decade since then fully a third of her rest days had been interrupted. It was, as she reminded herself every time it happened, simply something that went with the territory.

She expertly flipped the pager off the waistband of her dress and read the LCD screen. At least that was something that had changed since she had qualified: when she had first become a surgeon, the pager was a signal for her to scramble madly to find the closest telephone so she could call the hospital and find out what was going on. Now, thanks to advances in technology, she could read the reason for the summons directly off the LCD screen of the pager itself.

"Excuse me, ma'am," the young woman said, trying to get her attention as the total rang up, but Dr. Worthington was just standing there, looking at the screen, horror on her face.

She turned to the young woman. "My God. There's been an explosion at Gatwick."

For one long second, the two woman looked at one another without moving; then Dr. Worthington began to run for the door. Behind her a chorus of voices reminded her of the groceries and checkbook she had left behind, but she either ignored them or simply never heard. Pushing open the door of the supermarket, she dodged the startled people who were in her way and dashed for her car.

The East Surrey hospital where Patricia Worthington worked was a relatively new building, two miles south of Redhill and about ten minutes north of Gatwick by speeding ambulance. It was not the closest hospital to the airport, but it was the nearest with extensive facilities for dealing with a disaster such as the aftermath of a terrorist bomb. So it was to East Surrey that most of those injured in the blast were being taken.

Patricia Worthington blurred the two miles down the A23 in her mud-brown Renault, heedless of the speed limit and swerving around slower moving traffic in a way that would been reckless in anyone less controlled. The car slid to a halt in the hospital parking lot as an ambulance disappeared around a corner of the building, heading for the emergency entrance.

The doctor ran across the blacktop, hitching up her dress so she could run faster. Another ambulance entered the parking lot, its lights flashing and siren blaring. The siren died down as it made its way to the emergency entrance. In the distance, Patricia could hear yet another ambulance approaching. *My God!* she thought. *How many of them are there?*

Inside the hospital, she stopped and looked around desperately for someone to tell her where she could be of most use. A nurse, against regulations, entered the lobby area at a run, and Patricia called for her to stop. Realizing that she could easily be mistaken for a civilian in her green tartan dress, Patricia said, "I'm a doctor. A surgeon. I got a call on my pager. Do you know where they need me?"

Barely breaking her stride, the nurse called, "Follow me, doctor. They're just beginning to arrive. Good God, can you believe it?"

Hitching up her dress once more, Patricia followed the nurse at a run. They crossed the building to the far side, where, just as she arrived, someone was being wheeled in from an ambulance. Two nurses were standing near the door, waiting to take over from the ambulance paramedics. One of the nurses glared at Patricia, obviously wondering what fool had allowed a civilian into the room at such a moment. But the other nurse recognized the doctor. "Doctor Worthington, thank God you're here. The other doctors have all gone. We've had three emergency admissions already."

Patricia hurried to the gurney, issuing a flood of commands and questions. "Here, let me take a look. I'm a surgeon. How many of them are there going to be? Has anyone alerted any more hospitals? Is the chopper ready in case we need to transfer one of them? Oh Christ! It's a kid!"

Unconscious on the gurney was an intubated young girl, no more than five years old. She was unnaturally pale, and her pulse was so weak that for a moment Patricia thought the girl already dead. "She lost a lot of blood," one of the ambulance paramedics said. "And her right leg, above the knee. She's been dribbling blood from her mouth and ears."

The surgeon evaluated the situation quickly. There was already a saline drip attached to the girl's arm. Lifting the covering, she saw that a tourniquet had been applied above the place where her leg had been blown off. A blood pressure cuff wrapped around her thigh acted as an auxiliary tourniquet.

"Blood pressure cuff here, stat!" she shouted.

In moments a cuff was wrapped around the girl's arm. Patricia took the girl's pulse. She frowned.

"Blood pressure fifty over palp. Pulse 140 and damn weak. You, nurse, do we have any more IVs left? Then get one quickly. A large-bore catheter. Don't be pretty; just find a vein and get the stuff in her. Give her 800 cc. And we need blood here. Anyone know what the blood situation is?"

While one nurse scurried for the second IV, another answered, "The others who came in didn't look as bad as this. There should be some O still in the bank."

"Then get it!" Patricia snapped. She stopped for a moment and tried to control herself. It would do no good to rush things. That was how mistakes were made. "Wait a minute, nurse. Don't forget to check the O negative first. This is a girl, so if we have any negative that's what we want. Otherwise bring O positive."

The nurse nodded and hurried away as the second, larger IV was attached to the gurney and quickly injected into a vein in the girl's arm.

"Why the endotracheal tube?" Patricia asked the paramedics.

"She was dribbling blood out of her mouth."

"You told me that already, didn't you?" Dammit! She needed to concentrate on what she was being told. "Damn and blast! All right, we'll need an X-ray. Here, help me move her over here. Is there an X-ray tech around?"

The doors to the room swung open and another victim was wheeled in. Patricia looked at the prostrate form on the new gurney and wondered if she dare leave the girl to attend to the new arrival. She breathed a sigh of relief when another doctor ran into the room and quickly began to examine the newcomer.

The X-ray tech arrived, summoned from where he had been dealing with a previous arrival. Quickly, he slipped a plate under the supine girl, exposed a plate and ran out the room once more. From beginning to end, it took less than thirty seconds. "Three minutes," he yelled as he left the room.

Normally the emergency room was as smoothly efficient as any other vital organ in the hospital. Now it resembled a madhouse, with doctors, nurses, paramedics and technicians running this way and that, dodging one another, shouting names and numbers.

Patricia borrowed a stethoscope from another doctor and listened to her patient's lungs. She swore under her breath, then explained in answer to the questioning look on a paramedic's face, "Lungs sound wet on both sides."

She examined the girl's chest. "Fourth rib broken. Possible collapsed right lung." She paused for a moment, gathering her thoughts. She was not a trauma specialist. Doubtless there had been one available when the first victim had been wheeled in; but there was no time to find one now, not if the little girl was going to live. Patricia Worthington swallowed and told herself that all she needed to do was to be calm and to think carefully. Common sense would get her through this. She hoped.

"Set up for a chest tube. Pneumothorax here." A nurse — Emily Jones, her name badge said — hurried to obey.

By the time the X-ray technician returned, Patricia had made a small incision in the girl's side, and yet another tube led from the girl to a small bag hanging off the gurney. Patricia watched blood flow into the bag, anxiously waiting for the flow to diminish. It didn't.

"Doctor, she's swimming in there," the X-ray technician said, handing Patricia the film. Patricia glanced at it. She swore again.

"I'm going to need help. Are there any other surgeons available?"

"Sorry, doctor," said Nurse Jones. "I think everyone's busy."

"Any idea what the OR status is?"

"Number two was available when I went past a few minutes ago."

"All right. Get in there and don't budge. We'll be there in five minutes. Get swabbed, and have a pack of chest instruments ready. Go! Now! You, stay here and help."

Nurse Jones hurried away, narrowly avoiding another nurse on an urgent errand on behalf of yet another patient who had just arrived.

"We're going to do a thoracotomy. Then we'll go to the OR."

Oblivious to her surroundings, Patricia Worthington made an incision between the fourth and fifth ribs and applied a vascular clamp to the aorta below the heart. She winced at her first look at the girl's insides. Everything was swimming in a sea of bright red blood. "She's not going to make it," the watching nurse mumbled to herself.

"She bloody well is if I have anything to do with it," Patricia snapped as she tightened the clamp. "Come on; help me get her into Theater 2. You, come and help," she ordered the paramedics who had brought the girl in.

They wheeled the gurney at a jog out of the emergency room and down the corridor.

They halted outside the operating theater. For a second, Patricia hesitated. She looked at the door to the prep room, then down at the dress she was wearing. It was her favorite dress, casual and comfortable, and now filthy. It was no longer green, but literally dripped red on the floor of the corridor as she stood there, vacillating.

Then she looked at the girl.

With no further hesitation, she pushed open the doors of the operating theater. "Don't try to move her. Just leave her on the gurney. Get the blankets off. One of you, go and try to find an anesthetist. You, I want a continual supply of blood. Nurse, you have the chest instruments ready? Good."

"Doctor, I'm sorry, but surely you aren't going to operate like that? What about infection?" Nurse Jones asked.

Patricia kicked off her shoes, sending them scuttering to a corner of the room and then, in a motion that left the others in the room gawking, she loosened her belt and unzipped her dress, letting it fall to her feet, so that she was standing over the comatose child in only her underwear and stockings. She kicked the dress away. "When we have a spare moment, someone get me a mask and gown. In the meantime, we're just going to do the best we can. I'd rather have a patient who's alive but infected than one who's dead but clean."

Patricia selected a scalpel off the tray, and rested it against the girl's skin. She hesitated before making the first cut.

"If any of you is religious," she said, "now would be a good time to ask for divine intervention. This little girl is going to need all the help she can get."

Chapter 6
Friday, November 16
Surrey

Paul Kent arrived at Carltons' Bond Street offices at nine thirty, early enough to obtain a good seat. The room in which the auction was to be held was a relatively small one, capable of seating perhaps a hundred people. It was three-quarters full when the auction began with the auctioneer's words of welcome on the stroke of ten o'clock.

The sale was from the estate of John Harvey, a recently deceased wealthy collector of memorabilia from the Second World War. The lots moved quickly, and Lot 15, the one that had caught Kent's eye, was announced shortly after half past ten.

Lot 15 was Winston Churchill's Chippendale desk from the War Room in the basement of 10, Downing Street. At this desk, Churchill had written and delivered many of his most famous speeches, speeches that had stirred and exhorted a nation on the brink of disaster to fight on even in the face of overwhelming odds.

The bidding was short-lived but spirited, rapidly resolving itself into a two-man affair, with Paul Kent and Henry Parminter, a collector of Churchilliana from Essex, bidding against one another.

Parminter eventually dropped out, unwilling to match Kent's bid of £169,000. The hammer fell, and the desk became Kent's property.

Parminter caught Kent's eye and signaled that they should have lunch together. This pleased Kent, for it was not often that he could engage in intelligent conversation with someone whose knowledge and opinions of Churchill so closely matched his own.

Kent stayed for the rest of the morning to watch the remainder of the auction, his warm glow of success reflecting itself in the vaguely benevolent smile that was affixed to his face. Having won the prize he came for, he allowed Parminter to remain unchallenged and bid successfully for several smaller lots. At the close of the auction, Kent arranged with the auctioneers to have his newly-acquired desk delivered to his home the following afternoon. He made a note in his diary to call his insurance agent in the morning to ensure that it would be fully covered.

Parminter and Kent ate a long, gentlemanly lunch at a refined restaurant overlooking the Thames. They parted shortly after two and Kent took the tube to Oxford Street, where he occupied the afternoon purchasing Christmas gifts for his wife and daughter.

After a hurried and not altogether pleasant dinner in a small restaurant off Oxford Street, he crossed London by tube to the West End, where he browsed the playbills and finally selected a new play, *The Life and Times of Bartholomew Broadhurst*, which was earning favorable reviews in a small theater off the Haymarket.

It was getting late, past ten, when he was finally disgorged on to the sidewalk after the end of the play.

He reached Victoria Station just in time to catch the 10:30, and recovered his Mercedes from the station parking lot shortly after 11 p.m.

When he got home, a wave of exhaustion hit him. He dumped his bags of shopping on the floor of the living room, where he would deal with them tomorrow.

Remembering his promise to call Catherine, he lifted the phone and dialed the number of their house in Orlando.

To his surprise, there was no answer. He tapped the hook and redialed, but the result was the same. He grunted wordlessly. It was unlike Catherine to forget to set the answering machine. Perhaps it had broken since last year. He would try again in the morning.

Thinking no more of it, he put the phone down, turned out the light, and climbed the stairs to bed.

East Surrey Hospital

The operation to save the girl's life had been a success. Afterwards, Patricia showered and dressed herself in the blouse and slacks that she kept in her office for just such an emergency. Then she went to sit beside the girl to wait for her to wake up.

The girl's vital signs were now stable. Her blood pressure was up to 90, and her pulse was strong and steady at 62. Her breathing was calm and even. She was still in intensive care, and would remain there for some time, but Patricia could see no reason why, apart from the amputated leg, she should not make a full recovery.

She looked up at the clock on the wall, and did a quick calculation. She frowned. More than four hours had passed since the girl's arrival, and she was still unconscious.

No anesthetist had been available, so the operation had been performed without anesthetic, and more than once Patricia had wondered what they would do if she woke up in the middle of it. But she had slept soundly through it all. At the time it had seemed like a blessing, but now she was beginning to wonder. Was the damage more widespread than she had thought? Was it possible that, as well as the obvious physical damage to her insides, there had been brain damage as well?

Patricia pushed the thought out of her mind. She left the room in search of a mug of coffee.

In the doctors' lounge half a dozen surgeons were discussing the status of the people had been brought in after the explosion. A total of nine victims had been sent to East Surrey. One had died in the ambulance; another had died on the operating table. Six of the remaining seven had been operated on and their lives saved, although the same could not be said for all their limbs. All were now awake. The little girl, still without a name, was the seventh.

She poured herself a coffee and remained for a few minutes talking about the patients. The others congratulated her on saving the girl's life; Patricia told them how worried she was that her patient was still unconscious.

"After a trauma like that, I wouldn't be too worried," said Dr. Claybourne, the oldest and most experienced surgeon in the hospital. "Nature has a way of knowing what's best for the body. The girl probably just needs the rest to let the healing process begin."

Patricia nodded her thanks, grateful for the encouragement. She left the lounge and returned to intensive care, where she found her patient exactly as she had left her.

It was another two hours before she decided that something was definitely wrong. Pulling back the girl's eyelids, Patricia saw that her eyes were wildly dilated. Immediately she did something that realized with a sinking feeling she should have done much earlier: she ordered a CAT scan for the unconscious girl.

The results were worse than she feared. As well as an epidermal hematoma on the right side of her brain, it was immediately obvious that brain activity in the right hemisphere was far less than it should be, even for a patient in a deep sleep.

She located the resident neurologist, Dr. Samuel Higgins, a normally cheerful young man in his early thirties who, despite his youth, was beginning to gain a considerable reputation for successful brain surgery.

In his office she told him everything that had happened, while he sat on the other side of his cluttered deal desk, nodding continuously while he examined the results of the CAT scan.

"What do you think, Sam?" Patricia asked when she had finished.

"I think I'd better come and take a look at her. But you're right. It doesn't look good. Take me to her, and let's see what we can do."

Samuel Higgins took less than two minutes to arrive at a decision. "I want to go in and take a look. Did you see what kind of shape her carotids are in when you had her open, Patricia? It looks to me like there's a blockage, or more likely a break, in her right carotid. That would explain the epidermal hematoma, as well as the low level of activity on that side."

"I didn't see anything. But I wasn't really looking. I was too busy dealing with the damage in her trunk to take much note of anything else."

"Yes. Not your fault, of course. Don't blame yourself. Anyway, it might not be as bad as it looks. Come on, let's get her into surgery and take a look for ourselves."

But later, as Patricia looked in on the girl, once more back in intensive care after the second operation, she did blame herself. She should have realized much earlier that something was dreadfully wrong. Now the girl was sleeping soundly from the barbiturates that were used to keep the brain pacified after surgery. She would not wake up for days. If she ever woke up at all.

Chapter 7
Saturday, November 17
Surrey

Paul Kent came downstairs, still in his dressing gown, shortly after 8:30. After breakfast, he called his insurance agent at home. The agent told him that a slight increase in premium would be necessary, but if Kent put the check in the mail today, then the desk would be covered. Wasting no time, Kent got dressed, then wrote the check and ambled to the pillar box at the corner of Darnley Drive to mail it.

Yesterday the weather had been cool but clear. Overnight there had been a change. Now there was a low, heavy overcast, and the first light drops of rain began to fall as he returned to the protection of the house.

Idly, he picked up the day's newspaper where it had fallen, and turned it over to look at the headlines. He began walking slowly back towards the kitchen to make himself a cup of tea.

His mouth dropped open in horror and his legs stopped working in mid stride. The front page headline of *The Times* screamed at him in large, black type: *ILF blast at Gatwick.*

His mind leaping to make connections, he felt a sudden awful certainty that he knew why Catherine had not answered the phone last night. He shivered in the grip of an icy fear. Nightmares from his long-dead past began to intrude as he scanned the paper for details, his mind repeating over and over, *No! It can't end like this. Not now I've put it all behind me. It can't!* He tried to make the thoughts go away. They wouldn't.

The Times' article carried the essential facts in its first two paragraphs: the blast had occurred in the International Departures Lounge of Gatwick's South terminal; the time of the blast was given as 10:31; the Irish Liberation Front had claimed responsibility within minutes of the explosion; there was an unconfirmed report that the call claiming responsibility had been made immediately after the blast from the departure lounge itself; there were seven dead, but their names were not given "pending notification of next of kin"; another twenty, similarly unnamed, were wounded seriously enough to warrant hospitalization; one person had died on the way to hospital.

Forcing himself to be calm, he walked into the living room, all thoughts of tea gone, rereading the article but learning nothing new.

10:31. Catherine and Elizabeth must have been in the lounge at the time of the blast. And if they were all right, Catherine would have called as soon as she could get to a phone. He checked the answering machine. No messages.

He lifted the telephone, but his mind went momentarily blank. He struggled to remember the number in Orlando. When he finally dialed, he noticed that his fingers were shaking.

This time he let the phone ring and ring and ring. No matter that it was the middle of the night in Florida. He would stay on the line until Catherine picked up the phone and told him they were all right.

He tried to think rationally, arguing with himself that the odds were in favor of Catherine and Elizabeth; trying to persuade himself that even if they had been caught by the blast, the chances were that they had survived. Only eight were dead. Twenty were in hospital.

He realized that he was still standing, listening to the repetitive ringing of the phone thousands of miles away. He put the phone down. His hands were still shaking.

What should he do now? Just whom did one call to discover the fate of loved ones following a terrorist explosion? "The police," he said to himself, and he was just about to look up the number of the local police station when the telephone rang with a suddenness that startled him.

He lifted the receiver. Catherine, he told himself; it was Catherine calling to say that everything was all right.

"Good morning. Is Mr. Paul Kent available, please?"

It was a male voice, cultured, official. Kent opened his mouth and found that his throat was too dry for speech. He swallowed deliberately a couple of times, and then said as evenly as he could, "This is Mr. Paul Kent speaking."

The blue Mercedes slipped into a space in the parking lot of the East Surrey hospital at twenty minutes to ten. It had been raining for more than an hour, the kind of heavy, continuous rain that quells even the most optimistic of spirits. The hospital itself, even though almost new, looked as drab and cheerless as the countryside around it. Paul Kent gave it one glance as he opened the car door, and felt what little hope remained drain away.

He ran across the tarmac and into the foyer. Inside, a thirtysomething woman in the white gown of a doctor was waiting for him. She stepped forward and held out her hand.

"Mr. Kent? I'm Dr. Worthington. I operated on your daughter when she came in yesterday."

They shook hands perfunctorily. Kent thought she looked tired. Patricia Worthington thought he looked like a man who had lost everything.

Dr. Worthington began to lead the way down a corridor. "I'm sure you have many questions, Mr. Kent. But the most important thing is that your daughter is still alive. I'm sorry it took so long to find you. There was no identification on your daughter when she came in. The police tell me her name is Elizabeth."

"Yes," he said numbly. "Doctor, is she going to be all right?"

They halted outside a pair of swing doors marked "Intensive Care."

"I'm sorry, Mr. Kent. I don't know what the police told you, but I'm afraid Elizabeth is anything but all right; the prognosis, I'm sorry to say, cannot be good." She spoke carefully, choosing her words so that they contained no false hope.

"You must prepare yourself for a shock when we go inside." She laid a hand on Kent's arm, and Kent acknowledged it with a weak smile. "Your daughter lost a lot of blood. Did the police also tell you that she lost most of her right leg? We had to amputate above the knee."

She could tell by the look on his face that he hadn't been told.

"No," he said after the first shock had passed. "They didn't tell me much at all. Just that Elizabeth was here, in critical condition, and her mother...." He swallowed. "Her mother is dead."

"Oh! I'm sorry. I didn't know."

"They said she was close to the center of the blast. Someone was standing between Elizabeth and the bomb, otherwise she'd've been killed as well."

There was a brief silence. There was nothing the doctor could say.

After a few moments she continued, "Elizabeth lost her right leg, but most of the damage was internal. Her pulmonary vein was torn by the blast. When she came in she was bleeding internally from the break in the vein. We operated right away and I lost her briefly partway through the operation, but we managed to get her back again."

There was something more. Kent could tell from the way she was speaking that the doctor had not yet told him the most important thing.

"Please, what are her chances?" he pleaded.

"If it was just the physical damage, the leg and the internal damage, I'd be quite hopeful. But I'm afraid there's something else. The right carotid, you see...." The doctor paused for a moment, trying to think of some way to break the news.

She took a deep breath and said, "We each have two carotids. They carry oxygenated blood up into the brain."

Paul Kent swallowed hard. He understood now what it was that the doctor had been reluctant to tell him.

"There's brain damage," he said.

The doctor's hand squeezed his arm lightly, a gesture of support and hope. "We don't know that yet," she said. "I will be completely honest with you, Mr. Kent. There is no doubt that Elizabeth's brain was starved for oxygen after the... after it happened. But we honestly don't know how bad the damage is. The most important thing yesterday when she came in was simply to save her life.

"Afterwards, when she didn't wake up, we did a CAT scan and that showed us that the activity on the right side of her brain was considerably reduced from normal. Our resident neurosurgeon elected to perform another operation. We finished at around eight last night. We found a break in her right carotid. We fixed the break and, as far as we know, there was no other damage.

"After brain surgery like that we keep the patient asleep for several days and monitor carefully what's going on. Allowing her to wake up too early might send her brain into spasm. So when we go inside in a moment, she'll be asleep. The tubes and wires are to monitor her vital signs and keep your daughter's body supplied with a steady flow of nutrients and blood. Now, if you are ready...?"

Kent swallowed, then nodded. "All right."

The doctor pushed open the door and led him inside.

When they emerged five minutes later, Kent's face was haggard and his skin was gray. Patricia Worthington looked tired and depressed.

"I have one more question," said Kent in a voice that was weak and cracked. "Forgive me for asking, but I have to know. What would you do if you could get your hands on the person who did that?"

"You'd like to kill him, and you feel guilty about feeling that way? Is that it?"

"Something like that."

"Well don't. I'd like to kill him as well. I hope to God they catch whoever did it. The person responsible for what happened to your family doesn't deserve to live."

There was a sudden flash of steel in Kent's eyes. "Thank you, doctor. For everything. I'll see myself out." His voice was unexpectedly strong.

She shivered as she watched him walk away.

The weather did not improve much as the day progressed, and there was little traffic on the road as a blue Mercedes made its way down progressively narrower lanes in the south Surrey countryside.

At length, the car turned on to a road that was no more than a single-file track hedged in on both sides by thick woods. The car motored along the narrow road for about a mile as it climbed steadily, until suddenly the track opened out, the trees fell behind, and the car drove out on to the soft turf of the North Downs. The car moved about a hundred yards out beyond the perimeter of the woods, then came to a halt. Its engine stopped.

The only eyes that witnessed the arrival of the car belonged to the rabbits foraging nearby, who, alarmed by this unexpected intrusion into their domain, scurried for the safety of their burrows.

After perhaps five minutes of stillness, during which the rabbits ventured from their burrows and recommenced feeding on the damp, wet grass, the driver's door of the Mercedes opened and a figure stepped out into the light drizzle. The figure, a bearded man, was dressed in a warm overcoat. He wore no hat. Gently closing the door, he walked to the rear of the vehicle and opened the trunk.

There was a single, long, thin object lying in the trunk of the car, wrapped in a protective covering of green cloth. Slowly, the man carefully spread open the cloth.

Paul Kent stared for a full minute at the rifle, thinking of the past and trying desperately to shut out the present.

The rifle and the life that had gone with it were the only secrets he had ever withheld from his wife. To share either of them with her would have been to share what he had once been — and that was something she must never know, for that man had died, died at the moment that the man known as Paul Kent had been born.

He thought of Catherine the last evening they had spent together. He had come so close to telling her....

And now it was too late. She was gone; he could feel the past reaching out with an icy grip to reclaim him. And he willingly embraced it.

He shook himself. As the wet drizzle seeped down the back of his neck, Kent carefully lifted the rifle and balanced it in his hand. Perfect. Even after all these years he still marveled at the sheer beauty of such craftsmanship. Burned like a brand into the wood of the butt was the monogram *MB*. The man who had made the rifle, Maximillian Bücher, was a Swiss who took as much pride in his weapons as his father had once taken in his watches.

Kent cracked the gun and loaded a cartridge into each of the two barrels. The second bullet had never been necessary, but he had had Bücher make all his rifles with a double barrel, just in case. The barrels were mounted vertically, one above the other, with precisely one inch separating the centers.

Raising the rifle, he looked through the telescopic sight. The rifle was constructed so that the sight was an integral part of the gun, perfectly parallel to the two barrels over which it was mounted.

Reflexive Action

Kent walked slowly a short distance from the car, forcing his mind into the past, remembering. As he walked, the mid-afternoon drizzle began to turn into a heavy, rain-weighted mist.

About fifteen yards from the Mercedes he turned and unhurriedly raised the rifle. Looking through the sight, he released the safety catch and scanned the grass beyond the car, in the direction of the trees. After a few seconds he stopped: a rabbit about a hundred yards away was centered in the eyepiece, eating carelessly.

He slowly moved the rifle from side to side, holding the animal in the center of each arc, each sweep moving further from the rabbit than its predecessor. At last he found the entrance to the warren.

Rabbits rarely take food more than a three second sprint from the closest burrow, especially when there are nearby trees to shelter a potential predator. This particular rabbit, being near the limit of that range, was being especially cautious. When it was not actually engaged in the act of eating, it would sit up on its hind legs and cast around to make sure that there were no visible enemies within striking distance. It had marked the progress of the two-legged animal out on the downs, but had concluded that it posed no threat. Two-legged beasts travel slowly over the ground, and the rabbit was in no doubt that it could reach the safety of its burrow long before the slow-moving two-legs could be upon it.

Kent slowly marked the distance between rabbit and burrow. Then, holding his breath, he trained his sights at a point a hundred yards away and a little above the rabbit's head.

The image of his daughter as he had left her two hours ago forced itself on him. Lowering the gun he wiped away a stray tear. He pushed the memory aside and raised the rifle once more.

He squeezed the trigger.

The sound was not loud. Even without the rain to muffle the shot there would only have been a clean, sharp crack.

With the rain, the crack was drawn out into an indistinct thud.

The sound as it reached the rabbit's ears was muffled and did not disturb the animal unduly. What did disturb it was the bullet that hit the ground close by, at the edge of the woods. The rabbit knew nothing about bullets, but it did know that something nearby had suddenly moved. It started to bound towards the safety of its burrow.

Kent felt the recoil and heard the shot, but he kept his eyes firmly locked on the rabbit in the center of his telescopic sight.

As the bullet hit, he saw a small patch of earth shoot up a little below where the lines in the sight crossed, precisely on the line of the vertical hair. The bullet traveling from the upper barrel of the rifle traversed the hundred yards to its point of impact in roughly a tenth of a second. In that time, the bullet, falling under the influence of gravity, fell approximately two inches, so that the impact came slightly below the intersection of the lines in the sight. It had all happened just as it was supposed to.

There was a fractional moment of immobility, and then the rabbit was off, making for its burrow at full speed.

Kent counted slowly under his breath, following the rabbit as best he could with the sight. "One... Two...." At two and a half, the burrow came into view in the telescope. While the rabbit executed a speedy turn to its left before diving into the safety of its home, Kent shifted the rifle ever so slightly, so that the crossed hairs marked a spot in the top center of the burrow, which now nearly filled the field of view. The lower barrel, the second to fire, was mounted precisely one inch below the upper one, which was itself mounted exactly one inch below the telescopic sight. The second bullet would therefore hit its target some four inches below the position marked by the crosshairs.

Kent squeezed the trigger a second time.

There was a second crack, but this time the rabbit heard no distant thud. Traveling three times faster than the sound from the explosion, the bullet reached the rabbit first. The bullet broke the skin in the lower back and traveled the length of the animal's body, emerging from the top of its head a fraction of a second before the sound of the shot reached ears that sent electrical signals on a futile journey towards a brain that no longer existed.

Kent looked through the telescopic sight at the bloody result of his actions. He remained motionless for a few seconds, and then lowered the rifle, satisfied that if only he could find the Irish madman responsible for yesterday's blast, he would have no trouble disposing of him.

Chapter 8
Saturday, November 17
Surrey

Paul Kent stood motionless in the heavy, chill, moist air, his eyes fixed on the bloody body of the animal whose life he had just ended, his mind a mælstrom of conflicting emotions, tortured images and desultory thoughts.

He had driven to this deserted place with only one object in mind: to discover whether the skills of the man he had once been were still accessible, still ready for use when called on. Or had he succeeded, as he had so desperately wanted and tried to do for the past five years, in submerging the old irretrievably deeply beneath the veneer of the new?

The dead animal a hundred yards away gave him his answer.

Now, standing alone on the North Downs, Paul Kent knew that he had to commit suicide a second time. If Paul Kent was to have his revenge on the man who had killed his wife and damaged his child, he must himself die. For Paul Kent was utterly incapable of doing what had to be done. Only one man could do that. Paul Kent would die. And the man known as Kelton must be reborn.

He turned and walked back to the car. Paul Kent had driven the Mercedes on to the Downs; it was Kelton who drove the car away.

He returned to Darnley Drive, where he poured a glass of water and sat at the kitchen table. Slowly, he began to plan.

The first item of business was to discover who exactly was responsible for the blast at Gatwick. Assuming that he was successful, he then had to locate that person (or persons; surely more than one person must have been needed to plant the bomb?). Then, when the time was right, he would strike.

He twisted the glass of water in his hand. What about Paul Kent? If Kelton was to be the cold-blooded killer that he had to be, all traces of Paul Kent must be erased from his psyche; but five years' accumulated softness and weakness could not be obliterated merely by wishing them gone.

Kelton had to be absolutely certain that once he began his mission, all traces of Kent had been eradicated. A moment's hesitation, a fraction of a second of emotion, a single desperate failure to act reflexively and aggressively at the wrong moment could spell the death of both Kent and Kelton — and, what was much worse, might leave the person who had killed Kent's wife and maimed his child to go forever unpunished and free.

It would be easy to fool himself that Kent's emotions would be useful, that they would heighten his senses and increase his alertness, but Kelton recognized that such thoughts were merely self deceit. Any emotion, even anger or hatred, could fatally cloud his judgment, precipitating an error from which there was no recovery. If his thoughts were not absolutely clear, completely objective, he would jump to unwarranted conclusions, miss clues, fail to perceive warnings that would be obvious if he had a clear mind.

Kelton wondered if he had the strength to hold Kent's emotions in check. Deliberately, he made a promise to himself that he would make no move, initiate no contact, start no conversation without first asking himself whether it was necessary, what the likely outcomes were, and whether the risks involved were truly recognized and accounted for.

He raised the glass and drained it. Satisfied that he had made an important decision, he turned in for the evening.

His sleep was riven with nightmares that horrifically mixed the past and the present. One moment he would be standing in Elizabeth's hospital room, looking despairingly at the maze of tubes that led into her body from the machines that surrounded her; the next moment the tubes had transformed themselves into a forest and he was staring down at the mutilated remains of his first kill. Since then he had lost count of the number of people he had killed. Somewhere beyond the grave were they all watching him now, laughing at his confusion and dismay, revelling in their revenge?

He sat up bolt upright in bed, certain that he had heard a scream, followed by a chorus of laughter. The bedclothes were damp with his sweat. He waited, heart pounding, for the scream to be repeated. But there was nothing, just the gurgle of rain in the downpipe. It had been nothing but a dream.

Sometime in the past five years he had forgotten about the long nights and the dreams that haunted them. But now they had returned. The past was closing in. Kent was dying, and Kelton was being reborn.

Exhausted, he lay down between the damp sheets and willed himself back to sleep.

Next morning, his first, unformed thought was of Catherine. Sleepily, his arm drifted across to her side of the bed. A rapid series of thoughts followed: she was not there; she was in Florida; she was dead; Elizabeth was in hospital; he was going to avenge them both.

Before the train of thought could drag him further along this path and allow Kent's emotions to overwhelm him, he sat upright, balled his hands into fists, and brought them down hard on the bed. He screamed the word "No!" ferally to the empty room.

He would *not* permit himself to become emotional. Emotions were for Paul Kent; and Kent, for the duration, was no more.

Setting his lips in a line, he arose from the bed and went to the bathroom. The man who looked back at him from the mirror had a full, trim beard; his gray eyes had about them an aura of soft kindliness. The man in the mirror was Paul Kent. Kelton had always been cleanshaven, and the steel gray of his eyes had brought to mind death, not kindliness.

He opened a drawer and extracted a razor and a packet of blades. Ten minutes later he put down the razor and stared again at the face in the mirror. He looked at the thin horizontal line of the lips, the foreshortened aquiline nose, the uncompromising set of the square chin. Finally, he looked at the eyes. The muscles around his eyes tightened involuntarily, tensing and emphasizing the truth: a killer had been reborn.

Chapter 9
Sunday, November 18
Belfast, Northern Ireland

Sean O'Hannessy was in a deep sleep when the telephone on his bedside table began to ring. Reluctantly, consciousness percolated into his mind, and he fumbled drowsily for the instrument. His wife grabbed the sheets and blankets to stop him taking them all as he reached for the phone.

He lifted the receiver, resisted the temptation to say exactly what he thought of people who disturbed the sleep of good God-fearing Catholic folk at this time on a Sunday morning — especially those who had only just arrived from abroad late last night — and said merely, "O'Hannessy here. This had focking well better be good."

"Don't worry, you bastard, it will be."

O'Hannessy was instantly alert. He sat upright, his heart thudding.

He did not recognize the voice, except that it was upper-middle-class English — which was enough, for it meant that whoever was on the other end of the line was the Enemy.

"How was Libya, Mr. O'Hannessy? Hot, I imagine."

Barely keeping his temper in check, O'Hannessy replied reflexively, "What? Who the bloody fock are you?"

"All in good time, Mr. O'Hannessy. First let me ask you a simple question. Does the name Sir David Shackleton mean anything to you?"

"What the fock are you talking about?"

"Answer the question. Sir David Shackleton. Does the name mean anything to you?"

"No."

"I'm sorry but I don't believe you, you bastard. Your gang of mindless adolescent thugs went to considerable trouble to kill him while you were away chinwagging with that desert rat."

Now O'Hannessy lost his temper. "Look, you asshole, I don't know who the fock you are, what the fock you want, or even where the fock you got my phone number. And what's more I don't bloody care. You have ten seconds to make your point, and then I put the phone down."

"Oh, I don't think that would be wise, Mr. O'Hannessy. The ILF made a big mistake when it planted that bomb at Gatwick on Friday...."

O'Hannessy tried to interrupt, but the voice continued, refusing to be drawn into debate. "Whether by accident or design, that explosion took the life of Sir David Shackleton. Sir David was my boss, O'Hannessy. My name is John Pearce. Not Sir John yet, but it damn well will be after I've got my hands on you, you bastard."

O'Hannessy exploded. "Wait a focking minute will you? Who the hell is this bastard Shackleton, anyway?"

"Wrong tense, O'Hannessy. As I told you: 'was,' not 'is.' But just so you know, although I'm sure the papers will have it by now, Sir David was the director of the Government Communications Headquarters at Cheltenham."

The voice paused to give this time to sink in. For once, O'Hannessy was silent. GCHQ was the most secret of all Her Majesty's government agencies. The police, MI5 and SIS, the army, all these were fair game in the war the ILF had waged since 1969. But not GCHQ. That was the one agency that was untouchable. It was, if the truth were to be told, the one agency that the ILF was scared of.

Pearce continued, his words underlining this very fact.

"You're out of your depth this time, O'Hannessy. It's one thing to blow up civilians, politicians and soldiers still in nappies. That way you only have to deal with the police, the army and MI5. It's something else entirely to take down someone like Sir David. You're playing in the big leagues now, son."

O'Hannessy again tried to interrupt, but Pearce ignored him. "I am going to give you a phone number. Write the number down and ring it if there's anything you want to say. Take your time, there's no hurry. We're known for our patience here at GCHQ. Let's give it a week. If we haven't heard from you in seven days, we shall assume you have nothing to say. And if that's the case, then I hope that you have taken out good life insurance, because you and the entire membership of PexCom will cease to exist by the end of the month. The number is...."

"Wait! Wait a focking minute. I don't have a pen," O'Hannessy shouted.

He was trembling. His head was full of questions, but it was obvious that none of them was going to be answered by the man at the other end of the line.

"I trust you have a memory, O'Hannessy," was all he heard as he clumsily scrabbled around on the top of the bedside table for something with which to write. "The number is 0171-101-3462. You may call at any time of day or night. When you call, just identify yourself for the tapes, there's a good chap. Oh, and by the way, your man Shamus O'Riley is as good as dead, whatever you and your colleagues decide to do." There was a click on the line. Pearce had gone.

O'Hannessy slammed the phone down and jumped naked out of bed, frantically repeating the phone number to himself over and over. At last he found a sheet of paper and a pencil and scribbled down the digits. His wife, now thoroughly awake, turned in bed and asked, "What the hell do you think you're doing?"

"Fock off," he replied, then he grabbed his dressing gown from its hook on the back of the door and stamped out the room, heading for the kitchen where he intended to make himself a cup of strong coffee and have a good long think about the one-sided telephone conversation that had just taken place.

Five minutes later he settled himself in an armchair in the living room, his coffee on a table by his side. He steepled his fingers and began to think, for, notwithstanding his coarse language and proclivity for violence, Sean O'Hannessy was an intelligent, thoughtful man, with a first class honors degree in History from Durham to his name.

He replayed the conversation in his mind as carefully as he could, trying to make sure that he had missed nothing. It was all a puzzle, and he could make no sense of any of it.

O'Hannessy had no doubt that John Pearce was exactly who he had claimed to be. Who but GCHQ could know that the real power in the ILF had shifted six months ago from the Paramilitary Cabinet to PexCom, the Paramilitary Executive Committee? And who else would know that he, Sean O'Hannessy, was the leader of PexCom, and that he had returned from Libya only last night?

But what had Pearce been talking about? An explosion at Gatwick for which the ILF had claimed responsibility? Pex-Com had planned no such incident. There must be a mistake. He went to the kitchen, where, in one corner, a week's worth of newspapers were stacked.

Yesterday's paper was on the top of the pile. He bent down and picked it up. He could hardly miss the headline: *ILF carnage at Gatwick*. Walking slowly back to the living room, he read as he walked.

The report did not say much, but one of the few hard facts was the statement that the ILF had claimed responsibility. That, apart from the time, place, and number of dead and wounded, was about the only explicit statement of fact in the column; the remainder was gloss and speculation that this was merely the first in what promised to be a long series of explosions in public places in the run up to Christmas, still over a month away. He noticed that the article made no mention of a Sir David Shackleton.

As he read, he heard the Sunday paper being delivered. Picking up the new paper in the hallway, he saw immediately that the bombing was now, predictably, the object of front page excoriation by politicos of both major parties in Westminster. Leafing carefully through the paper, he saw no reference to Sir David Shackleton or GCHQ until he reached the stop press on the last page. The announcement was brief:

> *It is reported by the Home Secretary that amongst those killed in Friday's explosion at Gatwick was Sir David Shackleton, Director of the super-secret Government Communications Headquarters at Cheltenham.*

That was all.

He sipped his coffee, and tried to analyze the situation logically.

There had been a bomb blast at Gatwick, which had killed several people. Among the dead was, apparently, the director of the Government Communications Headquarters at Cheltenham. All right. But what was this about the ILF having claimed responsibility? That made no sense. No one in the ILF would dare explode a bomb at a major target without clearing it first with PexCom.

Pearce had given a name, what was it? A Shamus somebody... Shamus O'Riley, that was it. He had said that whatever PexCom decided to do, whether or not they agreed to talk with him, this Shamus O'Riley was "as good as dead."

O'Hannessy had never heard of Shamus O'Riley. He began to speculate along increasingly unpleasant lines. Suppose someone was trying to frame the ILF? What if one of the Protestant groups had been responsible for the blast, but were now trying to pin the blame on the ILF? Or even one of the more militant fragments of the much-divided IRA? It wouldn't be the first time. There had been some signs recently that *Saoirse Eireann*, the political wing of the ILF, might at last be asked to join the ongoing peace talks. There were plenty of people in the IRA who would like to stop that from happening.

It was now nearly eight o'clock. No longer too early to start rousing people on a Sunday morning.

O'Hannessy pulled a telephone towards him. Lifting the receiver, he dialed a local number.

The phone at the other end rang five times before it was picked up. O'Hannessy said, "Sean O'Hannessy here, for Gerry Connor. It's urgent."

A female voice said, dubiously, "Well, he's taking a shower right now. I can have him call you back."

"No," said O'Hannessy impatiently. "You just be a good girl and put the phone down and tell him right now that I want to talk to him. I'll wait."

"Well, I kind of hate to disturb him."

O'Hannessy's tone became several shades rougher. "Listen, you little bitch: you pass on my message or you'll regret ever meeting the focking bastard."

"OK, OK, keep your bloody hair on."

O'Hannessy heard the sound of the telephone receiver being rested on a hard surface. A few seconds later, O'Hannessy could just make out the voice of the woman shouting, "Oh, Gerry, it's only me," then the brief sound of rushing water as a door was opened and closed. Then a few more seconds and the sound of heavy footsteps coming quickly coming toward the telephone. The telephone was picked up. "This is Gerry Connor."

"Hello, Gerry. Sean O'Hannessy. Meeting at the usual place. Two o'clock this afternoon."

"Why? What's up? Is it to do with that bloody Gatwick thing?"

Typically stupid, thought O'Hannessy. As if he would say anything over an open telephone line. Although, he mused, perhaps there was no point in hiding anything — the English seemed to know everything in any case.

But he just said, "You'll find out then, Gerry. Don't be late." Then he hung up the phone.

He made three more phone calls, none lasting more than a minute.

Before the day was through, he would get to the bottom of this. Hell! What a mess to come home to.

Chapter 10
Friday, November 16
Orlando, Florida

Harris disembarked from the plane and, as soon as he had cleared customs and immigration, headed for a telephone.

He reached a recording that instructed him in a bland female voice to leave a message.

"The deal is concluded," he said, and put the phone down.

It was early evening. Too late to think of returning to his Vermont home today. He would stay overnight in one of the motels that lined Route 192. Tomorrow he would read what the papers had to say about the Gatwick explosion; then he would fly north, either tomorrow or the next day. He deserved a few days' rest before he embarked on his next mission: to kill the supercilious bastard Brezhnerov who had disturbed him at Kent's home two months before.

Harris slept well. Next morning he arose shortly after seven and breakfasted at a restaurant next door to the motel, outside which stood an enormous sign promising "Breakfast — All You Can Eat — $3.99."

As he stepped inside, he saw that perhaps a third of the small, square, Formica-covered tables were occupied, almost all by families with excited young children, restlessly anticipating the day ahead at Disney World. An aroma of warm, greasy food met his nostrils.

He chose a table as distant as possible from any children, and in less than a minute an attractive young woman in her late teens appeared, carrying a menu and a copy of the day's *Orlando Sentinel*. He glanced at the menu and ordered an omelet and large orange juice. The waitress left, and he turned his attention to the paper.

The bombing in Gatwick had, barely, made the front page of the local paper; the details, such as they were, were relegated to a large box in an inside page. It was a wire service story, probably repeated with minor variations in most of the country's local and regional newspapers.

Harris skimmed the boxed article. There were eight confirmed dead, with about twenty hospitalized. Harris nodded slightly, satisfied with the numbers. Had any fewer been caught in the blast, media attention might have been attracted to his actual targets. Any more injuries would have been, so to speak, overkill. He noticed with even greater satisfaction the statement that the ILF had claimed responsibility. There was a small additional sidebar summarizing bomb attacks in recent years that had been attributed to the ILF and another, somewhat longer one that tried to explain the tortuous relationships among the various factions on both sides of the Irish border.

Breakfast arrived. He reread the article more carefully while he sipped his juice. Satisfied that everything had gone exactly as he had planned, he put the paper down and attacked the omelet with gusto.

Back at the motel, he glanced at a complimentary copy of *USA Today* in the lobby, but its description of the bombing was even briefer than that of the *Sentinel*.

He paused in front of a rack of brochures that described the area's tourist destinations. Kennedy Space Center held a momentary attraction, but the shuttle had been rolled back a few days earlier, the victim of yet another in what seemed an eternal series of fuel leaks, and the launch that had been scheduled for Sunday had now been postponed. Nothing else on offer held any appeal.

He thought about catching a plane north, but on reflection decided against it. He deserved a rest. He would fly back tomorrow, but today he would kick his feet back and relax.

He drove aimlessly around the outskirts of Orlando, walked several times around one of the many small lakes nearby, and checked the television several times during the day for any additional news about the bombing on the television — but it was already yesterday's news, and by early afternoon did not rate so much as a mention.

He dozed lightly in the afternoon, made a reservation for a flight north for the next day, and spent $50 on dinner at a restaurant in Orlando. After watching a particularly vacuous movie on television, he went to bed early.

On Sunday, feeling fresh and relaxed, Harris arose promptly at 8 a.m. By nine o'clock he was at the airport, where he purchased a copy of the day's London *Times* flown in overnight, then hurried to the gate to catch his flight to Boston.

The index on the front page directed him to page 3, and he opened the newspaper to that page as soon as he was settled in his first class seat.

His heart skipped a beat.

Half the page was given over to the bombing; the headline blazoned *Spy Chief Killed In Blast* in 48-point type. Immediately underneath was a photograph of a man gazing out of the page.

Harris stared back into the eyes of the photograph. He recognized them instantly; the last time he had seen them they had been eyeing him suspiciously across an aisle in the Gatwick departure lounge.

He turned to the legend underneath the photograph. "Sir David Shackleton," he read. The newspaper began to shake perceptibly in his hands. What had he done? Whom had he killed?

His eyes returned to the top of the page, and he started to read.

LONDON. It was revealed early today by highly placed sources who wish to remain anonymous that one of the victims in Friday's bomb blast that claimed the lives of eight people at the international departure lounge of the South Terminal of London's Gatwick airport was Sir David Shackleton, director of the Government Communications Headquarters, GCHQ, in Cheltenham. GCHQ is responsible for the country's foreign intelligence surveillance.

Sir David, 52, was the youngest Director in the history of GCHQ when he was appointed to that post nine years ago. He has been credited with modernizing the country's eavesdropping and intelligence gathering operations.

Sir David was a career intelligence officer and an acknowledged expert in the fields of cryptography and computer controlled "expert systems." His thesis for his Cantabrigian doctoral degree, entitled "Heuristics and Problem Solving," although written thirty years ago, remains classified.

Sir David is said to have designed single-handedly the database handling techniques now used by GCHQ to collate intelligence information from widely disparate sources. The Irish Liberation Front has claimed responsibility for the bombing, but it is not yet known if Sir David was the intended target or merely an unlucky bystander.

Harris read the column three times, wringing the meaning from the words. He noticed that the paper was careful to state only that the ILF was "presumed" responsible, and that the organization had "claimed responsibility." Was this simply caution, or did the authorities already know that the explosion was not the work of the ILF?

Harris folded the paper across his knees and stared blankly into space, thinking. After all his careful planning, his endless hours considering possibilities, mentally rehearsing what his actions would be if any of a hundred and one things were to go wrong — after all that, something like this, something for which he could not possibly have planned, had to happen.

He felt like shouting at the unfairness of it all.

The head of GCHQ. GCHQ was the British equivalent of the National Security Agency. Without meaning to, he swore out loud, and received disapproving stares from a young couple across the aisle. He smiled weakly, and turned to look out the window.

He needed to think.

How good were the people at GCHQ? The NSA were rumored to be very good indeed, and were certainly more dangerous than either the FBI or the CIA. But what about their British counterparts? Were the British as inept as they were generally thought to be? Or was that just a carefully cultivated image?

What was GCHQ's brief? Did it simply collect and gather information, or did it include operations? Specifically, did it include wet operations?

The authorities would doubtless undertake their inquiry with increased vigor because one of the dead happened to have a knighthood, but even so surely they would not pursue the case with the same lethal energy that an American team of investigators would have demonstrated.

He thought about the clues he might have left.

There was the remote control; doubtless that had been found long ago, but there could be no fingerprints on it, and it was constructed entirely from unmarked parts readily available in England.

There was the explosive device itself. That he had been forced to construct in America; it was too risky to try to find a source of Foamtex or some similar explosive in the United Kingdom. But the force from the explosion should have been enough to destroy any traceable parts.

The sports bag, and the other items it contained apart from the Foamtex block, had been purchased in the UK in the days before the explosion.

That was all; there were no loopholes that he could see, no incriminating evidence left at the scene of the crime, certainly nothing that would point across the Atlantic. As long as the Brits treated this as a purely domestic affair, then he should be safe.

Or so he kept telling himself. The trouble was, he was unconvinced by the argument.

By the time he disembarked at Boston's Logan International Airport, Harris's inability to come to a firm conclusion about his degree of exposure had put him in a foul mood.

He was angry at fate for striking him such an unlikely and unlucky blow; he was angry at *The Times* for failing to carry a more complete story; he was angry at the weather — one of those deeply depressing wet, cold New England snows had begun to fall just as the plane had landed; and he was angry at himself for being angry.

He tried to console himself by thinking of the four and a half million dollars profit he had shown from the job, but the dollars had been in his Swiss account for so many months now that it was difficult to associate them with his actions of the past week.

He strode belligerently to a car rental stand and rented a small, front wheel drive Japanese subcompact that would handle well if the snow continued to fall.

Escaping the city as quickly as possible, he headed north towards New Hampshire. As he drove, the snow began to take its business more seriously. By the time he reached Manchester, New Hampshire, the snow was falling in large flakes. They were still melting when they hit the road, but the temperature was beginning to fall; it looked like the first true storm of the winter was under way.

In Manchester, he returned the car to the agency and recovered his own four-wheel-drive vehicle from a covered parking garage.

As he left Manchester, the snow began to stick to the black-top; by the time he reached the Vermont border, he had shifted to four-wheel-drive and the sand and salt trucks were out in force.

Nearly two hours later, he drove through the small town of Torrington, Vermont. Nearly home.

By now he was driving at a steady 25 miles per hour; darkness had fallen and the continuous stream of falling snow reflecting in his headlights was hypnotic. He followed a sand truck for the final two miles of his journey before, at last, he came to the place where an unmarked track, just large enough for a single vehicle, appeared in the trees to his right. He turned off the road and eased his way along the track, winding through the New England forest for nearly a quarter of a mile before opening out into a clearing in which stood a single, two storied dwelling.

The house had been built four years before, to his own design. Located in a fifty acre patch of forest owned by Harris, the nearest house was nearly a mile away, back in the direction of Torrington.

He drove into the garage, and turned off the engine. An exhausted sigh escaped him. Home at last.

He showered and changed, and heated a TV dinner from the freezer. As he ate, he kept pushing thoughts of Sir David Shackleton away. Time to worry about him later.

When he had finished eating, he went to his study, a small room about ten feet square, whose walls were covered from ceiling to floor with book-filled cases. In the middle of the room stood a solitary desk and chair, several papers strewn untidily across the surface of the former.

Ignoring the desk, he strode across the room, halting opposite the wall of books on the far side of the study. He ran his hand along the top of a row of books near waist level, and then pulled.

A length of about half a dozen books pulled away from the wall, swinging out and exposing a vertical steel handhold built into the wall itself. Grabbing firmly, Harris twisted, then pushed. The entire bookcase pivoted silently open.

Behind the bookcase, a light came on automatically, illuminating a room about twelve feet square. Harris stepped inside. Several filing cabinets with neatly marked drawers were stacked along one wall; along another was a stock of imperishable food and a bed. Opposite the bed, standing against a wall, was a table on which stood a small personal computer; a chair was tucked neatly under the table. In one corner, incongruous, stood a chemical toilet.

Harris turned on the computer. The monitor flickered into life and a series of messages flashed by on the screen far too quickly to be read, followed by a colorful screen with half a dozen icons. Harris clicked an icon twice, flexed his fingers, and began to type.

Within sixty seconds, Harris was connected to a large mainframe computer owned by the Secure Computing Corporation and located four thousand miles away, in Switzerland. This mainframe, among other duties, ran a confidential messaging service where people could leave electronic mail for other users of the machine, secure in the knowledge that the mail was beyond the reach of even the US government.

As he logged on to the remote computer under the account name *plethora*, it beeped once to inform him that there was a single message awaiting his attention, from Louise Smith — which was the pseudonym used by Vincent Cotterell.

He read Cotterell's message:

> Congratulations, Mr. Harris. I am informed that Mrs. Kent is dead, and her daughter in critical condition with brain damage – which is even better than if she were dead. We need communicate no more. The prearranged phone line will be disconnected immediately, as will my account on this computer. Once again, congratulations! Goodbye.

Harris looked at the computer screen in stunned disbelief.

What on Earth was Cotterell trying to do, using his real name in such a message? Even with the most secure system in the world, one did not take foolhardy, needless risks. Furious, he bashed at the keys, instructing the machine to delete the message; then he angrily terminated the connection.

Still angry, he turned his own machine off, and, closing the entrance to the hidden room behind him, he made his way back to the living room for a stiff drink.

Sipping his brandy, he forced himself to think calmly.

Perhaps he was simply being paranoid. After all, the computer was in Switzerland, and the Secure Computing Corporation stated baldly in its contract that it would coöperate with no requests for copies of messages stored on its system, except those received under direct order of the Swiss courts. But even so, one did not take unnecessary risks.

Was it simply a mistake on Cotterell's part? Or was there some deeper reason why he had linked Harris with the Gatwick bombing? Was there any chance that someone else could read the message from "Louise Smith"?

Harris did not know. But of one thing he was uncomfortably aware. Now that the job was over, he was suddenly expendable. Worse, Cotterell might even regard him as a liability, since Harris, if somehow apprehended, was certain to name the person who had bankrolled the job.

Was there any basis for his worries? Or were they merely paranoia? Harris finished his brandy without coming to any conclusions. Perhaps, he told himself, things would be clearer in the morning. It was getting late, and the exhausting drive from Boston, layered on top of the emotional baggage of his just-completed mission, made it too difficult to think clearly.

He set the burglar alarm, and made his way slowly upstairs for bed.

Outside, the snow was still falling. Six inches had already fallen, and as many more would be added overnight. Upstairs, in his bedroom, Harris looked out of the window into the falling whiteness. The very ordinariness and tranquillity of the falling snow calmed him. He climbed between the sheets more than half convinced that in the morning all his anxieties would seem faintly ridiculous.

A little after three o'clock, he was woken out of a deep sleep by a large red bulb on his bedside table, which was pulsing once a second, alternately filling the room with its lurid red glow, then plunging the room into darkness. Someone had broken into the house and triggered the silent burglar alarm.

He felt under his pillow for the pistol that was always there, then pressed a switch next to the lamp. The light stopped flashing and the room was plunged into a gray dimness, lit only by light seeping in from the partly-open doorway.

Keeping a firm hold on the pistol, he quietly rolled over the side of the bed farthest from the door, breaking his fall to make as little noise as possible in the room below. He rolled fluidly underneath the bed, until he was in a position where he could see the bottom of the door without being seen.

He calmed his breathing, forcing himself to take slow, even breaths, and waited.

He listened intently, but heard nothing except his shallow breathing for nearly five minutes, when at last he heard a distinct creak coming from somewhere beyond the bedroom door. It came from the stairs; there would be another creak in a moment, five steps higher.

The second creak came, quickly stifled but unmistakable. Without a doubt, someone was stealthily climbing towards his room.

His breathing now was quiet and steady. His muscles tensed as the bedroom door noiselessly swung open. Whoever pushed it was careful to remain out of sight.

There was a sudden movement. A pair of feet were suddenly in the doorway. There came two rapid, muffled shots, and simultaneously a jerk of movement in the bed above him.

Even in the midst of the attack, Harris was annoyed with himself for not being better prepared. He should have installed some sort of trap to spring on an intruder. Instead, he was the one that was trapped, underneath his own bed. He had a pistol, but there was no way to use it effectively until he could stand up and get a clear shot at whomever was standing in the doorway.

Light flooded the room.

The intruder had snapped on the overhead light; one look at the empty bed and he would know immediately that Harris was not there.

For several seconds the feet stood motionless while their owner silently surveyed the room. Then the feet began to move in a manner that could mean only one thing: their owner was bending down to look under the bed.

Harris shifted his weight noiselessly and aimed the gun towards the feet. A hand touched the floor to take the intruder's weight, and then a pistol came into view, pointing vaguely in Harris's direction.

For a fraction of a second, Harris was terrified that the intruder was about to take a blind shot under the bed, but then a face appeared next to the floor, looking directly into his eyes.

Nothing moved for several tenths of a second, as both of them registered the ludicrousness of the situation. But Harris had the advantage. "Hi," he said with a smile. He fired.

Blood spurted out in front of him, and he saw an arm jerk up as his opponent's gun fired, harmlessly shooting the ceiling.

Harris rolled out from under the bed in the direction of the open door; he kept rolling, crashing into the intruder's limbs just as he was trying to stand up. The force of Harris's momentum kept him moving, and the intruder fell forwards over him, the intruder's arms coming forwards to protect their owner as he crashed down against the bed.

As Harris turned, he pushed down with his legs and his right hand, so that in a single motion he was now standing, framed by the doorway, looking back toward the intruder. He brought his hands together in front of him, clasping his pistol, pointing it at the man who was struggling by his bed.

The intruder was stranded halfway between bed and floor. The man's — and it was a man, a man in his mid thirties with straggly hair that hung over his face in wet strands — the man's feet were on the floor, but the upper half of his body was on the bed.

He was trying to raise himself with his left hand. From the neighborhood of his right wrist blood was flowing; his pistol was still in his right hand, but his clumsy attempts to grasp it firmly seemed to be demanding his full attention. He made several attempts to clasp the pistol properly. Eventually, he surrendered the effort and, taking the strain off his good left arm, he lowered himself back on to the bed, beaten.

"Throw it on the floor," ordered Harris.

There was no immediate response from the other man.

"Do it. Now," Harris commanded.

"I c... c... can't," the man replied. "My hand hurts like hell."

"Then you will slowly stand and use your other hand, carefully, to drop the gun on the bed. Make it real slow. One move I don't like, and you'll never hold anything again."

With deep groans, most of which Harris suspected were unnecessary, the man shifted his weight and began to rise. Turning partway so that his left side faced Harris, he moved his left hand across in front of his body to try to hold his right hand steady. Without warning, the man threw himself sideways, away from Harris and on to the bed, turning as he did so. His hands swung around and for a fraction of a second, Harris stared straight down the barrel of a pistol. Harris fired as he bent his knees, dropping to the ground.

The intruder's head jerked back with the force of the bullet, his body following. As his backward jump ended, his head hit the bed first, followed by the rest of his body. Blood splattered over the bed. The man's arms landed on his torso, then the left hand loosed its grip on the pistol, and the right hand slipped down his side, leaving a trail of fresh blood, until it came to a rest, palm up, on the bed.

Harris could see none of this. He had fired his single shot and dropped to his hands and knees in a single reflexive action. All he could see of the intruder was a pair of legs from the knees down dangling over the side of the bed.

Harris leaned forwards and pressed the barrel of his pistol against the right kneecap of his assailant. "I'm going to count to three," he said. "At the end of that time, one of two things is going to happen. Either you are going to throw that gun of yours out through the door behind me, or I am going to blow your kneecap off."

The intruder did not reply.

"One... two... three. OK, here it comes." Harris pulled the trigger.

More blood, mixed with shards of bone, flew around the room. Then Harris, spattered with the other man's blood, stood up.

The sight that greeted him would have made lesser men turn and run for the bathroom.

Harris merely eyed the body on the bed critically for several seconds, then methodically set to work.

Putting down his gun on the bedside table, he leaned across the body. He removed the pistol from the sticky, lifeless hand, and placed it next to his own. Then he knelt on the bed and pulled the face towards him.

His second bullet had demolished the left side of the man's face. He pulled the pillow from the head of the bed and placed it so that the disfigured portion of the face was hidden, as he tried to reconstruct what the face must have looked like when it was whole.

It seemed familiar, ringing a bell somewhere in the recesses of his mind; but he could not quite place it. He went to the bathroom, returning a few seconds later with a small mirror.

94

Kneeling on the bed once more, he placed the mirror so that the reflection of the undamaged half showed in the reflecting surface. He recognized the completed face immediately: the man was one of Vincent Cotterell's Denver guards, the one who had greeted him at pistol point when he had stepped out of the elevator.

Harris remained motionless for a few moments, thinking. Then he dressed rapidly in warm clothes, ignoring the sticky blood that adhered to his body. Picking up both pistols, he went silently downstairs.

Staying in the shadows, he worked his way from room to room. The only thing out of the ordinary was a paneless window in the kitchen, where the intruder had entered the house.

Satisfied that no one else was in the house, he went to the study and entered the hidden room. The bed slid away from the wall easily and noiselessly on oiled castors, revealing a bundle of warm clothes, a garotte, and the outline of a square in the floor. Inside the square, near one edge, was a recessed pull ring. He slipped the garotte into a pocket, then he grasped the ring firmly and the trap-door opened.

Five minutes later and about fifty yards from the house, an accumulation of snow in the lee of a boulder shifted slightly. It moved again and then tumbled aside as a portion of the forest floor moved upward. Harris, now dressed in warm clothes, emerged into the still, cold, white forest.

He stood up, stretching his sore muscles, and listened intently.

The air was motionless; the only sound he could hear was the blood circulating in his ears. The snow had almost stopped falling and there were ragged gaps in the clouds. Light from the last-quarter moon joined with starlight to illuminate the forest with a ghostly pallor.

He took a firm grip of his pistol and began to walk cautiously towards the house.

Reaching the periphery of the clearing surrounding the house, he made his way around the boundary, keeping to the

shadows of the forest, until he could see the kitchen window.
There was no trace of anyone keeping watch. In the snow was
a single set of depressions where the intruder had walked up
to the house. Against the house, he could barely make out
the pane of glass, suction cups still attached.

Silently, he set off to follow the intruder's footprints, back-
tracking the way the dead man had come. They led down the
track toward the road.

He was nearly at the road when he saw the car.

It had been parked for some time. The ruts of the tire
tracks were partially filled with snow, and a layer of snow
covered the car's windows, almost hiding the light that was
on inside the vehicle.

Harris leaned against a tree and waited, pistol in one hand,
the other hand inside the pocket with the garotte.

The night was no longer silent. Now and then, overbur-
dened branches released their burden of snow, which fell to
the ground with a loud flurry. A branch high above the car
suddenly deposited its burden, causing a loud, hollow thump
that set off other flurries from branches nearby.

A few moments later, the driver's door opened. Harris
tensed, watching from a distance of ten yards as a short,
stocky man emerged.

The man closed the car door and began to trudge towards
Harris with his hands in his pockets and his eyes fixed firmly
on the path in front of him. He passed within six feet of
Harris without noticing him.

The man heard a thudding run behind him. Turning, he
was propelled forward as Harris kneed his back violently. He
fell forward, but his fall was arrested by something biting
painfully into his throat. He tried to scream, but no sound
could escape. Whatever was around his throat tightened. He
gurgled, dribbling froth from the corners of his mouth. His
hands went up to his neck, but they were powerless to move
the iron grip that was throttling him.

Harris counted slowly to twenty, then released the pressure on the garotte. The man fell forward into the snow, gasping for breath.

"How many of you are there?" Harris asked quietly.

No answer, just gasps.

Harris repeated the question, pulling on the handles of the garotte just enough to remind the man that it was still there.

Harris had to repeat the question two more times before the man had gathered his wits sufficiently to reply.

"Just me," he gasped.

Harris sighed heavily.

"Don't lie to me, you son of a bitch. I just shot the face off one of your friends. I'm freezing and in a bad mood and I'll be happy to finish this quickly if you try to screw with me. So I'll ask you one last time: how many of you are there?"

The man tried to lift himself on one arm; Harris kicked it away so that the man fell back to the snow. The man answered, "There were just the two of us. Honestly." There was a hollow sound to his voice, as if the garotte had done permanent damage to his larynx.

"Then let's go sit in the car where we can be comfortable and have a little talk."

Harris pulled the garotte away and dragged the man to his feet. Leading him to the car, he pushed him against the hood and said, "OK. Stop there and wipe the snow off the windshield."

The man turned to protest, but the sight of a pistol in Harris's hands instantly silenced him. He turned and began to wipe the windshield clean with his gloved hands.

"Now, get back in the driver's side. Do it slowly. One move I don't expect and it'll be the last move you make."

Harris hung back in the darkness of the forest, so as to be invisible to anyone inside the car. As the man opened the door, the courtesy light flooded the interior. The car was empty.

Harris stepped forward out of the shadows. "Get in and slide across to the passenger side."

Half a minute later they were seated side by side in the front of the vehicle.

Harris looked across at the man. The man was terrified. He wasn't going to give any trouble.

"Tell me everything," ordered Harris, glancing down at the gun to remind the man of its presence.

The man's eyes followed Harris's, then he looked up with an appeal in his eyes and, when he spoke, in his voice. "Please don't shoot," he began. His voice sounded unnatural. He put his hand to his throat. "You... you've done something to my voice," he said.

"I'll send you somewhere you won't have a voice to worry about if you don't start talking," said Harris.

"I'm just the driver. I have a wife and children, and...." His face was contorted, threatening to burst into tears.

Harris's voice softened. "Listen: I'm not going to shoot you unless you force me to. All I want is information. I'll ask the questions and you just answer them, OK?"

The man nodded, regaining a measure of control. "OK."

"First question. Let's make it an easy one. Who are you working for?"

The fear in the man's eyes suddenly quickened. No matter how much he feared Harris, there was someone of whom he was even more terrified. "But if I tell you that, he'll kill me."

"Possibly. But if you don't, I guarantee that I will. I'm cold, I'm tired, and I'm in a lousy mood. I don't give a damn about your problems. I'll ask you one last time: who are you working for?"

The man looked away. "A man named Brezhnerov," he said, his voice barely audible.

"And he works for Vincent Cotterell?"

The man nodded. "Yes. I'm a security guard for Mr. Cotterell in his Boston office."

"What about the man that you drove out here tonight?"

"Johnson? He's one of Mr. Cotterell's personal bodyguards now, directly responsible to Mr. Brezhnerov. He was a security guard out in Denver or somewhere until quite recently, I think."

Harris offered a crumb of encouragement. "Good, you're doing very well; that's exactly what he was. Now, Mr. Johnson was carrying a gun. Where's yours?"

The reply came without hesitation. "In my pocket. Please don't think I was trying to hide it from you. I didn't know you knew I had one, and I thought I'd only be making trouble for myself if I told you."

The fear on the man's face looked genuine enough; it was even possible that he was telling the truth.

"Which pocket?"

"The left one; I'm left handed."

Harris remembered back. Yes, the man had used his left hand to open the car door. Keeping his pistol aligned on the man's stomach, Harris withdrew the weapon and placed it in the left pocket of his own jacket.

"Good; we're doing fine, aren't we?" said Harris.

The man nodded reluctantly. His hands went to his throat and caressed the place where the garotte had been.

"One more question; then we're all done."

The man swallowed, obviously wondering what would happen to him once they were "all done."

"Who do you think I am?" Harris asked.

The man looked puzzled.

"Go on," urged Harris, "you must have some idea."

The man shook his head. "No. I was just the driver, and I got that job only because I was convenient. I'm sure Johnson knows... knew who you are, but my job was just to drive him here. I didn't even know where we were going; Johnson just gave me directions.

"We drove out here and parked and waited for a couple of hours. Then Johnson left the car and told me that if he wasn't back by three thirty I should come looking for him. In no event was I to enter the house. I was just supposed to look around outside and see if I could find him. If not, I was to come back to the car and wait another half hour. If he still didn't show up, I was to drive to the nearest public telephone I could find, dial a number, and explain what had happened to the machine at the other end."

"What was the number?"

The other man reeled off a ten digit number, with an area code in southern California. Harris repeated the number to himself.

"All right," said Harris. "Listen carefully. These are your instructions. When you leave here, find a phone and call that number. Tell the machine exactly what happened here. Also tell it that within an hour from now, I will have deposited a detailed account of Cotterell's association with me in a very safe place. If I should disappear, that information will be passed on to the authorities, who, I am sure, will waste no time in acting upon it. Do you understand?"

The man nodded; "Yes, I think so."

"OK, repeat it back to me."

The man did so to Harris's satisfaction.

"All right. Now, I'm going to get out of the car, and you're going to drive away from here. I never want to see you again, understand?"

"Yes, I understand." The man nodded vigorously. He never wanted to see Harris again either.

Harris grasped the driver's door, opened it, and began to get out of the car. He suddenly stopped. "That telephone number," he snapped; "what was it again?"

The man was taken aback for a moment; then he reeled off the ten digits. It was the same number he had given before. Harris finished getting out of the car and slammed the door behind him.

The man started the engine and jammed the car into gear. In thirty seconds he was gone, heading back towards Torrington.

The night was bitter cold. Harris, despite his jacket, shivered in the frigid air. He turned and began to trudge wearily back towards the house.

In the living room, he picked up the phone and dialed a ten-digit number. The phone rang once at the other end, then a recorded female voice said, "Leave a message after the beep. It may be as long as you wish."

Harris put the phone back on the hook and tried to think clearly. There was a lot to do.

He must deal with the body and the mess upstairs, and he must make good on his threat about leaving a message where it would be found if he were suddenly to disappear.

Which was more important? He tried to put himself in the enemy's shoes. What would Cotterell or Brezhnerov do when the phone call came from the terrified driver? One nasty possibility that occurred to him was that a tame judge might be disturbed in his sleep and a search warrant issued. Within an hour or two, there might be police on the premises, looking for evidence of a bloody killing.

It would have to be the body first, then. With a noise that was half sigh and half groan, he began wearily to climb the stairs. It was going to be a long night.

Chapter 11
Monday, November 19
Cheltenham, England

John Pearce was named Acting Director of GCHQ within hours of Sir David's demise. Pearce was forty eight years old, an Old Etonian and senior member of House, the son of an Old Etonian and senior member of House. He had known no employer other than GCHQ, and had risen through the ranks on a path parallel to, but quite different from, Sir David's.

Sir David had from the beginning been a technician, fully competent to understand the minutiæ of data acquisition and analysis. John Pearce had never shared Sir David's ease with mathematics and the day-to-day fieldwork of signals intelligence, having read English Literature at House; but he possessed a keen mind and those who underestimated him quickly learned the error of their ways. It was rumored throughout GCHQ that John Pearce was the highest scoring candidate who had ever taken the agency's entrance exam.

Although patriotism was an understood requirement for everyone who worked at GCHQ, in John Pearce it reached its apotheosis. While most of Britain had, albeit with reluctance, conceded that the British Empire was no more, in Pearce's mind one third of the map was still colored red.

Two years after moving to Cheltenham, Pearce had married a landed and monied family out of *Burke's Landed Gentry*, a union that gave him much happiness and, perhaps even more importantly to someone with his views, an unexceptionable social standing.

Pearce had now reached that happy stage in life where he knew what his future held — ten or so years as Deputy Director under Sir David, then a K and the Directorship for perhaps five years before retiring — and he was smugly and understandably satisfied with that future. He was forty eight, almost bald, slightly underweight (he played squash against his daughter twice a week) and almost completely content with his lot.

Then Gatwick changed everything.

The quickly-compiled reported stated that Sir David had been killed instantly; he was one of the closest people to the explosion. Witnesses said that he had purposefully thrust himself between the bomb and a small girl. Whether he was a specific target was something that was not yet clear.

The identification of Sir David's body had taken until 1 p.m. on Friday, almost two and a half hours after the explosion, and checking and confirmation required another ninety minutes. By four o'clock on Friday afternoon, the prime minister had contacted Pearce and confirmed him as Acting Director pending his appointment to the full Directorate.

By 11:30 a.m. on Monday, less than 72 hours after the bombing, a complete transcript of Sunday's hastily called meeting of the ILF's PexCom was on Pearce's desk, courtesy of a joint MI5/GCHQ surveillance team.

He digested the transcript with characteristic thoroughness but also with an increasing sense of dissatisfaction.

PexCom's discussion left no room for doubt. The ILF was *not* responsible for the bombing. No member of PexCom knew anything about the incident, nor was the name of Shamus O'Riley known to any of them.

There was considerable discussion whether the ILF should admit responsibility for the blast regardless of these facts.

After all, it might convince the British government that the ILF meant what it said when it insisted that *Sinn Fein* did not represent all Irish Catholics and *Saoirse Eireann* also deserved to be included in the peace talks.

Eventually, Sean O'Hannessy, who had refrained from mentioning the phone call from Pearce that had precipitated the meeting, convinced his colleagues that to claim responsibility would be counterproductive, and he was deputed to contact the authorities and to inform them that the explosion was not the ILF's doing.

So when O'Hannessy phoned Pearce early on Monday afternoon it was a short conversation; Pearce already knew exactly what O'Hannessy had to say.

Immediately afterwards, Pearce made a lengthy telephone call to the Director-General of MI5. Then Pearce called a GCHQ operative to his office.

A lanky man in his early thirties entered Pearce's office. The man sported short, thinning blond hair and wire-frame glasses. His long, thin face emphasized his hollow cheeks. A series of parallel lines crossed his brow, even in repose.

"You wanted to see me, sir?" In his voice, surprise was mixed with a hint of anxiety.

"Ah, Mr. Smith. Take a seat, and don't worry, I haven't called you in to bite your head off."

Nigel Smith smiled wanly as he sat. "That's good to know, sir."

"Rather the opposite, actually. I've been reviewing your file. Quite impressive."

"Thank you, sir. I do my best."

"Exactly. And that's why I've chosen you for an important job. Tell me, have you had any ideas about that terrible affair at Gatwick last Friday in which the Director was killed?"

Smith shook his head. "No, sir. Other than that the Irish Liberation Front must be off its collective rocker."

"What if I told you it wasn't the ILF's doing?"

"Sir?"

"We have unimpeachable evidence that, contrary to the reports in the media, the blast that killed the Director was not the work of the ILF. What we don't know yet is whose work it was. Would you be interested in being part of the effort to track down who was responsible, Mr. Smith?"

"Yes, sir, of course, if there's any way I could be of help."

"Good man. I'll outline the situation. The details are in here." Pearce pushed a folder across the desk. Smith picked it up as Pearce continued.

"The first thing you should know is that as far as Whitehall is concerned GCHQ will simply furnish any relevant information to Special Branch. Officially, this is their case. But, strictly unofficially, all their information, as well as any gathered by ourselves or the other security agencies, will be channeled through this office. We have the full support of both MI5 and SIS on this one. MI5 will provide whatever logistical support we need and SIS..., well, I don't think I need to spell it out. Let's just say that once we locate the person or persons responsible, SIS will take it from there if we feel it necessary. You understand?"

Smith nodded, aware of the sensitivity of what he had just been told. "Yes, sir."

"Good. Your job is to help find out who planted the bomb. You will report directly to me, although you will be using MI5 facilities. I've just got off the blower to the DG at MI5. He's making arrangements for you to work directly with his forensic people. Accommodation in Curzon House has been arranged. You're expected at MI5 forensics at nine o'clock in the morning. My secretary will give you the details on the way out. That folder is under no circumstances to be copied; nor is it to leave this building. I expect you to study it, memorize whatever portions of it you deem relevant, and return it to security before you leave the building this evening. You had no plans for the evening, I hope?"

"Nothing I can't cancel, no, sir."

"Right. Now, I realize this is all rather open ended, so I'm not setting a timetable, but I do expect to receive a detailed report from you at least once a week, and more frequently if any advances are made. The situation will be reviewed whenever it seems appropriate to do so. We will have our first review one week from today unless something breaks before then, in which case we'll just play it by ear. Any questions?"

Nigel Smith shook his head and said a quiet "No, sir." Pearce dismissed him.

The lines on Nigel Smith's forehead were deeper than ever as he left the office.

Monday, November 19
Near Torrington, Vermont

George Harris finally lay down to rest on the small, hard bed in the hidden room behind the study at half past five in the morning. He was exhausted, but for a long time his mind refused to let him rest. For more than an hour he remained trapped on the edge of sleep, occupied with thoughts of Vincent Cotterell and Victor Brezhnerov but unable to think constructively of how he might deal with either of these problematic characters.

Eventually, as the first unseen hint of the false dawn began to illuminate the forest outside, George Harris slipped into sleep.

He slept fitfully for about three hours. When he awoke, his mind was still wrestling ineffectively with the problems that had occupied it as he fell asleep.

He pushed Brezhnerov and Cotterell out of his mind to concentrate on more immediate concerns.

For five minutes, he reconnoitered the house. It was still empty. After showering and drinking three cups of coffee in a row, he returned to the hidden room and spent the next hour in front of the computer, composing a document that gave every detail of his association with Vincent Cotterell, and Cotterell's link to the blast at Gatwick.

Pausing only for another coffee, he uploaded the document to the Secure Computing Corporation's computer in Lucerne.

He then sent a short note to the system administrator requesting that in the event that his account was not accessed for a period of a month, or if payment on the account were ever to become delinquent, the administrator should immediately extract file number 12,683 from the archives and forward it to the United States Federal Bureau of Investigation.

As soon as this was done, he called the number in Southern California.

"This is George Harris and I have a message for Vincent Cotterell and Victor Brezhnerov," he said to the machine. "As promised, I have taken out an insurance policy. I do not recommend a repeat of last night's efforts. If anything happens to me, a full report of Cotterell's association with the events of last Friday will automatically be sent to the FBI."

He dropped the handset back on the hook, satisfied that, one way or another, Cotterell and Brezhnerov would receive his message.

How long it would stop them from trying again was another matter entirely.

Chapter 12
Tuesday, 20 November
New York

George Harris was under no illusions that his precautions would do more than delay Vincent Cotterell for a while. He also knew that he could not expect to survive a second attack. In the circumstances, he was left with no alternative: he had to strike first.

By lunchtime on Tuesday, Harris had formulated a plan. He lost no time putting it into effect.

By mid afternoon, he was driving south in a rented Ford. He drove until well after sunset, until he reached Sherbourne, a narrow concentration of commercial buildings and tract housing some forty miles north of New York City. There he checked into a small, shabby motel adjacent to the freeway, its sign advertising rooms "by the hour and by the day." He paid cash in advance for one night.

He slept well, oblivious to the patter of insects, and next morning he showered and dressed at a leisurely pace, ignoring the peeling paint and the stale, cockroach aromaed air. After a solitary breakfast at a greasy hamburger joint, he returned to his room, where he picked up the phone and dialed a New York City number. The telephone was answered on the second ring by a honeyed female voice.

"Good morning; Cotterell Industries. How may I help you?"

"Good morning. Could you please give me the extension for Mr. Victor Brezhnerov?"

There was a barely perceptible pause, during which Harris heard the rapid clicking of a keyboard, then the woman said, "Mr. Brezhnerov's extension is 249. Would you like me to connect you?"

"Yes, please."

A phone rang. On the third ring, the receiver was lifted.

"Brezhnerov," said a male voice.

Harris depressed the hook with a finger and killed the connection. He had confirmed what he had needed to know: Victor Brezhnerov was employed at Vincent Cotterell's corporate headquarters. That meant that he lived either in, or at least close to, the city.

He lifted his finger, waited for the dial tone, then dialed a number in western North Carolina.

Denzel Burton did not look like a man with an annual income well into six figures. His hair was unfashionably long and kept under control by a rubber band that forced it into an untidy ponytail. His chin was stubbled and his eyes bloodshot as they peered closely at the screen in front of him. He wore a crumpled tee shirt that displayed the credo "Reality is for wimps" in garish neon colors. His jeans were faded and worn ragged at the base of the legs, and sported the beginnings of a hole on the left knee. His feet were bare: a pair of cheap plastic flip-flops lay discarded on the floor nearby.

He was bleary eyed as he leaned forward, frowning at the screen in front of him — not because it was early, but because it was late. On the left side of his stained keyboard stood a nearly empty can of *Jolt*. Five empty cans of the caffeine-laden cola lay in the trash can. Half obscuring a mouse pad to the right of the keyboard were two mugs, one half full of cold coffee, the other empty but its inside stained a heavy walnut.

Denzel was concentrating on the screen on front of him, frowning deeply. He was connected to a machine that stood on the desk of the president of a major computer manufacturer in which he owned a considerably quantity of stock. The reason for his frown was the contents of the memo that he was reading:

From: Tom Stiles, VP R&D
To: George Levanworth
Subj: X3J16 development

Tom, I regret to have to tell you that the cause of the failures in the X3J16 motherboards has yet to be found. Because of the importance of this product to our earnings, I have OKed an additional $1m. The engineering team is working round the clock to locate and fix the problem. I am confident we'll find the source of the trouble within the next week. Depending on what that source is, the fix may take anywhere from a few hours to several weeks.

I'm sure you're as disappointed in the lack of progress as I am. At this point, I think it would be prudent to let the release schedule slip by approximately six weeks. I am aware of the damage this would likely do to our stock price. However, I see no practical alternative. Give me a call in the morning if you want to discuss any of this further.

Six months ago, Denzel had purchased $15,000 of stock in the company in the hope of doubling his money. Right now his stock was worth just over $13,000, and it would plummet as soon as this news hit the streets. He scribbled himself a quick reminder, "Call broker."

A window on the screen suddenly opened with a blare of trumpets. "Incoming call," the window flashed.

He leaned back and listened while his computer answered the phone.

"Denzel is not available. Please leave a message. Thank you."

In New York, George Harris listened to the familiar, terse message. "Good morning. This is George Harris. I would appreciate a rapid response...."

He was interrupted as Denzel, always appreciative of a client who paid his bills quickly and without argument, and whose jobs demonstrated a healthy lack of respect for privacy laws, lifted an extension phone.

"Good morning, Mr. Harris. What can I do for you?"

"Good morning, Denzel. A simple request this time, I think. I need to find someone's address. I have his name and roughly where he lives. Would you be able to do that?"

"Does he live under the name you're going to give me?"

"As far as I know."

"No problem, then."

Denzel did not have to give the matter a moment's thought. Property tax records; utility and telephone payments; if necessary, credit card records or driver's license records: one of those should suffice to locate the person in whom Harris was interested.

"I need to know the home address for a Mr. Victor Brezhnerov," Harris spelled the name, "and I've reason to believe he lives in or near New York City. Do you need any more information?"

"Age or any description?" Denzel asked, in case he had to try the more obscure sources of information.

"Early to mid forties. A big man, maybe six three, two hundred and fifty pounds, maybe more. Works for Cotterell Industries in their headquarters building in New York."

"OK, that should be more than enough. A thousand dollars sound reasonable?"

"How long will it take?"

"Half an hour if we're lucky. If it looks like it's going to take much longer, I'll call you back and let you know. The price remains the same either way."

"OK. You can reach me at the following number." Harris gave the motel's number and the extension of his room. "I'll stay here until I hear from you."

Denzel scribbled the number on his pad, said goodbye, and put down the phone. He rubbed his eyes. He had been about ready to go to bed, but that would have to wait for a while now.

In the event, his sleep was not long postponed. Victor Brezhnerov was easy to trace. The first place that Denzel looked, the NYNEX billing records — there was no point in accessing the listed telephone numbers; it was just as easy to go straight to the billing records, which were more complete because they included the unlisted numbers that were not in the directory database — contained the information Harris needed.

Twelve minutes after his conversation with Denzel, the phone rang in Harris's motel room.

"Hello?"

"Denzel here."

"Go ahead."

"There is a Mr. Victor Brezhnerov residing at 12450 South Brentwood Circle, Collingswood, New York, 10154. There are two telephone numbers at that address, neither of them listed. The first is 914-242-3005; the second is 914-242-7451. I didn't try to check whether this guy fits your description. I can do that if you want, but it would take a while and I probably couldn't get started until later in the day. I haven't gone to bed yet and I need some sleep."

"OK. I'll check this out. I'll be in touch if it's the wrong man. Payment by the usual method?"

"Sure. Bye."

The line went dead. Harris looked at the information he had scribbled on a sheet of paper. Collingswood; where was that? He opened a drawer and removed a two-year-old telephone directory. Riffling quickly through the book, he stopped when he reached the maps.

Tuesday, 20 November
Collingswood

As George Harris reconnoitered the neighborhood, he could not help being pleased with what he saw. Collingswood was a quiet, heavily treed, discretely expensive retreat for well paid professionals; South Brentwood Circle, where his quarry lived, was perfectly suited to his purposes.

It was a small cul-de-sac, around which were ranged five houses, all standing in the shadow of a tree-covered ridge that climbed a hundred and fifty feet above the level of the houses. A narrow road ran along the top of the ridge. The trees that clung thickly to its slopes were a mixture of evergreen and deciduous, and provided Harris more than enough cover, even in November.

He soon found a place about halfway down the escarpment where he was hidden from the road by a dense thicket of bushes, and which afforded him a nearly complete view of the rear yard of number 12450, as well as a good view of much of the front of the lot on which the house stood.

Number 12450 was a trilevel house with a detached garage to the left of the house as Harris looked at it. Harris could not see the front of either the garage or the house, but he had a clear view of a concrete path that appeared around the corner of the garage and ended in front of a door on the left side of the house. He could also see the far end of the graveled driveway where it joined South Brentwood Circle.

Satisfied with the geography, Harris returned to his car and drove away, constructing a shopping list in his head.

By the time that the sun rose at 6:50 the following morning, he was hidden among the trees halfway down the hill, bundled warmly against the chill of the late fall morning. His car was parked nearly half a mile away, in the far corner of a convenience store's parking lot. He looked down on number 12450 through a pair of binoculars. Beside him, lying on a towel to protect it from the damp ground, was the elongated shape of a rifle.

He ignored the weapon, concentrating instead on the house below. There was movement behind the panes. The kitchen was on this side of the house, as were the two bedrooms. The curtains of the bedrooms opened, first one belonging to a boy of around ten, then his parents', revealing the occupants already dressed. He shifted his attention to the kitchen window and watched the three of them eat a breakfast of corn flakes, orange juice and, for the adults, coffee.

The three left the house within minutes of one another: Victor Brezhnerov in a BMW, his wife in a Toyota, and the child, dressed in an overcoat against the damp, cool air, walked to the end of the graveled drive, kicking the gravel as he went. Two minutes later, he boarded a school bus.

Harris waited for thirty minutes. Then, keeping a careful watch for any sign of interest from the neighboring houses, he scrambled down the side of the hill, using the trunks of the trees for cover. It was an easy jump at the bottom of the hill into the Brezhnerovs' back yard.

He reconnoitered the exterior of the house. There was a red box attached to the front of the house, warning away burglars. Harris confined himself to looking in at the windows before climbing back to his position in the trees.

Settling himself into the hollow his body had created, he settled down to a long wait.

The boy was the first to return, at about half past three.

The school bus entered the cul-de-sac, stopped outside the Brezhnerov's house to deposit him on the sidewalk, then pulled away and quickly became lost in the tangle of trees that grew throughout the subdivision. The boy kicked the gravel as he walked up the driveway, looking neither to right nor to left.

He opened a screen door covering the door in the side of the house, fumbled with a key, then disappeared inside. A couple of minutes later, he appeared in the kitchen, where he made himself a snack and poured a glass of milk. Then he carried the food and drink away into some other room that Harris could not see.

Mrs. Brezhnerov returned about an hour later. Harris watched as she made them both a meal, something heated in the microwave, that was taken into another room to be eaten. After a while, she returned to put the dirty dishes in the dishwasher, and then disappeared once more.

Lights were turned on somewhere in the front of the house; Harris could see their spill on the grass. The sun set, and another light came on above the side door, illuminating the pathway between garage and house.

It began to get cold. Harris pulled his coat tighter and put on a pair of leather gloves. Every minute or so flexed his fingers, telling himself that, no matter what the weather, if the opportunity did not present itself today, then he would just try again tomorrow.

In the next hour and a half, several cars drove into the cul-de-sac and entered neighboring driveways. At last, a pair of headlights trundled slowly up to the entrance of the driveway of number 12450 and then swung off the road and on to the gravel. In the pool from the light above the garage, Harris saw Brezhnerov's BMW. He lifted his binoculars to his eyes just in time to confirm that the car had only one occupant before the car went into the garage and was lost to view. He let the binoculars fall and lifted the rifle.

Shifting his position slightly, he let his weight fall on his left side. His right hand, now ungloved, gently pressed against the trigger and moved backward a fraction, taking the slack.

Harris looked through the gun's telescopic sight and moved the rifle slightly, until he was eyeing the edge of the garage around which Brezhnerov must walk as he headed for the house.

It took longer than Harris had expected, and he was beginning to wonder if something had happened to Brezhnerov when suddenly the large man turned the corner and came into view in the telescopic sight.

He was walking slowly, deep in thought. Harris dropped the sights lower, away from Brezhnerov's head, to the larger target of the man's torso.

Brezhnerov halted, just for a moment, and stretched out his arm to open the screen door. He was brightly lit by the light above his head, and his profile almost filled the telescopic sight. Harris took a deep breath and smoothly squeezed the trigger. He felt the sharp kick of the recoil and heard the spang of the shot reflecting from the ground below; his eyes remained on the man in the sight.

Brezhnerov jerked backward as if he had been kicked by a large animal. For a second, he was out of the field of view of the telescope. Harris searched for him, then found him. He smiled.

Brezhnerov was lying on the ground, a pool of dark liquid spreading near his right hip. He was on his back, trying to rise. As Harris watched, an enormous fatigue seemed to come over the man, and his head gently fell back to rest on the concrete of the walkway.

Harris aimed carefully and fired a second shot into the man's ample trunk. The body jerked and a new pool of maroon liquid spread from the man's side. Harris scrambled to his feet, scuffed the area to hide his presence, and climbed the hill toward the road.

Five minutes later, he was starting the engine of his rented car. Three minutes after that, he passed the sign that greeted drivers travelling in the opposite direction: "Collingswood — Population 4,506 — Please Drive Carefully."

In the distance he could hear the ululant wail of sirens.

Chapter 13
Friday, November 23
Cheltenham

The first report from Nigel Smith landed on John Pearce's desk at Friday lunch time. Bypassing the usual interdepartmental mail, it had been carried by a motorcycle courier who had blurred down the M4 from London. It was the first thing Pearce saw when he returned from lunch. Opening the sealed envelope, he saw that it held several loose sheets of A4 paper covered with double spaced typing.

Attached to the top sheet was a yellow square of sticky paper on which was a handwritten message, initialed "NJS": "Please let me know if you have any questions, sir. This is only an initial report, but I thought you would like to see what progress we've made."

Pearce settled himself comfortably into his chair and began to read.

From: N. J. Smith
To: J. Pearce, Acting Director, GCHQ
Date: 23/11
Subject: Gatwick bombing
Classification: Eyes Only, Acting Director

This is the initial report into the investigation of the
explosion that occurred at approximately 10:31 a.m.
on Friday, 16 November in the international departure lounge of the South terminal at Gatwick Airport.
This report is authored by Nigel Smith of GCHQ Cheltenham, currently assigned to MI5 Forensics at the
personal request of the Acting Director of GCHQ. This
report focuses on the forensic aspects of the case; other
aspects are mentioned only briefly as and when necessary to an understanding of the forensics.

This report is being written in the early hours of 23 November; investigations into the subject matter are continuing, and a series of similar reports is expected. However, progress has been so rapid that the author feels
it appropriate to document the substantial successes as
quickly as possible, so that they may be brought to the
attention of superior officers.

1. Background

At approximately 10:31 a.m. on Friday 16 November,
there was an explosion in the international departure
lounge of the South terminal at London's Gatwick Airport.

The explosion was of sufficient force to kill immediately
a total of seven persons, amongst whom was the Director of GCHQ, Sir David Shackleton. A further twenty individuals were hospitalized from injuries received

during the explosion; one additional person died on the way to hospital. To date, two of those hospitalized have since died from those injuries, twelve have been released from hospital, and the remainder are still hospitalized, undergoing various degrees of care. No warning of the explosion was received by the airport, the police or any of the mass media.

Immediately following the explosion, at 10:33 a.m., a 999 call was received at the emergency dispatch centre that handles the Gatwick area. Automatic call detection and tracing circuits indicate that the call was placed from a public telephone kiosk in the lounge in which the explosion occurred.

The caller, who spoke with a Northern Ireland accent, possibly assumed, gave his name as Shamus O'Riley, and stated that the Irish Liberation Front was responsible for the explosion. It is worth noting that none of the usual passwords was given. Later evidence, acquired outside the scope of this investigation, indicates that the ILF was not responsible for the explosion (see below, section 6).

2. Proximate Cause

There are no gas lines in the area in which the explosion occurred. There is no substantive doubt that the explosion was the result of a device planted within the lounge itself by a person or persons as yet unknown (but see below, section 6).

Eyewitnesses, not interviewed specifically for this report but whose evidence was given to the police and is available as transcripts, described the explosion variously as "slow," "making a sort of 'whump' sound" and "more of a sudden strong wind than the kind of thing one expects from an explosion"; all of these indicate that the explosion was caused by a particular class of explosive (see below, section 5).

The local constabulary, acting under the direction of Special Branch, performed a praiseworthy job in examining the area for clues. Retrieved from one waste paper basket, located about 60 feet from the blast itself, was a small radio transmitter (see below, section 3). The transmitter carried no fingerprints. The blast itself left little debris from the original explosive device; however, sufficient evidence has accumulated that certain salient facts appear to have been established (see below, section 4).

3. The Radio Transmitter

The transmitter is a small blue plastic box, measuring about 7.5 cm x 7.5 cm x 5 cm. In the centre of one of the 7.5 x 7.5 faces is a red push-button, and across the opposite face a length of 22 gauge wire is taped. The wire runs backwards and forwards across the 7.5 x 7.5 face a total of three times. The total length of wire is approximately 48 cm. One end of the wire punctures the plastic box and is connected to the internal electronic components.

The transmitter has been dismantled by MI5 forensic personnel and the electronics examined in detail by MI5 radio experts. No fingerprints have been found anywhere on the device, either on the box (inside or out), or on any of the electronic components inside the box.

The electronic components inside the box constitute a small oscillator generating about 1 watt of power, obtained from four alkaline AAA sized cells which are seated inside the device. The oscillator is activated by depressing the red button on the outside of the box. The signal produced by the oscillator is on a radio frequency of approximately 150 megahertz (MHz), in what is known as the Very High Frequency (VHF) portion of the radio spectrum.

Output from the oscillator is fed directly to the wire taped to the outside of the box. This configuration permits the wire to act as a primitive radio antenna. At the transmitter frequency of 150 MHz, and with an output power of about 1 watt, the radio waves would be detectable by a primitive receiver over a distance of at least several hundred feet, providing that there were no substantial intervening objects.

The AAA cells would be sufficient to operate the device continuously for a period of several minutes. No detectable voltage reduction is exhibited by the cells that were present in the device at the time at which it was found. This implies that the device was operated for only a short period of time, less (and possibly much less) than approximately one minute, before being discarded.

Each component of the transmitting device has been examined with care. All components are freely available over the counter throughout the United Kingdom and in most other technologically advanced countries. Two items displayed lot numbers which are currently being traced. It is known that the lots concerned, at least in part, were shipped to the United Kingdom from their overseas manufacturers, one of which is in Korea and the other Taiwan. We do not yet have a listing of the precise retail outlets in which these lots were finally placed for sale to the public.

The plastic box encasing the transmitter electronics was manufactured in Britain. The box is of metric dimensions and stamped with the name of the manufacturer, "Box Plastics," a company based in Huddersfield. The manufacturer has informed us that the entire lot of which the box forms a part was sold to a national chain of hardware stores (Gringer and Galt's); this chain operates no stores outside the British mainland. In particular, it has no outlets in Northern Ireland or Eire.

We conclude, tentatively, that the radio transmitter was hand crafted using materials purchased entirely in Great Britain. It seems at least plausible, if not highly likely, that the Gatwick explosion was initiated by the reception of a 150 megahertz radio signal produced by this device.

4. Materials From The Explosion Itself

Special Branch informed us at the start of our investigation that, although numerous people in the vicinity of the explosion have been interviewed in depth, they had obtained no useful information regarding physical descriptions of either people who might have been associated with the explosive device or of the device itself. Accordingly, the following has been deduced entirely from remnants obtained by police and Special Branch forensic experts from the site of the explosion.

Very little of the explosive device has been recovered. From the configuration of the wreckage, it is believed that the explosive device was placed underneath a seat.

In the departure lounge the seats are arranged in groups of four, the groups being scattered throughout the available floor area. The seats are constructed of foam plastic on a steel frame and covered with a hardwearing fabric. There is ample room for storage of small, hand carried items of luggage underneath the seats.

Several scraps of material have been recovered from the area, which are, as yet, unaccounted for. The most likely container is probably a light blue canvas bag or case. Several fragments, quite widely dispersed, of a light blue canvas fabric were recovered. Two of these were scorched badly. Forensics experts have examined these fragments in detail, and have discovered traces of a foam explosive adhering to strands of the material of one of the scraps (see below, section 5).

Several small fragments of metal from the explosive device itself have been recovered. The largest of these has attached to it three relatively undamaged electronic components.

Two of these components were a resistor and a capacitor of quite standard design, available almost anywhere in the world at a cost of a few pennies. The third was an Integrated Circuit (commonly called an "IC" or a "chip"). MI5 electronics experts have deduced that the chip was a VHF FM radio receiver, which could act as the basic component for the detection of the signal produced by the transmitting oscillator. The frequency to which the receiver was tuned was determined by the values of the capacitor and resistor. The experts have concluded that this receiver was set to operate somewhere between 120 MHz and 175 MHz.

The common black elongated "beetle" shape of an integrated circuit is merely a protective case, inside which is embedded the electronic chip itself. Although the casing of this chip was substantially damaged, the bulk of its visible face was intact. The protective packaging of chips is typically marked with a wide variety of information, including chip number, lot number, manufacturer name, and other similar information. In this case, all of these details had been deliberately erased from the IC package, apparently by rubbing its surface with sandpaper.

However, the chip type and the name of its manufacturer is commonly microscopically etched into the circuit that is embedded in the chip casing. The receiver chip has been extracted from its casing and appears to be undamaged. The etched information indicates that this chip was fabricated by the TransChip Corporation of Santa Clara, California. From coded information etched into the chip, TransChip confirms that the chip is a VHF radio receiver capable of receiving signals at 150 MHz.

TransChip Corporation state that the chip was produced sometime between March and September of this year. Chips with these etchings were purchased by distributors in the United States, Canada and Japan. No direct sales to European distributors were made.

5. The foam explosive

Foam explosives are a relatively recent innovation. Their construction lends them ideally to a situation where a small, "soft" explosion is desired, using only a light, easily carried, highly portable explosive device.

Foam explosives have numerous advantages over older conventional plastic explosives in such circumstances. Of primary importance is the fact that whereas plastic explosives have a distinctive look, feel and odor, foam explosives possess none of these. They are undetectable by smell, and have a look and feel very similar to those of blocks of ordinary polyurethane foam, although they are generally considerably more dense.

Several kinds of foam explosive are now available — although not widely — especially in the United States. MI5 experts have used a gas chromatograph to determine the composition of the explosive used in this device from the tiny fragments adhering to the blue fabric of the bag believed to contain the device.

The explosive used at Gatwick goes by the commercial name "Foamtex." This is one of the newer, denser and more powerful foam explosives. A cube measuring between 20 and 25 cm on a side would have been sufficient to cause the damage at Gatwick.

Foamtex is manufactured only in the United States, by a company called Explosives Unlimited, which is based outside of Kansas City, Missouri. This company is preparing for us a complete list of the customers who have purchased Foamtex in the six months that it has been on the market. They have informed us, however, that, with the exception of a single shipment to Australia, all of their customers are located in the United States.

United States law requires that a permit be issued for the export of any explosive material, although it has to be conceded that it would be a simple matter to smuggle a 15 cm cube of Foamtex out of the country. The US Department of State Bureau of Munitions Control, which is responsible for the issuance of export permits, has assured us that only a single permit for the export of Foamtex has ever been issued, for the shipment to Australia. In particular, no permit granting permission for export to the United Kingdom has ever been sought.

6. Tentative conclusion

From the evidence gathered so far, it is clear that the Gatwick explosion was a premeditated act.

The questions remain, however: by whom, and for what purpose? The second of these questions is beyond the scope of this investigation. However, we believe that some progress, if only of a negative kind, has been made with regard to the first question.

The Irish Liberation Front appeared initially to accept responsibility for the explosion. They have since rescinded that claim, leaving it unclear who the perpetrators might be. The forensic evidence from the radio transmitter and the explosive device itself tend to support the independent evidence gathered by MI5 and GCHQ that the Irish Liberation Front was not responsible. Further, this same forensic evidence indicates that the perpetrators may well be based outside Great Britain, most likely in the United States.

The radio transmitter was, clearly, meant to be discovered. There is no doubt, however, that it is not a "plant" in the usual sense of the word. It was not left, superficially, to deceive, because it seems fairly clear that it was, in fact, the device that was used to initiate the explosion. However, it is likely that the construction of the device was meant at least to misdirect. Such information as the transmitter does furnish goes to support the notion that the explosion was the product of a domestic, rather than foreign, organization.

The shreds of evidence from the explosive device itself, however, tell a quite different story. Perhaps most telling is the deliberate erasure of the information from the casing of the IC used in the radio receiver. This action would only be necessary if that information would be valuable should the chip survive the explosion and be found by the authorities. And the most valuable information that those markings could have provided would be to discredit the picture that was carefully painted by the one piece of evidence that those responsible for the bomb knew would be found — the transmitter.

7. Speculation

The use of a foam explosive which is available only in the United States, but which could easily be smuggled from country to country in small quantities, coupled with the erasure of identifying marks from the casing of a radio receiver chip that was not distributed in Europe, indicates that a fruitful working hypothesis might be that the bomb itself was constructed in the United States and then carried to this country. It also seems clear that, whoever the culprits may be, they do not want to be found, and have gone to considerable trouble not only to cover their tracks, but even to plant information to draw the authorities away from arriving at this conclusion.

John Pearce frowned when he reached the end of the report. He read it a second time, this time taking copious notes. When he had finished, he pushed himself back from the desk and stretched.

All in all, Smith had made excellent progress. But how serious were his speculations about the US? If Americans were involved, he would have to tread very lightly indeed.

He buzzed his secretary. "Mrs. Johnson, get me Mr. Nigel Smith. He is currently seconded to MI5. Try their forensics first."

"Certainly, sir."

127

He stood up and gazed out the window at the gray day, deep in thought.

A minute later, his ruminations were disturbed by the buzz of the intercom. "Mr. Smith on the line for you, sir."

"Thank you, put him on." Pearce seated himself and lifted the telephone. "Ah, Mr. Smith, I wanted to thank you for the report. It arrived over lunch. You've made good progress. Well done."

"Thank you, sir."

"And I was wondering if you've given any thought to what you're going to do next?"

"Well, sir, I'm not sure how much more use these forensics chaps are going to be. And I gather that a lot of it comes down to how many resources we are willing to allocate."

"It always does come down to money in the end, doesn't it? What exactly do they want?"

"There are a couple of things they'd like to look at, mostly trying to pin down where the bomb was manufactured. They can do some kind of advanced testing on the aluminium from the fragment of casing which was attached to the electronics from the bomb. They seem to be pretty sure just from looking at the stuff and doing some simple tests that it's from the United States, but they aren't quite ready to go on record about that yet. And, apparently, the way these foam explosives are made, each batch is slightly different, so they will be able to tell precisely which batch our sample came from if we let a couple of them fly to the States for about a week or so."

"What are they doing right now?"

"They're looking for skin cells abraded on to the electronics. If they can find several matching cells from different components, it might be useful later in confirming the identity of the person who constructed the bomb."

"It doesn't sound like progress is going to be particularly swift from now on."

"No, sir, although I wouldn't want to bet against something useful coming out of their work eventually."

"All right. Stay there for another couple of days. I'll talk to Sir Harry about letting his boys take that trip to the States; it might be useful to know the life history of that foam stuff. Now, Mr. Smith, do you have anything in particular planned for the evening?"

"No, sir. Why?"

"Let me give you the phone number of a friend. Give her a call, and ask her out. Tell her I gave you her number."

"Sir, I don't think that's really...."

"This is strictly business, Mr. Smith, although what the two of you get up to afterwards is no affair of mine. She's a reporter with *The Times*. Take her out somewhere fancy and charge it to us. Don't tell her anything about anything, except that we no longer believe that the ILF was responsible."

"But I'll have to explain how we came to that conclusion."

"Simple, tell her that the caller claiming ILF responsibility gave a non-existent name and a very bad impression of a Northern Irish accent."

"And I suppose I'd be stupid to ask if any of that is true?"

"On the contrary, there is no one by that name known to have ILF connections of any kind. Also, we've had the dispatcher's tape played to a phonologist. He said that there was not a shred of doubt that the man was not Irish."

Pearce paused for a moment, considering whether he should tell Smith what else the phonologist had said: that the man was undoubtedly an American, most likely from the midwest, although there were also traces of New England in his speech. He decided against saying anything. Jane Mathieson had an uncomfortable habit of prising too much information from those to whom she spoke.

"And to give her more confidence in the reliability of the information, you can tell her the name that the man on the phone gave: Shamus O'Riley. So far, we've kept that from the press, but we might as well release it now we know that it's meaningless. It's just the sort of irrelevant detail that the press love. The reporter's name is Jane Mathieson, and her private number is 0181-321-4539. Make sure that this is all attributed only to the usual 'well-placed source.' The paper won't publish without some effort at corroboration, so you may tell Miss Mathieson that she can reach me at home on Sunday morning if she feels it necessary. She has the number."

"OK, sir, I have all that; thank you, sir."

"Good, and, by the way, I don't think you'll be disappointed." Without giving time for a response, Pearce put the phone down with a slight chuckle. Jane Mathieson should remove a few of Mr. Smith's worry lines.

He became serious once more as he tried to think through the ramifications of what he had just done. How would the bombers would react to the news that their attempt to blame the ILF for the explosion had failed? There was always the faint hope that it would draw them out, causing them to reveal themselves somehow... if the bombers really had intended to kill Sir David, and if they really were an organized quasi-military group. So far, he had no proof of either assumption. It was always possible, although it seemed increasingly unlikely, that Sir David's death had been a mistake, an unfortunate coincidence. But if that were true, then why go to all the trouble to disguise the country of origin of the bomb?

But if it were not true, why a bomb? If someone had wanted to kill Sir David, there were so many much cleaner ways of taking him out; bombs, after all, were so confoundedly messy.

There was still an awful lot about this affair that simply did not make sense.

Chapter 14
Thursday, November 22
Dun Laoghaire, Eire

Kelton, dressed expensively in a dark wool custom-made suit, and carrying a United Kingdom passport in the name of Patrick Brosnan, passed easily through Irish immigration and customs with his rented vehicle. The customs officials were cursory in their nominal inspection, and the pistol parts hidden inside the door of the Ford Escort went undetected.

It was late in the day by the time he drove out of the port and took the T44 northeast towards Dublin. He arrived at his destination, the swank Shelbourne Hotel off St. Stephen's Green in the south-east corner of the city, just as it was getting dark. He informed the clerk at the registration desk that he would be staying only the single night and paid cash in advance for his night's stay. He ate a solitary meal in the hotel restaurant, after which he made one phone call and then retired early.

The following morning dawned gray, with low, threatening cloud.

After breakfasting at the Shelbourne, Kelton checked out and made his way on foot down the crowded streets in the direction of Leinster House, the building that houses the Irish parliament, the *Dail*. A short distance from Leinster House,

Kelton climbed a short flight of dirt-streaked granite steps and entered a shabby-looking house that had been converted into offices.

Inside, he found himself in an unimpressive entrance hall whose air was tinged with a faintly medicinal odor. Half a dozen painted doors lined the hallway, each marked with the names of one or more companies; a stairway covered with threadbare carpet hugged one wall. At the foot of the stairway was a black directory board with removable white letters.

He found the office he was looking for and climbed the narrow staircase, the stairs creaking uneasily as he ascended.

A vertical series of three signs was affixed to the door of room 201, the signs decreasing in size from top to bottom. The uppermost sign said SAOIRSE EIREANN — IRISH FREEDOM PARTY. Below that, in smaller letters, Kelton read: ARDRÚNAÍ — GENERAL SECRETARY. The last sign said simply LIAM O'CONNAUGHT.

Kelton remained outside for several seconds, listening intently. The faint sound of typing came from beyond the wood. He knocked on the door.

"*Tar isteach*," said a woman. Kelton took this as an invitation to enter.

He found himself in a small, cluttered room. A large bookcase stood against one wall, filled with legal-looking volumes. Old periodicals were strewn on a coffee table that stood in front of a pair of chairs upholstered in green leather. Opposite the chairs was a desk, from behind which a young woman looked at him, her hands hovering above a computer keyboard. Behind her, against the wall, stood a line of filing cabinets. Across the room was a second door, partly open, through which Kelton could see another office. Inside, a man was leaning back in a chair, talking into a telephone.

The woman smiled, exposing a row of even, white teeth behind her lipsticked lips. She had short, auburn hair and wore a hint of blush on each cheek and sufficient eye shadow to draw his attention to her large, limpid eyes. She was in her early twenties. As he closed the door behind him, Kelton caught a whiff of perfume.

Kelton waved to the man in the inner office and mouthed "Hello."

The man looked momentarily puzzled, then acknowledged the silent greeting with a wave and an uncertain smile. He dropped his feet to the ground and turned away, and Kelton shifted his attention to the young woman. He returned her smile.

He spoke first: "Good morning."

"Good morning. May I help you?" The woman replied in English with a tilt of her head, the smile still fixed in place and now extended to her eyes. She spoke in the rich brogue of the west coast.

"I happened to be in Dublin on business, and I had a spare hour and I thought I'd just drop by and say hello to Liam for a few minutes."

"Oh! Mr. O'Connaught is not expecting you, then?" The smile weakened slightly.

"No. Sorry. I'm only in Dublin for the day, and it was an unexpected diversion. I thought I'd take the opportunity to renew our acquaintance. We were at Trinity together. Long time ago now of course, but I like to catch up with old friends when I get the chance."

"I'm afraid Mr. O'Connaught has a meeting in half an hour, but I expect he might be able to see you for a few minutes before then. He's on the phone right now" — she waved vaguely in the direction of the inner office — "but I'd be glad to tell him you're here. What was the name, sir?"

The man in the inner office put the telephone down, and as he did so he cast another puzzled glance in Kelton's direction.

"Mark Temple," said Kelton, catching the general secretary's eye, "but that's all right, I'll just be a minute." He took four quick steps and was in the doorway of the inner office before anyone could move. He went through and smoothly closed the door behind him. In a loud voice, easily audible to the secretary outside, he said "Liam, Liam, It's me, Mark Temple, from Trinity. Long time no see, eh?"

The man behind the desk rose to his feet, a frown on his face.

"Temple? I don't know...." His voice trailed off. Out of the pocket of his raincoat Kelton had pulled a small pistol with a silencer attached. The barrel pointed straight at Liam O'Connaught.

Kelton spoke quickly in a quiet whisper. "Greet me and tell me to be seated. I won't give you a second chance."

There was an extended silence while the general secretary digested the situation. Then he said, "Oh, er...."

"Louder."

Liam O'Connaught raised his voice, "...Mark. How good to see you. I didn't recognize you for a moment. Here, have a seat."

"Good," said Kelton. He stepped forward, away from the door, confident that all that the receptionist could hear was the subdued, muffled tones of ordinary conversation. "This will only take a minute. I just want some information. Write it down for me. I work for MI5, and a paper crossed my desk yesterday that would be worth a lot to the ILF. I must get the information to them."

"You want to get some information to the ILF?"

"Right."

O'Connaught tipped his head and eyed Kelton suspiciously. "If that's all you want there's no need to go through this rigmarole. Anything you tell me will be passed on to them. We contact one another frequently," he said, adding quickly, "although, of course, *Saoirse Eireann* in no way condones their paramilitary tactics."

"Sorry, that's not good enough. I need to talk to someone directly, without the risk of an intermediary garbling the message. In any case, I don't have any time to waste. My information concerns the explosion at Gatwick last week, and that man Sir David Shackleton they killed. They made a big mistake there. Heads are going to roll, their heads"

"Oh...." O'Connaught drew the syllable out into a sigh. "That cock-up. I'm getting mixed signals about that, but my information is that the ILF wasn't involved, no matter what the papers say."

For a moment, Kelton was caught off guard. Was O'Connaught telling the truth? A flicker of doubt flashed through his mind. He suppressed it. He could think of no reason to trust the ILF's mouthpiece, and several reasons not to.

He gestured with his pistol; when he spoke his voice had acquired a dangerous edge. "Listen. Save that shit for the politicians. I don't have either the time or the inclination to listen to your disavowals. All I came here for is information."

The general secretary shrugged. "OK; but, like I said, if you have a message for the leadership of the ILF, I'm sure I could arrange to have it passed on."

"Not good enough. I want the name and address where I can find the person or persons responsible for the Gatwick bombing. Just write them down and I'll be gone."

"Now, wait a minute," O'Connaught raised his voice and was shushed by Kelton. "Wait a minute, you can't seriously expect to walk in here, threaten me with a gun, and then walk out with information like that. Besides which," he added suspiciously, "if you are from MI5, how come you don't know all this already?"

Kelton thrust the pistol forward until the barrel of the silencer was within six inches of the Irishman's face.

"Look, I'm not going to stand here arguing with you. The ILF made a big, and I mean a *big*, mistake killing Shackleton. You've no idea what the English have planned for you. Personally, I don't give a shit about the ILF, the IRA or any of the whole sorry lot of you, but it suits my purposes to have the English tied up in Northern Ireland as long as possible. Once the ILF is decimated by what's about to be unleashed on them, they'll no longer exist as an effective irritant to the English.

"So I'm going to give you one last chance. Start writing. If you don't, then two things are going to happen. The first is that I will pull the trigger on this gun. The second, which you will no longer care about, is that the entire leadership of the ILF will wake up one morning soon with bullets through their brains, courtesy of the SIS, acting on information supplied to them by my bosses at MI5. Now, I'm going to count to three. If you haven't started writing by the time I reach three, I pull the trigger. One...."

O'Connaught was a politician, not a hero. He grabbed a pen and started scribbling. A few seconds later, he handed over a sheet of paper.

"That's the man in charge of making decisions about targets. I don't know anything definite about the Shackleton killing. I know the newspapers reported that the ILF was responsible, but like I said don't think they really had anything to do with it. Talk to this man; he'll know for sure whether they were involved, although whether he'll tell you anything is another matter."

The possibility that his colleague in the north might stand up to this aggressive stranger apparently gave O'Connaught new strength, and he continued more belligerently, "If you're planning on killing him, I'll tell you right now that he'll be warned. If you shoot me, he'll automatically be on guard, and if you don't, I'm going to pick up the telephone the moment you've gone and tell him myself."

Kelton backed away, lowering his pistol. "Look, if I were really a killer, I'd kill you now that you're no further use to me, wouldn't I?"

O'Connaught gulped. "Yes, I suppose so. *Are* you going to kill me?"

"Of course not. You've given me what I came for, and I'm a fair minded man, not a cold-blooded killer. Now, if you'll just act normally while I let myself out, I'll be on my way. Don't try anything though; I'll still have the gun in my pocket, and if you force me to, I will use it."

In a loud, friendly voice, he said, "Well, Liam, it's been good seeing you again. I hope it won't be so long again next time."

Kelton retreated backwards. He backed out of the door, waving cheerfully at O'Connaught. He glanced at the secretary, whose face lifted to meet his. She threw him another of her smiles.

"Good day," Kelton said, then he turned, walked quickly to the outer door, and was gone.

An hour later, a blue Ford Escort with English license plates was heading northwards on the T1 trunk road towards Belfast.

Friday, November 23; evening
Redhill, Surrey

Patricia Worthington was at home. It was her first day off since the explosion the Friday before. This week she had completed her shopping without interruption. The same young woman had been at the checkout counter, and after a few moments, she had recognized Patricia as the woman who had run out the store last week leaving her groceries and checkbook behind.

"You were here last week, when that awful explosion happened at Gatwick, weren't you?" she ventured.

"Yes. I'm a doctor. The hospital paged me. Sorry I had to leave in such a hurry."

"Awful business, that. I hope they catch whoever did it."

"When they do, I hope to God someone makes them pay. I operated on a little girl. Four years old, she is."

"Is she going to be all right?"

The doctor shook her head. "We don't know yet, but I doubt it. She needed two operations, and we've kept her asleep since the second one. We took her off the drugs yesterday, but it'll probably be a day or two before she wakes up. If she wakes up. The flow of blood to her brain was restricted, you see. We're afraid there's been permanent brain damage."

"Oh, the poor thing."

There was nothing more to say. Patricia paid for her groceries and then, even though it was several miles out of her way, went home via the hospital on the offchance that Elizabeth Kent's condition had changed. It hadn't.

The ringing of the phone shook her from her recapitulation of the events of the day. A glass of wine, almost empty, was in her hand. She downed it gratefully before answering the phone.

It was highly irregular, but something about Elizabeth's plight had made it seem perfectly natural that Mr. Kent should make a point of contacting the doctor every day for a bulletin on his daughter's condition. According to the standard procedures, Patricia was supposed to route all such enquiries to the hospital. But in the event of a change, all they would do would be to pass on to Mr. Kent the words she had given them. So surely, as Mr. Kent had pointed out, it would do no harm for him to contact her directly instead.

Normally, Patricia Worthington would have rebuffed his request as a matter of course. But things in this particular case were far from normal. There was something about Paul Kent that worried her. There was even something that almost scared her, although she had been careful to give no hint of that fact to anyone else.

That first morning, the day after the explosion, he had reacted to the sight of his daughter in a way that had puzzled and worried the doctor.

For a while he had stood there, saying nothing while she tried to explain what the hospital would do for his daughter. He had listened silently, nodding at the right places, but his eyes had been fixed vacantly on his daughter as if, although he was looking at her, he was seeing something else entirely. She would have thought that he was simply remembering their family life as it had been, except that on his face was no trace of the sad, those-days-are-gone-for-ever melancholia she would have expected. Instead his face was taut and tired, as if he had finally given up a long struggle with himself.

"Perhaps you could bring in some of her soft toys?" she had suggested. "That way, if... when she wakes up we can try to make her feel more at home."

He had nodded silently, his eyes still on his daughter.

She had led him from the room, and once they were outside he had asked her, "What would you do if you could get your hands on the person who did that?"

"I hope to God they catch whoever did it," she had replied. "The person responsible for what happened to your family doesn't deserve to live."

For the first time, he had seemed to register what she had said. He had straightened as if her words had removed an unbearable burden from his shoulders. And in his eyes had been a flash of something she had never seen before in her entire life: a surge of powerful hatred that even now, a week later, caused the hairs on the back of her neck to prickle. She shivered, put down her empty glass, and stretched out her hand for the phone.

"Good evening, Dr. Worthington."

"Good evening, Mr. Kent."

"Any news?"

"Not really. It was supposed to be my day off, but I dropped by the hospital at lunchtime anyway to look at Elizabeth; I'm sure they'd have called me if there was any change after I left."

"Should I be worried? She's been asleep for a week now."

Patricia weighed the question. She would answer it honestly, just as she had answered all his questions. But what was an honest answer? "No, not really," she said at length. "We took her off the barbiturates yesterday, but she's been very deep for a week. Her metabolism is still weak. It might take as long as three or four days for her to metabolize the drugs out of her system. I had hoped she might wake up today, but no, I wouldn't really be worried yet. If we get to Tuesday or Wednesday and there's still no sign of consciousness, then I'd begin to worry."

She thought about telling him that worrying would change nothing; they had done everything they could for Elizabeth Kent. But she said nothing — Mr. Kent knew that without being told.

"All right. Thank you. I do appreciate this, you know."

"That's all right, Mr. Kent. How are you doing?" She was no psychiatrist, but she knew how vulnerable people in Paul Kent's position were. And yet "vulnerable" was the last word she would have used to describe Mr. Kent. The last time she had seen him, on a visit to the hospital three days ago, she had noticed that he was cleanshaven, and the change had made him look even more like someone to be scared of.

"I'll survive," Kent replied. "I'm in Ireland on business at the moment. I'm afraid I'm not always near a phone, but I'll keep calling you every day if that's all right with you."

"Yes, certainly. Please don't work too hard, though. It's good to occupy yourself, but you've had enough stress recently. If you feel it catching up with you, come home."

"Dr. Worthington, I appreciate your concern, but I assure you that you would approve of this particular piece of business. Goodnight, doctor."

"Goodnight, Mr. Kent."

She put the phone down and sat looking at it for a long time, wondering what he had meant by his final words.

Chapter 15
Sunday, November 25
Belfast, Northern Ireland

By Sunday morning, Sean O'Hannessy had almost forgotten the telephone call he had received two days earlier. It had been a puzzling call, one that made little sense at the time and even less so as the hours rolled by without any contact from Liam's crazed Englishman. O'Connaught had called to warn O'Hannessy about a gun-toting Englishman who had walked into his office and demanded to know who in the Irish Liberation Front was responsible for the Gatwick bombing. At gunpoint Liam had given him Sean O'Hannessy's name.

"Why the fock didn't you tell him Gatwick wasn't anything to do with us?" O'Hannessy had demanded.

"I tried to, what kind of fool do you take me for? But he wasn't interested."

"He was from MI5?"

"That's what he said."

"Was he telling the truth?"

"How the fock should I know, Sean? He was pointing a gun at me. I wasn't in much of a position to make demands."

"But he was English? You're sure of that."

"Yes. North of England, I'd say."

"Describe him again."

"Early forties. Clean shaven. Hair light brown. A little under six feet. Lean face. Roman nose. Narrow, gray eyes. Expensively dressed, much better than I'd expect for someone from British intelligence."

"OK, Liam. Well, I'll keep my eyes skinned. I'll let you know if he turns up."

At first, O'Hannessy had been deeply disturbed. Why was a lone MI5 operative wandering around with a gun trying to find out who was responsible for the Gatwick bombing? O'Hannessy had already made it clear to GCHQ that neither he nor anyone else working for the ILF was responsible. Any well-placed agent of the British Secret Service would have access to that information by now, and even if he did not, it had been made painfully clear by John Pearce's telephone call of last Sunday that GCHQ and, presumably, MI5, knew exactly how to reach him if they wanted; there was certainly no need to go through Liam O'Connaught.

Was this agent a renegade then, as he claimed? Or was he something else entirely? A dissatisfied loner out for revenge? And if so, against whom? The British, as he had cryptically claimed? or was his real target the ILF? With the peace process moving slowly forward in Ireland, the ILF was now the only real thorn in the Brits' side. It would be very convenient for them if something were to happen to O'Hannessy or one of the other leaders.

But nothing happened, and by the time he went to bed on Saturday night, O'Hannessy was more than half convinced that the whole thing was a false alarm.

He arose early on Sunday, leaving his wife asleep, and went alone to early Mass. It was good to get these things out of the way early, leaving the rest of the day free for other matters. When he returned home, his wife was preparing breakfast. They ate together and then O'Hannessy retired to the spare bedroom upstairs that served as his office while his wife read the Sunday paper. She left at 10:35 for eleven o'clock Mass.

142

The doorbell rang at 10:45, and O'Hannessy paused in the midst of the paragraph he was writing for his pseudonymous column in the *Republican Weekly*.

Putting down his pen, he wondered who could be calling at this time of day. Friday's telephone conversation came sharply back to mind.

Opening the drawer of his desk, he removed a pistol from underneath a stack of papers. Even though the house was in an estate that was solidly Republican, a lifetime of warfare had taught O'Hannessy that he could never be too careful.

He walked to the window of the study, which overlooked the tiny front garden and the road beyond, and looked through the net curtain down on to the short path that led from road to front door. Standing on the threshold was a portly priest whom he did not recognize, dressed in dominical black. O'Hannessy looked both ways along the street. There were no cars parked on the road that he did not recognize; the priest must have walked to the house.

It was difficult to see any details of the priest's physiognomy, but the man appeared to be quite different from the description that Liam O'Connaught had given of the rogue Englishman. This man, apart from tending to embonpoint, had a head of gray hair and wore rimless spectacles. Feeling more at his ease, O'Hannessy moved away from the curtain and walked downstairs to the ground floor.

The doorbell rang a second time just as he reached it.

Keeping a grip on his pistol behind his back, O'Hannessy unlocked the door and opened it halfway. The priest smiled at him from the threshold.

No one could reasonably describe his face as lean, as Liam had described his attacker's visage; the priest's cheeks protruded visibly, and his eyes were brown, not steely gray. O'Hannessy relaxed further. Vaguely, he thought that he had seen the priest somewhere before, but he could not quite place where. In church, perhaps?

"Good morning, Father, what may I do for you?" he asked.

"Good morning."

An Englishman's voice. O'Hannessy tensed slightly. The priest nodded respectfully.

"Good morning, sir. I'm very sorry to bother you, but I was at Mass this morning and afterwards a man gave me this to give to you."

So that was where he had seen the priest before. O'Hannessy recognized him now. He had been in the congregation at early Mass, seated near the back of the church. The priest held out an envelope and continued, "He was a compatriot of mine, I think, and he asked me to give it to you and wait for a reply."

O'Hannessy took the envelope. "Why didn't he bring it himself?" he asked suspiciously.

"I asked him that, sir, and he said that he thought you would not trust an unknown Englishman arriving on your doorstep unannounced. I think, if you'll forgive me saying so, that he was perhaps scared for his life."

"Well that shows more intelligence than usually comes from the English," said O'Hannessy. Quickly he added, "Sorry, Father, I didn't mean to offend."

"That's all right, my son, I understand; no offense taken." A smile crossed the priest's face. "Are you going to open the letter?"

"The man who gave this to you, what did he look like?"

The priest considered for a moment. "Oh, he was about my height, maybe a bit younger, his hair was not yet the color of my own." The priest smiled, and O'Hannessy caught a glimpse of a twinkle in his eyes behind the rimless spectacles. "He was dressed very well, obviously a man of some material substance. Thinner than myself... Oh yes, his eyes were gray, I remember that...." The priest's voice trailed off, unable to think of anything else.

"This man; if I give you a reply, how are you going to meet him?"

"He said he would meet me at Mass tomorrow morning to see if I had a reply for him."

O'Hannessy considered this for a moment, and decided that it was a reasonable answer. He stepped back and gestured. "Do come in, then."

O'Hannessy moved to one side of the narrow hallway to allow the priest to pass, placing his pistol in his right pocket. He closed the door.

The priest regarded O'Hannessy as the latter tore the envelope open. Inside was a single folded sheet of paper. O'Hannessy unfolded it and saw that it was covered with closely spaced handwriting.

He started to read. The writing was difficult to make out. The letters were small and ambiguous. O'Hannessy furrowed his brow in concentration, trying to make out the words.

"Ahem." The priest cleared his throat.

O'Hannessy looked up and his heart momentarily stopped. In the priest's right hand was a silenced pistol, pointing directly at O'Hannessy.

With his left hand, the priest took something out of his mouth. O'Hannessy recognized a pair of cheek pads, which the priest put into a pocket. The priest's face became suddenly leaner.

"Now then, Mr. O'Hannessy, let's not waste any time. First, I warn you to keep both of your hands in full view. Second, let me assure you that I have killed many times in cold blood and I would have no hesitation whatsoever in pulling this trigger on such a man as yourself. Third, please hand over that letter and envelope."

The letter and the envelope disappeared into the Englishman's soutaine.

"Now, turn around and place your hands on the wall while I remove that gun from your pocket."

O'Hannessy did as he had been ordered. The Englishman stood directly behind him and jabbed the pistol sharply into his back.

O'Hannessy winced in sudden pain and let out an involuntary "Ow." The Englishman did not react; the pistol remained firmly planted in O'Hannessy's back.

The Englishman removed the gun from O'Hannessy's pocket, then quickly frisked him. The pressure of the pistol against O'Hannessy's back disappeared.

"You may turn around now," the Englishman said.

O'Hannessy turned. The Englishman's pistol was pointing at his torso. There was no sign of his own weapon.

The man in the soutaine spoke, his voice crisp and clipped. "I am going to ask you some questions. I want answers, I want them quickly, and I want them to be accurate. I can always find your colleagues if you don't furnish the information I want. In other words, to put it bluntly, you are highly expendable. Do you understand that?"

The Irishman nodded.

"Right. First question. How many superiors do you have?"

"What do you mean?"

The pistol came closer. "Listen, you son of a bitch. Don't try to mess with me. I know exactly who you are. Answer the question. How many people above you?"

"None. There's a small council that oversees all policy and activities, and I'm the current chairman. There's an odd number on the council and all decisions are made by majority vote."

"So if a major action was planned, such as a bombing on the English mainland, you would know about it?"

"Sure. Someone else is in charge of mainland actions. He'd arrange the details, but only after the action had been sanctioned by the council."

"So, purely as a matter of interest, which way did you vote when the matter of killing Sir David Shackleton came up?"

So there it was. Shackleton again. Everything came back to him. This man must have been sent by the English. But why? Hadn't Pearce believed him?

"Listen, there's been a mistake. We didn't kill Shackleton. We didn't plant that bomb."

"That's not what the papers say."

"Surely you don't believe what you read in the papers? Some clown called in claiming ILF responsibility for that bomb, but we had nothing to do with it. I told the Brits that early last week. Your information is out of date. Go back and check with your boss, whoever he is. You've got it all wrong."

The Englishman was visibly taken aback. There was an awkward silence. When at last he spoke, he sounded unsure of himself.

"Let me make sure I understand this. You're claiming that last weekend's explosion at Gatwick wasn't the ILF's doing?"

"Damn right. Somebody obviously wants to pin the responsibility on us but we had nothing to do with it. Nothing. And we've been asking questions ourselves. As far as we've been able to find out, it was nothing to do with an Irish group of any kind, Republican or unionist."

"So who was responsible then?"

"No idea."

"You know what I think? I think you were unlucky. You set that bomb and accidentally killed Shackleton. Now you're running scared. You can't kill the head of one of the branches of the secret service and hope to get away with it. Once you saw in the papers what you'd done, you decided the only thing to do was to try to cover it up and deny responsibility."

"No, that's not it at all." O'Hannessy began to take a step forward, then thought better of it as the Englishman's pistol prodded him in the stomach. "We had nothing to do with it. We know nothing about it. Really."

"Convince me."

"What more can I say?" O'Hannessy was beginning to shout. "We are as much in the focking dark as you are. Who the hell are you, anyway? Who do you work for? You told Liam you worked for MI5, but you don't, do you? If you did work for them, you'd know I was telling the truth."

The Englishman ignored the outburst. "I want a list of the names and addresses of every person on your council. I'm going to talk to every one of you, until I find the bastard that set that bomb."

147

"Look, you focking fool, I don't know who the fock you are, who the fock you work for, or even what the fock it is you're really after. All I know is that you have the focking gall to dress up as an honest Catholic priest and then you push your way in here asking questions about a bombing which you've already been told had nothing to do with us. And now you expect me to just hand over a list of names and addresses? Those people would only repeat what I've already told you. You've outstayed your welcome, you English bastard. I think it's time you left."

Now he did take a step forward, albeit a small one.

The Englishman's eyes narrowed, but he stood his ground. When he spoke, it was calmly and deliberately. "You seem to forget who has the gun here."

"I forget nothing, you focking English bastard. We're at war with you. If you want to regard me as your prisoner, fine, go ahead. I'll give you my name and rank, and that's all. Otherwise, get the fock out of my home."

The muscles in the Englishman's face tensed. "How many civilians have you killed in the last ten years, O'Hannessy?"

O'Hannessy recited: "My name is Sean O'Hannessy, and I hold the rank of General in the Irish Liberation Front."

"Answer me, you bastard."

Something in the Englishman's eyes changed.

"My name is... uh...."

O'Hannessy never ended the sentence. He was thrown backwards against the wall, blood spewing from his open mouth.

The Irishman leaned against the wall for a second, his face tense in pain. Then his muscles relaxed and slowly he slithered to the ground, where he slumped face down, blood pumping out of his chest on to the worn carpet of the hallway.

Chapter 16
Monday, November 26
Surrey

Patricia Worthington looked at the pot and wondered if another mug of tired coffee was a good idea. No, she decided. Although she felt drained, that was preferable to the tremors that another coffee might bring on. She glanced at the clock on the wall of the doctors' lounge; her last scheduled surgery for the day was not for another hour. After that she would do the rounds, checking up on her patients. Perhaps she would be able to catch up on her sleep with a nap this afternoon.

She heaved herself out of her chair.

"Tired, Patricia?" Dr. Higgins looked at her sympathetically over the top of the day's *Times*.

"Yes." She crossed the room to the sink and began to rinse her mug.

"Can't say I blame you. Bloody terrible what happened to that girl. That what's keeping you awake?"

"Yes. I know its stupid, but I keep thinking it's my fault. I keep thinking that if only I'd thought to do a brain scan earlier we might have been able to do something for her."

"It's not over yet, Patricia," Dr. Higgins said with a kindly smile. "Anyone who's been in neurosurgery any length of time has seen plenty of miracles, and here's always room for one more." He pointed to a story on the front page of *The Times*. "Anyway, whatever *The Times* says, I still reckon the ILF is to blame, and it looks to me like someone gave them a taste of their own medicine. Did you see this article... Patricia! What's the matter?"

The mug had slipped out of Patricia's hand and shattered in the sink. For a moment she stared at the smashed mug, oblivious to her surroundings. Her own words echoed in her head. "I know I shouldn't say this, but to be honest, I hope they kill whoever did this to your daughter." That's what she had said, wasn't it? And hadn't he said he was in Ireland "on business" on the phone the other day?

"Patricia?"

"What? Oh. No. I'm all right." She turned off the faucet and began to collect the shards of the mug.

It was impossible though, wasn't it?

She looked at her hands. Even though she had decided not to drink the coffee, they were trembling.

Kelton was tired. He was also furious with himself.

His tiredness was a direct result of his anger, for he had spent a restless and unpleasant night reliving the events of yesterday. As well as his anger, in the moments when he was being brutally honest with himself, there was a nagging worry that perhaps this time the task that he had set himself was simply too much. Was it the five years of retirement? or the fact that, not matter how hard he tried, it was proving impossible to divorce himself completely from the stark truth that it was his own family whom he was trying to avenge?

All night, whenever sleep had finally overtaken him, he had woken after only a few minutes with a picture before him, the same picture that even now kept thrusting itself forward: Sean O'Hannessy refusing to cow before his weapon, steadfastly repeating his name and rank.

It was not that O'Hannessy's death was to be particularly regretted. His death was surely a service to mankind. What appalled Kelton was that, when faced with a stony refusal to coöperate, he had lost his temper and, in his frustration, he had used the simplest and most direct available method to silence the man.

Never before had Kelton killed needlessly. That he had done so now demonstrated how treacherous was the state of his emotions.

To cap it all, the whole affair had been unnecessary, as he had discovered when he bought a copy of *The Sunday Times* after disposing of his disguise in the waters of Lough Neagh.

ILF not responsible for Gatwick bombing, read the page two headline. In the column underneath, written by Jane Mathieson, she reported that "well placed sources in the security forces" believed that they had proof that the bomb had not been planted by the Irish Liberation Front. There was speculation that the bomb had originated abroad, possibly in North America.

If Kelton had read the paper first, he would never have visited O'Hannessy, the ILF leader would still be alive, and Kelton's emotions would still be intact.

He purchased a copy of Monday's *Times* just before leaving Belfast on the morning ferry. The paper contained no followup story, just an item on O'Hannessy's death, which served merely to augment Kelton's bleak mood. He sought out a seat on deck and tried to think. Everyone else crowded inside, away from the cold wind. After a while it began to rain. Kelton barely noticed.

Still unsure what his next move should be, he rented a car when the ferry docked in Liverpool, and began to drive south.

As he drove, the late autumn clouds dropped ever lower, and what light there was became thinner and grayer. Passing a signpost that informed him that Woodstock was eight miles ahead, he turned on his car headlights, even though it was only 3 p.m. The persistent light rain that had followed him all the way from Liverpool became heavier.

He had reached a dead end. What should he do now? Yesterday's *Times* article had suggested the possibility of an American involvement. Should he go to Mike Downing for help? Surely Downing would want unofficially to avenge Shackleton's death. Or would he be better off remaining undercover and acting alone?

It was as he drove into Woodstock, the small, studiously picturesque town that abutted Blenheim Palace, that he finally reached a decision.

He turned off the road and parked the car in one of the three cramped spaces that constituted the parking lot of the Royal Churchill Hotel.

Royal the hotel might have been in name, but it was so in nothing else. It stood in a terrace of houses; only its whitewash, the awning over the entranceway, and the fact that its tiny parking lot stood in the place of a front garden rendered it distinct from the neighboring dwellings.

Kelton climbed a small flight of narrow stone steps and entered a gloomy, overwarm reception area. A fire flickered in the grate and a radio tuned to a Radio 4 play stood on the countertop of the reception desk. A man in his early fifties with a newspaper spread before him stood behind the desk. There was no one else in the room.

"May I help you?" the man asked with a marked lack of enthusiasm, as if he expected Kelton simply to be a lost tourist wandering in from the rain and requesting directions to Blenheim Palace.

"A room please, for one night," Kelton said.

The man became more welcoming, and he quickly turned down the volume on the radio and spirited the newspaper away.

Kelton signed himself in at the hotel registration book, giving the first name that came into his head and a fictitious home address. He told the owner that he expected to stay only the single night, news that the proprietor, with a nod, took in his stride.

After installing himself in a second floor room, Kelton returned downstairs. He briefly exchanged pleasantries with the owner, deriding the weather and agreeing that they were "in for it tonight," then walked out into the street.

Kelton was no stranger to Woodstock, having visited it often as he researched his book on Churchill. But the book was now far from his mind. Now he half walked, half ran through the rain, heading down the narrow street in the direction of the A44. Reaching the main road, he waited on the sidewalk for a quarter of a minute before the traffic left a gap large enough for him to dash wetly across the road. Dodging under an awning, he entered the cozy dryness of a small shop with a sign outside proclaiming "Genuine Cream Teas with Clotted Cream and Strawberry Jam."

The interior of the tea shop was rendered gloomy by the November weather, but, unlike the Royal Churchill, the little tea shop was doing a brisk business, with patrons at more than half the tables. Looking around the tea room, he realized that most of the customers were local folk, not travelers passing through. The tea shop must be a recognized meeting place where the locals congregated in the late afternoon to exchange gossip.

He seated himself at an empty table near the rear and waited for service.

It was about half a minute before a homely waitress in her early thirties appeared and asked for his order. He requested a cream tea, then added, "Excuse me, do you have a telephone I could use?" He reached for his wallet.

"No, sir, not really. There's a public telephone just across the street there." The waitress pointed past the other tables and out through the window into the gray downpour outside.

Kelton opened his wallet and removed a twenty pound note. "I have to make an international call; I expect it will take only a minute or two, and I'd be happy to pay for it with this." He pushed the note across the table towards the waitress. "I'm sure the total cost of the call will be only a pound or two, but it's such a nuisance to make international calls from a public telephone kiosk, and, as you can see, the weather is not very coöperative. You'd be quite welcome to keep this note if you would oblige me."

The waitress eyed the note but left it untouched.

"Sir, would you mind waiting for a minute?" she asked. "I'll be right back."

She smiled, then turned and wove around tables and chairs until she reached a small, curtained doorway at the far end of the shop. She disappeared through the doorway and returned about a minute later, accompanied now by a second, older woman, who was attired casually in a manner that suggested that she did not often enter the public portion of the building.

The older woman spoke. "Now, sir, is there something we could do for you?"

"I hope so. You see, I was just explaining to this most excellent waitress" — he cast a warm smile in the direction of the waitress — "that I would like to place an international phone call if it wouldn't be too much trouble. It would take only a minute or two, and I'd gladly let you keep this twenty pound note in exchange for the service."

The woman eyed him suspiciously, then picked up the note from where it lay on the table. "You don't mind, do you?" she said, opening out the note and snapping it sharply. Without waiting for a reply, she held the note up to the light from one of the shaded ceiling lights. She examined it for a couple of seconds, turning it around several times. "Seems OK," she said in a tone that indicated mild surprise. "Follow me."

Turning to the waitress she said, "Now, Suzanne, you take care of the gentleman's tea. He'll be back in a couple of minutes."

Kelton followed the woman, noticing that she surreptitiously folded the bank-note and secreted it somewhere in the folds of her dress. He made a mental note to make it right with Suzanne.

They passed through the curtained doorway into a short hallway and then entered a kitchen in which a young man was working, transferring small dabs of strawberry jam from a large container into small china dishes. A radio on a shelf was tuned to Radio 4; the play was still in progress. At the far end of the counter was a battered black telephone.

The woman gestured toward the telephone and said, "There you are, just help yourself."

Kelton asked, "You wouldn't have anywhere a little, er... quieter, would you?"

"Well...," the woman looked dubious, "there's another telephone upstairs. I suppose you could use that."

"That would be most kind. I'd hate to get in the way down here."

"Come with me, then," said the woman brusquely.

They continued down the hallway past the kitchen, and then turned sharply and climbed a flight of narrow stairs. Arriving at the top of the stairs, Kelton found himself on a small landing, on one side of which was a small table supporting an old rotary telephone and assorted pens, pencils and scraps of paper. Several doors, all closed, lined the landing.

"Here you are, then," said the woman, "and if you want me, I'll just be in here," she said, pointing towards one of the doors.

Kelton thanked her and the woman went into the nearby room, closing the door behind her.

Wrapping a handkerchief over his right hand, he lifted the telephone. Using one of the pencils from the table, he began to dial.

In Woodstock it was 3:50 on a rainy, windswept afternoon. Three thousand miles and five time zones to the west it was 10:50 in the morning of a gray, wintry day. Fifteen seconds after Kelton finished dialing, a phone rang in a small cubicle in which a woman in her mid thirties was reading the latest Danielle Steel paperback. A headset with a boom microphone sat snugly on the woman's head.

She put the paperback down. By the beginning of the phone's second ring, a computer screen in front of her had flashed a message on its screen:

Phone number dialed: 202-292-2442
Caller: Unknown — Deep cover, DD Only
Callee/contact: Mike Downing
Answer code: Mike's Used Books
Validation code: None
Originating phone number: tracing

The last word on the screen was flashing. The woman leaned forward and pressed a button; simultaneously, the ringing in her headset ceased and, in a building several hundred feet distant, the capstans on a large reel-to-reel tape recorder began to turn.

"Good morning," the woman said. "Mike's Used Books. May I be of assistance?"

She heard the echo of her voice, indicating an international, probably transatlantic, satellite connection. She made a bet with herself that whoever was calling would disconnect before the trace was completed. The last line on her computer screen changed to "tracing — International." It continued to flash.

"Good day," a clipped English voice came down the line. "I have a personal message for Mike. I will return a call to this number in precisely one hour. At that time, I want to speak with him directly. It will be to his advantage not to have the conversation recorded."

"I'm sorry, which Mike to you mean?" asked the woman. It was a standing order that she should try to keep a caller on the line until the trace was completed. But she already knew that there was no point with this call. Tracing overseas links took too confoundedly long, and the caller obviously knew what he was doing. As she expected, the screen status changed again, now reading "tracing — International — Europe." It still flashed.

"That's all," said the voice.

"Wait a minute, who shall I tell him is calling?" Too late. The telephone went dead. The computer screen read "tracing — International — Europe — UK." It was still flashing. She leaned forward and pressed a button on the computer keyboard. The woman smiled to herself, pleased that she had won her bet.

Two hundred yards away, in a receptionist's plush office, a telephone rang. It was one of four telephones arranged in a neat row on a desk. A harried secretary paused and in the midst of a conversation on one of the other phones he abruptly said, "Sorry. Please hold"; without waiting for a response, he stabbed the hold button. He wondered how often the Chairman of the Joint Chiefs of Staff was put on hold. He lifted the telephone that was ringing. "Office of the Deputy Director."

"Good morning. Covert front desk here. I just received a phone call which is marked eyes only for Mr. Downing. The call is coded number 43256."

"Thank you, I'll forward the message immediately."

Inside his office, Mike Downing was tired and generally dispirited. Any minute now the Chairman of the Joint Chiefs of Staff would be calling to hound him to provide SIGINT backup for a planned wargame in the Indian Ocean. How many more times did Downing have to tell the military that he had better things to do with his resources than to squander them on a never-ending series of war games? Didn't they realize that now the Cold War was over the NSA was forced to work harder than ever?

The intercom beeped. Downing leaned forward ready to grasp the telephone to begin the weary explanation of why he would not devote resources to a third series of games this year. "Yes, Mr. Jackson?"

"Sir, an eyes only message just came in from the covert front desk. Message number 43256. Oh, and the Chairman of the JCS is on hold."

Downing could not suppress a grin; Jackson understood him perfectly. "Then tell him to take a hike. Or words to that effect, anyway."

"Certainly, sir. With pleasure."

Still smiling, Downing wheeled his executive chair across to a corner of the office where a table supported a computer workstation. Donning the headset that lay on the table next to the computer, he typed a series of characters on the keyboard.

Seconds later, the recorded conversation played itself back in his headphones. The computer screen showed that there had been insufficient time to trace the telephone call completely, but it had originated in the United Kingdom. Downing listened to the conversation a second, and then a third time. He looked at his watch. Eight minutes had elapsed since the call had completed; that left him another fifty two minutes before Kelton called back. He knew from experience that Kelton would be punctual to the second.

Downing wheeled his chair back to his desk and stabbed at the intercom. "Mr. Jackson, please come in here."

"Yes, sir." Moments later, Mr. Jackson entered the room, notebook in hand.

"Make some arrangements, Mr. Jackson. In about fifty minutes from now, that would be," Downing looked at his watch, "at about ten of noon, a phone call will come in to one of our covert numbers, 202-292-2442. I want that phone call to be secure on this end, unrecorded and routed directly to this office. There is to be no trace placed on the call, and no record anywhere in the Palace that the call ever happened. If anyone gives you grief, tell them to check with me personally. Do you have that?"

Jackson had been scribbling furiously. He looked up from his shorthand and read back Downing's instructions.

"Fine. Get to it. I assume your notes will be shredded at the end of the day?"

"Of course, sir."

"Good. And now I don't want to be disturbed until after the call is over."

The secretary said, "Certainly, sir," and left the office.

Mike Downing looked out of his window and steepled his hands in thought. Kelton's call had resurrected a lot of ghosts.

Mike Downing had risen through the ranks. He had been present at the birth of the NSA, on November 4, 1952, when he had been merely one of ten thousand employees of the newly formed agency, a mathematician who had recently received a Ph.D. from Harvard in the not-quite-respectable area of number theory at the impressively young age of 21.

Over the intervening years he had held a number of posts, moving gradually from active mathematician to competent administrator, his career paralleling, although somewhat more slowly, that of the man across the Atlantic who came to be a close friend over the years. No one had been more thrilled than Mike Downing when David Shackleton was named to head GCHQ, the closest thing Britain had to an NSA, an appointment that had been followed in the next New Year's Honors List by elevation to a knighthood.

Downing had never expected that his congratulations would have cause to be reciprocated, but five years ago, the last in a series of political appointments to the position of Deputy Director had resigned "for personal reasons," and Downing had been speedily appointed in his stead. The position of Director at NSA was a rotating service appointee who had little contact with the day-to-day running of the Puzzle Palace (as the NSA facility was known to its occupants); the true power lay in the hands of the agency's Deputy Director.

He wondered what Kelton wanted with him. Kelton had been the one major blunder of his career. In a world in which it was his job to discover, tabulate and store other people's secrets, Kelton was his secret, his one weakness — a fact of which he was all too aware.

There was no way to know why Kelton had suddenly renewed contact after all these years.

He tried to work on paperwork, but was unable to concentrate. Time dragged, but at last the fifty minutes were up.

Exactly on schedule, the telephone rang. He opened a desk drawer and pressed a button to start a tape recorder. Then he reached out for the telephone handset.

"Hello, this is Downing."

"Hello, Mike, it's been a while, hasn't it?"

That's right, thought Downing: establish the fact of a previous association right away, just in case tapes were running.

"Yeah, five years or so, I guess," he said.

"That's right, I retired shortly after that job I did with you, so I guess that does make it a little over five years." More unnecessary words just for the tapes. "So, to business, Mike. I assume my request has been honored. This isn't being recorded anywhere, no tracers, or anything like that?"

"No trace, no, and no official recording either. I'm recording to my personal machine, unless you'd rather I didn't."

"I made the stipulations for your protection, not mine. I'm sure you don't want the fact of our previous association on record."

"To be honest, I'd be much happier if you gave me a number and let me call you back. After all these years, open lines make me nervous."

"And give away my location? Not a chance, Mike. Anyway, I was only calling to commiserate with you that Sir David was killed by those Irish maniacs."

Mike's mind raced. What was Sir David Shackleton to a killer like Kelton? Had David, like Downing himself, availed himself of Kelton's services at some time in the past?

"Yes," he agreed guardedly, "it was an awful waste. But what do you care about David? Did you know him?"

"Slightly. He did me a favor once, and I feel like I owe him one in return. The least I can do for him now is to find the madman who killed him."

Mike Downing digested the implication of Kelton's words. Slowly, he said, "Much as I might applaud those sentiments I don't see what that's to do with me."

"I just returned from a brief visit to Northern Ireland. I assume you know that the ILF took responsibility for Sir David's death?"

"Yes, that crossed my desk."

"And perhaps you're aware that yesterday's *Sunday Times* reported that there is now considerable doubt whether the ILF were actually responsible for the bombing."

"No, I hadn't seen that." Speculation of that sort would not have been forwarded up the chain by the western Europe desk. "What was the basis of the report? Did it say?"

"No. It merely quoted what it called a 'well-placed source.' But it doesn't matter. I can attest to the fact that it's accurate. The ILF had nothing to do with it at all."

"How can you be so sure?"

"Perhaps you noticed that a senior member of the Irish Liberation Front was shot dead yesterday in his own home in west Belfast?"

"Yes, I saw that. But what does that have to do with Gatwick?"

"I was in Northern Ireland yesterday, and spoke to my own 'well-placed source' who was not in a position to lie to me. He convinced me that the ILF was not involved."

There was silence while Downing assimilated what Kelton had just said. "I understand," he eventually said, "but I still don't see what this has to do with me."

"My source told me that your British counterparts have shown a lot of interest in the bombing. Maybe you could make a few discreet enquiries with people at GCHQ if they haven't already contacted you?"

Downing weighed Kelton's suggestion. On the one hand, he had not the remotest desire to renew his association with a professional killer; on the other, Sir David had been a close friend and respected colleague. He owed him something.

"I suppose I could try, but I still don't see why you expect me to get involved at all. It's a British matter until they come to me and ask for help."

"True, but you knew Sir David well, and I think you cared about him as a friend and colleague. I thought you might like to help out, that's all. People shouldn't be allowed to get away with killing nonpolitical targets like Sir David." And, by extension, although Kelton never said as much, Mike Downing. The unspoken message was clear: if they — whoever "they" were — got away with killing Sir David Shackleton, maybe they would try for Mike Downing as well.

Downing was not fooled for a moment — at the right price, Kelton would have no qualms about killing Downing himself. Downing wondered what really lay behind Kelton's desire for retribution. Owing David a favor was at best an excuse. But it was not the real reason, Downing was sure of that.

"All right," he agreed, "I'll make a couple of discreet phone calls, but I won't promise more than that."

"That's all I'm asking. If you find anything, I'm sure you remember the communication channel. It's still open."

"I'll let you know what I find out. It'll probably take a few days."

"I look forward to hearing from you."

There was a click in the receiver at Downing's ear. He replaced the telephone on the hook and switched off the recorder, then walked thoughtfully to the window.

The weak sun filtered through a layer of thin cloud, highlighting the NSA campus. He looked at the sight for a full two minutes, his mind buried in the past, before he turned away from the window. His face was grim.

D. R. Evans

Chapter 17
Monday, November 26
Cheltenham

It had been a trying weekend for John Pearce.

Saturday had passed peacefully enough, the only intrusion being Jane Mathieson's mid-morning telephone call requesting confirmation of what Nigel Smith had told her at dinner the prior evening. It was not until Sunday afternoon that the telephone rang again, ending both his afternoon nap and his weekend.

His wife brought the cordless telephone into the bedroom, where Pearce was blearily rubbing the sleep from his eyes.

"For you, darling. Sorry to disturb you, but she says it's important."

Pearce mouthed the word "Who?" but his wife merely shrugged and whispered "Work" as she handed over the telephone. She turned and left the room. Since the earliest days of their marriage, she had learned to quell all curiosity about her husband's telephone calls.

"Pearce here," he said into the phone.

"Good afternoon, Mr. Pearce. Sorry to bother you twice in one weekend. This is Jane Mathieson, with *The Times*."

"Yes, Jane. Is something the matter?"

"I'm not sure. I was wondering if there's anything you'd like to add to the conversation we had yesterday. I would keep the source confidential, of course."

Pearce was puzzled. What did she have in mind? "No, I don't think so," he said.

"You're sure?"

"Yes."

"You are aware of what happened this morning, aren't you, Mr. Pearce?"

"What? What happened this morning?"

"We received the news here about an hour ago. Apparently Sean O'Hannessy was killed at home sometime late this morning. Mr. O'Hannessy, as I'm sure you know, was widely believed to be one of the most important leaders of the Irish Liberation Front."

Pearce was silent for several seconds as the last of his lethargy left him and his mind began to race. When he spoke again he was businesslike. After all, he was the head of a quasi-secret agency talking to a reporter.

"I'm sorry, Miss Mathieson, I was unaware of that news. I'm afraid I have no comment. Do you have any details you could give me?"

"We're working on it, but we don't have much yet. O'Hannessy's wife found him when she got home from Mass this morning shortly after twelve. He had been shot with a single bullet and he was already dead when she found him. That's all we have so far. If we get anything more, I'll let you know."

"Yes, yes. Thank you." Pearce switched off the phone. A muted four letter word escaped his lips.

He immediately called the Director of MI5 at home and told him the news. Within the hour, both men were at their desks, awaiting further information.

But little was forthcoming. As the Director of MI5 had warned Pearce, it was extraordinarily difficult to obtain reliable information from the West Belfast Catholic community when that community closed ranks as it was now doing. By the time that Pearce headed home long after sunset, the only additional news was a rumor that a Catholic priest had been seen entering the O'Hannessys' house at about the time of the murder. The only bright spot in the whole affair was that a hurried series of telephone calls had confirmed that the murder was nothing to do with any branch of the British security forces.

Pearce was at his desk again early the next morning. *The Times* carried the news of the killing on page one, but the article contained nothing more than the same speculation about the priest that the Royal Ulster Constabulary and Jane Mathieson had already provided the prior day.

It was long-established practice at GCHQ that the Director spent Monday morning closeted with his section chiefs, going through reports of the last week's work and discussing items of mutual interest. The morning dragged for John Pearce, who found it difficult to keep his mind on a heated exchange between two of his subordinates about the possible purchase of a new and more powerful supercomputer from the Japanese, whose main purpose would be to attempt to break the newest internal NSA ciphers.

Eventually, the meeting broke up for lunch, with no decision made but a vague commitment from Pearce that he would make one within the next day or two.

Over a tasteless meal of fried chicken and mashed potatoes, Pearce took no part in the conversation that surrounded him, pondering instead the events of the weekend and how they meshed with his own hunt for Sir David Shackleton's killer.

Maybe there was no connection at all, for he was certain that Sir David's death had nothing to do with the ILF. And yet it was difficult to believe that O'Hannessy's death was completely unrelated to the Gatwick bombing.

It was a disturbing coincidence, made more so by the manner of O'Hannessy's death. The method used in the killing, a single bullet delivered from a gun carried by a man dressed as a Catholic priest (a "priest" who it was now confirmed had attended Mass at the Church of Our Lady of the Angels at the same service as O'Hannessy only a couple of hours before the killing) was unlike any of the usual methods of assassination favored by the various Irish groups. Instead, and worryingly, it bore the hallmark of a single person, acting alone.

Yet such a person would have to be amazingly cool and determined to have carried out the act. So much so that it was difficult to believe that an amateur could have pulled it off. To have gone to so much trouble, the killer must have been certain of Sean O'Hannessy's leadership position in the ILF, and while there had been much speculation on the matter in the press, the truth was far from common knowledge.

Was it possible, Pearce wondered, that the same man had been responsible for both the Gatwick explosion and O'Hannessy's murder? But if so, why?

He shook his head; there were too many unanswered questions; he needed more information before indulging in wild speculations.

He returned to his office and held a brief and unsatisfactory telephone conversation with Nigel Smith, who unhelpfully told him that the MI5 forensic specialists had taken the weekend off and therefore there was nothing to add to his report of the prior Friday.

Putting the phone down, Pearce spoke to his secretary on the intercom. "Mrs. Pettigrew, when am I scheduled to meet the Deputy Director of the NSA?"

"Hold on a moment, sir. I believe you have a reservation on a flight next Sunday and the first meeting is scheduled for Monday morning." There was a rustle as Mrs. Pettigrew flipped through the appointment calendar. "Yes, that's right, sir. You leave Heathrow at half past noon on Sunday, and meet in the DD's office at 9 a.m. on Monday. You return on Wednesday."

"OK. Thank you."

He leaned back in his chair, deep in thought.

The likely origin of the bomb was something that had been weighing heavily on his mind since Friday, and doubly so since Jane Mathieson's call yesterday afternoon.

The question was: should he should talk to Downing now about a possible American connection? or should he wait until next week, when he might have more solid evidence to place before his counterpart?

It was one of those questions that would have been easy for Sir David to answer. Sir David knew Downing well, both as a peer and as a friend, and he doubtless would not have hesitated to place an immediate exploratory call. But Pearce was well aware that in Washington he was an unknown quantity; if the first impression he made betrayed insecurity or inadequacy, it might be a long time before he could repair the damage.

He decided to wait. He was still too uncertain about the bomb's origin, and the last thing he wanted was to be written off as an incompetent doomsayer at his first meeting with the Americans in his new capacity. He would look inept (and thereby simply confirm the common American assumption of British incompetence) if it transpired that the guesses of the forensic experts were wide of the mark. So, unless new evidence came to light, he would do nothing until next week, when he would to his best to introduce the matter delicately in his private discussions with the Deputy Director.

He pushed the matter firmly out of his mind. Lifting a thick file from the "In" tray, he was soon absorbed in the problem of weighing the relative merits of continuing to fund the Port Stanley listening post or using the money towards the purchase of an Hitachi supercomputer to try to break the NSA's new Mirage class codes.

Chapter 18
Monday, December 3
Fort Meade, Maryland

John Pearce tried not to look nervous.

He had met Mike Downing several times, and the two had always gotten along with one another well enough. But now that Pearce was Acting Director things were bound to be different. And he knew that he could not, at least not for many years, presume to the level of familiarity and friendship that Downing and Sir David Shackleton had shared.

The guards who had escorted him from the main gate opened the door of Downing's office for him, and he walked inside. Downing rose to greet him. The two men shook hands and surveyed one another briefly before Downing opened the conversation.

"Take a seat, John. Glad to see you again. Sorry it's in such unhappy circumstances."

The two quickly settled into conversation.

They chatted for over an hour, getting to know one another and, generally, each liking what he saw in the other.

Even so, it was more than an hour before Pearce felt comfortable enough to introduce the topic that was uppermost in his mind.

168

"We miss Sir David at GCHQ, you know," he said. "Especially those of us who worked closely with him."

The sadness in Downing's face was both immediate and unfeigned.

"I'm sure you do. He was a great man, you know, a great man. I miss him as well."

Silence fell on the room. Both of them were professionals who had reached the highest pinnacle that his country could offer. Both knew that the agency for which he was responsible had a brief that was limited to matters of signal intelligence. Neither man officially had the power to do more than give verbal vent to his feelings of loss and frustration.

Pearce waited, holding his breath, to see whether Downing was prepared to step beyond the boundaries that theoretically proscribed his actions. And if he did not, would Pearce have the fortitude to raise the idea himself? Now that the moment was here, he was not sure.

The silence passed from respect for the dead to something more, an expectant waiting for something to be said. And Pearce became increasingly certain that Downing had thought through the situation and come to exactly the same conclusion as himself. But as long as that conclusion was left unsaid it could be denied. Was either of them willing to say out loud what had to be said if David's death was to be avenged?

Downing, whose gaze was purposefully avoiding Pearce while he thought, was facing a dilemma. From the very beginning he had understood that the real reason for Pearce's visit was to enlist his aid in helping with an unofficial effort to track down Sir David's killer. But why did Pearce think that the NSA would be able to help? The answer to that question was not yet clear to him.

The whole subject was a minefield, and Downing was all too aware of how carefully he must tread. Did Pearce know anything about Kelton? Did he know what Kelton knew: that the Irish, who initially had been so firmly blamed by the newspapers, were in fact not responsible for Sir David's death?

He shifted his gaze and tried to read the answers in Pearce's face, but the man, an awfully *young* man to head up one of the most respected SIGINT agencies in the world, was playing his cards too close to his chest.

In the intelligence business, one learns quickly that information, once given, cannot be retrieved. For now, it would be safest to act uninformed.

"I gather that the Irish got him. Any idea why they chose him as a target?"

Pearce replaced the coffee cup he had been nursing, exhaling audibly as he did so. If this was not an offer of assistance, then he had no place sitting in Sir David's seat. He chose his words carefully, aware that it was entirely possible that the meeting was being taped, and if something illegal was to be agreed, then it had to be done covertly, the words ambiguous, the meaning unclear to anyone who might hear them, except for the two men seated on either side of Downing's desk.

"Since you mention it, there is something suspicious about that whole Irish connection. If there is an Irish connection."

Downing permitted himself to look intrigued.

Pearce continued, "We've been working on the case, you know, sort of semi-officially because it's not really within our purview, but we've been trying to help out MI5 and Special Branch and, quite frankly, the whole affair is not quite as simple as we thought at first."

Downing raised an interrogative eyebrow. He was as anxious to hear what Pearce knew as Pearce was to have Downing's assistance, although it was impossible to guess from their mien or the studied indolence in the delivery of their words that either man was more than casually interested in this topic of conversation.

"Really?" Downing asked. "What's the complication?"

"We got a lab report from MI5, and actually it doesn't look like the Irish did it at all."

"It doesn't?"

"No. In fact, as you may know, the ILF officially denied responsibility a couple of days after the explosion, although it was not widely reported at the time, and in any case no one really believed them. Anyway, we have intelligence that informs us that they were telling the truth."

"Reliable intelligence?"

"Absolutely."

Pearce used the word on purpose. There were many grades of intelligence, depending on its source and on many other factors. If the Director of GCHQ said that an item of intelligence was "absolutely reliable," its validity was beyond question.

"But I thought I read that the ILF claimed responsibility at the time of the explosion?"

"You probably did. A phone call was made moments after the explosion from the departure lounge itself. The caller claimed that the ILF was responsible. We are sure now that that call was placed simply to distract and mislead us. The caller was apparently an American, probably originally from the mid-West but now living in New England, doing his best to imitate a Northern Ireland accent. Not with a great deal of success, according to our phonologists."

"An American? Anything we might be able to do to help, do you think? Bearing in mind of course that the only support we could provide is SIGINT." The caveat, of course, was for the benefit of any tape recorders that happened to be listening.

"Possibly. I have a copy of our file on the bombing right here. Maybe I should leave it with you." Pearce lifted his slim attaché case, spun the thumbwheels and, for the first time that morning, opened it and extracted a file.

He thrust the file across the desk. Neither man commented on the fact that the presence of the file in his attaché case was clear evidence that Pearce had arrived that morning with the specific goal of asking Downing for assistance in tracking down Sir David's killer.

"I think you'll find it interesting reading," Pearce said.

Downing resisted the urge to thumb through the file immediately. He swung his chair and turned away from Pearce to look out the window. It was a cold, gray day outside, the bare branches of the trees moving slightly in the breeze. Snow looked possible before the day was out. But any further discussions would have to take place outside the office and away from the microphones.

"Did you bring a coat, John?" To preëmpt the possibility of a negative reply, Downing continued, "I wondered if perhaps you'd like to take a quick stroll? Just for a few minutes, to restore the circulation."

"Yes, good idea," Pearce agreed, and the two men quickly rose from their chairs.

"Anything you want to tell me that isn't in the file?"

Downing and Pearce were bundled tightly against the biting wind. Even so, they hurried as they walked along the path. The wind whipped away the condensed moisture from their breaths almost before the droplets had time to form. "Is there anything to go on apart from the phonologist's report? What did you learn from forensics?"

"Quite a lot really. Most of it's in the file."

The cold caught at Pearce's throat. Even though Washington was at a much lower latitude than Cheltenham, still it was colder here than it ever was back home. He wondered vaguely how Washingtonians could stand the bitter winters and the hot, sticky summers. "The file includes a report prepared by one of my people who was working with the MI5 forensic team. When you read it you'll see that it seems possible, even likely, that the explosive used in the bomb was of American origin and smuggled into Britain.

"In the last few days they've confirmed that the VHF receiver chip was an American part, manufactured mainly for your Department of Defense for use with its field-mobile packet radio network. Unfortunately, in these free-trade days, the same part is widely available in most developed countries. The mask number etched on to the chip showed that it was made recently, so it was probably purchased in the United States, Canada, Australia or Great Britain, since it usually takes a while for parts to filter out to other countries; but that hardly narrows the field very much.

"MI5 has sent a small cadre of chemists over here, but they arrived only yesterday, so it will be a while before we get anything from them."

"Any leads at all about the person or group responsible? Do we even know if it was an individual or a group?"

"No, nothing on that yet at all. The bomb was built very carefully, and, as you will read, everything we've found so far indicates that we were supposed to be misled into believing that the perpetrator was British, whereas, in fact, as I told you, he seems to be American. We are hoping that maybe his trail will be a little easier to follow if we can pick it up over here."

Downing nodded. "Anything else?"

"I don't think so."

"OK. I'll take a careful look at it, and see if I can't think of some way we can help out." He paused. "It's the least I could do for David."

"He meant a lot to you didn't he?"

The question marked a change in subject. The two continued walking, hurrying even more quickly against the biting wind. The file was not mentioned again.

When they returned to Downing's office, the two spent the rest of the morning discussing matters "of mutual concern," mainly centering on the neverending political shifts in Eastern Europe.

At lunch they were joined at their table by the chief of the NSA's Office of Telecommunications and Computer Services. The topic of conversation shifted to the subject of inter-service electronic communication in general, electronic communication between the NSA and GCHQ in particular, and the ever increasing and somewhat worrisome reliance that was now placed on the world-wide Platform computer network that, since the early 1980s, had linked many of the world's intelligence gathering agencies.

After lunch, while Pearce was occupied in discussions with Downing's Deputy Director for Operations, Downing returned to his office, where he twice read slowly through the folder Pearce had given him. Then he dictated a short advertisement to be placed in the next day's London *Times*. He followed that with two short memoranda for immediate delivery, one to the DDO, and one to the man with whom Pearce and he had shared lunch.

If anyone could trace Sir David's killer from the information in the folder, it would be one of these men.

Chapter 19
Tuesday, December 4
Chapel St. Leonard's, Lincolnshire, England

The east wind blew directly across the North Sea, whipping the water into dirty white-capped peaks, until it reached the long, almost horizontal stretch of mud-colored sand that was the shore along the Lincolnshire coast. Walking across the sand, his footprints leaving marks that would soon be erased by the incoming tide, a single figure walked, his collar upturned, his head hunched down to protect it from the worst excesses of the biting, salt-laden wind.

It was just before eight in the morning and the sun was not yet up, although it would rise above the watery south-eastern horizon within the next few minutes.

The man presented his profile to the wind, his left cheek burning where the cold air slammed into it. His walk became a sort of jog, his hands thrust deeply into the pockets of his raincoat, his arms straight. He turned around and the wind assaulted his other cheek. He began to jog back in the direction he had come.

Ten minutes later, he climbed the small rise that separated the dirty brown sand from the road that led to the village of Chapel St. Leonard's. The sun had risen now and, for a moment, to an observer on the road (had there been one that blustery morning) he would have seemed like an apparition, silhouetted against the bright background of the sky. Then the man dropped down the leeward side of the slope and stopped to catch his breath, free at last from the buffeting of the chillsome wind.

Kelton looked around; he could see no movement except pieces of paper, skittering here and there where they were exposed to the whim of the wind.

He breathed deeply, and began to stride in the direction of the village.

Kelton had returned to Surrey the day after his telephone conversations with the head of NSA. Within minutes of arriving at the house on Darnley Drive, he had realized it was a mistake to come home.

At first he thought that it was only his imagination, but by the end of the second day, he knew that it was going to be impossible for him to stay in the house. This was not Kelton's home, and Kelton did not belong there; it was Paul Kent's home, and Kelton was nothing but an intruder. Every hour, almost every minute, he would look up at some sound, expecting to see Catherine popping her head around a door-jamb to ask if he wanted a cup of tea, or Elizabeth wandering in wanting help with a broken toy.

The urge to get in the car and drive to the hospital and simply sit and look at Elizabeth, still unconscious in her bed, became almost unbearable.

The very air in the house was heavy and oppressive, and he continually found himself beginning a train of thought that wondered: *why is it so quiet?* and *where is Elizabeth?*

No matter how much he tried to fool himself that Elizabeth was Kent's daughter, no matter how often he reminded himself that he was Kelton and not Kent, his brain refused to accept the charade.

The evenings were the worst, when he made his daily call to Dr. Worthington; for then he had to cease being Kelton for a few minutes and once more become Kent. And once he acknowledged Kent's presence inside his head, it was impossible to pretend any longer. It was his own wife who was dead, his own daughter who might never wake up. After the call he would go to bed, where he stared sleeplessly up at the ceiling, remembering.

It was too much. He got up at four o'clock and, after wandering aimlessly around the house for half an hour, he convinced himself that he had to leave, to distance himself from the hospital. He pored over an AA book for five minutes, then quickly packed a small suitcase. Just as it was getting light, he got the car out the garage and began to head north.

He could have chosen anywhere, really. He needed isolation and an environment completely unlike Surrey, and at this time of year there were many places in England that could have offered both. For no deeper reason than that this was one part of England that he and Catherine had never visited — and hence it held no memories for him — he drove around the London Orbital and then headed north, past the signs for Cambridge and Peterborough. In Boston he began to drive parallel to the coast, looking for somewhere to stop.

He found the village almost by accident, driving down an unmarked road that did not rate even a "B" classification. In the summer, Chapel St. Leonard's was an overflow for nearby Skegness. But now, as winter began to bite deeply across the flat, drear fenscape, the noticeboards and the ruts of the vanished caravans in the fields were all that remained to remind the stranger of the bustling place it became in the summer months.

Driving slowly through the village, he had found the bungalow some distance from the village center, not far from a newish estate, looking forlorn and unloved and in obvious disrepair, its battered "For Sale" sign swinging in the easterly breeze in a way that inspired no confidence that it would see the winter through.

He had not purchased the house, and the sign was still on the far side of the privet hedge, now more firmly staked in the ground against the biting east wind, but the elderly female owner had been only too pleased to rent the one-bedroomed bungalow for three moths to the pleasant middle-aged man who drove an expensive car and was happy to pay cash in advance. A writer, he said he was, who needed to "get away from everyone for a bit" so he could finish work on his latest book.

She asked what kind of books he wrote, but his only response had been: "novels, under a pseudonym." She wondered if she had read any of them. Probably, she decided, for she was a voracious reader and from his unconcern about money it was obvious that her tenant sold a lot of books; she was thrilled at the thought that she had met someone famous.

That was five days ago, and Kelton had known instantly that coming to this remote and windswept place was the best thing he could have done, for in this place it was much easier to pretend that Kent was far away, still living his comfortable life in suburban Surrey.

The only exception came at nine o'clock every evening. Unable to give up the only contact with his daughter, he still called Dr. Worthington every day. For a few minutes, Kelton was replaced by Kent; but as soon as the doctor had delivered her news that there was no change, Kent would hang up and Kelton would take his place. With the distance he had placed between them and the daily unchanging report from Dr. Worthington, it became easier every day for Kelton to gain control.

Still walking briskly, Kelton arrived at the first shop in the village.

The handwritten notice in the newsagent's window declared that the shop opened at eight thirty during the off-season, but, as usual, Kelton had arrived a few minutes after that time and the sign on the shop door still announced: "Sorry, we are closed. Please call back later when we are open for Lyons cakes."

Inside the shop the lights were on. Kelton tapped on the door. Within a few moments, an elderly man, rotund and with a red face that was topped by an arc of white hair, unlocked the door, flipped the sign over, and opened the door to Kelton.

"Good morning, sir; bit nippy this morning. Take your walk did you?"

Kelton stepped into the shop and was immediately assailed by the distinctive mixture of smells — bread, soap and newsprint chief amongst them — that seems to pervade such places.

"Yes," he replied. "Bit chilly, though. Looks like rain later, too. Did you hear the forecast?"

"Aye. Rain coming in from the east. The wind should die down by midmorning. There'll be a frost tonight, I shouldn't wonder. Here you are then."

While they exchanged pleasantries, they walked to the rear of the store and the shopkeeper snipped open the string on a bundle of papers and extracted a copy of the day's *Times*. As always, Kelton gave the front page no more than a glance, just enough to be sure that he had the right paper, then he dug in his pocket and extracted a pound coin. The shopkeeper made change and, with a cheerful farewell, Kelton stepped out once more into the chill morning. Tucking the paper under his arm, he walked smartly back to the bungalow.

While he waited for the kettle to boil, he settled down at the kitchen table and spread the paper open before him. As always, he turned directly to the classifieds. He squinted as his eyes ran down the columns of tiny print, aware not for the first time that most people his age wore reading glasses. He tried to ignore the niggling thought that he was not immune to the vicissitudes of growing older.

Halfway down the third column, his finger stopped. There it was, a typical *Times* coded personal, uninformative to anyone except its intended recipient: "K. Looks hopeful. Please call UK number. D."

Kelton smiled, just as the kettle began to spew a mist into the kitchen, to be followed moments later by the loud,

179

reluctant thud as it switched itself off. Standing to make his pot of tea, he could not help a smile of satisfaction. Downing's ad was surely a good sign. He poured the hot water on to the teabags, and let his mind wander.

It would be early afternoon before the East Coast of the United States arrived at work, which gave him plenty of time to drive some distance from the village to find a distant public telephone kiosk.

He drank his tea, two cups, thoughtfully, then gathered his coat and a warm wrap, locked the bungalow, and got in his car.

He drove south, skirting Skegness and then heading towards Boston. There was no great hurry, and as he drove he listened to a violin concerto on Radio 3 and looked out over the wintry fens that stretched as far as he could see to the west, north and south, and as far as the slight rise of the coastal berm to the east.

He pulled off the road a little before one o'clock and began threading his way down country lanes. He passed through three villages before he found what he sought: a sleepy pub with a public telephone kiosk — a proper red one, not one of those newfangled flimsy yellow affairs — standing across the road from the pub's car park.

He entered the pub — *The Fox and Hounds*; hardly original, but at least it was appropriate in this part of the country — and ordered a pint and a ploughman's. Beer in hand, he went outside while he waited for the meal to be prepared. A farmer on his tractor drove noisily past, then he crossed the road and stepped into the telephone kiosk.

He dialed an Oxford number. The sound of the phone ringing at the other end halted after a single ring, to be followed by clicks and whistles as the scrambler came on line and the call was automatically forwarded through secure cable 3,000 miles across the Atlantic. After about ten seconds, a distinct click came as the telephone was picked up at the far end.

A homely female voice with an American, slightly southern, accent came on the line. "If you would wait a moment, your call is being transferred automatically to your party."

Kelton said nothing. The voice, he knew, was a recording. Another thirty seconds went by. Then another click, particularly clear, and a flat American voice said, "Mike's Used Books. This is Mike."

"Good morning, Mike. I received your message in today's paper."

"Good. I was expecting your call. I think maybe we need to talk."

"OK. Go ahead. What have you found?"

"No, I mean really talk. Face to face. Does the name John Pearce mean anything to you?"

Kelton paused for several seconds, trying to place the name. Somewhere at the back of his mind it rang a bell, but he couldn't remember where he had seen it. In a newspaper, perhaps?

"No. Who is he?"

"The new head of GCHQ since David died. He was here yesterday, and he left behind a file with some information in it that would interest you."

Kelton made a thoughtful moue. So GCHQ were on the trail as well, were they? He supposed he shouldn't be surprised. But what, he wondered, did Mr. Pearce intend to do when he found his man?

"What information?" he asked.

"The Brits agree with you that the ILF had nothing to do with it. They are still working on it, but they seem pretty certain that the killer, or at least the bomb, came from this side of the pond."

Kelton could not suppress a smile of satisfaction as a weight was lifted from his shoulders.

He had not dared to admit it even to himself, but these past few days he had been wondering more and more whether there was any chance that he had got it all wrong. What if

O'Hannessy had been lying? What if it really *was* the ILF that was responsible?

Now his doubts were washed away. Here was the first truly independent evidence, apart from a single week-old hint in one newspaper, that he had been right, that O'Connaught and O'Hannessy had been telling the truth, that the trail pointing to them was false, nothing but a blind to disguise the identity of the real perpetrators.

Kelton tried to keep his relief from his voice as he said, "Good. What else do you have?"

"There's plenty in the file to keep you interested for a while. But I'd like your help in following up an idea I have. With any luck, between ourselves and the British, we might be able to get this thing sorted out pretty quickly."

"So what do you want me to do?"

"Could you meet me at 9 a.m. Thursday outside the National Air and Space Museum in downtown Washington?"

Kelton thought for a couple of seconds. It was now midday on Tuesday. At this time of year there should be no difficulty getting a flight at short notice. "OK."

"Just look like a lost tourist and I'll come and help. I'll have a safe meeting place arranged."

"See you Thursday, then."

The line went dead. Kelton put the phone down and looked absentmindedly at his beer for several seconds.

"I'm coming for you, you bastard, whoever you are," he said with satisfaction. Then he picked up his glass and quaffed deeply of the drink.

Back in the pub, as he settled himself at an aged table in front of the warm fire that cast its heat throughout the lounge bar, Kelton found his mind wandering back to the last time he and Downing had worked together.

Chapter 20
Five years earlier

A terse advertisement had appeared in *The Times*: "K. Please call. Mr. Downs." It was followed by a central London telephone number.

Kelton recognized neither the name nor the telephone number. When he dialed the number, from a public kiosk on the A44 not far outside Worcester, a hand at the other end lifted the telephone almost before it had started to ring.

"Cultural attaché," said a youngish male at the other end of the line, his voice carrying the unmistakable twang of the American South.

Kelton raised an eyebrow. Why would someone at the American Embassy want to talk to a professional assassin?

"Er... yes. I'd like to speak with a Mr. Downs?"

"Mr. Downs? I'm sorry sir, but there's no one here by that name. I'm afraid you must have the wrong number."

Kelton waited to see if the man would cut the connection. He did not. The suggestion of a wrong number was simply to discourage callers; the man had remained on the line to see if Kelton had a legitimate reason for this call.

"Mr. Downs placed an ad for me in today's *Times*. I assume that he is interested in availing himself of my services."

"Yes? and what services would those be?"

Kelton could play games too. "Oh, excuse me. I think I've made a mistake. Goodbye."

"No, wait a minute," said the American quickly, "perhaps I can find Mr. Downs for you. Can you please hold?"

"Sixty seconds, and then I'm gone."

"I understand, sir. I'll be as quick as possible." The man was suddenly professional.

Kelton counted as he waited. Forty-eight seconds elapsed before there was another sound in his ear.

"Could I have your name please, sir?" asked the man.

"No, you may not."

"Sir, I'm afraid that Mr. Downs is not presently available. However, if you could call back in an hour, he would be able to talk to you then."

"Just now you said there was no person there by the name of Downs."

"Oh, yes; sorry, sir. I apologize for the confusion, but I understand that he is *most* anxious to talk with you, and hopes very much that you'll be able to call again."

"I'll call back. One hour."

Kelton put the telephone down, puzzled and intrigued. *What am I getting into here?* he wondered.

He drove east along the A44 for fifty minutes before pulling into a layby with a telephone kiosk just outside Chipping Norton. He picked up the telephone and dialed the London number again.

As before, the phone barely had time to ring before it was snatched up. "Cultural attaché," the same voice said.

"I'm calling for Mr. Downs. I rang about an hour ago."

"Certainly, sir. Please hold while I connect you."

The connection took some time to go through, and there were several ticks and other odd noises on the line before he heard a phone ringing: not the distinctive *brrr-brrr* double ring of British telephones, but the long single ring of an American instrument. It was answered on the third ring.

"Mr. Kelton?" enquired a pleasant-sounding voice that was indubitably American.

"I'd like to speak to Mr. Downs."

"Certainly. You got him," the voice said. "Thanks for calling. Now, what do you know?"

"I don't play guessing games. Who the hell are you and what do you want?"

"Whoa, steady on. I just wanted to know if anyone had told you anything. First of all, though, I need to know that I'm talking to the right man. Where were you on January 16 of last year?"

"How should I know? That's eighteen months ago now."

"Perhaps you have forgotten that on January 16 of last year Monsieur Georges Lebeq, the French ambassador to the United Nations, was shot and killed. Does that jog your memory?"

"Oh, yes, then I do remember. I could hardly forget, since I also happened to be in Guadeloupe when it happened. Although I was staying in Port-Louis, while I believe that Monsieur Lebeq was killed in Basse-Terre, on the western island if memory serves me correctly."

"Are you still in the same line of business?"

"You obviously know I am. But I don't have the faintest idea who you are. How about establishing *your* identity with me?"

"Mr. Kelton, I can't do that. At least not right now. Not even over a fully secure line, which I understand this is not. However, once we've gone through some preliminaries, I'd be only too happy to meet with you."

"What sort of preliminaries?"

"They won't take a moment. We've established that you are the correct man. I repeat my earlier question: are you still in the same line of work that you were eighteen months ago?"

"I'm thinking of retiring. But I'd be willing to listen if the right job came along."

"I can assure you that for this job you would be paid most handsomely. I can't discuss a figure with you over an insecure phone line, of course, but I'm sure you'll find it a very satisfactory payment for a relatively simple job."

Kelton knew better than to accept this at face value. People did not contact him for "relatively simple" jobs. People called Kelton only when a nasty, complicated and usually political assassination was on the cards.

Rather than respond he kept silent.

"You still there?" asked Downs.

"Yes, and I'm still listening, though you haven't given me any reason to stay on the line much longer."

"Maybe we had better meet somewhere so I can give you all the details in person. Let me think a minute. Hang on, I'll get my calendar and I'll be right back."

The line went relatively quiet for about thirty seconds, only the occasional click and a quiet, repetitive tapping greeting his ears. Downs came back on the line. "OK. I could spare some time next week. How's your schedule then?"

"Monday and Tuesday would be fine. After that I'm tied up."

"How well do you know Washington?"

Washington. So this *was* a transatlantic call. "As well as the next tourist," he said noncommittally, wondering just who this Mr. Downs really was.

"OK. How about Monday, 10 a.m., outside the main entrance to the National Air and Space Museum?"

"No good," he replied. "At 10 a.m. on Tuesday next you will be standing on the pavement on the west side of the university engineering building in Oxford. You can't miss it, it's the tallest building around. You will be wearing a carnation in your buttonhole."

"Now, wait a minute, I can't just...." The protesting voice was cut off as Kelton hung up the phone.

Now we'll find out how much Mr. Downs needs me, thought Kelton.

At five minutes past ten in the morning on the following Tuesday, which was a comfortable, somewhat windy autumnal day in late September, a man walked quickly north along the Banbury Road in Oxford.

The man crossed Keble Road and hurried past the building that houses Oxford's Department of Nuclear Physics, the massive Van de Graaff generator clearly visible from the street through the windows. He glanced at his watch as he left the Nuclear Physics building behind and drew level with the engineering building, slowing to a stroll and looking around as if searching for someone. He continued northward until he reached the point where Banbury Road meets Parks Road; then he turned and slowly retraced his steps.

The man was wearing a suit, and looked somewhat out of place in the ancient university town with its casual lecturers and even more casual students. It was a couple of weeks before the commencement of Michaelmas Term, so there were few undergraduates to be seen, but there still enough postgraduates around for him to feel both old and conspicuous. He wore a yellow carnation in his buttonhole.

Reaching Keble Road, he turned around and began to stroll northwards once more, retracing his steps. He glanced at his watch. Twelve minutes past the hour. He showed no sign of displeasure. The opposite, in fact. He continually looked around as if enjoying the sights, even if they were the very ones he had seen but minutes before.

He walked north to the conjunction of the roads and turned south once more. Seventeen minutes past the hour. As he passed the engineering building for the fourth time, a needlessly raincoated figure with his hands in his pockets walked past him, then turned and said "Mr. Downs?" to his retreating back.

The suited figure turned around, both hands rising, preparing to greet the other and simultaneously showing that his hands were empty. "Mr. Kelton?"

Without answering the question, the other man drew close and said, "In my right pocket is a gun. It is pointing at you. Let me check you for wires and weapons."

"What? Oh, yeah, sure," said Downs, while the other rapidly brushed his left hand lightly over his clothes.

Kelton withdrew his right hand, empty, from his coat pocket, and extended it towards the other. "Good morning, Mr. Downs. I'm glad you came."

"Is there somewhere we can talk? You wouldn't believe the strings I had to pull to meet you here like this. It's very irregular, you know."

Kelton frowned. "You know a lot about me, Mr. Downs, but I know nothing about you. It seemed only reasonable to even things up a little by having us meet on my home territory rather than yours."

The American responded with the first of many things that were to lay the foundation of their relationship of mutual respect. "I understand. I can tell you that I don't like it any more than you. I find all this undercover work thoroughly distasteful, and personally I don't think we should be messing around doing jobs like this anyway; but since we have to do it the two of us might as well get along as best we can. For my part, I'll tell you as much of the picture as I can, and I'll try to trust you to do your job well. I hope you'll try to trust me the same way."

"All right. Sounds reasonable to me."

The two men shook hands firmly. "By the way," said the American, "my name isn't really Downs. It's Downing, Mike Downing. Call me Mike. Let's not stand on ceremony. And, to be honest, I've quite enjoyed the morning. I studied in Oxford for a couple of years, more years ago now than I care to remember, and this is the first time I've been back."

"In that case, I'm glad to have been the cause of your return. And my name isn't Mr. Kelton. It's just Kelton."

"No first name?"

"Maybe yes, maybe no. But to you it's just plain Kelton."

"Whatever you say... Kelton. Look, is there anywhere we can go to talk? All the restaurants have changed since my day."

"This is Oxford, Mike. You can talk almost anywhere. Surely you haven't forgotten that? Anyway, there's a little coffeehouse off St. Giles where we can get both privacy and good coffee."

The two men walked south towards the center of town. Kelton led Downing into a side street and thence into a small coffeehouse. With the undergraduates still on vacation, the coffeehouse was quiet and almost empty.

Over coffee and warm, fresh rolls, Downing attempted to establish his trustworthiness. Without asking Kelton a single question, he talked about his own life: his marriage and divorce; the two children, both now in college on the west coast; stories from his time as a student of P.P.E. at Oxford.

"They didn't have a one-way system here then," he observed, "and you could actually get where you were going without first taking a tour of the city trying to find a parking space. Things don't always change for the better."

To Kelton it was obvious that the man was suffering from the bittersweet feeling that comes from revisiting somewhere that long ago provided many happy memories, but on which time has wrought many changes.

Eventually, Downing's nostalgia ran its course.

"So," he said, "I suppose we should discuss the purpose of our meeting."

"Yes," agreed Kelton. It was about time.

"How much do you know about the various security agencies in the United States?"

"Not much."

"Here's a quick rundown, then. There are three main civilian agencies, as well as many military ones that don't concern us. The three civilian agencies are: the Federal Bureau of Investigation, the FBI; the Central Intelligence Agency, the CIA; and the National Security Agency, the NSA. Each of the three has its own charter, and, generally, the charters are mutually exclusive."

"Meaning?"

"Meaning that, generally, in any particular operation, only one of the three agencies can legally be involved. Basically the FBI has jurisdiction over domestic matters and the CIA has jurisdiction over foreign cases. If a CIA operative was caught working on a domestic case, there's a good chance he'd end up behind bars."

"That doesn't seem to leave much for the NSA," observed Kelton drily.

"We tend to be rather more coy about the NSA," said Downing. Downing unfortunately chose that moment to look at the surrounding tables suspiciously, in the manner of a second-rate actor trying to portray a spy. The action was rendered even more humorous by the fact that none of the tables was occupied, and Kelton had to stifle a laugh. "Generally," Downing continued, satisfied that they could not be overheard, "the NSA confines itself to foreign intelligence gathering. Officially, they do nothing domestically."

"So, you imply that there is unofficial domestic surveillance? But only intelligence gathering, no field operations?"

"I'm not going to confirm anything or deny anything. It's more than my job is worth. If you make some smart guesses, that's not my problem, is it?"

"And what happened to all that talk about trust?"

"I'll tell you what I can. But if I sit here and tell you everything you want to know, I'll fail the polygraph test that I'll be forced to take if you seem to know more than you're supposed to. Understand?"

Kelton nodded. "OK. Makes sense. So, which one of the three do you work for? Presumably you can tell me that."

"No, I can't. At least, not yet. I can tell you that I work for one of them, and that all three have been working together, along with the DEA, the Drug Enforcement Administration, for the past two and a half years trying to infiltrate and smash what we believe to be the world's largest heroin smuggling operation."

"OK. Fine so far." Kelton was ambivalent. Political killing was his forté; he knew little about drug smuggling. "I don't see how I fit in the picture though."

"You will," said Downing. "Have you ever heard of a wealthy American businessman called Carl Cotterell?"

Kelton thought for a moment. "No, I can't say I have."

"We've been trying to nail Mr. Cotterell for several years. He's the man behind the smuggling operation I mentioned. As far as we can tell, he supplies both the money and the brains. The operation itself is called the Golden Pipeline. He siphons off the profit and launders it through any number of his tame overseas holdings."

"Well, if you know all this, why don't you just put the man away?"

"Don't think we haven't tried. Twice we thought we had him nailed. We indicted him and brought him to a jury trial. Both times the jury let him off. The last time this happened was four weeks ago. We're sure he bought the jury somehow, although of course we can't prove a thing. The government had the strongest case the prosecutor had ever seen in a major drugs case like this. The newspapers had him convicted and sentenced before the trial was halfway through. And then the jury let him off."

Downing paused before continuing. He lowered his voice so that Kelton had to lean forward to hear properly, "So my superiors have decided it's... er... time to take matters into our own hands."

"Ahh... I see," Kelton nodded. "And that, presumably, is where I come into the picture?"

"Exactly. My superiors have decided that we've wasted more than enough time doing things by the book. We've spent millions and wasted goodness knows how many man-decades of effort, and it's gotten us nowhere. Worse than that, it's terrible for morale. What's the point of us wasting

our lives going after scum like Cotterell if they can subvert
the system and escape justice once we've delivered them to
the courts?"

"I see your point. So what's the deal?"

"Simple. I'm authorized to offer you the sum of one million
US dollars in return for your services. We want him dead,
cleanly and at your earliest convenience. And, obviously, we
must be sure that there's no possible traceable connection
leading back to us."

Kelton frowned. "You don't have to worry about it being
traceable. But one million dollars? I don't know. Expenses
can add up quickly, you know. Normally, I would add my out-
of-pocket expenses to the bill, but I think it would be wise
if we minimized contact between us. So let's make it two
million up front, expenses included, and I think we'll have a
deal."

"I'm not sure I can negotiate. One million was the figure I
was authorized to offer. I'm sorry."

Kelton shook his head. "Your bosses wouldn't send you
over here on a moment's notice like this if it wasn't important to close this contract. And they certainly wouldn't send
you without some sort of negotiating power. I'm sure you've
been given a ceiling over which you can't go. I'm also reasonably sure that that ceiling is at least two million and possibly
considerably more. It's not an outrageous price for the job,
especially given my record. So why don't you just count yourself lucky that I haven't pushed harder, and let's get on with
it? You wanted us to trust one another, remember?"

Downing smiled, then laughed. "Yeah, you're right on all
counts. So, two million it is."

He held his hand out across the table, and the two men
shook to cement the deal.

"So, what do we do now?" asked Downing.

"Now we refill our coffee cups and get down to some serious
discussion."

The money arrived three weeks later. Not long afterward,
Carl Cotterell was killed without warning in New York: a

single shot from a sniper's bullet as he was bending to enter a car.

The man who pulled the trigger was never caught.

———————————

All that was five years ago now.

Kelton had read in the newspapers that the Cotterell fortune had passed into his brother's hands, and in the intervening years he had seen occasional references to the Golden Pipeline, which, as far as he could tell, far from suffering at the loss of Carl Cotterell, had flourished under its new management.

"So perhaps Robbie Burns had it right after all," he said to himself as he lifted his beer. He looked at the cheerful fire burning in the grate and was lost for a moment in a reverie.

Then he pressed the glass to his lips and drank deeply.

Chapter 21
Wednesday, December 5
Cheltenham

John Pearce said, "OK; well, thanks anyway" in a grudging tone, then slammed the telephone down into its cradle in disgust.

"Damn!" he swore, giving rare voice to his frustration.

He tried to calm himself, forcing himself to breathe deeply and evenly. He knew it was the tiredness caused by jet lag as much as the sense of defeat.

The MI5 chemist had just called from Missouri with his news. (*Missouri? Where the devil is that? Out west somewhere, isn't it?* thought Pearce.)

The deep breathing worked. Gradually, Pearce became calmer. He had not realized how much he had been pinning his hopes on the chemists' efforts; hopes that, as he had just learned, were to be unfulfilled.

The chemists had had no trouble determining the lot number of the Foamtex explosive from which the Gatwick device had been constructed. Foamtex was sufficiently new that only a couple of dozen 2-ton lots had been made by the explosive's manufacturer. Of the roughly 25 tons that had been manufactured, all except a fraction of one lot was accounted for. That lot had been manufactured just four months ago, and the entire 2-ton output from that manufacturing run had been purchased by a concern called Australian Outback Mining, based in Queensland.

It had arrived in Australia little more than a month ago, at the end of October, and the mining company had immediately notified the manufacturer that several cubic feet of the explosive were missing. The explosive was shipped in cubes exactly one foot on a side: five such cubes had disappeared in transit.

According to the experts, between a half and a full cubic foot would have been adequate for the Gatwick explosion. Investigations by Customs officers from Australia, New Zealand (where the ship transporting the cargo had briefly put into port) and the United States, as well as operatives from the United States Bureaux of Alcohol, Tobacco & Firearms and Munitions Control had been unable to determine even the simple fact of where in the transportation process the missing cubes had been removed. So all the chemists could report from Missouri was that they had reached a dead end.

Pearce looked at the telephone. He had better call Downing and tell him that it was all up to him now. It seemed highly unlikely that anything else useful was going to turn up from the British investigations.

Kelton left the bungalow in Chapel St. Leonard's shortly after three thirty in the afternoon, after removing everything that showed he had ever been there. He drove south, and did not stop until he had driven around London and found an anonymous hotel for the night near Crawley, south-west of the city and close to the airport. He had already booked a business-class seat on a Delta flight to JFK for the next day.

He debated with himself whether he should visit the hospital or simply call Dr. Worthington as usual that evening.

Then he asked himself, *What kind of a person are you, that you can even ask such a question?* That settled the matter, and for a few hours Kelton was pushed firmly into the background while Paul Kent visited his daughter.

She was in a different room now, but there was still a cat's cradle of tubes and wires connecting her to the machines that clustered around her bed. On a table next to her bed were the soft toys he had brought from home. He almost cried when he saw that they had been joined by Mr. Bear, somewhat the worse for having been caught in the explosion but still recognizably Elizabeth's favorite toy and constant companion.

In Elizabeth herself there was no obvious change. She still lay there with her eyes closed, breathing evenly as if merely asleep. The top of her head was hidden under a swath of bandages into which disappeared several wires. Her face was paler than he remembered it.

He pulled up a chair and talked to her for a while, reminding her of shared memories, of times they had been together as a family. It seemed fantastic now that they had never realized how precious those times were, how soon they would be gone forever.

After he had been there a few minutes, Dr. Worthington came into the room. They shook hands and greeted one another.

"Still no change then, doctor?" he asked, although he already knew the answer.

"I'm afraid not. But our resident neurologist says not to give up hope. Miracles happen every day. And I'm glad you could come by. Business trips over for a while?"

She had spent a lot of time thinking about what had happened in Ireland ten days ago, and had come to the conclusion that it was impossible that Mr. Kent could have had anything to do with the death of Sean O'Hannessy.

"Unfortunately no," he replied. "I just drove down from Lincolnshire today and I'm off to the States early tomorrow. I've no idea how long I might be gone. Is there some other time of day I could call about Elizabeth? Because of the time difference, I mean. Or am I being stupid to keep calling? Is there really any hope she'll ever come out of this?"

"Like I said, Dr. Higgins says it's never hopeless, and he's the expert. You can reach me here at the hospital most days. I'm usually in surgery in the mornings, but you should be able to reach me any time after noon." She gave him her office number. Then, deciding that she might as well put her imagination to rest once and for all, she asked, "Tell me, Mr. Kent, if you don't mind me asking, what line of business are you in?"

Kent looked away, suddenly unsure of himself. It was crazy and he knew it. Kelton would have had no compunction about lying, saying the first thing that came into his head. But Kent could not lie, not to the doctor who had saved his daughter's life.

He racked his brains for a sensible answer, but none came. "I'm afraid I can't tell you," he said lamely. "Really, I'd tell you if I could. But I can't."

"That's all right," said the doctor. But it wasn't. She had given him the perfect opportunity to quash her suspicions, and he had evaded the question. Even so, she told herself that there had to be a perfectly simple explanation.

She watched Mr. Kent carefully. She wondered if there was anyone with whom he had shared the pain of his loss. Everyone should have someone to turn to at such times, but she was sure as she watched him that Mr. Kent had not unbent to anyone.

"Mr. Kent?"

"Yes?" He did not turn to look at her.

"Please, would you do me a tremendous favor?"

"If I can."

"Would you do me the honor of having dinner with me tonight?"

Now he did look at her. He shook his head. "I'm sorry, I can't." His regret seemed genuine.

"Can't? or won't?"

"Daren't. I'm sorry, I think I'd better leave."

Before she could respond, he had brushed past her. She heard the sound of his steps almost at a run dying away in the distance.

She turned to look at Elizabeth.

"Who are you, Mr. Kent?" she wondered aloud to the silent room.

Next morning, Kelton arrived at Gatwick an hour and a half before his flight was due to leave, dressed like an overworked midlevel executive, and carrying a small but new suitcase stuffed with items hastily purchased that morning. He checked the suitcase, passed quickly through security and passport control, and soon found himself in the departure lounge.

It was the same lounge in which, just a few weeks before, the bomb had exploded, changing his life forever, yet there was no more trace of the explosion in the lounge than there was of emotion on his face. Kelton looked impassively at the place where Catherine Kent had died and Elizabeth Kent had been destroyed.

The woman and her daughter belonged to Kent, not to this middle-aged businessman who simply scanned the lounge in search of a convenient place to pass the time while awaiting his flight to begin boarding. For one brief instant the illusion wavered and the mask flickered; but a moment later his face was impassive as ever. He had a job to do. Later there would be time for Kent to have his way. Later Kent would have the rest of his life in which to grieve.

As luck would have it, the flight was overbooked in both first class and business sections; the only empty seats were in coach class. No one was willing to give up his seat voluntarily, and Kelton found himself bumped down into coach class, and provided with a worthless round trip business class ticket between London and New York "for your future use, sir." It was not an auspicious beginning.

Things got worse when he discovered that he was condemned to the center seat of a group of five. Worse yet, immediately behind him was a child throwing a tantrum about having to fly. The tantrum lasted until they were well over the Atlantic, and even when she fell quiet, she continued to kick Kelton's seat every few minutes.

Landing at Kennedy in a murderous mood, things only got worse. After passing through Immigration, which took the best part of an hour because he was travelling on a (forged) British passport instead of an American one, he moved on to Customs, where an agent for some reason took a dislike to him and spilled the entire contents of his luggage on to the counter, and then proceeded to search the contents as if he was surprised not to find contraband oozing out of every item. Even the toothpaste tube was carefully opened at the wrong end and the toothpaste tasted to ensure that it was not tainted.

By the time that Kelton was allowed out the Customs hall, he was seething with barely restrained anger. It was already evening. According to the schedule that Kelton had set himself, he should be on his way to Washington by now.

He strode furiously to the front of the taxi rank and glowered at the driver of the yellow cab.

Unlike Kelton, Frederico Lopez, "Freddie" to his friends and associates, and owner of the Airport & Downtown Cab Company's car number 136, was having a good day. This was a good run, driving between Kennedy and the downtown hotels. It cost him a bit, of course, to bribe the bastard who scheduled the runs for the company, so that Freddie had the run more than twice as often as he should, but the cost of the bribe was more than offset by the profitable naïveté of foreign businessmen visiting the Big Apple for the first time.

He had done well today, pocketing over $150 in profit, all of it unreported either to the company or to the government. And he still had time to make maybe three more runs before going off duty for the night.

Early though it was, Freddie was already considering the possibility of sleeping away from home tonight. Sabrina was an expensive bitch, but at least she pleased him, unlike the woman to whom he had pledged undying love and devotion twenty-one years ago in San Juan's *Iglesia de los Niños* back on the island. *Por l'amor de Dios.* Twenty one years! and what did he have to show for it? Just a cow of a wife who was now so fat that she made even her mother seem thin, two bratty sons who were roaming the streets somewhere probably getting it twice as often as their father, and a lousy, menial job as a cab driver who didn't get no respect from no one.

But it was a job, he reminded himself, and one that was not without its compensations. Like the $150 in his money belt. And Sabrina. Yes, he knew where he would spend the night.

He looked up as a figure blocked the light. A well dressed, middle aged businessman was scowling at him from the curb. English, Lopez decided immediately, basing his guess on the man's clothes and the way he was looking down his nose at Freddie. Freddie sent a "phut" of spit through the window, landing barely four inches from the Englishman's polished black shoes.

Well, Freddie decided, this one would pay for that look.

"Put it in the back," he said, jerking his head to the rear of the car where the trunk lid had risen in response to his pull of a lever. *New suitcase*, he thought as the man moved to stow it in the trunk. *That's good, he'll pay more to get it back.*

The man got in the back of the cab. New York cabbies are undecided on whether to separate themselves from their customers. Some have a sheet of glass, often bulletproof, to separate them from their paying customers. Freddie had rejected the precaution as both needless and too expensive. In his eight years on the job, he had been threatened often enough, once even with a gun, but only by people who had already got out of the cab. Bulletproof glass, he had long ago decided, was just one more lousy American con. He glanced in the rearview mirror. "Where to?"

The man, definitely English, the cabbie noted with satisfaction as soon as he spoke — he was good at this, he got them right nine times out of ten — gave him an address downtown. Freddie cast a single momentary glance in his nearside mirror then shot out in front of a shuttle bus, tires squealing.

It was not a long journey. Traffic was lighter than usual tonight, which gave Freddie Lopez the opportunity to consider how much he was going to charge the man. He tried to size up his passenger. It was not his first visit to New York: those he could spot a mile away. On the other hand, he looked distraught.

"Bad flight?" he ventured.

"Yes." The monosyllabic reply did not invite further questions.

Fifty dollars should be about right, Freddie decided. He looked like a hard-assed kind of a guy, the type who might make trouble if he was pushed too far. Fifty dollars plus two more runs tonight. Maybe he could take Sabrina out for a few drinks before they went back to her place. Yes, now that *was* a good idea. It warmed him just to think of it.

He pulled over to the sidewalk and turned to his passenger without a glance at the meter. "That'll be $75," he said.

The man looked at the meter, then at the cabbie. "The meter says $25," he said, as if he were drawing a pupil's attention to an elementary arithmetical error.

"You want to see your suitcase again? $75."

Slowly the light dawned on the Englishman. His eyes narrowed, then flicked to the identification sheet mounted on the dash, then returned to engage the cabbie's eyes momentarily. Freddie did not flinch, and after a moment the passenger looked away and glanced at his watch, then back at the driver. He took a deep breath then asked, "How often do you do this?"

Lopez had almost decided that this was one dangerous dude — that moment in which their eyes had locked had worried him — and perhaps he should say it was all a mistake. One more try though. Sabrina would do even more than usual if he gave her a $50 bonus.

"Seventy five dollars," he repeated, not answering the man's question. For a moment he steeled himself against the possibility of an unpleasant scene, but the Englishman seemed to wilt.

"OK," the Limey agreed, and reached into his coat. He withdrew a wallet and handed the bills across. Lopez nodded, then released the lid of the trunk. The man got out and recovered his suitcase.

"Close the fucking trunk," the cabbie called, but the man simply turned and began to walk down the street. "Fucker," the cabbie shouted, then pulled out into the street, relying on the cab's acceleration to close the lid of the trunk for him.

Kelton walked half a block, not once looking back.

He halted outside an old stone edifice, one of a row that sported a series of brass plaques mounted next to ostentatious doors several feet above the level of the sidewalk. He ascended half a dozen stone steps and then passed through a pair of doors made of heavy, mottled glass.

Inside the lobby, he removed a key ring from his pocket, selected a key and walked across to a metal door marked "Personal Security, Inc." He unlocked and opened the door and walked through the doorway to find himself in a small, well lit, windowless hallway.

There was one other door in the corridor, halfway down its length and in the wall to the left. Beside the door was a chair and a table on which sat a television monitor, a telephone, a walkie talkie, a Rolodex and a paperback novel that had topped last year's bestseller lists as a hardback. Rising from the chair and looking in his direction was an armed guard, his hand moving casually towards an open holster on his right hip. The door behind Kelton swung closed with a thud, followed a moment later by a click as the automatic lock secured itself.

His hand resting casually on his gun, the guard said: "Good evening, sir. Could I have your number and password please?"

"Number 219," Kelton replied, "and the password is Terminate."

"Just one moment, please."

The guard twirled through the Rolodex. He found the card he was looking for.

"OK; thank you, sir."

The guard unlocked and opened the other door. Inviting Kelton to follow, he walked into the room beyond.

Kelton found himself in a brightly lit room that was the almost the length of the hallway he had just left, but considerably wider.

The air was stale and stagnant. On the opposite wall was an array of small, sturdy metal doors, each engraved with a number and bearing a double lock. The guard located door number 219, inserted his key into one of the two keyholes and turned his key in the lock. Kelton fitted his key in the lower lock and turned it.

The guard gestured towards a door in the wall to their left. "There's a private room in there, sir."

"Thank you," said Kelton. "I don't expect to be more than about five minutes."

The guard returned to his post, closing the door behind him and leaving Kelton alone.

As soon as the guard had gone, Kelton opened the door to his safety deposit box. The face of the box was perhaps a foot square, and the box extended back some four feet. Inside was a brown leather case, roughly nine inches by six inches by three feet. On top of the case was a heap of drab, olive colored cloth, wrapped around a small object of indeterminate shape.

Kelton removed the case, put the cloth-wrapped object in his pocket, and walked to the private room. The room was recently painted yellow and was quite small, about eight feet by four. A workbench ran across the width of the room along the opposite wall; there were two stools adjacent to the bench.

He opened the case on the bench. Inside was a rifle, the letters *MB* etched into the wood of the butt. The rifle was broken down, and he lifted the pieces out the case and expertly fitted them together. They fitted into position smoothly and with sharp, positive clicks. Kelton balanced the completed rifle on his right hand and then turned it around to look through the telescopic sight. Satisfied, he broke the rifle down again.

He withdrew the olive cloth from his pocket. Unwrapping it, he exposed an FN-Browning High Power pistol.

He lifted the pistol, checked that it was loaded, and examined it to make sure that it was none the worse for its long sojourn in the box. Then he replaced it in his pocket.

The guard looked up from the television monitor and nodded as Kelton entered the hallway. "Good night, sir."

"Good night."

Kelton walked to the end of the hallway, opened the door, and was gone.

Descending the steps to the street, he hailed a cab and, pointedly keeping his belongings beside him on the seat, he told the driver to return him to Kennedy airport. The trip was uneventful, and the driver charged him no more than the fee on the meter. Kelton gave him a $10 tip.

Reëntering the terminal, Kelton went to the car rental booths, where he spent the next quarter of an hour filling out apparently endless forms. At last, the girl behind the counter seemed satisfied and she handed over the keys and gave him directions to his car.

He was just turning away when something caused him to do a double take. At a nearby booth a man had just finished renting a car from another agency. Kelton was sure that the man had been on his flight from London. But why was the man only now renting a car? Their flight had arrived several hours ago. What could have delayed the man so long?

The man took his key and turned and walked away without a glance at Kelton. Kelton shrugged, and went looking for his car.

It was only after nearly ten minutes of wandering through a vast, nearly full lot that he found it, two rows away from where it should have been. Given the way the day had gone so far, he was hardly surprised that car number 11 was in parking space number 121.

He placed his case in the trunk of the blue Oldsmobile, then carefully locked the car. He glanced quickly around the parking lot. A man some distance away turn sharply away, as if he had been watching Kelton. Kelton was almost certain it was the man from the airplane.

Kelton frowned, then dismissed the incident. He was tired and jumpy, that was all. It was just a coincidence. And anyway, there was something more important to think about. With a grim expression on his face, he began to walk toward the cab stand.

He hovered in the shadows, watching the people and the cars; but not for long.

Car number 136 of the Airport & Downtown Cab Co. was fifth in line. As he watched, a door into the terminal opened and disgorged a stream of people. He hurried over and joined the stream, barging through the people, heading for car 136.

An overweight man blocked his way momentarily, complaining, "Hey, waddya think you're doing?"

For answer, Kelton merely looked downward. The man's eyes followed Kelton's, and rested on a metal barrel that glistered ominously in the artificial light. The barrel was pointing directly at the man's stomach.

"Shit!" the man exclaimed, backing away in alarm. "Take the cab if you want it." He turned and hurried away, not looking where he was going, almost knocking an elderly woman to the ground in his hurry to escape the madman who had pulled a gun on him over a mere taxi cab.

Kelton opened the door and climbed into the cab.

He slammed the door and Frederico Lopez said, "Where to?" half turning in his seat, but not giving his new fare so much as a glance.

Freddie had decided that he had had enough for one day. This would be his last fare, then he would drive across town to the apartment where Sabrina and her attendant pleasures awaited. The thought spurred him to press the pedal even more enthusiastically than usual as the car pulled away from the rank, hurrying to reach the address that Kelton had just given him.

It was some moments before Freddie realized that the address was strangely familiar. He had taken someone else to the same block already this evening. Who was it? Oh yes, that fucker of an Englishman with a crumpled business suit and expensive coat and who had, just for a moment, looked dangerous when Freddie had demanded his "bonus" fare.

Freddie glanced in his mirror. A startled frown crossed his face.

"¿Qué pasa?" he asked, suddenly alarmed.

Kelton raised his hand and leaned forwards slightly. The barrel of a pistol nestled snugly against the back of Freddie's head.

"How's your day been?" asked Kelton pleasantly.

It was several seconds before Freddie was able to reply. He could not believe this was happening. A fare did not simply draw a pistol and point it at the driver's head. At least, he didn't if he was sane. They were in the middle of traffic. Surely the Englishman couldn't be that mad.

"Shit!"

"Answer the question," the Englishman demanded.

"How's my day been? Are you fucking serious?"

"Completely. It's a simple question. Answer it." Kelton stabbed forward with the pistol, jabbing the cabbie's head painfully forward.

"Er, OK, I guess" the driver said, trying to keep his suddenly sweating palms from slipping off the steering wheel. He felt an urgent desire to wet his pants. The fucker *was* mad.

"Well I'm afraid it's going to go seriously downhill from here, you little bastard. So you like to fleece people, do you? Fun, is it? Gives you a feeling of power, does it?"

The driver did not respond. What sort of answer could he give? His head was forced painfully forward another inch by the barrel of the gun. It hurt, and he groaned.

"Does it?" the passenger repeated.

He was obviously a madman. What does one do if a madman with a gun gets in your cab? Freddie had no choice. He had to humor him until he could find some way to get away.

"Oh, er, yes." What else could he say?

"Would you like to know what I do for a living?"

Freddie didn't reply.

"Not interested, eh? Well, I'll tell you anyway. I kill people."

The steering wheel slipped in Freddie's hand, and the car swerved dangerously into the adjacent lane, to the accompaniment of a blare of horns. For the first time, Freddie began to fear for his life. The desire to wet his pants increased.

"Drive carefully. You wouldn't want me to pull the trigger by accident, would you? The gun is loaded, by the way."

Freddie brought the car back into its lane, while the Englishman continued, "I've had a bloody miserable day, and I feel like killing someone just for the hell of it."

Freddie was trembling now. Loco. The Englishman was truly loco. He could feel the barrel of the gun tapping rhythmically now against the back of his head.

But even a loco Englishman wouldn't kill someone over a matter of fifty lousy bucks. Would he?

"Señor. It was a mistake," Freddie said, gulping.

"Shut up. I'll tell you what I'm going to do. I'll give you a choice. I can pull the trigger, or we can pull over and discuss this whole thing. Which would you prefer?"

The driver looked almost relieved. "Señor, I can pull off the freeway in one minute. There's a parking lot. We can talk there."

"All right," said the passenger, not changing the pressure of the gun as it continued tapping against the driver's head.

Terrified, Lopez pulled over to the right hand lane and then exited the freeway at the next opportunity. Immediately adjacent to the ramp was a café, its half-broken neon sign flickering nervously high in the air. Lopez pulled into the parking lot; he stopped in an empty parking space and turned off the engine. The tapping on the back of his head ceased, and a wave of relief swept over him.

He turned towards the passenger. "What are you going to do, señor?"

"Nothing," replied the passenger. "At least, not if you empty out all your pockets on the seat beside you."

The driver did as he was told, fumbling in his haste to empty his pockets.

Kelton eyed the pile of money, the keys, the grubby handkerchief. It looked like about $350 in cash.

"Now, out you get. Leave the keys in the ignition." He stabbed his weapon forward to emphasize his words.

The driver almost fell out the door in his haste. Kelton opened his door, got out, and slammed it shut, keeping the pistol carefully pointed at the cabbie, who had backed nervously away a few feet and now stood wringing his hands and rocking nervously from one foot to the other.

Kelton got in on the driver's side and slammed the door closed. He turned the keys in the ignition with his free hand, then, gunning the engine, he slammed the vehicle into reverse. Tires squealed in protest as he shifted through the gears and he raced out the parking lot and merged with the passing traffic.

The cabbie stared after his disappearing vehicle, then turned and ran for the safety of the café, shouting at the top of his voice.

Kelton laughed out loud. It was the first thing that had gone right all day.

It was as he was driving back to the airport that he realized the enormity of what he had done. *He had taken revenge on someone while on a job.*

He started to tremble. It was unthinkable. All his training, all the years he had been a professional killer, never in all that time, no matter what the provocation, had he permitted himself to deviate from his assignment simply to satisfy a momentary hurt or anger. And now he had done that very thing. He had drawn attention to himself needlessly.

This was even worse than the loss of control he had experienced in Belfast. Then he had had an excuse, but now he had taken a needless risk simply because a grubby little man had robbed him of fifty dollars. He had let the man have his money, and then calmly returned later with the sole intent of scaring the man half to death.

What a fool he had been. Kelton would never have been so stupid. Only Kent could have done something so foolish. He had hoped he had left Kent safely behind in England. But he was still here, inside his head, as dangerous as ever.

If he had let his emotions cloud his judgment once, he might do it again. *Get a grip on yourself. Catherine and Elizabeth can't afford to have you screw up on this one. Step back from it all. When it's over, that's when you can become human again. That's when Kent can come back. But until then, no more unnecessary sideshows. You're a professional, and it's time you started acting like one.* It was part command, part vow.

He dumped the cab in a short term parking lot at the airport. He removed the mound of money, then wiped all the surfaces he had touched, still berating himself for his stupidity. He closed the door and looked at the car. The idea of disabling it was instantly dismissed. He had done enough damage already; there was no need to make the situation worse. Without looking back, he walked away.

It was as he started the Blue Olds and began to make his way out the parking lot that his anger with himself was suddenly replaced by a more ominous feeling.

Seconds after he had started his car and switched on the headlights, another car some distance across the lot did the same thing. The moment the headlights flared in Kelton's mirror, the memory returned of the man from the airplane who had waited so long to rent his car. The headlights came from the same place he had been standing when Kelton had last seen him.

The conclusion was inescapable. Someone was following him.

Chapter 22
Thursday, December 6

It is a 230-mile drive from New York to Washington. It had already been a long day, and the prospect of five hours on the road before he saw a bed was not pleasing to Kelton, but if he was being followed, then the person doing the following was going to be equally tired and, he hoped, even more prone to errors. And in any case Kelton had an appointment at nine the next morning that he could not afford to miss.

Keeping a careful eye on his mirror, Kelton crossed Brooklyn and Staten Island and then joined the flow of traffic heading south-west on the New Jersey turnpike. The traffic thinned as the road turned south and now he was all but certain that he was being followed. It was still impossible to be completely sure, for even in the dead of night the road was busy, but every time he speeded to pass a vehicle, or slowed a little to let a stream of traffic pass him in turn, there was one pair of headlights several hundred yards behind that quickly mimicked his actions.

It was nearly two o'clock before Kelton reached the Washington beltway. He traveled around it for a short distance, then pulled off at the exit for College Park. Five minutes later, he pulled into the parking lot of a motel close to the campus of the University of Maryland. There was no difficulty in obtaining a room for the night and, by twenty past two, he was sound asleep.

At seven o'clock the next morning the alarm clock woke him from a deep sleep. A cold shower prepared him for the day ahead. As he crossed the blacktop to the lobby for a cup of caffeine laden coffee, he was not surprised to see a rental car with New York license plates parked in a space that had been empty when he had arrived.

He poured himself a cup of sour coffee, drinking it while appearing to peruse a copy of the day's *Washington Post*. The curtains of the room adjacent to his own were open; inside, he could just make out a man seated at a table, apparently working at paperwork. Every few seconds, the man looked up and cast a glance toward the lobby.

Kelton threw away the acidic dregs of the coffee, quit the lobby and walked across the parking lot to his car. Settling himself into the driver's seat, he saw the door of the room next to his own open, and a man exited the room and began walking swiftly across the parking lot, directly towards the car with New York plates. The man did not look in his direction, but now Kelton was certain beyond any doubt: it was the same man who had been on yesterday's flight from London.

He set off along the beltway in the direction of NASA's Goddard Space Flight Center. Pulling off the beltway shortly after the exit for the Center, he parked at the closest *Kiss 'n' Ride*, and joined the throng of morning commuters on Washington's billion-dollar subway system. He did not bother looking behind him. If his tail was at all competent, he would still be there when Kelton had decided what to do with him.

Kelton disembarked at the downtown mall and climbed the steps to ground level. He emerged into the dull, chilly, leaden gray of a December morning, then walked to the center of the mall and casually surveyed his surroundings to get his bearings.

The Supreme Court and Capitol buildings were atop a rise to his right; to his left rose the spire of the Washington Monument. Hidden but not far away to his left was the White House. Kelton glanced at his watch. Only a few minutes before nine. He walked rapidly along the mall; at eight fifty-eight he was standing in front of the National Air and Space Museum.

Looking northwards along the sparsely populated mall, he could see Mike Downing carrying a small briefcase and striding towards him, perhaps a hundred yards away. Kelton scratched his head and looked around in puzzlement, a tourist who had lost his bearings.

Downing broke his stride as he approached. "Excuse me. Are you lost? Can I help?"

Kelton saw that Downing had aged. His hair was gray now. And the lines on his face remained even when he stopped talking. *But then*, Kelton thought, *it's been five years. We've all aged.*

"Hello, Mike. Good to see you again."

"The *Has Beans* coffeeshop. Walk towards the monument. About a hundred yards on your right you'll see a small alley. Go down that; about fifty yards on your left, on the corner, you'll see the store. Tell them you're with the Smith party."

"Thank you; you've been most helpful." Kelton nodded his thanks, and Downing moved off down the mall.

Kelton began to follow Downing. The American passed the alley entrance and was lost to view as Kelton turned and ducked into the alley. The *Has Beans* coffeehouse was a short distance down the alley to the left. He pushed open the door and walked in.

It was a bustling coffee shop, about half full and noisy with conversation. The *maitre d'* was a pert young girl who looked up and smiled as Kelton entered the restaurant. "With the Smith party," Kelton said.

"Ah, yes. Wait a moment and I'll be right with you." The girl moved away towards a long counter at the far end of the coffeehouse, where a tall bearded man was working an espresso machine.

Kelton cast his eyes over the patrons while he waited. At the tables and booths sat an eclectic mixture. Striped suits of bankers, lawyers and politicians sat only a few feet from long-haired, scruffily-clad youngsters. Over in one corner a middle aged man with thinning hair and bottle-lens spectacles was puffing away at a pipe while peering myopically at the screen of a portable computer. At an adjacent table, a young woman was ostentatiously leaning forward to drink, her breasts barely held in place by a meager, low-cut jersey. Kelton observed that several pairs of male eyes were fixed on her breasts.

"This way," said the young girl, who had reappeared without Kelton noticing, and he followed her across the room into a small segregated area where a row of empty booths lined the walls.

Within a minute, Downing appeared and sat down heavily opposite Kelton.

"Hello, Kelton," he said, holding out his hand.

"Hello, Mike." The two shook hands.

"I figured that if a coffeehouse was good enough for Oxford, it should be good enough for Washington as well." Downing smiled.

Kelton returned the smile and nodded, conveying his understanding that by referring to their previous meeting Downing was telling him that this conversation was not being recorded.

Wasting no time on preliminaries, Kelton cut to the heart of the matter. "Nasty business, this mess with Sir David."

"Yes, but we've made quite a bit of progress, and we're hoping that maybe you'll be able to offer us some guidance about where we go from here."

A young waiter appeared. They ordered coffee and waited silently until their order was filled.

Then Downing opened his briefcase, removed a folder and passed it across the table to Kelton. Wordlessly, Kelton reviewed it, reading it carefully from start to finish, pausing only occasionally to sip from his coffee while staring into space, his thoughts obviously far away.

As he turned the final leaf of paper, he looked up at Downing "Well," he said, "this is fairly convincing evidence that it was an American job. Is that how you read it?"

"We're inclined to agree that it was an American, at least on the basis of this evidence." Kelton noticed that Downing spoke in the plural. He wondered how many other people had seen the document. "What puzzles us is motive. Neither we nor our British counterparts have been able to find an adequate motive for the killing. We've been wondering if David was simply unlucky: in the wrong place at the wrong time."

"Possible, I suppose," conceded Kelton, "but it doesn't seem very likely. And it still doesn't bring us any closer to knowing who was responsible, does it? And don't forget the obvious attempt at misdirection — to make it seem as though the ILF were responsible when in fact they weren't. That must have been planned. It happened immediately after the explosion, and before Sir David's identity was generally known."

Downing said nothing, mulling over the puzzle yet again but still unable to come up with a single solution that fitted all the facts.

"You don't have any more to go on than what's in this?" asked Kelton, tapping a forefinger on the folder.

"No, that's the lot, right there, uncensored, at least by us. That's everything the Brits gave us, plus what we've come up with ourselves."

"Hmmm...." Kelton furrowed his brow and looked blindly at the surface of the table, his head resting against his steepled hands. He remained this way for half a minute, ruminating. Eventually, he leant back and withdrew a small black book from the pocket of his coat.

"Do you have a pencil and paper?" he asked.

"Sure," Downing replied, opening his case. "Just what do you have in mind?"

"One of my erstwhile colleagues may have heard something. One of them might even have done the job."

"You think this might have been the work of a professional?"

"I'm not sure. But something about this whole thing just doesn't make sense. If you try to put the pieces together in any of the obvious ways, there's always a piece that doesn't fit. But how's this for a crazy scenario? What do you think would have happened if you had double crossed me five years ago?"

"We wouldn't do that. I wouldn't have allowed it," Downing objected. But he and Kelton both knew that he would have, if enough pressure had been applied.

"Perhaps not, but just suppose for a minute that you had. Suppose that somehow you had put one over on me: been short on your payment, or not played straight about the target or the real reason for of the contract; what do you think might have happened?"

Downing shrugged. "Tell me," he said.

"You'd be dead, along with any of your bosses that I could have traced," Kelton said, matter of factly.

Downing nodded slowly and thoughtfully. "So you're suggesting...."

"It's just an hypothesis, of course, with no proof. But at least it, or something like it, is possible, don't you think?"

"Yes; yes, I suppose it is."

"Besides which, this is beginning to smell more and more like it was the work of a single individual, not an organization. One individual who thought, rightly or wrongly, that Sir David was responsible for cheating him, and who decided to exact his revenge. It fits, doesn't it?"

"Almost; except that that file was given to me by Sir David's successor. The British know everything in this file. Surely the Brits will have investigated anyone who might have a grudge against David?"

But Downing knew the answer to this as soon as he had asked the question.

"Mike, surely you don't think that everything Sir David did was on the record? There's no reason to believe that anyone else knew of whatever arrangement he might have had with the person who eventually killed him."

Downing nodded. "Yes. You're right, of course. So you're suggesting there's a chance you might know the person responsible?" It was as much a question as a statement.

Kelton shook his head.

"It's possible, but no, it's not very likely. But one of the people I have in mind might have heard something. For the most part, professionals use guns. They're clean, quick and relatively certain. Bombs are just too messy and unreliable as a rule. Besides which, most of us do have consciences, you know, and bombs generally lead to the deaths of too many innocent people. No, about the only person I know of who would even consider using a bomb is George Harris."

Kelton stopped and considered that thought. "Yes, you may want to look at him carefully; he used a bomb once before, in Italy, to misdirect the Mafia. It worked, too. Also, for what it's worth, he's an American."

"You seem to know a lot about him," said Downing, inviting further comment.

"Just the usual professional hearsay. We've never met. The only reason I know about the Mafia business is that I was approached with the job and turned it down. I heard that the client's second choice was Harris, and that he accepted. That's all. I do know that he's supposed to be good, though. Anyway, here's a list of five of my colleagues — names and how to make initial contact. Are you ready?"

Downing held the pencil above the paper and said, "Yep, go ahead. Shoot."

Kelton went through the names. They included an Italian, an Englishman, a man who could be reached only through a phone number in Wyoming, an Eastern European, and George Harris.

217

"George Harris. Believed to be American, but country of residence unknown. You reach him through a computer mailbox. Send an electronic mail message to the computer address *plethora@secure.swsec.com.*"

"OK, got it all," said Downing as he scribbled the electronic mail address. "Anything else I should know, especially about Harris?"

"Not really. They're all good men, if you follow my meaning. Harris in particular has built a good, solid résumé. When I retired he was the one most often mentioned as my successor, if you'll pardon my immodesty. He'd be the first one I'd go to. He's a good all-rounder. Favors the garotte when circumstances allow, but accomplished with almost any other weapon you care to name, including explosives."

"And how should we go about introducing ourselves to these people? We can hardly say, 'Good morning. We're one of your local friendly US government agencies and we were wondering if you could give us some information about a killer?'"

"No, of course not. Make them an offer. These are honest people. You can't be in that line of work and expect to live very long if you're not honest.

"It seems to me that you can take one of two approaches. You could offer them a reasonable sum of money, say a hundred thousand dollars, for information regarding last month's Gatwick bombing. The other approach is simply to string them along for a while. Tell them you're interested in having a job done. Tell them it will require knowledge of explosives and say that you need references. Either way should work."

"Good idea. Thanks. I'll start on it as soon as I get back to the office. What are your plans for the next few days while we work on this?"

"I don't know. There's nothing much for me back home, so I guess I'll probably hang around in the Washington area... take in some of the sights, you know. That way I'll be nearby in case you need me. I'm staying at the Capitol Luxury Motel in College Park. You can leave any messages there. I'll let you know if I leave, and give you a new number or address. Obviously, I'd be interested in hearing about anything that turns up." *What I really want to know is whether you're going to let me waste the bastard when you find him*, Kelton wondered, but refrained from putting the thought into words.

"You'll hear, don't worry," said Downing, jotting down Kelton's temporary address and conveying by his tone of voice his answer to the unasked question. Kelton nodded, and allowed himself the smallest of smiles.

They finished their coffee and stood to leave.

"Oh, by the way," said Kelton as if the thought had only just occurred to him, "you aren't having me followed, are you?"

"No," said Downing. "Why?"

"I think I'm being watched. Don't worry. I'll deal with the problem." In other words: *if he's yours, Mike, you'd better pull him off my tail before he gets hurt.*

They shook hands and each said what a pleasure it had been. Kelton left the coffee shop while Downing went looking for a rest room to relieve himself.

As he drove back along the beltway towards the motel, Kelton watched his tail in his rear view mirror. But as he approached the motel, the car from New York suddenly slowed and fell way back. When he arrived at the motel, he discovered that a new occupant was moving into the room next door. The man was short and sallow, and his eyes shiftily refused to meet Kelton's. The man's car, parked outside his room, carried Virginia plates.

A short while later, Kelton left his room and drove out of the parking lot. In his rearview mirror, he saw the car with Virginia plates easing out into the traffic behind him.

Downing entered his office shortly after lunch.

He turned to his computer terminal and initiated a request for information about George Harris. Within ten seconds, the machine had flashed up a list of five people with that name, along with a couple of lines of identifying information next to each one.

Three of the five entries appeared in green, indicating that the files were "live and unclassified"; the last entry of the five was in yellow, indicating that that particular George Harris was deceased. Downing's eyes were drawn to the fourth entry, below which was flashing, in red, the words "DD EYES ONLY — FILE KEDGFQ." The six letter group was a random sequence generated by computer, so that not even the date of the file might be guessed from its name.

Downing clicked on the line; a full screen of information appeared before him. "DD EYES ONLY — FILE KEDGFQ" flashed in red on the top line. Downing quickly reviewed the screen of information, but little of it seemed important, except that it confirmed that this had to be the George Harris of whom Kelton had spoken.

The computer screen indicated that Harris was a contract killer and listed several targets for whose demise he was suspected of being responsible. There was no mention either of explosives or of an Italian contract, Downing noticed. So much for the efficiency of the NSA.

The entry under "Address" read: "Unknown. Believed to be in New England." No telephone number was listed. Under "Known aliases" was the comment: "See next page; no known pattern, never known to use the same alias twice." Downing clicked the mouse again and a second screen of information appeared. The screen was half filled with aliases. The only thing they had in common was that each of them could reasonably be applied to a white American male. Downing ran his eyes down the list, but he recognized none of the names.

He went back to the initial screen. The "DD EYES ONLY" message intrigued him. What about the man could be so sensitive that it had not been transcribed to the computer files?

Downing wheeled his chair back to his desk and pressed the intercom. "Mr. Jackson, please come in here a moment."

He scribbled a note on a piece of paper, signed it with his spidery signature, and tore it from the pad as his secretary entered the room. He held out the paper.

"This is authorization for you to retrieve an 'eyes only' document for me. Get me the file as quickly as you can."

The secretary grasped the paper. "Yes, sir," he said smartly and promptly left on his errand.

He returned some fifteen minutes later, bearing a very thin file that he handed to the Deputy Director. The file was sealed with striped tape. Downing took it and waited until Jackson had left the room before breaking the seal. The file contained but a single sheet of paper, on which was a handwritten note. The note was undated and unsigned, but Downing recognized the handwriting of his predecessor. It took only seconds to read the note in its entirety.

> *It is my belief, from conversations with a well placed source at the CIA, that George Harris was named by that agency as their second preference to be an operative for the joint CIA/KGB operation codenamed LUM-BERJACK, which, to judge from subsequent events, was successful. The name of the first choice operative is unknown, although, given the sensitive nature of LUM-BERJACK it is highly unlikely that an in-house operative would have been nominated. Judging from the method by which Andropov was removed from power, it is my opinion that CIA nominations were not used for the operation, and that ex-KGB operatives and methods were utilized instead. My source indicated, however, that Mr. Harris was approached concerning the operation in its broad terms and expressed willingness to participate.*

Downing closed the folder and stared into space.

After a long pause, he resealed the file with fresh striped tape then called his secretary into the room. He handed the file back to the secretary. His hand, he saw, was trembling, and he wondered if he looked pale.

"Thank you, Mr. Jackson. Please return this to the secure file room. And leave instructions that the DD is to be informed should this file ever be requested by anyone else."

"Thank you, sir. Certainly, sir," said the secretary as he unknowingly accepted the time bomb. He wondered why the DD looked as if he had seen a ghost.

As Jackson left the room, Downing placed his head in his hands and tried to put out of his mind forever the words that he had just read.

Chapter 23
Friday, December 7
Fort Meade, Maryland

Frances Tabor slipped her pass into the slot and waited impatiently for the buzzer to sound. After a few moments, there was a low pitched electronic buzz and her card was ejected from the slot. In one motion, she grabbed the card and leaned against the door, which now yielded to permit her entrance to the lobby.

She was in a hurry this morning, anxious to see the results of the night's work. She glanced at the two elevators in the small bay at this end of the building; both cars were on upper floors, so she opened the door to the stairwell and began climbing to the fourth floor.

She opened the door to her office just in time to see the digits of the clock on the wall change from 8:59 to 9:00.

She was breathing hard, a result of the unaccustomed exertion, and she took a moment to recover herself, smoothing her skirt and then wiping the incipient perspiration from her brow.

Her office displayed the clutter that she liked to think demonstrated the presence of an active mind. On the wall was a photocopied bromide, "A clean desk is a sign of a sick mind." Underneath was scrawled, "You have the healthiest mind I know" in the hand of her thesis advisor. Papers were strewn all over her desk in untidy piles, leaving only a few square inches here and there where the brown plastic laminate surface was visible.

She slipped into her chair and wheeled it sideways to the computer table next to her desk. This too, no doubt, would have been occupied with papers were it large enough, but her Sun workstation, with its keyboard, monitor and mouse almost covered the surface. She switched on the computer and logged in.

The computer began to wade through the lengthy script that personalized the machine so that it would work in a way that suited Frances. It was a process that would take a couple of minutes, and she picked up her stained coffee mug from its resting place next to the mouse pad and walked to the coffee room. If she was aware of the covert appreciative glances that followed her as she walked past the open doors of male colleagues, she made no sign of it.

Had Frances Tabor accepted a job at one of the corporations that had been so assiduously courting her just a few months before, she probably would have arrived at work dressed in tee shirt and jeans, with her hair unbrushed and her face overly made up. Here, where the young members of the elite Computer Security group were expected to pay no attention to the agency's unofficial dress code, she displayed her rebellious nature by dressing immaculately. A young, hormone-driven, red-blooded male would have had to have been blind not to have watched her appreciatively as Frances swept down the corridor to the coffee room, her ocher skirt making swishing sounds as it rubbed against her nyloned legs, the cream color of her Aran sweater contrasting with the negricity of her unblemished skin.

She returned two minutes later, sipping her coffee. Thirty three e-mail messages had come in overnight. She glanced down the list of subjects; one jumped out of the screen at her: "Subject: APPOINTMENT 9:30 DDO." It had been sent, according to the computer, by the Deputy Director for Operations himself, shortly after she had left the office yesterday evening.

She clicked to open it. The message was brief and to the point: "Please report to my office at 9:30 Friday morning. DO NOT MENTION THIS TO ANYONE."

She was intrigued. She barely knew Harold Perkins, the Deputy Director for Operations, having met him only once, when he had made a point of greeting her on her first morning at Fort Meade. What could the DDO possibly want with her? She wondered for a moment if she had done anything particularly worthy of either commendation or reprimand, but she could think of nothing. She glanced at the clock on the screen and realized that she would have to hurry if she was to avoid being late for the appointment.

Frances locked the screen and hurried out of her office, heading for the stairs. She arrived at the DDO's office with less than two minutes to spare, and as soon as she identified herself to the DDO's secretary, the secretary guided Frances directly into Perkins' office.

Harold Perkins looked up from the paperwork on his desk and he smiled widely in greeting. He rose and offered her his hand, not something that he would have done with most of his employees, but the thought of simply touching the hand of someone so attractive and seemingly innocent was enough to put him in a state of muted benevolence for the rest of the morning.

"Take a seat, Frances. Glad you could come. I hope you didn't mention this appointment to any of your colleagues?"

"Good morning, sir." Frances settled herself as best she could on the hard chair. She was nervous, and was embarrassed at the thought that the DDO's hand must now be damp with her sweat. "No problem, sir. I got your e-mail message this morning. No, I didn't talk to anybody about it."

"Good, good." Perkins continued to smile, trying to put the obviously anxious young woman at her ease. "I have a little job for you. I think you'll enjoy it."

He extracted a memo pad from a drawer, and tore off the top sheet and handed it across the desk. Frances looked at it as she took it. Penciled on the sheet was a computer address.

"On that piece of paper is an e-mail address," the DDO said. Frances nodded; she already knew that. "I want you to find out if we have any way of tracing activity in and out of that address. If so, I want a complete listing of all the traffic at that address for the past year."

"How fast do you need this, sir? It may turn out to be difficult, or even impossible, depending upon the location of the address." Even as she spoke, she was working how she would go about accomplishing the task.

"My orders came directly from the Deputy Director. This is a priority job. You'd better drop all your other work and concentrate on this. Send me e-mail or call me later in the day and give me a quick situation report so I can tell the DD how long it's likely to be before we have anything substantive for him. Don't make it long or detailed, just an overview of the situation. I want you spending your time working on the problem, not trying to look good for the boss. OK?"

The smile, which had briefly departed while he described her task, now returned. He wondered whether there was some way he could promote Frances so that he could find an excuse to spend more time with her. He hadn't realized before how attractive she was....

"Yes, sir." Frances returned his smile, happily unaware of what was going on in the DDO's mind. "I assume I'm working alone?"

"Yes. Unless you decide you need help, in which case don't hesitate to contact me."

"I'll let you know, sir."

"Now, I've taken enough of your time. Off you go, and don't forget to let me know how things are going later in the day. Thank you."

"Thank you, sir," she said, and swished out the room. Perkins let his eyes follow her; then, with a sigh, he bent his head and returned to his paperwork.

Frances returned directly to her office. The last of the coffee was cold. She refilled the mug, still thinking about how to attack the problem.

Taking the paper from her pocket, she looked at the address more carefully. *plethora@secure.swsec.com*. It was a strange name, *plethora*; usually usernames were immediately identifiable as the name of a person. Well, the first thing to do was to try to track down the location of the computer. That shouldn't take long.

secure.swsec.com was a standard Internet address. That meant the address would be registered in the central depository.

Access to the outside world was through a firewall machine located in the basement of the building in which Frances Tabor worked. The machine's name, appropriately enough, was *basement*.

It required less than a minute for Frances to log on to *basement*, and thence to connect with the Internet Network Information Center computer to see what was listed under *swsec.com* in the machine's service database. The *.com* part of the address meant simply that the computer belonged to a commercial organization, most likely based in the United States but not necessarily so; the *.swsec* was an indication, probably some sort of contraction, of the name of the company.

In seconds, the InterNIC computer, located across the country in California, told her what she wanted to know. Computers with names ending in *.swsec.com* belonged to the Secure Computing Corporation, registered in Lucerne, Switzerland.

The company ran a class C computer network, number [192.136.26], which meant that the company was a fairly small concern, with at most about 250 computers attached to the

Internet. Larger companies had class B networks, with up to 60,000 networked computers. The very largest companies, governments agencies and other huge autonomous organizations had class A networks, each with enough addresses to permit several million computers to be connected simultaneously to the Internet.

She closed the connection to the InterNIC computer and, extracting a yellow pad from a drawer, began to make notes.

A small Swiss company with only a relatively few computers; that probably meant that they were all, or nearly all, located abroad, although the fact that the network name ended in *.com* implied that the company probably maintained at least one office in the United States. Still, it was promising. Next, to find out where the machine *secure.com* was physically located.

Still connected to the machine in the basement, she issued the command *ping secure.swsec.com*, telling the basement machine to bounce signals off *secure.swsec.com*, similar to the manner in which sonar is used to ping submarines, and to display the round-trip time taken by each ping.

A numerical address, [192.136.26.2], appeared on the screen: the address by which the machine *secure.swsec.com* was known to the Internet. She scribbled the numbers on her pad.

basement pinged *secure* every few seconds, displaying the total round-trip time each time. After about half a minute, Frances hit Control-C and studied the listing on her screen.

The displayed round trip times varied, but they averaged out to about 1800 milliseconds, a little under two seconds, just right for a slow serial link into Europe. The pings were too fast for a satellite connection, which was unfortunate, as that would have made tracing past activity a little easier; instead, the route across the Atlantic was most probably a permanently leased line on a transatlantic cable. Still, that would not delay her long.

She wondered if any of the information about the account was public. Deftly, she typed the command "finger plethora@ secure.sec.com." In moments, the computer responded by displaying:

[swsec.secure.com]
Login name: plethora   *In real life: M. Atkins*
Directory: /home/mailclient/plethora
Last login: Wed Nov 30 17:30 on ttya
No unread mail
No plan.

M. Atkins. She wondered idly what the "M" stood for. Then she picked up the telephone and dialed the DDO

"Perkins," said the DDO.

"Yes, sir, it's Frances Tabor here."

"Is there a problem?"

"No, sir, not really, but I'll need some assistance. It looks like the computer is located offshore, probably in Europe, and traffic from the U.S. reaches it through a transatlantic cable. I'll need your authorization to have operators load some cable playback tapes for analysis."

"All right. Give me a few minutes to arrange it, then call across and they'll load whatever you need."

"OK. Thank you, sir."

A few minutes later, Frances Tabor dialed across campus to a massive room which, filled with computers though it was, nevertheless housed but a tiny fraction of the agency's eleven acres of high-powered computers.

"Good morning," she said. "This is Frances Tabor with SIGINT, Computer Security Group, code 1264."

"Good morning, ma'am. We were expecting your call. What may we do for you?"

"How much data from TATs 5 and 6 would you be able to bring online simultaneously?"

"The Transatlantic Telephone cables? Give me a minute." There was a pause during which Frances heard the rapid clicking of computer keys. The operator asked, "How much do you need? A month would be easy. A year would take a little while for us to bring online."

"Let's start out with a month and see how it goes. I'll probably need the whole year eventually, though. How long will it take to get a month?"

She heard the sound of more keys being punched, then, "It'll be online in about five minutes. You'll find the data stored in SCAN format in the files tat4.cur.11 and tat5.cur.11 in the directory /data/scan/tmp."

"OK. I assume from the filenames that those will be the data for November of this year?"

"Yes, ma'am."

"Do you have a way to make data for the current month available?"

"Yes; wait a moment." More keys being pressed. "OK. We don't need to load tapes for that. The data are being moved over the network right now. They should be pretty much there by the time you've changed directories. The filenames are the same as for November, but ending in the digits one-two instead of one-one."

"Thank you," said Frances. "You've been most helpful."

"Sure, no problem."

Frances put the telephone down and logged on to a Cray YMP-48, one of the most powerful computers in the world.

The files of December data were already there, and the first of the November data files was growing rapidly in size as the data moved from nearline optical storage media to fast, online magnetic media.

Frances pulled up one of the standard NSA sniffer programs that were used to examine telephone traffic for patterns. Glancing at her pad of yellow paper, she thought for a moment, then told the computer to begin searching. The estimated time to complete the search flashed on to the screen: 23 minutes at the current level of activity on the Cray.

She had set the machine to work scanning the current month's data files looking for data packets marked with the computer address [192.136.26.2] as either originator or respondent. The machine would copy all such packets into a separate area on the disk, ready for secondary analysis.

As soon as the November data were complete, she instructed the Cray to do the same to those data. According to the machine's estimate, extracting all the relevant information from five weeks of transatlantic cable traffic would take until shortly after noon.

As always, the machine's guess was reliable. When she returned from an early lunch at ten minutes past noon, the Cray had finished, and it took only a few moments to send a copy of all the traffic that had entered or left *secure.swsec.com* on to the disk of her own machine. She also called across to the archives to request that all the TAT 5 and TAT 6 data for the past year be made available before the end of the day. Then she leaned back in her chair and pondered her next move.

She brought up the SCAN program again, and requested a listing of the total number of data packets now on her hard disk. There were only a few million, a small number, but still far too many to inspect them visually.

What was the name of the account? She looked at the yellow pad. *plethora*, owned by M. Atkins. *All right, M. Atkins, whoever you are, let's hack your password*, she thought.

She told the computer to extract only those data packets which contained the word *plethora*. The machine took about a minute before it informed her that of the several million data packets, a total of 25 contained the word *plethora*.

Now she told the machine to rebuild all the sessions that contained those 25 packets. Because, of course, when one logs on to a remote computer, the first thing it asks for is your username — in this case, *plethora*. And the second is the password.

But there is one other occasion when computers use usernames: when delivering mail. When Frances's computer finished, it would provide a copy of all the mail into and out of the account, as well as a complete log of every session when M. Atkins had logged in.

It was 3:30 before the computer finished. Giving herself only a few moments to gloat, she picked up the phone and called the DDO's office.

"Good afternoon, sir. Frances Tabor here again. I have copies of all the activity on that account for the past month. They are loading the tapes and by morning we'll have a complete listing for the past year."

"Excellent! Could you e-mail copies to me directly?"

"Certainly, sir. I'll do that right away. The computer will work overnight on the last year's data. I'll come in early to tidy things up. Give me a couple of hours or so to collate and format everything, and the whole lot should be in your mailbox by 10 o'clock."

They quickly concluded the conversation and Frances sent the messages electronically to the DDO's office. He sent copies to the Deputy Director, gratified that Frances was not only extremely attractive, but that her efficiency would redound to his own credit. He would have to give her more work in the future.

––––––––––––

Mike Downing was in the city that Friday afternoon, testifying to the Senate behind closed doors, so it was not until Saturday morning that he checked his e-mail. He was pleasantly surprised by the DDO's efficiency: he had not been expecting anything from Perkins for several days yet.

He printed out copies of all of George Harris's electronic mail and began to study the messages carefully.

A smile formed on his face, and quickly erupted into a grin. Paydirt!

George Harris, using the pseudonym M. Atkins, logged on to check for messages nearly every day, although he rarely left or received mail. The most recent mail message from Harris, dated nearly two weeks ago, was the most damning. In it,

George Harris referred to a file that contained a record of the entire Gatwick affair, and had left instructions with the computer system administrator that the file was to be read and passed to the proper authorities should his account fall delinquent.

Every word of the file had passed down the transatlantic cable. Frances Tabor's program had reconstructed the file, and now it sat, complete, along with the electronic mail printouts on Downing's desk.

Downing read the file with an increasing sense of wonder. The narrative made it quite clear that Vincent Cotterell — Downing's eyebrows rose in astonishment at that unexpected name — had bankrolled the entire operation and that Harris himself was responsible for exploding the bomb. But there was one obvious oddity about the account: nowhere did it specify that Sir David, or any other particular individual, was the intended target of the bomb.

Downing pondered for some time what might have led George Harris to write the file. The most likely answer seemed to be found in his instructions to the system operator. Harris must have thought he was about to be double-crossed by Cotterell, and was using the narrative as an insurance policy.

Downing quickly leafed through the remaining papers, but there was little else of interest, just one message immediately after the bombing, from someone called "Louise Smith" — a pseudonym that appeared in several other communications and that Harris's narrative made clear was Vincent Cotterell himself — that unambiguously linked the name of Harris to the bombings. Downing separated that message and the narrative, and shredded the others.

As he stood over the shredder, he pondered his next move, weighing everything he now knew. He was certain that he knew the name of Sir David's killer. Although he did not yet know where Harris was, it would be a simple matter to obtain a warrant to trace the telephone line the next time that Harris connected to the network. Harris was still alive, that much at least was certain, for the last time he had logged on to the overseas account was yesterday. So the insurance policy seemed to have worked, at least so far. With any luck, then, a telephone trace should lead him to Harris within the next twenty four hours. But what then?

On the one hand, he could hardly let his personal anger and disgust at David's killing get in the way of the law. He had taken the law into his own hands once, but only under duress and because the law had been made powerless by subversion. There were no such justifications this time.

Grateful though he was for Kelton's help, would it not be irresponsible of him to return the favor by telling Kelton where Harris could be found? Kelton's response to that knowledge, Downing knew, would be both swift and unmerciful.

But that raised once again the puzzle of why Kelton was so concerned about finding David's killer. David had never mentioned Kelton to him, although there was probably nothing surprising in that: David had known nothing of Downing's involvement with Kelton either. But Downing could not escape an uneasy feeling about this unexplained connection between Kelton and Shackleton.

And what about John Pearce? What should Downing tell him? Surely Pearce had a right to know what Downing had discovered?

So should he tell Kelton, or Pearce, or both?

If he told Kelton, the consequences were predictable. But what if he told Pearce? Why was Pearce so anxious to find Sir David's killer? When Pearce had come to Downing, he must have known that anything Downing produced could not be used in court. So what was he going to do with the information?

Downing could think of only one answer to that question: the British government, through Pearce, intended to eliminate David's killer. And if that were true, then both Kelton and Pearce had the same goal. So nothing would be gained by withholding the information from Kelton.

He moved away from the machine, his decision made. He would tell them both what he had discovered; he owed David that much. But how much should he tell them? Would it be enough just to give them George Harris's name, or should he involve Vincent Cotterell as well?

What grudge could Vincent Cotterell possibly have against David Shackleton? It seemed unlikely that the two men had ever crossed paths, and even if they had, what could David have done to deserve what had happened? Perhaps, after all, David was not the intended target. Yet no one else of consequence had been killed or hurt in the blast, so what else could have prompted Cotterell to instigate the bombing? He pondered this problem for a long time, always coming back to the same conclusion: there had to be a connection he didn't know about between Cotterell and David Shackleton.

But Pearce would know. And if he didn't, he would be able to find out. That would be the *quid pro quo*. Cotterell's name for an explanation of why Cotterell might want David killed.

Had David somehow found a weakness in the Golden Pipeline? Was that the answer to all this?

Five years ago they had all thought that Carl Cotterell's death would mean that the Golden Pipeline would rust away into nothingness. But instead his younger brother had stepped into the breach and maintained the flow of heroin even while he was doubling, then redoubling, then redoubling again, the size of his brother's legitimate business.

Then something had happened. Late last summer, the amount of heroin flowing into the US had suddenly skyrocketed, and the DEA was certain that the Golden Pipeline was the source. Cotterell was exploiting a new route somehow, some recently-discovered loophole in security. That much was obvious, but no one had been able to guess what the new route might be. Had David found out? And had he paid for that knowledge with his life?

He shrugged. Too many speculations, and not enough data. But the noose was tightening around Vincent Cotterell, and the first order of business was to find George Harris. To do that, he would need a warrant to put a trace on the line as soon as Harris next logged on to read his mail. And for that, he would need the help of the FBI. Downing stretched out a hand and lifted the phone.

Chapter 24
Saturday, December 8
Surrey

No one was in the room when Elizabeth Kent opened her eyes. None of the monitors attached to various parts of her body was triggered by the movement, so no one knew for certain when the change occurred. All they knew was that the nurse was sure that Elizabeth had still been asleep when she had checked on her shortly after ten o'clock, and when Dr. Worthington looked in three hours later, Elizabeth was staring at the ceiling.

Dr. Worthington spotted the change as soon as she entered the room. Letting out a cry of delight, she ran to the bedside. Elizabeth, if she was aware that she was no longer alone, did not react to the fact. But she did react when Patricia waved a hand in front of her eyes. She blinked.

Patricia repeated the motion. Elizabeth blinked again.

Patricia ran to the nurses' station and grabbed the telephone. Her hands were trembling as she dialed the doctors' lounge. "Is Sam there? Put him on, please."

The nurse at the station looked at her speculatively. "It's the little girl," Patricia said. "She's showing signs of coming out of it." The nurse smiled broadly. There would be a celebration in the nurses' lounge later.

"Sam? It's Patricia. Can you come to Elizabeth Kent's room? Her eyes are open and she's responding to simple stimuli. I'd like you to take a look and tell me what you think."

She put the phone down and, unable to contain their excitement, she and the nurse hurried together back to Elizabeth's room.

The girl's eyes were still open. The doctor repeated her test, and Elizabeth blinked again. Doctor and nurse grinned at one another.

"Can you hear me, Elizabeth?" Patricia asked. There was no response. "Blink if you can hear me, Elizabeth." Still nothing; but Patricia refused to be downcast. She had been on the verge of giving up hope. Now she could hope again.

Sam Higgins bustled into the room. He took one look at Elizabeth's open eyes, and nodded to himself with a smile.

"This is good, isn't it, Sam?" Patricia asked.

"Probably. At least it means that things are happening in there." He repeated Patricia's test, waving his hand in front of Elizabeth's eyes. She blinked again. "Good," he nodded to himself.

He probably said more, but Patricia didn't hear. She was too busy crying.

———

Because it was the weekend, Paul Kent called Patricia at home early that evening. She picked up the phone as soon as it began to ring.

"Dr. Worthington? Paul Kent here. I'm sorry I'm a bit late. How're things? Any change?"

He could hear the delight in her voice as soon as she spoke.

"Yes, Mr. Kent, there is. Elizabeth started responding to stimuli early this afternoon."

Kent's heart leapt.

The doctor told him what had happened. "When I left the hospital an hour ago, she had just fallen asleep again. But all afternoon she was consistently responding to basic stimuli. She feels pain, and she reacts when you wave a hand in front of her face. I know it doesn't sound like much, but it's great progress."

"I'll be on a plane tonight. I can be there by nine tomorrow morning."

"I think that would be wonderful, Mr. Kent." She paused for a moment. She didn't want to raise his hopes too much, but she didn't want to dampen his enthusiasm either. She cautioned him: "Remember, she's not really conscious yet. She won't recognize you. But it's the first sign of progress. We took another CAT scan and the neurosurgeon says that things are definitely changing inside her head."

She wondered if she should also tell Mr. Kent of Sam's warning that such changes sometimes led to brain spasms, and even death. No. Kent had been hurt enough.

She continued, "She's a fighter, Mr. Kent. Somewhere deep inside her head she's struggling to find a way to make her brain work again. If you could be here just to talk to her, it might be just what she needs."

"I'll see you... I'll see you *both* in the morning."

He put the phone down and let out a whoop of joy.

She was going to make it. Tomorrow he would see her again. If necessary, he would sit by her bed day and night until she recovered. And then.... And then what? Catherine was dead. Nothing could change that fact. He pushed the thought aside and concentrated instead on Elizabeth. Elizabeth needed him, that was what was important.

Revenge would just have to wait.

Chapter 25
Saturday, December 8
Boston, Massachusetts

Vincent Cotterell knew that he should have been satisfied, but he could not escape a nagging worry that something somewhere was slightly awry; somewhere inside his head a voice was whispering something that he could not quite make out.

He was seated in his Boston apartment overlooking the Charles River, a half-finished vodka Martini in his hand to aid thought.

He tried reviewing everything one more time, the Golden Pipeline first.

His latest expansion of the Pipeline, a scheme entirely of his own devising, had succeeded so well that it might have been scripted. Its only drawback was that too many people were involved, and that meant that it was only a matter of time before it was discovered and infiltrated. The Pipeline would have to be broken up then. But Cotterell hoped that that would not be for many months yet — and possibly not for years if his characteristic luck held.

He was not worried that his own relationship to the Pipeline would be uncovered; he was far too carefully insulated for that to be a concern. To make doubly sure of his safety, he had carefully "promoted" an unwitting stoolpigeon as CEO of PlanetAir; Cotterell's only connection to the airline was that he held 51% of the company's stock.

Not that the CEO would ever have to worry about a trial should he ever be accused of running the Pipeline. There would be a fatal shooting, and all that would be left would be a trail of circumstantial evidence leading in circles of ever-decreasing radius around the sap.

But that was all insurance for the future. At the moment, the Pipeline was functioning perfectly. Not a gram of heroin coming through the new PlanetAir route had been taken by the authorities since he had shipped a few tentative kilos in early September. Each day now, several tens of kilograms of Pakistani heroin were arriving in the United States, smuggled by his well-paid carriers; lesser amounts were appearing in other countries with less well-developed appetites for the drug and fewer hard dollars to pay for the habit.

The ruse was simple, but it worked, possibly because of its very simplicity.

A carrier would strap to himself (or herself; almost half the carriers were female) several pounds of heroin, in the form of a string of small brown sausages tied around the waist, and then board a predetermined international PlanetAir flight. It was a glaring loophole in international security that governments concerned themselves almost completely with drugs being smuggled *in* to their countries. Carriers taking drugs out ran almost no risk of detection — a fact amply proven in the past three months.

Shortly after take-off, the carrier would go to the lavatory, at which time he would strip and remove the small brown plastic containers of the drug. He would pull them apart and drop them, one by one, into the toilet. From that point on the carrier was completely clean, and could travel through immigration and customs at the far end without fear. While the carrier walked free, a special honey truck belonging to a Cotterell-owned company emptied the tanks from the flight and, later, the brown bags were retrieved. So simple, yet flawless.

Cotterell's thoughts turned from the Golden Pipeline to the Kelton operation. Although that seemed to be progressing a little less smoothly, there was no obvious cause for concern here either.

His first attempt on Harris's life had failed, but that was only a temporary setback. Harris's unexpected tracking down and shooting of Brezhnerov had been the cause of some rapid rearrangements, but all was back on track again now. He expected to receive the good news of Harris's final elimination before he left for Denver on Monday afternoon.

As for Kelton, the man tailing him reported that he was in Washington nosing around and, apparently, spending most of his time sightseeing. The only incongruity had been a single meeting in midweek with an unidentified man in a downtown coffee shop. Photographs of the stranger had been taken, but as yet there was no word on his identity.

Cotterell wondered if Kelton had yet understood the true purpose behind the explosion at Gatwick. He doubted it; Kelton's actions were hardly consistent with a man bent on revenge. The only nagging puzzle was what was the man doing in Washington at all? What kind of man could leave the country while his daughter lay unconscious in hospital?

But it hardly mattered. There was no way that Kelton would ever be able to connect Cotterell with what had happened at Gatwick. The only connection was Harris, and Harris would soon be dead.

And then... then Cotterell would turn his attention to the man who had killed his brother. He could imagine the scene now: the shock on Kelton's face when Cotterell confronted him with the truth; the desperate attempt to negotiate; then, at last, the despair as Kelton realized that there was no escape. Cotterell's hand clenched, mimicking the imagined act of pulling the trigger.

The anticipation of the moment caused him to cast his mind back to the event that had come to define his life.

He had just left a particularly dull meeting, one of the few each year that Carl insisted he attend so that he had at least a basic understanding of the overall workings of the Cotterell empire.

He could remember nothing about the meeting now except that it had been in downtown New York and he had spent most of it fantasizing about one of the secretaries. A blonde, if he remembered correctly.

As he and Carl left the building, they were escorted by two inconspicuous armed guards. But the guards had been useless. Not that it was their fault. There had been no sound, no warning of any kind, nothing anyone could have done to prevent the tragedy.

Vincent was looking idly up and down the street, waiting his turn to enter the car behind his brother. He turned toward the limousine just in time to see his brother's head explode. Red blood, white bone, and gray brain cells disgorged themselves from Carl's head; one red fountain above the right ear, and another whose exact position was hidden somewhere below the left ear, erupted into being.

For a fraction of a second, nothing moved, and all the eternal cacophony of New York's streets seemed to become utter silence in the shock of the moment. That frozen moment was painted like a canvas in Vincent's memory. Then, slowly, his brother's body caved over to one side, as if he had fallen asleep on his feet. His momentum carried him forwards so that he hit his head clumsily on the leather of the seat in front of him, leaving a gruesome, slimy trail of commingled remains as his head slid across the leather, crashed sickeningly into the metal step of the car, and eventually came to rest on the sidewalk.

Vincent stood stock still, his mind trying to grasp what had just happened.

He was thrown to the ground as one of his brother's security guards felled him and then dragged him behind the shelter of the car. The other guard had a weapon in his hand; after looking around for any sign of a sniper, he leaned down and cursorily felt Carl's body for a pulse. There was little point; it was quite obvious that Carl had to be dead.

After a moment, the guard confirmed the fact, not a shred of emotion in his voice as he said: "He's dead." The guard who had dragged Vincent to the rear of the car crouched by Vincent's side, scanning the windows of the tall buildings all around, looking for some sign of movement that would betray the sniper's position.

Vincent looked at what remained of his brother and retched. Turning his head away, a small metal object lying on the sidewalk caught his eye. Without thinking, he stretched out his hand and picked up the bullet. It was still warm.

He turned it around in his hand, examining it. The front was squashed from the force of its impact with the sidewalk. There was a small crack in the concrete where the bullet had landed and spent its energy, before bouncing once and rolling to a stop where Vincent had found it. Absent-mindedly, he pulled a clean handkerchief out of a pocket, wrapped the bullet in the handkerchief, and stuffed both back into the pocket.

None of this was done consciously, they were the automatic acts of a man whose mind was trying desperately to come to grips with the terrifying events of the past few seconds. Later, when he found the wrapped bullet, he looked at it with puzzlement, trying to fathom how it had come to be in his pocket.

But for now he looked up at the featureless windows of the high rise office buildings towering over the street. Somewhere, behind one of those blank windows, was the man who had killed his brother.

A scowl of hatred showed on Vincent's face. All around him now was a bustle of activity as passersby began to realize that there would be no further shots and their curiosity drove them from the hiding places to which they had instinctively scattered. Vincent spoke, his voice muted, for no one's ears but his own and those of the unknown killer hidden somewhere behind one of the myriad panes of glass. "I'll kill you for this, you bastard. By God, one day you'll pay for this."

"Come on, sir, let's get you inside," the guard at his side said, and Vincent allowed himself to be hurried away from the car and bustled into the building he had left not two minutes before. He glanced back at his brother, spread-eagled unnaturally on the sidewalk in a pool of his own blood. It was the last time he ever saw him.

Some people go through life without ever being tested. These are the unlucky ones, for they never truly know the stuff of which they are made, and without that knowledge no person can ever truly know himself. Some people are tested and, at the moment of destiny, find that they are incapable of the strength required to fulfill the rôle that could have been theirs. These are the ones to be pitied, for evermore they must live with the knowledge of what might have been. But others come to their moment of truth and, recognizing it for what it is — their very reason for being — refuse to be intimidated by their weaknesses and emerge with a new strength, their feet set firmly on the path for which destiny has made them. These are the ones who have fulfilled all that it means to be human. They know that their ideas, thoughts and actions prior to this one moment have been instantly made irrelevant, for they were no indicator of the person who now walks the path of his destiny. The person is truly born only at the moment of this confrontation, and each, for a single moment, holds his destiny in his hands and can choose what to make of it.

For Vincent Cotterell, that defining moment was the death of his brother. Prior to that moment, he had seemed — and indeed was — but a shallow playboy, a hedonist interested solely in the pleasures of this life; but that was no more than a shell, not the essential Vincent Cotterell. As he stared up into the windows reaching up to the sky and almost without thinking swore his oath, Vincent Cotterell was staring at the reason for his being, and in that moment he became something new.

———————

Vincent Cotterell was smart enough to realize that, once it became clear that no one was going to be quickly apprehended for the killing, there were other things of more immediate importance than trying to find the killer himself. Carl Cotterell had been head of a large business empire, and the wolves were circling, waiting for the brother to make a mistake.

So Vincent Cotterell put his personal feelings aside, and threw himself into the business of learning business. It turned out that he had a natural talent, never before tested, for making money.

He discovered that there were only a few simple rules to making money, lots of it, providing one started with a sufficiently large ante: be decisive; don't be afraid to make mistakes; and when you do make them, learn from them, cut your losses and get out quickly. He applied these philosophies to both the legitimate and the illegitimate sides of the Cotterell interests, and under his care both sides of the operation flourished as never before.

Life became hectic and busy, and remained so for nearly four years.

Amid the quotidian busyness of running the conglomerate, Vincent never forgot either his brother or the oath of revenge he had sworn while hiding behind the car, looking up at the windows that hid his brother's killer; but no one had ever been apprehended, and the cops had long ago given up the case, the trail by now so cold that Vincent had no idea where to turn. One day, he still hoped, a clue would come his way and he would be able to begin his manhunt in earnest, but as time passed this became more and more a wishful dream, with little expectation that it would ever be realized.

When the clue came, he barely recognized it.

He was interviewing a candidate to be his new head of personal security, a position which, in Vincent's scheme of things, was one of the highest trust. Not only was the head of personal security responsible for Cotterell's personal safety; he also played the part of Cotterell's confidant, his eyes and ears in the organization, his most trusted deputy. It was not a position of obvious power — from it, one could form no power base, build no coalitions — yet it was, perhaps, the single most powerful appointment which it was in Vincent's power to bestow.

Cotterell had reviewed his personnel files carefully, and chosen four long-standing employees to interview for the position. The candidates themselves would never know that they were interviewing for the job, although perhaps the more astute of them might understand that before the interview ended. They were merely invited to Cotterell's office; once there he simply engaged them in conversation. After two or three hours they left. The unsuccessful ones would hear no more; the successful candidate would be told of his appointment.

It was Victor Brezhnerov, a large-framed bulldog of a man who was in charge of security at Cotterell's New York headquarters, who mentioned Kelton.

Cotterell had asked Brezhnerov whom he would most like to meet.

"I don't suppose you'll have heard of him, sir, but I'd have to say that a man named Kelton is probably the person I'd most like to get to know."

"Kelton?"

"Yes, sir. Please don't get the wrong impression when I tell you he's a paid assassin."

"An assassin?" Cotterell could not conceal his surprise.

Brezhnerov shrugged. "Yes, sir. In fact, I've always wondered if it was Kelton who killed your brother."

Cotterell snapped upright in his chair. "The man who killed my brother? What makes you think that?"

"Let me tell you what little I know about him, sir. I first heard about Kelton from my brother, who was with Delta in 'Nam and then became a mercenary after the Americans left.

"Stories began to circulate in the closing months of the war about a young assassin working for the VC. After the Americans left, my brother stayed on in 'Nam along with some of his friends from Delta, hiring themselves out as mercenaries.

"One of the provincial high-ups heard that Kelton had accepted a contract on his life, and he responded by bringing in my brother and his team to protect him. My brother thought it was easy money; it was safe, and what sort of a madman would set himself up to get past a former Delta group just to kill a politician?

"It turned out that this man Kelton was not only crazy enough to try, but the mucky-muck took it in the head one evening right in the middle of enjoying one of his harem of whores. It impressed my brother no end. No one ever found a trace of Kelton. To this day, whenever my brother comes to town, we sit down over a beer and try to figure out how Kelton did it. We haven't worked it out yet. My brother swears blind that not so much as a fly could have gotten into that house without being seen. But Kelton did it. Got out again, too.

"I've kept track of him ever since. At least, I've tried to. Someone like that doesn't advertise himself, of course, but after a while you get to recognize his genius. He gives no warning, leaves no traces. It's always a clean kill, always a single bullet; usually, although not always, from a rifle. You never have to worry about conspiracy theories if Kelton's involved. It's one man, one bullet, no warning, no clues. Perverse though it may be, I have to admire such quality."

Brezhnerov paused, seeming unsure whether to continue, and a heavy silence descended on the room. "He seems to be retired though, now," he eventually added.

"Go on."

"The last assassination I'm certain he did was more than five years ago now, the French Ambassador to the U.N., who was killed while vacationing in Guadeloupe. There have been a couple of possibles since then, but I'm less sure of them."

The heavy silence continued. Eventually, Cotterell spoke. "This man Kelton; did he kill only political targets? Why do you think he might have killed my brother? What reasons do you have other than the fact that my brother was shot by a sniper?"

"Sir, you shouldn't underestimate the strength of that circumstantial evidence. Your brother was shot from a considerable distance. A single shot was fired. It takes an extraordinary marksman even to consider making such a shot. That it was successful speaks volumes about the man who pulled the trigger. But there is something else. When my brother was in 'Nam, he learned how to contact Kelton if you want to set up a contract on someone. It's by a coded advertisement in the London *Times*. Such an ad was placed only a couple of months before your brother's death.

"I agree that it's all circumstantial; but you have to admit that it all fits."

Cotterell promoted Brezhnerov on the spot to be his new head of security, and the next day, Cotterell took the new appointee to lunch. While waiting for the entrée, he pulled a matchbox out of his pocket and handed it across the table. "Open it," Cotterell ordered.

Brezhnerov did so. Inside, nestled on a bed of cotton wool, was a bullet, its head flattened.

"May I take it out of the box?"

"Be my guest."

Brezhnerov carefully removed the bullet from its resting place and rotated it several times in his hands, inspecting it closely. It was a used .38 caliber bullet. The rifling marks were clear, the lines etched permanently into the metal as the bullet had spun down a rifle barrel. The nose of the bullet was compressed on one side; it had struck a glancing blow against something unyielding after being fired.

Brezhnerov replaced the bullet in the matchbox without comment. He looked up at his employer, a query on his face.

Cotterell said, "Suppose I thought that this bullet had been fired from a gun owned by the man Kelton that you mentioned yesterday. How might I go about testing that hypothesis?"

Brezhnerov looked down at the bullet nestling in the matchbox. "You mean that this...?"

"Yes. That's the bullet that killed my brother."

Brezhnerov closed the matchbox slowly, using the time to think. "It shouldn't be too hard. Kelton prefers rifles made by a Swiss named Bücher. He has left behind Bücher rifles on two occasions when he had to escape unencumbered. I'd try to track down Maximillian Bücher and try to match the bullet against his records."

"Maximillian Bücher... tell me more about him."

"He's probably the best designer and craftsman of precision hunting rifles in the world. A man like Kelton would be unlikely to use a rifle built by anyone else. If I was in his position, I certainly wouldn't. I'd like to own one of his rifles myself one day, but I'll probably never be able to afford it."

Cotterell sat, thinking deeply, for some considerable time. The food arrived, and Brezhnerov waited, fork in hand, for his employer to begin eating. Cotterell's eyes cleared, and he said, "Well, maybe we can do something about getting you one of those rifles. Do you have any idea how to find Bücher?"

"As I said, he's Swiss. At least, I think he is. I don't know any more than that, but I doubt that it would be hard to find him. He's not particularly secretive."

"OK. Give me back that matchbox and get yourself ready for a trip to Europe. I'll have a cast made of that bullet and a duplicate poured. This time tomorrow, I want you on a plane to Switzerland carrying the duplicate. I want to know if Bücher made the gun that killed my brother."

D. R. Evans

Chapter 26
Geneva, one year ago

Maximillian Bücher's small shop was located in a wide alley off the *Bahnhofstraße*.

On this particular morning, a large man stood on the far side of the alley, studying the store. Above the storefront was a sign: *Waffenschmied Handlling* written in gold against a dark maroon background above the storefront. Underneath was written, in smaller gold lettering, *M. Bücher*. The window was opaque, painted glass. The paint on the sign and the woodwork, as well as that on the window, looked recent.

The large man crossed the alley, pushed open the door, and entered the shop.

Inside, it was small and poorly lit. A pair of low-wattage bulbs hung from the ceiling; what little light entered from the alley outside was sharply attenuated by the painted glass of the window. There were two glass counters, placed in the form of an "L," one at the rear of the shop, one to the left. The counters were supplied with fluorescent lights, which concentrated their light downward to highlight the objects for sale. Small cases, some of them lit by tiny fluorescent tubes, hung from the walls. The smell of wood, leather and metal combined to create a pleasant, full scent that was greater than the sum of its parts.

In so much a man's world, Victor Brezhnerov was taken aback to see a pretty young dark-haired girl behind the counter. She looked up as he entered the shop, interrupted by the jangling sound of a bell above his head. He appeared to have interrupted her in the process of making entries with a pencil in a paperback book. She looked up and smiled.

"*Guten morgen*," she said.

"I'm sorry. Do you speak English at all?"

The smile did not waver. "Certainly, sir. Are you an American?"

"Yes. From New York."

"Ah yes, New York. I have seen it on the television, of course. Tall buildings, yellow taxis. The Statue of Liberty."

Brezhnerov returned her smile. She had spoken with an accent, but one that took him a moment to place. English, that was it. Perhaps she had spent time in that country.

"Your English is very good," he complimented her, closing the door behind him.

She shrugged. "Oh, it's so-so. In Europe we have to learn many languages. French, German, Dutch, Italian, Spanish, English. You Americans have it easy." Her eyes seemed to twinkle, turning the criticism into a shared joke. Brezhnerov decided that he liked her.

"You're right, of course. We do have it easy. Now, I wonder if you could help me? I'm over here to buy some of your renowned Swiss craftsmanship." He swept his hand to include the store. "We have nothing half so good at home."

"Well, sir, it would not be right if all the world was the same, would it?" She did not wait for an answer. "Here in Switzerland we are good at making money, watches and guns. If you have come to purchase a hunting rifle, then you have come to the right place."

"Yes, that's exactly it. Do you mind if I browse for a while?"

"Not at all; feel free. And just ask if you have any questions." The girl, still smiling, dropped her head and picked up the book in which she had been writing. Brezhnerov saw that it was a book of crossword puzzles.

He began to examine the contents of the glass cases. He was looking for a rifle with the initials MB carved into the butt. After about five minutes, he had examined every rifle on display, but none displayed the looked-for signature. He did a calculation in his head, converting currencies. The typical price of these rifles was a couple of thousand dollars. Hardly in Bücher's price class. He stepped towards the counter and coughed tentatively. "Excuse me."

The girl looked up again, the furrows of concentration on her brow disappearing and her smile returning as she met his questioning gaze. "Yes, sir. May I help you?"

"I'm not sure. These rifles are OK as they go, but I was looking for something a little more, shall we say, classy. I had heard that the best rifles are built by a man named Bücher. Do you have any of his work here?"

A new respect appeared in the girl's eyes. "Maximillian Bücher. Oh yes, he is the best in the world. We here in Switzerland are very proud of his work. But you will not find any of his work on sale here, or in any other shop. He makes rifles only to special order. To buy one of his guns, you must first be measured by him, pay your money, and then be prepared to wait for as long as two years while he builds your rifle exactly to your specifications."

"Ah, I see. I did not realize. Well, how might I go about finding Mr. Bücher?"

"His rifles are very expensive, you know."

"I assure you that's not a problem. I do want to own the best in the world, and if Mr. Bücher makes the best, then I need to talk to him."

Her smile became wider, almost a grin. "In that case, I think that can easily be arranged. I believe he is working out back. If you would be so good as to wait here." Without waiting for an answer, she turned away, pulled to one side a maroon colored drape that covered an open doorway behind her, and disappeared through the doorway.

A minute or so later she returned, accompanied by a man in his late forties. Brezhnerov wondered if he was the girl's father; there did seem to be a certain resemblance between them. He was shorter than she, and wore spectacles far down on his nose, looking at Brezhnerov over their rims. His hair was thick, gray, and well coiffed. He was dressed in a neat, button down, open-necked Oxford shirt and dark trousers.

"Good afternoon, sir," the man said. "I understand you wish to speak with Maximillian Bücher?"

"Indeed I do."

"At your service, sir." The man gave a jerky little bow, like a cuckoo in a clock. "Would you please follow me?"

Bücher walked behind the counter that made the second leg of the "L." At the far end was a doorway set in the rear wall; he opened the door and passed through into the room beyond. Brezhnerov followed, and found himself in a small room dominated by a round table around which were placed several chairs. On the table were several pads of writing paper and a penholder. Bücher switched on a light as he held the door open for Brezhnerov. He closed the door behind the American, then gestured toward the table. "Please, be seated."

Brezhnerov sat down, and Bücher took a chair on the opposite side of the table. He studied Brezhnerov for several seconds, then said, "Now, my daughter informs me that you would like a rifle built to your personal specifications?"

"Well, not exactly." Brezhnerov reached into his coat pocket and withdrew a matchbox, which he placed on the table. "But first, I want to be sure I'm talking to the right man. You are Maximillian Bücher, aren't you?"

"I have that honor; yes, sir."

"Good. Then I have something here that will pay you just as well as an order for a rifle would, but which will take considerably less of your time. Would you please open this matchbox?"

He pushed the small box across the table toward the Swiss.

Bücher leaned forward, his face expressionless, and took the matchbox. He opened it and, seeing the bullet inside, asked, "May I?"

Brezhnerov nodded and Bücher withdrew the bullet carefully. He held it up to the light and turned it around. He pushed the spectacles up his nose then peered closely at the bullet. Finally he looked at Brezhnerov and spoke. "So, it is a .38 caliber bullet. It has been fired. It struck a hard object. What more do you wish to know?"

"I wish to know whether it was fired from one of your guns. Ten thousand dollars if the answer is 'yes.' And another fifteen if you can tell me precisely for whom that gun was made, and where I might find the owner of the gun."

"You are not the police?"

Brezhnerov shook his head.

"Nor a government agent?"

"No."

"Ah." Bücher smiled. He closed the matchbox and pushed it back across the table. He leaned back in his chair and crossed his arms. "I see," he said, nodding. "And you think my life is so cheap that I would risk it for a mere 25,000 dollars? Obviously, this bullet has been used in some way of which you do not approve. And now you, Mr. Mysterious Stranger, want me to tell you who fired the shot, eh? And what do you think my life would be worth after I gave you that information? I am sorry, but I am afraid I cannot help you."

He did not stop smiling pleasantly at Brezhnerov.

Brezhnerov did not move to pick up the matchbox. It was a pity; he rather liked this dapper Swiss craftsman. It would be shame to have to hurt him.

When he spoke, he leaned forward slightly to emphasize his words. "Mr. Bücher, I came here today under orders. I am to leave this building with certain information. Either I go to my boss and give him the name of the man that owns the gun, or I go to him and tell him you are dead. I'm sorry,

I truly am. You seem like a sensible person. Now, which is it
to be?"

Bücher slumped back in his chair and raised his hands to
the ceiling. "All I do is make guns. And I make them well,
perhaps the best in the world. So why do you need to come
here and threaten me like this?"

"I came here for information. Information that only you
can provide. I will pay well for it, and you have my word that
I will never divulge my source. You know," Brezhnerov's voice
was calm, dripping reasonableness, "I don't think you really
have much of a choice, do you?"

Bücher sighed as he leaned forward and picked up the
matchbox once more. "Twenty five thousand dollars, you
say? Well, I suppose it could be worse." He lifted himself
out of the chair, and Brezhnerov quickly stood. "Come with
me," Bücher said.

Bücher led the way out of the room through the door
through which they had entered. Brezhnerov trailing him,
he walked the length of the "L" of counters, edging past his
daughter, who was now engrossed in conversation with a potential customer in some language that Brezhnerov could not
immediately place, and then the two passed through the doorway behind the maroon drape.

They walked together through a passageway, out into a
small half-covered courtyard, then across the open space until they were standing at the door of a small, single storey,
detached building. Bücher unlocked a padlock on the building's outer door. He pushed open the door, turned on a light
switch and entered the building.

Brezhnerov followed, closing the door behind him.

The room was long and narrow, with walls of whitewashed
stone. It was some kind of office, although obviously not one
that was often used. One of the long walls was lined with
filing cabinets. There were no labels on the drawers. A large
desk stood at one end of the room, a powerful light directly
overhead, a lamp and a magnifying glass mounted on separate
Anglepoise fixtures on the edge of the desk.

Bücher opened the matchbox and took the bullet out. "I would imagine," he said, "that you have some idea who might possibly be the owner of the gun?"

Brezhnerov said nothing.

"Only," continued Bücher, "it would make things a lot easier if we checked a couple of the more likely candidates first."

Brezhnerov paused for a moment, and then said, "All right then. A man by the name of Kelton."

Bücher's mouth tightened and then he nodded slowly. "Ah, yes," he said. "I was hoping it would not be him. But," he added, more to himself than the other, "who else would it be?"

Looking at Brezhnerov, he continued, "I keep a sample bullet fired from every rifle that I make. They are all in this filing cabinet here."

He touched the third cabinet from the left. "It is not locked. And now I think it would be best if I left the room. You will find everything neatly filed. There is light and a strong magnifying glass at the desk. I do not want payment. Maximillian Bücher does not sell his clients for money. I will leave now. I do not want to see you again. I will lock up after you have gone."

"You don't want the twenty five grand?" Brezhnerov asked incredulously.

"That is correct. I have my pride and my principles. There is little doubt that I will be killed because of your visit here today. I do not want to die knowing that I deserved death."

"But surely you have spoken to the police about Kelton and your guns? It is an established fact that he has used your rifles in the past. They must have questioned you."

"That is true. But the police... they are expected, and, in any case, they are not very competent. You... well, that, I think, is quite a different matter."

Brezhnerov shrugged. He was no philosopher.

"Before you go," he said, "there's one more thing."

"One more thing? What else could you possibly want from me? I have given you my life. Is that not enough?"

"You've seen this man Kelton. What does he look like? The police must have asked you that too."

"Seen him? Oh, yes, I have seen him, twice. First when he came to talk with me about his requirements, and one more time when we checked the first gun for balance and accuracy in his hands. But it was a long time ago now. As I told the police, I don't remember so well these days, and we all change, you know. I don't think I could be of much help to you."

Brezhnerov looked menacing, which was not difficult for someone a good foot taller and a hundred pounds heavier than the man he was trying to intimidate. He raised his hand to hit Bücher, then thought better of it.

"Mr. Bücher, you must understand; I won't hurt you if you coöperate. Now, I'm sure you'll remember something if you think carefully enough. Height, build, age, color of hair, manner, that kind of thing."

Bücher resigned himself to utter defeat. "Yes. I do remember. But it is true what I have told you. It was all a long time ago now.

"He was quite tall. I would say about your height, maybe a little less, one meter eighty or so; very athletic in build. I would think that he would be a little older than you — between maybe 35 and 40 now, perhaps a little older. The one thing that made a strong impression with me was his manner. He seemed to be the personification of the English gentleman that one reads about in books but never seems to find in real life. Perhaps you do not know what I mean." Bücher evidently had doubts that Brezhnerov would recognize a gentleman if one was presented to him already labeled. "You understand, he was quiet and polite and seemed interested in learning about how things worked. Just a very nice person to be around. That's all I remember." Bücher shrugged his shoulders.

"Any accent or other distinctive mannerisms that you remember?"

"No. Very English. That's all. I remember nothing else."

Brezhnerov said nothing, unsure whether more threats or bribes might not extract further information from the Swiss. Bücher, suddenly seeming much older, pressed the matchbox into Brezhnerov's hand; then he turned away, opened the door, and was gone.

Brezhnerov looked down at the matchbox, then at the open doorway. He shook his head uncomprehendingly, then closed the door.

He dropped the matchbox on the table, then crossed to the third filing cabinet. He opened the top drawer. The drawer was full of folders, arranged alphabetically from A to J. He closed the top drawer and opened the next one. K, there it was, right at the front: Kelton. And another and another. Seven folders in all with Kelton's name carefully written in a neat, diminutive script.

Brezhnerov withdrew the first folder, took it to the table and opened it out on the flat surface. The folder contained a one-page description of a rifle, a photograph of the weapon, and two bullets wrapped in plastic bags. He looked at the photograph and understood why there were two bullets — one for each barrel. He had never seen a double barreled rifle with the barrels arranged vertically before, but, as he thought about it, he recognized that there was a certain logic to such an arrangement.

Opening one of the plastic bags, he carefully removed the bullet. He switched on the light and compared the bullet under the magnifying glass with the newly cast duplicate of the bullet that had killed Carl Cotterell. Superficially they were the same, apart from the blunted head of the American bullet, but he could see differences in the details of the patterns of scratches on the two pieces of metal.

He tried the bullet from the second plastic bag, with the same result. He returned to the filing cabinet and brought all of the folders marked with Kelton's name to the table. Methodically, he began to go through them, comparing each bullet in turn against the one from the matchbox.

It was the seventh bullet.

Carefully, he rotated the two bullets together under the magnifying glass. There could be no doubting it: apart from the impacted head, they were identical.

He looked at the sheet of information in the folder to see if it might provide some clue to Kelton's identity, but there was nothing significant, only the vital statistics of the gun that had fired these bullets.

There was no photocopier in the office, so he quickly copied down the numbers on to another sheet of paper. Then he carefully replaced the bullet in its plastic bag — it had come from the upper barrel he noticed, the one that fired first, according to the rifle's information sheet — closed the folder and replaced it, along with the others that he had disturbed, in the filing cabinet.

Early that afternoon, Brezhnerov made a telephone call back to the United States.

"Brezhnerov here, Boss. It's Kelton. I'm sure of it now."

"How so?"

"As I hoped, Bücher keeps meticulous records. I compared the bullet with the ones in his files until I found a match. It didn't take long. It was a double-barreled rifle built for Kelton nine years ago. The bullet came from the barrel that fired first. There's no doubt about it."

"And Bücher?"

"Refused payment. Said something about how since he was going to be killed, he didn't want to take the money. Can't say it made much sense to me."

"OK. Well, forget him now. I've budgeted the money. Keep it for yourself."

"Thank you, Boss."

"Now all we need is a way to track down Kelton's where-abouts."

"I've been giving that some thought. Can I have a few days to try something?"

"Take as long as you need. This is important to me."

"Yes, Boss. I'll get in touch as soon as I find out anything."

Brezhnerov put the phone down. He could almost feel the net tightening around his quarry.

In the center of London, off the Strand and backing on to the Victoria Embankment, stands Somerset House. Within the walls of this building is deposited the statistical history of the British people. Each birth, each marriage, each death is recorded on a sheet of paper and carefully filed away. Summary books are maintained and easily accessible. Any member of the public may go to Somerset House to read the summary records and, for a nominal sum, obtain a full copy of any document contained in the records. In this computerized age, many of the records have been copied from paper to optical storage media accessible through a series of computer terminals placed in private study carrels.

Brezhnerov entered Somerset House shortly after it opened at 9 a.m. one warm early autumn Monday morning, and requested access to the computerized records. He was directed to a small carrel by a uniformed attendant. The carrel held a chair and a table, on which stood a computer terminal and a binder that held half a dozen laminated sheets describing the Somerset House computer system. He sat down at the terminal and began to read.

He had little to go on. There was the name itself, "Kelton," which was unusual but, almost certainly, a pseudonym. But there was one more thing.

Kelton had retired about four years ago. Why would a man in his mid thirties retire when at the height of his profession? Perhaps he had died, the victim either of disease or another man's bullet? Perhaps he had simply lost interest in his occupation and decided to try his hand at something new? Both of these were possible and, if either were true, then he was wasting his time here. But there was a third possibility. A man of Kelton's age might easily have undergone within the past few years a change of circumstances that would encourage him to retire from his financially rewarding but unusually hazardous occupation: he might have gotten married.

Brezhnerov opened a pad of paper, twisted his propelling pencil to provide a sharp point, and began to make his acquaintance with the Somerset House computer system.

He worked steadily all of that day and most of the following one, until his notepad was covered with notes to a depth of nearly fifty pages, a written record of disappearing trails, sudden flashes of inspiration, disappointment and, at last, possibly, an answer. Or at least a pointer to one.

Four years before, a marriage had been registered. In Holy Trinity Church, the parish church of Wallington, Surrey, the marriage of Paul Michael Kent to Catherine Elizabeth Warner had taken place. There was nothing remarkable about the record of the wedding itself; it was no different from any of the hundreds of others that Brezhnerov had looked at in the past two days. But what was remarkable was that, prior to the wedding, there was no record of Mr. Paul Michael Kent.

Brezhnerov had combed the computer records and, as a last resort, the summary books that were still on the shelves; there could be no doubt that Paul Michael Kent had no official existence prior to the wedding day. He did show up once after the wedding; ten months following the marriage, the records showed that the birth of Elizabeth Josephine Kent had been registered in Chipstead, Surrey, south of London. Paul Michael Kent was Elizabeth's father.

Brezhnerov left Somerset House and ten minutes later he was in a post office, flicking through a telephone directory. He found the name, P. M. Kent, next to an address in Chipstead, Surrey. He smiled. Now it was just a matter of digging into Kent's past. But he already knew what he would find.

Brezhnerov had found his man.

Chapter 27
Saturday, December 8
Surrey

Patricia kept telling herself that she was getting too sentimental in her old age. She had been a surgeon for more than a decade, and she thought she had seen it all: children dying of leukemia; babies born without limbs; a bride maimed for life in an accident on the way to church. But Elizabeth Kent was different. Someone had done this to Elizabeth Kent on purpose.

Patricia told herself that of course no one had actually intended Elizabeth Kent to be caught in the blast; the girl had simply been an innocent victim, that was all. But even so, it was something new in Patricia's experience to have to deal with the direct results of man's inhumanity to man, and Patricia found that whenever she was not thinking of something else, her mind would wander of its own accord to the little girl who was struggling to find herself.

Patricia usually treated herself to something special on Saturday evenings: perhaps a meal out, either alone or with a friend; sometimes a trip to the cinema; occasionally even a visit into the city to see a West End play. Tonight she was supposed to be going out to dinner, but the events of the afternoon kept intruding on her preparations.

Normally she had a good clothes sense and had little trouble finding something suitable to wear for an evening out. But tonight she had tried on half her wardrobe, finding fault with everything. She was still trying on dresses when the doorbell rang.

"It's open," she called. "I'll be with you in a minute."

She could hear Dan pottering around in the living room while she cast her eyes desperately over the remainder of her wardrobe. "Get yourself a drink," she added. "I'll drive."

That was a change. Normally this was the one evening of the week when she allowed herself a couple of drinks to help her relax. But tonight she didn't feel like a drink. To be honest, she didn't even feel like going out, even with Dan. It slowly dawned on her what it was she really wanted to do.

She stood there for several seconds, hesitating, wondering if there was any chance that Dan would understand. Then she pulled a thick patterned sweater and a pair of slacks from their hangers and quickly put them on.

Dan Major arched an eyebrow in surprise when she walked into the room. He was standing next to the small drinks trolley in the corner; in his hand he held a small glass half filled with an amber liquid. He was wearing a jacket and tie.

"Hullo. You don't look like you intend going out tonight."

"Sorry." She walked across to him and gave him a kiss on the cheek. She caught a light whiff of cologne. "I'm not in the mood. Would you mind awfully if I changed our plans?"

"Ah! My lucky night has arrived at last," Dan said with a smile. "I knew when I ran over that black cat yesterday my luck was going to change."

He knew instantly from the shadow that crossed her face that he had adopted exactly the wrong tone. Soberly, he said, "I'm sorry. Has something happened?"

Patricia shrugged. "Not really. I don't know what's got into me. I've got a patient.... I know I'm being stupid, but would you mind terribly if we ate at the hospital tonight? The café stays open all night, and the food's really not that bad. I'm really sorry. Perhaps you should just go home."

Dan put down his drink and placed an arm around Patricia's shoulder. "No. That's all right. If you want to go to the hospital café to eat, that's where we'll go. The Royal Windsor's overrated anyway. But I'll drive, I've barely touched the drink, and you can tell me about it in the car. How's that?"

She gave him a squeeze. "Thank you, Dan. You keep doing things like this and one day I think I'll fall in love with you."

"I live in hope." He kissed her on the cheek.

They arrived at the hospital twenty minutes later and went directly to Elizabeth's room.

She was much the same as she had been when Patricia had last seen her, except that someone had put Mr. Bear on the bed next to her and draped her arm around the cuddly toy.

They both tried talking quietly to her, repeating her name and stroking her arm, but there was no visible response. Her eyes were still open, and Patricia waved her hand in front of her face. Elizabeth blinked. Patricia and Dan smiled.

They stayed for a few minutes, then Patricia suggested that they go down to the cafeteria.

"I'm sorry," Patricia said when they had chosen their food from the buffet and sat down to eat. "I know this isn't what you had in mind."

"It's all right. Really. I understand how you feel. If I were you I don't think I'd want to go out either." After a pause, he asked, "What are her chances?"

"Realistically? Not very good, I'm afraid. But Sam Higgins, our resident neurologist, says that one should never give up hope. It's a good sign that she's beginning to respond to stimuli, but she's been under for a very long time and her recovery will probably be neither quick nor complete."

"And her parents?"

"The mother was killed outright in the blast. Her father...." She stopped, unsure of what she truly thought of Mr. Kent. "I don't know," she eventually said. "He's a bit of a strange fish. But I suppose anyone would seem a bit strange after a loss like that."

"In what way is he strange?"

"I don't really know. Sometimes when I look at his face I break out in goose pimples. Sometimes I'm almost scared of what he might do if he could get his hands on the person who did it."

"You mean you think he'd like to kill whoever was responsible? Who wouldn't? If someone killed my wife and did that to my daughter, I know what I'd want to do to him."

"Yes," she nodded. "But there's something different about Mr. Kent. He's lonely, that much is obvious. But there's something else, something I can't quite pin down. I don't know...."

She thought about telling him about her reaction when she had first learned of the coincidence that Mr. Kent had been in Ireland when Sean O'Hannessy had been killed. Then she pushed the thought aside. She liked Dan, and she certainly didn't want him thinking she was crazy.

"Come on," she said. "Let's talk about something else. It's bad enough that I dragged you to the hospital to eat. You don't want conversation like this as well."

So conversation turned to more everyday subjects, but after they had finished coffee, Dan suggested that they go back to see Elizabeth.

"You're sure you don't mind?" Patricia asked.

"Sure I'm sure. I can see how much she means to you. And anyway, maybe it does some good for her to hear us there in the room with her."

Patricia smiled her thanks, and they made their way back to Elizabeth's room.

They saw the change instantly.

Instead of lying peacefully with Mr. Bear in her arm, Elizabeth's face was twisted to one side, facing the bear. Her arm was wrapped so tightly around the bear's middle that its head and legs stuck out at odd angles. For a moment, Patricia thought that Elizabeth was awake; but then she saw her face.

The right side of Elizabeth's face looked pale but normal; but the left side was rigid, her mouth partway open in an unnatural snarl. At the corner of her mouth bubbled a small mass of frothy bubbles.

Patricia rushed to the girl and tried to pull her arms from around Mr. Bear. Elizabeth's arms were locked tight and refused to move. Her eyes were dilated so much that the irises were all but invisible.

"Dan, go get a nurse. There's a nurses' station down the corridor to the right. Hurry!"

Dan stood rooted to the spot for a fraction of a second, just enough time for Patricia to shout, "Now!"

He dashed out of the room in search of help.

When he reappeared with a nurse in tow, Patricia said, more calmly, "You two look after her and make sure she doesn't hurt herself. I'm going to call Sam Higgins."

She hurried to the station and looked up the neurologist's home number. She dialed. The clock at the nurses' station stood at a few minutes before ten.

Someone picked up the phone.

"Sam?"

"Yes. Who is this?"

"It's Patricia. I'm at the hospital. Elizabeth's having a stroke."

"Damn! Right now?"

"That's what it looks like."

"All right. I'll be there in fifteen minutes. Do the best you can."

Struggling not to think of what might be happening to Elizabeth, Patricia hurried back to girl's room.

College Park, Maryland

It was just after seven o'clock in the evening. Kelton turned the key in his motel room and walked inside. A car with

267

Virginia plates entered the parking lot and drew into a space. A man got out and began to walk toward the room next door.

Kelton was booked on a flight that left Washington at eleven. His bags were already packed. All he needed to do was to put them in the car, check out, and drive to the airport.

The phone began to ring. He stopped in the act of lifting a bag off the bed, and looked at the phone. Only two people had this number: Mike Downing and Patricia Worthington. He didn't particularly want to hear from either of them. He wanted to be with Elizabeth when she woke up, that was all.

He put the bag down and picked up the phone.

"Mr. Kent?" It was Dr. Worthington, and he knew instantly that something was wrong.

"Dr. Worthington? Is something the matter?"

"Yes." He could tell that she was trying not to cry. "I'm terribly sorry, Mr. Kent. Elizabeth's had a stroke."

There was silence for a few moments as the doctor pulled herself together before continuing. "It happened about two hours ago. I'm afraid it was fairly major. Sam Higgins, the neurosurgeon, came in straight away and took a CAT scan. He decided we'd better get her into surgery immediately. We've only just finished. I'm sorry, but I'm afraid there's not much hope any longer."

There was a long silence, broken only the sound of the doctor sniffing back her tears.

"When you say there's not much hope...."

"She's still alive. Her vital signs are weak, but not dangerously so. But Sam says it'll be a miracle if she ever wakes up."

"And if she does...?"

"If she does, she won't be aware of what's going on around her."

"A vegetable."

"I'm so sorry, Mr. Kent."

So Elizabeth was gone again. She wasn't going to recover. They would never be together again. The past few hours had been nothing more than a cruel mirage.

The doctor continued. "I'll stay here overnight, and I'll call if there's any change."

"But there's not really any chance of that, is there?" he heard himself talking as though from a great distance.

"Not really, no."

He put the phone down and stared sightlessly at the packed bags.

The news reached Mike Downing at home that evening: the *plethora* account had been accessed, and the number that made the call had been traced. It took Mike only a few minutes to add an address to the number.

He called England first. Then he called a motel in College Park.

The telephone in the motel room rang. Kelton was seated on the bed, his back propped against the veneered chipboard of the headboard. Beside the bed were his bags, unpacked once more. The reservation to England had been canceled. He was staring blindly at the wall.

The sudden ring of the phone startled him. He looked at the phone, dragging his mind to the present. What news did Dr. Worthington have now? Was Elizabeth dead? He picked up the phone.

"Good evening, Kelton."

It took him a moment to realize that it was Mike Downing calling about the search for the Gatwick bomber, not Dr. Worthington calling with news about Elizabeth. With a tremendous effort, he shifted mental gears.

"Hello, Mike. Have you got something?"

"It was George Harris. I have his phone number, his address and his current alias. Are you ready?"

"You're sure it was Harris?" Kelton's brain was beginning to function, taking over from the benumbed Paul Kent.

"Certain."

Kelton reached for a pencil and writing pad. "Ready."

Downing recited the information, and Kelton scribbled it down.

"Thank you, Mike. Is there anything else you want to tell me?"

"No. Except... be careful. He's a professional. And he hasn't been retired for the last five years."

"I appreciate the vote of confidence," Kelton replied icily. He put the phone down and looked at what he had written.

George Harris.

Kelton spoke out loud: "You bastard. I'm coming to get you." Kent might be numb, but Kelton knew exactly what had to be done. It was time to forget about playing mind games with Paul Kent and to let Kelton to do what he knew best. It was time to kill.

A few minutes later, Kelton settled his bill in cash, paying for one final night and telling the desk clerk that he would be leaving very early the next morning.

"You won't be making any more telephone calls?" the clerk asked suspiciously.

"No."

"All right then." The clerk annotated the room's card. "Come back and see us again, Mr. Kensington."

Kelton grunted noncommittally and walked out the lobby. As he strolled back to his room, the door of the room next to his opened and a man came out, heading for the lobby. Kelton smiled and said "Good evening" as they passed. "See you in the morning," added Kelton to himself as he let himself into his room.

He packed quickly, then turned off the television and lay down on the bed fully clothed. He was asleep by 10 p.m.

D. R. Evans

Nurse Emily Rogers came to the end of the short story and flipped the page of this week's *Woman's Weekly*. An interview with a prominent female politician filled the next several pages. She flicked through them quickly, looking for something more interesting.

An article comparing working women in the UK and the US caught her eye, and she began to read.

The second hand on the clock on the panel at the ICU station swept past the 12. It was five o'clock in the morning.

Emily raised a hand to her mouth as she read, unconsciously stifling a yawn.

The penetrating buzz of an alarm brought her instantly back to the here and now. All thoughts of the article fled from her head as she took in the status board at a glance. ICU 3. That was the little girl who had been in the bomb blast. The poor mite. She'd been in surgery when Nurse Jones came on duty. A major stroke, they'd said. They'd brought her into intensive care around midnight. Dr. Higgins had looked all in; Dr. Worthington had looked as if she was never going to smile again.

Dr. Worthington's boyfriend — at least, Emily assumed that he was her boyfriend — had been with them. He had wanted to drive her home, but she had insisted that she was going to stay the night at the hospital. Visitors were not allowed in the doctors' lounge where she intended to sleep, so the boyfriend had reluctantly departed by himself.

Dr. Higgins had gone home and Dr. Worthington had sat with the girl for more than an hour before tiredness had overcome her and she had retreated to the doctors' lounge to try to get a few hours' sleep.

Nurse Jones rolled back her chair and walked quickly toward ICU 3.

She stopped in the doorway, horrified. The sight that met her eyes was both terrible and terrifying.

Elizabeth's eyes were open unnaturally wide. Her normally peaceful face was as taut as a tight mask, and her body was writhing this way and that, her back arching so violently that there seemed a real possibility that she would break one of her own bones. The movement had caused the monitor leads to be pulled out of the machine. As she watched, Emily saw one of the IVs surrender to the stress and snap, sending a dribble of saline trickling to the floor.

Emily dashed to the bed and tried to hold Elizabeth down, but the little girl's muscles were too strong for her. The girl bucked wildly under Emily. Her lips were pulled back ferally, as if she were about to scream. Yet in the midst of the chaos, Emily noticed that apart from the clatter caused by her thrashing around, Elizabeth was completely silent. Not so much as a grunt or groan escape her bared teeth.

The nurse gave up after a few seconds. Leaving Elizabeth, she ran back to the ICU station and lifted the telephone to call for help.

Washington, DC

Kelton's wristwatch alarm went off at 1:30, interrupting a dream. Silencing the alarm, he stole out of the room. He left the door ajar, then padded silently across the parking lot towards the car that had been following him for the past several days.

Stuck to the rear window was a small helical antenna, betraying the presence of a carphone inside the vehicle. Kelton made sure that he was unobserved, then removed a pair of wire cutters from his pocket and cut the antenna near its base. Holding the antenna, he returned to his room, closed the door, and put the antenna in the trash can. Then he returned to bed.

An hour later, his alarm woke him again. This time he arose, grabbed his bags where he had stacked them five hours before, and noisily left the room. He banged the door behind him, then crossed the parking lot towards his car.

As Kelton slammed the trunk of the car, he smiled to see the light come on in the room next door. The light went off again, and in the spill of a lamp attached to the motel wall he saw the curtain move to one side. A dark shadow was all he could see of the man inside looking out. Kelton was tempted to wave cheerily, but checked himself in time. The man had done a good job. It was not yet time to spoil his fun.

Kelton ostentatiously looked at his wristwatch, nodded as if pleased with himself, then walked casually around to the driver's side and opened the door. He eased himself slowly into the driver's seat. On the passenger seat he placed a long, cylindrical sports bag. From the bag he removed a rifle and propped it against the seat where he could grab it in a hurry.

A man dashed across the parking lot, racing for his own car. Kelton turned the key in the ignition and eased his car out of the lot. Thirty seconds later, the tail followed.

Unheard, the phone in Kelton's room began to ring. It rang for two minutes. It stopped briefly, then rang for a further minute. Three thousand miles away, Patricia Worthington put her phone down. She pulled a handkerchief from a pocket and wiped the tears from her eyes.

Kelton made his way around the beltway and headed west. The two-car convoy crossed the border into West Virginia before sunrise.

In West Virginia, the roads were narrow, and twisted and wound their way up, down and around the rural hills. Traffic was almost nonexistent.

Dawn came, the sun rising to peer through the lowering cloud in his rear view mirror, and still Kelton drove westward. Patchy cloud covered stretches of the road and Kelton kept his lights on. Those of the car behind were extinguished in a futile effort to become invisible.

Kelton began to look for the right place to spring his trap.

They drove another ten miles, the mist gradually clearing as the sun slowly rose.

At last, Kelton's car broached a ridge, and he saw what he had been looking for.

The road turned a corner as it surmounted the ridgeline, and spread out before him Kelton saw a picturesque valley filled with evergreens and no obvious signs of habitation. About a quarter of a mile ahead, partway down the hill, a track left the road to the left, heading steeply down the incline.

The tail had not yet turned the corner. Kelton estimated he had thirty seconds in which to act. He gunned the car, heading for the opening where the track met the road.

Kelton's car sprang forwards as it accelerated; as he approached the track, Kelton turned the wheel violently and slammed his foot on the brakes. The car spun through ninety degrees and slipped sideways across the left hand side of the road, coming to rest just off the road, its front pointing towards the road, its rear facing along the track.

Kelton grabbed the rifle from the seat next to him and dived, clutching it, out the driver's door. He hit the ground, ran forward at a crouch, and threw the barrel of the rifle across the hood of the car, pointing back the way he had just come. He tapped his pocket, checking for his pistol. He looked through the rifle's telescopic sight. Moments later, his pursuer came into sight around the corner at the top of the ridge.

Kelton aimed the rifle towards the left side of the windshield as the car approached. He fired; the windshield turned instantly opaque.

The car's wheels locked as its driver slammed on the brakes. The car slid off the blacktop and hit a rut; it bounced back on to the road and finally came to a halt a couple of hundred feet up the hill and on the opposite side of the road from where Kelton crouched.

For a few seconds nothing moved; then the passenger door, on the far side of the vehicle, opened. Through the sight, Kelton caught a glimpse of a figure exiting the car.

The driver of the other car used the bulk of the vehicle and the windshield as a screen, keeping them between himself and Kelton. Kelton waited patiently for him to show himself. He was in no hurry.

After about half a minute, a head poked around the rear of the car and peered down the road toward Kelton. As soon as the man saw Kelton's rifle, he quickly disappeared again.

Kelton dropped to the ground and wormed his way through the muddy, damp grass under his car. From here he could see his quarry's feet on the far side of the other car. He watched, and he waited.

For a long time, nothing moved.

Then, without warning, Kelton heard a shout: "Look, there's no need for shooting."

The sound echoed off the pavement and the hillside before becoming lost in the still, crisp air. Kelton made no reply.

"I'm going to come out now with my hands up; OK?" the man shouted.

Still Kelton remained silent and motionless. He saw the figure straighten itself. The legs came out from behind the car and the man stood in the open, fully exposed, several feet from his car.

Kelton watched silently as the feet hesitantly began to walk towards him. Kelton eased his pistol from his pocket.

The man stopped about ten feet from Kelton's car. "Why don't you come out?" the man shouted, more loudly now, a frightened edge audible in his voice.

The man turned around, trying to see where Kelton might be hiding. As he did so, Kelton slid forward a few inches, until he could see the man's back. The man's hands were partially raised. In his right hand was a small handgun. Kelton brought his pistol forward, took careful aim and gently squeezed.

Under the car, the sound of the gunshot was deafening, and by the time Kelton had recovered his senses, the man had dropped his pistol, and was now facing Kelton's car.

He was young, in his early thirties, and his left arm was lifted across his chest, his left hand reaching over his right shoulder to clutch at the point where the bullet had entered his body. There was a bloody exit wound high on his chest. The man's face was contorted in pain, his eyes squeezed almost closed, and his breath coming in punctuated gasps.

"Back away from your gun," commanded Kelton.

The man ignored him. His face was draining of color, and Kelton wondered if he was going to faint; his eyes were glazed over and he stared vacantly toward Kelton's car.

"Take five steps backward," Kelton said. "I'll count them for you. One."

The sound of Kelton's voice penetrated to the man's consciousness. He withdrew his hand from the wound and looked at it. It was scarlet. As he looked, several red drops fell to the pavement. He took a step backwards.

"Two," Kelton said. After a pause, the man stepped backward again. The man took three more steps as Kelton slowly counted them off. Then, as the glazed eyes of the man watched him without really seeing, Kelton wriggled his way out into open and stood up.

"Here, let me look at that," said Kelton. Gently, he moved the man's hand away from the shoulder, and touched the area lightly with his own hand. The man backed away from the touch, but the pain of the contact seemed to bring him back from wherever he had been. His eyes began to clear and, for the first time, he looked at Kelton with eyes that held intelligence.

"You'll be fine," Kelton pronounced. "Come with me, we need to get your car off the road." He held out his hand to the man, and gently, as if leading a child, walked him back to his car, a process which occupied two full minutes. The man walked unsteadily, his gait more a shuffle than a walk.

"What happened?" the man asked as they reached the car.

"Don't worry. You'll be fine now. It's really only a flesh wound. Hurts like hell, but no real damage." Kelton opened the passenger door and eased the man into the vehicle, then got in and sat beside him.

He turned the car around so that its shattered windshield could not be seen by any chance passerby, then turned to look at the man beside him.

Color was returning to his face. Deliberately, Kelton pointed his pistol levelly at the man's stomach, less than a foot away. He looked the man straight in the eyes. "Now, if you know who I am, you know that I wouldn't think twice about pulling the trigger."

The man shook his head weakly. He tried to say something, but his speech was merely a hoarse groan. He stopped, swallowed several times, and tried again. "I don't know who you are, but you don't have to do anything to convince me. It's obvious you'll kill me if you want to."

"You're telling me that whoever sent you on this job didn't tell you that you were tailing an assassin?"

The man's eyes grew wide with fear. He shook his head violently, then stopped as a spasm of pain wracked him.

"No. I had no idea. Oh, God! Please don't kill me."

"Who sent you?"

"No. Please anything but that. He'll kill me if I tell you...."

The man's eyes dropped down to the pistol, and Kelton waited while the man worked it out for himself.

Eventually, the man said, "But you'll kill me if I don't, won't you?"

Kelton did not reply. The man tried to meet Kelton's steel-gray eyes, but he held them only for a moment before he was forced to look away.

"Vincent Cotterell," he said.

The man unexpectedly burst into tears, but Kelton hardly noticed; his mind was too busy racing.

Cotterell! *Cotterell!* Why the hell was Cotterell having him followed? Did he know that Kelton was the man who had killed his brother? Was that possible? Was Cotterell now planning to take his revenge for his brother's death? Was that what this was all about?

The man in the seat beside him mumbled something as he sniffed back his tears.

"Shut up," said Kelton. "I need to think."

The man shut up.

Kelton's thoughts were swirling around crazily inside his head. Could it be true? Or was he just jumping to conclusions? Did Cotterell really know, or did he just suspect? He needed to get away somewhere quiet and think it all through. But first he had to be certain the man was telling the truth.

"Are you sure it was Cotterell? Think carefully before you answer. I'll kill you if I think you're lying." Kelton raised his gun and pressed it against the man's temple.

The man swallowed nervously; sweat dribbled unheeded down his face. "He didn't give me the orders himself," he sniffed. "I'm only his head of security in Washington. But the orders came from him."

"How can you be certain?"

"I report directly to his head of personal security in New York, a man named Victor Brezhnerov. He was the one who gave me the orders. He made a point of telling me that Vincent Cotterell was taking a personal interest in you and would be watching me carefully to see how well I did. There was to be a big bonus for me if Cotterell liked the way I did the job."

"But you aren't the first man to follow me. Someone else followed me from England to Washington. When did he first pick me up?"

"I don't know. All they told me was that they'd been tailing you for a couple of weeks. That's all I know."

A couple of weeks.

Kelton thought back. Two weeks ago he was in Ireland. Surely he would have spotted a tail. Wouldn't he? But perhaps not. He had had no reason to believe he was being followed; it was all too possible that he had been careless.

"Bastard!" said Kelton involuntarily. His grip on the pistol tightened.

"Please, please don't shoot me. I'm telling the truth. I don't know any more," the man shouted, certain that he was about to die.

Kelton realized that his knuckles were white with pressure. Slowly, he pulled the pistol away from the man's head.

"Do you know why Cotterell was having me followed?"

"No. But please, he'll kill me if he ever finds out what I've told you."

"What exactly were your orders?"

"To follow you and call in whenever I saw anything out of the ordinary. If you met anyone, I was to report a description and to try to take a photograph if possible. If you took a journey anywhere, I was to follow and report in with the car telephone every hour. You made that impossible this morning," the man finished ruefully.

Kelton was silent for about ten seconds, staring out the window. Then, coming to a decision, he said, "All right. I'm sorry about the shoulder, but you'll live."

He removed the car keys from the ignition and opened the door to leave.

"Wait," said the other. "You aren't just going to leave me here, are you?"

"You aren't going to die from that wound, and there's bound to be someone along soon."

Kelton got out and returned to his car. With a squeal of tires, he pulled out into the road and raced back towards Washington.

The man watched the car disappear around the nearest bend; then he leaned forward and threw up.

Chapter 28
Saturday, December 8
Cheltenham

Mike Downing had called John Pearce at home on a private, and very secure, line. The line, after wending through the switching and scrambling circuits at GCHQ, dived underground to emerge outside Pearce's study, where it penetrated the brick wall and made its way to an old fashioned gray rotary telephone that sat on the polished oak desk that hugged one wall of the study; the line between Washington and Pearce's study was as secure and untappable as modern technology could make it.

Pearce replaced the receiver on its cradle and discovered that he was distractedly gazing at a painting of the Duke of Wellington routing Napoleon from the Belgian countryside. His mind was somewhere else entirely, trying to decide what he should do about what Downing had just told him.

The name of Sir David's killer was now known. An American called George Harris had made and exploded the device. This was exactly the information that he had hoped to get from Downing, but now that he had it, what next?

He knew what he should do, of course: call the prime minister and tell him exactly what Downing had told him. And he would do that. But the question he was wrestling with was whether to make another phone call first. If Downing's information were somehow to reach the ears of the chief of SIS, by this time tomorrow it would all be over. David's death would be avenged.

But could Pearce really do that? It was what he had been planning to do, but now that the moment was here, it was much harder than he had expected. It would mean going against everything he stood for. Did he have the right to take a man's life just for the sake of revenge?

He looked at the picture of Wellington, and was in no doubt about what that great man would have done. But Wellington had lived nearly two hundred years ago, and he was a general, a military man through and through. Pearce turned to look out the window at the drab December garden beyond the pane. It was raining.

For a long time he just sat there, without moving. At last, he picked up the telephone and dialed a Buckinghamshire number from memory.

"This is the Acting Director of GCHQ. Please tell the PM that I would like to talk with him."

The prime minister listened without once interrupting. When Pearce had finished, he asked, "And do the Americans propose to do anything with this information?"

"I don't know, sir. We did not discuss that point. But I doubt it. I strongly doubt that the information was obtained by methods that are deemed legal in the United States. Although the head of NSA is certain that Mr. Harris is the culprit, they would not dare bring him before an American jury."

"But we could bring him before a British one, could we not? The testimony relating to how he was caught can be heard in camera. The hard part would be persuading the Americans that they should extradite him." The prime minister's voice dropped as he spoke, so that it was difficult for Pearce to be certain of what he was saying; he realized that these were merely thoughts spoken out loud. The prime minister's voice became stronger again. "And you, Mr. Pearce, do you have any ideas of your own?"

There was a strained silence while Pearce struggled with his conscience. Eventually, it won. Duty first. He could not lie. "Yes, sir; I have an idea. But you won't like it."

"Does it involve, shall we say, an operation on foreign soil?"

"Yes, sir. You might call it that."

"Then I must ask you this: do you have any reason to believe that Sir David was the target of this attack? Or might he simply have been an unlucky victim?"

"The head of NSA wanted to know that as well, sir. I'm afraid that the most diligent efforts have revealed no one who might have wanted Sir David dead, except insofar as he was a political target by virtue of his position."

"Then I think we need say no more. I hereby order you to refrain from issuing any orders that might lead to action abroad. Do I make myself clear?"

Pearce nodded gratefully, even though the gesture could not be seen by the Prime Minister. The weight of responsibility had been lifted, the decision taken out of his hands. The fate of George Harris was a political matter now.

"Yes, sir; I understand."

"Good. I will discuss this matter privately with the Foreign Office and I dare say they will be in touch with you sometime in the next few days. And now, Mr. Pearce, I have visitors to entertain. Thank you for your telephone call. We shall discuss this matter further at the appropriate time."

There was a click, and the line went dead.

Chapter 29
Sunday, December 9
Between Washington, DC and New England

Reaching Interstate 81, Kelton turned his blue Oldsmobile northwards. He drove automatically, the cruise control set a couple of miles per hour above the posted limit. The morning passed almost without his noticing the fact, his mind still trying to process what the man in the car had told him.

His stomach growled, awakening him from his reverie and reminding him that he had eaten no breakfast. He pulled off the freeway and drove into a small, unmemorable town a short distance from the highway, choosing a nondescript restaurant that grandly advertised "Champagne Sunday Brunch."

He dallied over lunch, trying to decide what to do. There was no hurry. He knew where George Harris lived, and it was only a matter of time before he and Harris were alone together.

He realized that in anticipation of that meeting, he had compressed a bread roll almost to nothingness. The thought of the revenge that would soon be his was pleasant, like a child's anticipated Christmas present. But another part of his mind warned him that such emotion could be dangerous, possibly fatal. Every time he thought of how close he was to his ultimate objective, it became more difficult to remain cold and dispassionate. The ghost of Paul Kent had not been exorcised; Kent had refused to remain far away in comfortable, suburban Surrey as Kelton had intended. Instead, he was here again, once more at Kelton's shoulder, ready to invade his body and cloud his mind if Kelton let down his guard, even for a moment.

Kelton made a conscious effort to think about something else. Soon enough now, Kent would have his way, but not yet, not just yet.

What about Vincent Cotterell? How sure was Cotterell that Kelton had killed his brother? Once Kelton had dealt with Harris, would he then have to do the same with Cotterell?

The thought soured his stomach. He had thought he had put the killing behind him. It was one thing to come out of retirement to kill Harris, who deserved it for what he had done. But Cotterell was part of the past. Couldn't he just stay there?

Kelton pushed the rest of his lunch away. He was getting nowhere. But one thing he did know: George Harris had killed his wife and all but murdered his child. For now, that was all that mattered.

He paid for his meal and strode grimly from the restaurant, his face a warning to anyone who happened to glance his way.

He drove more quickly now, overriding the cruise control. Several times he discovered that he was driving too quickly, much too quickly. He forced himself to keep his foot off the accelerator, matching his speed to the trucks on the highway. Even so, his knuckles were white as they gripped the steering wheel.

It was well past midnight when he reached Manchester, New Hampshire and stopped for the night. He thought about going all the way to Torrington, but knew that when he confronted Harris he needed to be fresh. He forced himself to stop at a motel.

It was early morning in England, and he wondered what time Dr. Worthington woke up. He stretched out his hand to call her, but then changed his mind. He didn't want to know. Too much was at risk. Tomorrow, after it was over, he would call. Until then, he had a job to do.

He went to bed.

He awoke a little after six and stripped and forced himself to suffer the agony of a cold shower. The frigid water had the desired effect: when he left the bathroom he felt cleansed both physically and mentally, and his body was tingling with anticipation as he dressed.

Not much longer now.

The sun had not yet risen as Kelton left Manchester. The morning was crisp, clear and very cold, and the antelucan stars hung luminously in the sky without a trace of a twinkle. Kelton left Manchester behind, driving now along winding country roads at whose edges stood shallow banks of snow. He drove slowly, mentally preparing himself for what lay ahead.

He reached Torrington shortly before nine o'clock. The car needed gas, and hunger pangs told him that his body needed breakfast. He stopped at a service station and purchased a tank of gas and a couple of fresh doughnuts and a pint of orange juice. He ate and drank in the warmth of the station, staring blindly out the window.

Before he left, Kelton got precise directions to Harris's house from the owner of the service station.

He went to his car and started the engine. The clock on the dashboard said 9:02.

The clock on the bedside table read 9:02.

George Harris looked at it, thought about staying in bed a while longer, then told himself he was getting soft. Reluctantly, he got out of bed.

Things were back to normal, and he no longer went to sleep each night wondering whether an unwelcome visitor might decide to drop in on him before morning. He had called Vincent Cotterell the day after he had killed Brezhnerov. It had been a brief conversation in which he told Cotterell what he had done, and reinforced the message that if anything were to happen to him, the FBI would automatically be told about Cotterell's involvement with the Gatwick explosion.

Cotterell had seemed shaken by Brezhnerov's death. "I think," he had said when he had heard Harris out, "that the killing should now cease. You've also convinced me that to try to threaten you any further would be counterproductive. Let me then simply congratulate you on a job well done and let us part, if not as friends, then at least as mutually respectful colleagues."

Harris paused by the window on his way to the bathroom. There had been no fresh snow overnight, but the area surrounding the house was still virgin white from yesterday's fall. The sky was mazarine blue. He would go for a long run later; he was beginning to feel the need for exercise. He opened the window a crack, and took several deep breaths of the cold, scented air.

He showered unhurriedly. Afterwards, clad only in a dressing gown, he walked downstairs to the kitchen, where he poured himself a tall glass of orange juice and covered two slices of bread with strawberry jam while waiting for the coffee to brew.

As soon as the coffee was ready, he poured himself a cup and ambled into the living room. He put on *Abbey Road* and sat in an armchair, munching toast and sipping the hot coffee.

A few minutes later, he returned briefly to the kitchen, and came back with a fresh cup of coffee and another slice of toast. He was humming along with *Maxwell's Silver Hammer*.

His eye was caught by a movement at a window. He turned to look at it, and froze. An eternity passed in a fraction of a second. His muscles were on the point of obeying his brain's command to fling himself to the floor when the bullet hit.

The first thing he felt was the impact. There was no pain, just a sudden, irresistible force applied sharply to his right thigh.

He staggered backward, but did not immediately fall. Looking down, he saw a gout of blood coming from a small, clean dark hole in his leg.

His mind seemed to accept the fact that he had been shot, and almost immediately encouraged itself with the sequential observations that he was still standing, that there was no pain, and that the thigh was probably the best place one could ever hope to be shot.

Then two things happened, almost simultaneously. One was that the pain suddenly impacted itself on his brain. The other was that his right leg buckled without warning.

As he fell, a pistol butt smashed into the window from outside, scattering splinters over the floor. A gloved hand reached in and began to brush away the remnants of the pane from its frame. Upstairs, next to his bed, a red light began to flash.

Harris tried to rise, using the table for support, his eyes fixed in disbelief on the window through which the shot had come. It couldn't be. It was simply impossible. His eyes must be playing tricks.

He tried to stand, but his body shot through with pain as soon as he tried to put any weight on his right leg. He looked around for a weapon, but the best he could come up with was the plate and glass from his breakfast, which were hardly likely to be effective against a man with a gun.

The man was forcing himself with difficulty through the gap he had made. He was wearing a dark green balaclava that hid all of his face except for two narrow slits for the eyes. But there was something horribly familiar about the man's bulk and the way he moved.

Eventually, the man was through, and he dropped heavily to the floor. He turned to face Harris. He was swathed in heavy, dark clothes, protection both against the cold outside which now began to invade the room and against being seen at night. Harris realized that the man must have been waiting in ambush. Normally, Harris would have risen earlier, and it would still have been dark when he came downstairs.

If only he had looked more carefully when he had glanced out his window, perhaps he would have seen traces of the man skulking in the woods. But such thoughts ebbed from his mind as the man stopped in front of him and raised his hand to remove the balaclava.

Harris gasped. "You."

Brezhnerov smiled, then gave a little bow. "I trust you will forgive the somewhat melodramatic entrance. But yes, indeed, it is I." The smile broadened to a smirk.

"But you're dead."

"If you say so."

"But I killed you. I saw you go down. I saw your blood." Harris was almost shouting, as if by protesting loudly enough and with sufficient conviction, he could send this ghost back to the grave where it belonged.

Brezhnerov shook his head gently, then tutted. "Never believe everything you see, Mr. Harris. Also, never believe everything you are told, especially by a very smart multimillionaire who is used to getting his own way."

Harris lapsed into silence. But his eyes remained riveted on Brezhnerov. It couldn't be. It just couldn't be. He had killed the man himself. Two shots, both into the man's trunk. Even if the man had been miraculously lucky and the bullets had somehow failed to kill him, it was not possible that he had had time to recover. Even if he wasn't dead, he should still be in hospital. And the blood; Brezhnerov had lost too much blood for him to survive. No. Brezhnerov was dead.

Or was he? Maybe it hadn't been Brezhnerov.... It was a ringer! He'd killed a ringer. He groaned as it all became clear.

"Ah, you have a theory," said Brezhnerov. "Good. I am glad you haven't let the inconvenience of a bullet in your thigh affect your thought processes. Incidentally, you are almost right. It was me that you shot. And it hurt like hell, let me tell you that."

"But it couldn't have been you. I killed the man I shot."

Brezhnerov shook his head.

"No. You hurt me. That's all. But I deserved it for underestimating you.

"I made a mistake by not coming here to kill you myself. I realized that as soon as the call came through that night you let the driver go. I think, Mr. Harris, that perhaps that fiasco encouraged you to sadly underestimate our efficiency. By the time you left here next morning, you were under surveillance. We followed you to New York, and I kept asking myself what you were up to. It wasn't until you went to Collingswood that I understood that you meant to kill me.

"From that point on it was easy. When you shot me I was wearing a Kevlar jacket augmented with bags of artificial blood. The demonstrations I saw beforehand were most impressive, and of course we both know that it convinced you as well. Although I must ask if that second bullet was really necessary."

"But why did you do it? If you were having me watched, you could have picked me off at any time."

"I wanted to come and get you myself, in my own time, on your own territory. You were obviously bent on revenge. The simplest course was to let you believe that you had killed me, that Mr. Cotterell had succumbed to your demands, and that you were safe. That meant I could deal with you at my leisure. Which is exactly what I'm doing now."

Brezhnerov sat down in a comfortable chair, his back to the window through which he had entered the room, and looked across the short distance that separated him from Harris.

"But what about your family?" Harris persisted. "I might have shot them."

Brezhnerov shook his head. "No. You were being watched the whole time. If you had looked like you were about to shoot my wife or son, you'd have been shot before you could pull the trigger. Fortunately, that was not necessary."

"So what happens now?"

"You and I, Mr. Harris, have a brief chat about the ways of the world, and then you get a second bullet somewhere where it will do permanent damage and make you very, very dead."

Harris's mind was beginning to clear, the urgency of the situation forcing the pain in his leg into a corner of his mind. Surely there was something he could do to turn the tables on Brezhnerov. All he needed was a little time to think.

But there was no time.

"Now," Brezhnerov said, "let's see if you can come up with a good reason why I shouldn't kill you right now." He raised his gun so that it pointed directly at Harris's head. There was not the slightest tremor in Brezhnerov's hand. Harris looked along the weapon, beyond it, directly into Brezhnerov's unblinking right eye.

"I don't understand," Harris said, genuinely puzzled. "I meant what I told Cotterell. In the event of my sudden death, the information about his part in the Gatwick bombing will be made public."

"Is that all? Or is there more?"

Harris did not immediately answer the question, because at this moment he heard something that momentarily distracted him. While Brezhnerov had been talking, the music had continued playing on the stereo. Harris knew the music well, and he was certain that the track just ending contained no sound like a distant gunshot. The gunshot, he was almost certain, had come from outside.

Brezhnerov seemed not to have noticed, either because he was unfamiliar with the music or because he was seated closer to the speakers.

Harris clung to the sound of the gunshot; the possibility that something was going wrong outside was his only hope of getting out of this situation alive. He had to keep Brezhnerov talking.

"Isn't that enough?" he asked.

"Mr. Cotterell says it's not." Brezhnerov closed his left eye, and sighted down the barrel with his right.

"But what about the contract on Cotterell's life?"

The words came out without any thought, and Harris had no idea what he was going to say next, but he knew that if he did not divert Brezhnerov, any help from outside would arrive too late.

Brezhnerov opened his eye and lowered the gun, pointing it now towards the floor near Harris's feet. He frowned. "What contract?"

"Is it past nine o'clock yet?"

Brezhnerov glanced at his watch. "Yes. Why?"

"Because Vincent Cotterell was going to be shot at 9 a.m. EST this morning. And if the message I sent warning him didn't get to him in time, you've seen your employer for the last time. If it did, how are you going to explain to him that you just killed the man who saved his life?"

Brezhnerov sat without moving, his brow corrugated as he tried to decide if he should believe the man on the floor before him. He was probably lying. But the risk was too great to take a chance.

"Wait a minute," he growled, "let me see if I have this straight. Are you trying to tell me that someone was going to make an attempt on Cotterell's life this morning? And that you sent him a message to warn him?"

"Exactly," nodded Harris. He suddenly winced, holding tightly to his thigh and catching his breath, as if in agony, although in fact the pain in his thigh was now no more than a deep, penetrating throb.

"You're bluffing."

Harris looked up, pain all over his face. "All right, I'm bluffing. So shoot me," he said, drawing his breath in shallow pants.

Brezhnerov lifted the pistol, and took aim. Then he lowered the weapon again. There was no pleading in Harris's face; nothing was written there except the agony of his wound.

"When should he have received this message?" Brezhnerov asked.

"I've no idea. We communicate through an electronic mail system, using computers. It would be about a week ago now that I sent him the message. I've no idea when, or even whether, he received it."

"A week ago? I was with Mr. Cotterell yesterday afternoon, and he never said anything to me about it then."

There was a telephone on a table within reach of the armchair in which Brezhnerov was seated. He put the pistol down and pulled the instrument towards him.

Harris watched him through half-closed eyes. He forced himself to ignore the pain in his leg, but maintained an expression of wracking agony on his face. If only he could catch Brezhnerov somehow off guard. A flying leap using his good leg, and the mug of coffee thrown in Brezhnerov's face, might just do it. If he could rely on his body to do as he commanded it.

Brezhnerov lifted the phone. Behind him and framing his face was the window through which he had earlier entered. Then, astonishingly, for a fraction of a second, another man's face appeared around the frame of the window. The man looked into the room, then just as suddenly he was gone, so quickly that Harris was not completely certain that he had not imagined it.

Brezhnerov began to stab at the digits on the face of the telephone. Harris's eyes flickered between Brezhnerov and the window. The face returned.

From where he was slumped, Harris could not see any of the man's body below the face; the bulk of Brezhnerov and the chair in which he was sitting made that impossible. Noisily, Harris began to drag himself across the floor, away from Brezhnerov and towards a sofa. Brezhnerov watched him disinterestedly, engrossed in conversation on the phone.

Harris propped himself against the sofa and glanced back toward the window. Now his view was unimpeded, and it was difficult to stop himself from smiling at what he saw, for the man's arm was raised, and in it he held a pistol that wavered midway between Brezhnerov and Harris, as if the man was unsure whom he should shoot.

Harris did not recognize the man, who was about his own height, but somewhat older, with hair beginning to gray at the temples. The man's eyes, even at this distance, looked like cold steel.

Brezhnerov interrupted his examination of the man at the window. "You will be pleased to hear that Mr. Cotterell is alive and well, Mr. Harris. He knows nothing of any message from you about an attack on his life; he is checking right now whether any messages have come in from you in the past week. I hope for your sake that you're telling the truth, because if you aren't, my orders are to kill you without wasting any more time."

"Don't worry. The message will be there. I even signed it with my real name, George Harris."

The man at the window was craning forward in an effort to hear the conversation between Brezhnerov and Harris, his task made difficult by the sound of the Beatles still coming from the speakers. But he must have caught Harris's name, because now the man nodded.

A wave of relief swept over Harris as the man's arm swiveled slightly until it was pointing squarely at the back of the chair in which Victor Brezhnerov was seated.

Chapter 30
Sunday, December 9
Torrington, VT

Kelton spotted the turning off the road with no difficulty. It was a narrow track, just wide enough for a single vehicle, disappearing quickly into the woods to his right. There were car tracks in the snow, which had been crushed until it was no more than a thin, dirty layer over the frozen mud of the track. He pulled off the road and began to follow the twin ruts.

He was surprised to see, a short distance down the track and completely hidden from the road by a bend, an empty Range Rover parked off to one side, tight against the trees. Kelton stopped his car in the middle of the track. Cautiously, he picked up his rifle and pistol and flicked the safeties off.

He slowly opened the car door, then got out, locking the door behind him, and disappeared into the forest. He listened for any unnatural sound. The air was quiet and still, the snow and the trees deadening all sound. Cautiously, he began to move through the trees toward the house.

He had taken no more than half a dozen steps when the unmistakable sound of a gunshot shattered the still air. The shot was from a small caliber weapon, a pistol rather than a rifle, and it had come from somewhere in front of him. The shot was followed by flurries of snow falling from trees all around.

He halted, holding his breath, trying to filter out the sounds of the falling snow and the blood pumping through his ears, listening intently for any more unnatural sounds. From the same direction as the shot had come, he thought he caught the faint sound of tinkling glass.

He waited, and the tinkling sound abated. He counted to one hundred, slowly, taking a full two minutes to do so. Then he resumed moving, slower and even more cautiously now, moving directly towards the sounds that had disturbed the still morning air.

Kelton reached the edge of a clearing and looked out from the shadow of the trees at the house that stood before him.

It was a moment before he saw the anomaly: immediately to the right of the front door, a window was missing its glass, and through the breach he could make out the sound of music. It was some sort of rock music, something he recognized but could not immediately place. He watched the house, looking for any sign of movement.

After a few moments, a man appeared around the left corner of the house. Kelton froze, afraid that if he drew back further into the shadows, the motion would give him away. The man was short and bundled warmly against the cold, looking like a bloated animal readying itself for hibernation.

The man stopped and looked at the forest surrounding the house, his eyes scanning the trees warily. They swept past Kelton without pausing.

Apparently satisfied that no untoward danger lurked nearby, the man leaned against the wooden siding of the house. In his hands he held a small handgun. With some difficulty, for he did not relax his grip on his weapon, he extracted a pack of cigarettes and a lighter from an inner pocket of his coat. He removed a cigarette, lit it, and returned the lighter and pack to their place of safety. Putting the cigarette to his mouth, he closed his eyes as he enjoyed the first lungful of smoke. The hand holding the gun hung limply at his side, his left hand keeping a careful grasp of the cigarette.

Kelton dropped his pistol into a pocket and swiftly lifted the rifle to his shoulder. It took only a single shot. He did not even bother to watch while the man crumpled to the ground, but instead turned his attention to the open window, waiting expectantly for some indication that the shot had been heard.

But nothing happened and, after half a minute or so, Kelton stepped out into the clearing. The tracks in the snow made the story clear enough. There had been two men: one he had seen and already dealt with; the second was responsible for the broken window and was now inside the house. Kelton safed the rifle and leaned it against the trunk of a tree.

Pulling the pistol from his pocket, he raced from the trees to the house, where he flattened himself against the siding near the corner where the dead man's body lay sprawled on reddened snow. He began to move along the side of the house toward the open window. He passed the front door without incident, took two more steps, and was now immediately adjacent to the opening. The music was louder now. Kelton realized that the music was loud enough that it was possible that the gunshot might not have been audible inside the house.

Underneath the music, a conversation was taking place inside the room. He could hear the sounds of speech clearly enough, but it was impossible to hear exactly what was being said. He inched towards the window frame, then, in a single rapid motion, thrust his head into the opening, looked inside, and withdrew once more.

He examined the eidetic image that had been imprinted on his mind.

There appeared to be only one occupant of the room — at least, his mind had registered only one in that fraction of a second. A man in his mid-thirties was slouched on the floor roughly in the middle of the room. He was dressed only in a loosely wrapped bathrobe. Most of the man's inner thigh was exposed, and although Kelton could not recall the details, it was impossible to miss the fact that both the thigh and the floor were drenched in red. The man was looking up into an armchair whose back was toward Kelton.

Was there another person in the room, someone who had wounded the man, someone who was now sitting in the armchair? Slowly, Kelton inched forward until he stood clearly framed in the window, his pistol pointing into the room.

Now it was obvious that the room did indeed have a second occupant, seated in the armchair, the top of his head barely visible over the back of the chair. He was leaning forward across the arm of the chair, dialing a telephone that sat on a small table.

Kelton watched the wounded man as he dragged himself across the floor and came to rest slouched with his back against a sofa. The man returned Kelton's gaze, just for a moment, before his eyes went back to the man in the armchair. Kelton directed his pistol halfway between the room's two occupants, prepared to let events inside to continue, but also ready to interrupt at any moment if it became necessary.

One of these men was almost certainly George Harris. And whoever the other one was hardly mattered, for Harris belonged to Kelton and Kent, and to them alone. He waited, arms outstretched, the pistol steady in his hands, waiting for the first sign of a suspicious move from either of them.

The man on the floor was indeed wounded in the thigh. The wound did not look too bad, certainly not life-threatening, but it would be enough to slow the man down. The man at the telephone looked away from the instrument and addressed the other; Kelton craned his neck so that his head was now completely inside the room, but still the music drowned out the words of the man in the chair.

But he heard the response clearly enough, even if he did not understand it: "Don't worry. The message will be there. I even signed it with my real name, George Harris."

The wounded man was Harris. That was all he needed to know. Kelton nodded his recognition of Harris's name, then swung his arm slightly, until the gun was aimed at the back of the armchair. After coming all this way, Kelton had no intention of letting someone else deny him his revenge.

The man in the armchair spoke briefly into the telephone, then replaced it on the hook. He turned to Harris, said something that Kelton could not make out, and raised a gun.

Kelton did not hesitate; he pulled the trigger twice, not wanting to risk the possibility that the first bullet might be deflected by the armchair.

There was an involuntary cry of pained surprise, then the arm of the man in the armchair spasmed and fell limp; the gun that he had been holding clattered to the floor, his arm dangling loosely over the arm of the chair and almost touching the floor near the gun.

Kelton waited. There was no more movement from the chair.

Kelton watched Harris's eyes slide across the floor to the gun. They looked at it for a moment, and Kelton could see that Harris was deciding how long it would take him to cover the distance to the weapon. Then Harris's eyes rose and met his own. One look at the steel of Kelton's eyes was enough to convince Harris to stay where he was.

Never letting the pistol in his hand waver for more than a moment, Kelton made his way through the smashed window. Once inside, he walked to the armchair and wordlessly picked the gun off the floor. He safed the weapon and put it in his pocket.

He did not recognize the man in the armchair. He was, or had been, a large man: not stout, but with a heavy build on a large frame. The man's head lolled to one side, his mouth slightly open. There was a tiny dribble of blood leaking from the lower corner. His eyes were open. His face was already turning the flaccid pale yellow-white of Caucasian death.

Kelton turned to Harris.

"How do I turn off the music?"

Harris, now that the twin shocks of the shot in his leg and Brezhnerov's miraculous appearance alive here in his own house were no longer important, suddenly felt very weak and tired. He had no idea who this stranger might be, nor did he care very much. All he knew was that he had been about to die and this man had saved him. He felt lightheaded, as if the whole thing might have been nothing but a dream. Suddenly, all he wanted to do was to close his eyes and sleep.

Kelton repeated his question, and it slowly penetrated Harris's mind that the man who had saved his life was asking him something. He tried to concentrate on the sounds the man was making. "The music? Over there," he said, but his voice came out as a weak mumble that would have been incomprehensible were it not for the slight nod that accompanied it.

Kelton walked to the stereo and pressed the switch. The Beatles were extinguished, and silence fell on the room.

Kelton went back to the armchair and looked down at the man who still leaned against the sofa. His face looked unnaturally pale.

"George Harris, I presume," Kelton said. He spoke gently, and his face softened to match the words. "I'm a friend," he seemed to be saying without actually saying so.

Harris nodded. He made an effort to speak clearly. "Yes, and thank you. I'm afraid I'm not feeling up to much. I've been shot." He smiled feebly. Then, without warning, his body went limp.

Kelton slapped him back to consciousness. "Bite your lip and the inside of your cheek. Try to stay awake," he said as he pulled back the dressing gown and quickly examined the wound.

It was superficial, the bullet still lodged somewhere inside the fleshy part of the leg. The real danger was from loss of blood. He came to a quick decision.

He looked up from the wound. Harris's eyes were on him, but they were having difficulty staying focused.

"Right," said Kelton, "I'll need a couple of pairs of good, stout tweezers, a box of matches, whatever bandages you have in the house, a drinking glass and a good sized bottle of some spirit with a kick to it. Do you have all those in the house?"

It was several moments before Harris understood what the man had asked. He nodded. Kelton went through the list again, item by item, and to each Harris grunted a word to tell him where the required object might be found.

Kelton said, "Don't move. Keep your hand on the wound. Try to stop it from bleeding any more."

Then he moved away in search of everything he needed. It was less than three minutes before they were in a neat row on a towel on the floor beside Harris. Harris had lain down on the floor in the meantime, and there was a tinge of color now in Harris's cheeks and his eyes were beginning to focus again.

"What are you going to do?" Harris asked.

"Take the bullet out."

Harris accepted this at face value. His brain was beyond questioning the logic of events as they unfolded.

Kelton opened the bottle, and filled the glass to within half an inch of the rim with golden Mount Gay rum. He handed it to Harris, helping the wounded man to hold the glass steady. "Right. Drink this, as quickly as you can."

He helped Harris to tip the glass. Some of the liquor dribbled down Harris's face, but most of it went into his mouth and then down his throat. Kelton poured a second glass, as large as the first one.

"Now drink this one, only more slowly this time. Don't try to talk."

Harris seemed stronger, and drank from it without help this time. He drank more slowly, as Kelton had ordered him, taking a large sip every few seconds.

The glass was about half drained when the tiredness, which had retreated, suddenly returned with a vengeance. Harris found the glass suddenly too heavy to hold. Kelton took its weight just as Harris's hands relaxed. His eyes closed, his head lolled to one side, and he lapsed into unconsciousness.

The operation took about half an hour. There were no complications, and afterwards Kelton could not resist a feeling of satisfaction as he dressed the wound.

The job done, Kelton found a couple of blankets to keep Harris warm and a pillow to keep his head comfortably raised from the floor. That task accomplished, Kelton looked across to the body in the chair and remembered that there was a second body outside. Even though this was a remote place, it would be folly to leave bodies in plain view.

He spent the next quarter of an hour dragging the two bodies into the woods, then another ten minutes scrubbing himself clean. Neither of the bodies carried identification. A search of the Range Rover also revealed nothing.

When Kelton returned from the car, Harris was sleeping comfortably in the middle of the living room, his chest rising and falling peacefully in sleep. Kelton walked to the sofa and sat down. Absent-mindedly he pulled out his pipe and a tin of tobacco. For half a minute he concentrated on the job of cleaning out the pipe and packing it with fresh tobacco. Then he spent another half minute carefully lighting it and ensuring that it drew properly. That done, he leaned back contentedly, and stretched his legs out before him. He lifted his eyes to the ceiling and began to ponder his position.

Harris presumably knew the identity of at least one of the two men Kelton had killed. But Kelton could not guess who he might have been. Was it a business deal gone sour? Gatwick, perhaps? Or was it something else entirely?

He thought about calling Downing. Kelton would not have been at all surprised to learn that Downing was somehow involved in whatever he had interrupted. He weighed the thought carefully, then decided that it would cost him nothing to wait until Harris was conscious and could give him his side of the story.

When he had finished his pipe, he explored the house, checking on Harris every couple of minutes. But he found nothing, and after a while time began to hang heavily.

It was past two when Harris awoke for the first time.

Harris knew instantly that waking was a mistake. He had a vague recollection of the events of the morning; but his leg was agony, making it difficult to think. Even worse, he was drunk.

By itself, being drunk may not have been such a bad thing, but to be drunk and to know it and to want desperately not to be drunk is a singularly unpleasant and frustrating state in which to find oneself. Harris opened his eyes, made a few incoherent grumbles to the stranger standing over him, and then passed out once more.

Kelton looked at his watch, and decided that it was late enough now that he could call Dr. Worthington. Harris would sleep for another hour or more yet. He could afford to let Kent have his way for a while.

He made the call in the kitchen. The phone was answered before it had completed its first ring.

She interrupted as soon as he identified himself. "Mr. Kent. I tried to call you as soon as it happened, but no one answered the phone. Then I expected you to call yesterday, but somehow I missed you."

"I'm sorry. I've been very busy. What's the matter? Is something wrong?"

"Oh, Mr. Kent. I'm so sorry. It all happened without warning in the middle of the night. Elizabeth's dead. It happened a few hours after her stroke. She had some kind of a fit; the nurse couldn't restrain her so she went to get help. When she got back, only about a minute later, Elizabeth had stopped breathing. We couldn't resuscitate her. We did everything we could, but her systems simply closed down one after another." The doctor's voice began to break up. For a moment, he thought it was the connection, but then he realized that she was crying.

"Thank you," he said mechanically. A long silence hung in the air, punctuated only by the sound of sniffles coming down the line. "Thank you, doctor, for everything you've done."

He put the phone down.

For a long time he stared vacantly at the phone. Then he turned and went back into the living room where Harris still slept on the floor.

His fists clenched, he stood over the inert form. "It was you, wasn't it? I'm going to kill you, you bastard."

He fought the temptation to get it over with, to smash the bastard's head to a pulp in his drunken sleep. But that was what Kent would do: that would be the act of a normal man given his chance to vent his anger on the man who had killed his wife and daughter. But he was Kelton, not Kent. Now more than ever he had to be Kelton, otherwise everything would be ruined and he would lose his chance for real revenge. Before Harris could die, he had to condemn himself out of his own mouth. There must be no uncertainty.

And he had to give Kelton a name.

Kelton was beginning to get nervous long before Harris woke the second time. It was only a matter of time before the two men he had killed were missed. What then? He decided that if Harris was not awake by six, he would wake him himself.

It was ten minutes before six when Harris awoke for the second time.

The pain in his leg was considerably less now. Instead of a deep throb that was accentuated with every heartbeat, the pain was now merely a general, diffuse ache down the entire length of the leg. Even better, although his head still felt as if it were packed with some sort of woolly material through which each thought had to struggle, at least he could think, which was a definite improvement.

He tried to prop himself up on his arms, but gave up on that exercise as the room began to spin dizzily around his head. Lying down once more, he looked up at the man who had saved his life.

The man began to speak. His accent, Harris now noticed, was English.

"Ah, good; you're awake," the man said. "Hang on a minute, and I'll get you something."

Vaguely, part of Harris's brain realized how ridiculous was the admonition to "hang on a minute"; even better, some other part of him realized that his brain must be functioning reasonably well if he were capable of such a logical deduction. He mused on these thoughts for a while before realizing that the man was now bending down beside him and offering him a glass almost filled with a muddy red liquid.

He raised his head a little, and managed to bring a hand around to steady the glass. He spluttered and nearly spat the liquid out as it hit the back of his throat with an unexpected sharpness. He recovered himself, and at the man's insistence continued drinking, more cautious now, until, suddenly, he discovered that the glass was empty.

"How do you feel?" the man asked.

Harris was surprised at the strength of his voice as he replied. Indeed, his entire body seemed considerably strengthened by the draught he had just taken.

"I've been better, but not too bad, considering," he said. "What on earth was in that drink?"

Kelton told him, while wondering how sober Harris really was. How long did a man's liver take to process the alcohol in two long glasses of Bajan rum?

Harris was becoming agitated, as the full memory of the morning's events returned like an avalanche. Who was this man who had saved his life? And what was he doing here? As to the man's profession, Harris could make an educated guess. The way that the man handled a gun showed him to be more than usually conversant with weapons. A soldier, perhaps?

"Who are you?" he asked at last.

"My name is Kelton," the other said.

Harris's jaw slackened. Kelton. For a moment his mind refused to function.

Kelton was explaining, "I used to be in the same business as you. Perhaps you've heard of me," but Harris was not listening. Two thoughts had struck him, stark in their juxtaposition: this is a man who used to kill for a living, perhaps the best there's ever been — and this is the man who saved my life.

It was several seconds before Harris recovered sufficiently to speak.

"Kelton," he said, nodding. "Of course I've heard of you. You were the man I modeled myself after." But there was a question that had to be asked, needed desperately to be answered. "Thank you for what you did. I owe you my life. But how did you know that Cotterell's hitman would be here?"

It says much about Harris's state of mind that he failed to notice Kelton's reaction to this question. For a long moment Kelton's shock was nakedly apparent; then he turned away. When he looked back, his face was composed, relaxed. But behind the face, his brain was working overtime.

What the hell did Cotterell have to do with George Harris?

It was one more unanswered question; and somehow, everything led back to Cotterell. For five years, the man had been just a name from the past, his brother a contract fulfilled. Now, all of a sudden, Cotterell's name seemed to be everywhere. Cotterell had been having him followed. To what purpose? Cotterell had been on the point of having George Harris killed. Why? What was Harris to Cotterell? Somewhere, there was a link that tied everything together. What was it?

"Cotterell? You mean Vincent Cotterell?" he asked.

Harris nodded.

"Are you sure they were Cotterell's men?"

"There was more than one?" Harris looked puzzled. He looked across the room to the armchair and realized for the first time that it was empty. He looked quizzically at Kelton.

"There was another one guarding the place outside. Don't worry, I got him first."

Harris remembered the gunshot that Brezhnerov had failed to hear, and nodded to himself. "I heard it."

"I dragged the two of them out into the woods. We'll have to do something about them, but not right now. How can you be sure they were Cotterell's men?" Kelton asked again.

"The guy in the armchair, that was Cotterell's head of personal security. We've met before. And anyway, he was on the phone to Cotterell just before you killed him. There's no doubt about it: they were Cotterell's men all right."

Kelton made a snap decision. Now there was nothing for it. He needed answers. He had to talk to Downing.

"OK," he said smartly. "You stay here and rest. I'll be back shortly."

Kelton went into the kitchen. *Damn it*, he nearly swore out loud. What did Downing know that he hadn't told him? Something, he was sure of that. It had been Downing who had given him the contract to kill Carl Cotterell, and it was Downing who had directed him here, obviously intending that Kelton would kill Harris. What sort of game was Downing playing? It was time he started answering some very pointed questions.

Kelton lifted the telephone receiver from the cradle on the kitchen wall, and dialed a Washington number from memory.

Before the first ring had ended, the usual nondescript female voice came on the line and said, "Good morning. Mike's Used Books. May I help you?"

Kelton struggled to restrain himself, knowing that losing his temper with the hired help would get him nowhere fast.

"This is an urgent message for Mr. Downing," he said in forced, level tones. "My name is Kelton, K-E-L-T-O-N. Have him call me at 802-447-9275 immediately. Tell him that lives may depend on it."

"Mr. Downing? I am afraid we don't have anyone by that name here. Are you...."

"He's your bloody Deputy Director," interrupted Kelton curtly, and immediately hung up. The explicit statement would ensure that his message reached its destination in record time, even if Downing was on the other side of the world.

He walked back to the living room and resumed his place on the sofa. In his absence, Harris had managed to shuffle across the floor so that he now leant against the armchair, looking quite comfortable.

"How's the leg?" asked Kelton.

"Hurts like hell. But thanks anyway."

"For asking, or for fixing it?"

Harris laughed. Not a deep, full laugh, but the tightly controlled laugh of a man in pain, who is afraid that too much movement will simply make the pain worse. "Both, I guess. Why'd you fix it, anyway?"

"It didn't look too hard, and it would have been pretty difficult to explain the situation to a doctor, especially with one corpse outside and another in the armchair. Now, if you'll forgive me, I think, under the circumstances, that I should be the one entitled to ask questions first. Why is Cotterell trying to kill you?"

"Well...." Harris was cut short by the sound of the telephone ringing.

Kelton stood up, and Harris said, "Don't worry, the answering machine will get it in a couple of rings."

Kelton did not pause. He ran for the kitchen, where he would be safely out of Harris's hearing, and grabbed the telephone just as it began its third ring. "Hello," he said breathlessly, barely preëmpting the machine.

"Good evening. I am looking for a Mr. Kelton. I was told that I might reach him at this number."

"Hello, Mike."

"Hello, Kelton. Sorry, I didn't recognize your voice for a moment. You sound as if you've been running. Not from anyone, I hope?"

"Why? Did you have someone in mind?"

There was a pause, slight but noticeable. "No, of course not."

"Mike, do you know where I am?"

"If I remember the number right, you're at Harris's house."

"Got it in one, Mike. I'm in Harris's kitchen. Harris is in the room next door, recovering from a gunshot wound. He'll live."

"Kelton, I don't think I want to know any of this...."

"Just listen to me, you bastard. And don't you dare put the phone down on me, or I swear I'll come after you as well."

"What's the matter? Something's happened to you, hasn't it? What is it?"

"Answer me one question: what does Vincent Cotterell have to do with George Harris?"

There was a long silence.

"Let me tell you what I know," continued Kelton. "I know that the man who was following me worked for Cotterell. I also know that I arrived here just in time to stop Harris being killed by one of Cotterell's men. Would you like for me to draw the obvious conclusion?"

"I'm sorry, Kelton."

"Why the hell didn't you tell me, Mike?"

"Because it wasn't necessary. And because the killing has to stop somewhere. And, I guess, because we can't figure out why Cotterell would want to kill David."

"So Cotterell goes free?"

"Listen, Kelton. We took the law into our hands once before. I realize now I shouldn't even have told you about Harris. My fondness for David got the better of me. I should...."

"David be damned! You haven't got it yet, have you, Mike?"

"Got what? What are you trying to say?"

"David Shackleton had nothing to do with any of this. He wasn't the intended target, and he wasn't the reason I came after Harris."

"What are you getting at? I don't understand."

"Cast your mind back five years, Mike. What was the last job I did, just before I retired?"

"The one you did for me."

"Say it, Mike. Say it out loud. What was that job?"

"Are you recording this, Kelton?"

"You have my word. No. Now say it."

"You... you killed Carl Cotterell."

"And do you know why I didn't take any more jobs after that?"

"No."

"Because I got married, Mike. I got married, and settled down, and after a while we had a little girl.

"One last question. Where do you think my wife and four-year-old daughter were on the morning of the sixteenth of November?"

There was a drawn out silence before the Deputy Director of the NSA exclaimed hollowly, "Oh my God! No!"

"Yes. It wasn't Sir David that Cotterell was after. It was my family. My wife was killed outright. My daughter has lain in a hospital bed unconscious ever since it happened, fighting for her life. I talked to her doctor only a few hours ago. She's dead, Mike. My wife and my daughter are both dead. So don't try to stop me. Harris and Cotterell are both mine."

He slammed the phone down, paused to gain control of himself, then turned away. If Downing interfered, he too would be a dead man.

A minute later, Kelton entered the living room with two large glasses of orange juice. He offered one to Harris with a smile, then settled himself on the sofa. "Now, where were we? Oh yes, you were about to explain why Vincent Cotterell wants you dead."

"I did a job for him. Now he wants to get rid of me because I'm the only one who knows about the job who isn't directly on his payroll."

Kelton looked as if he were digesting this information, then he asked, "Isn't he risking a lot? I mean, surely it should be obvious to him that you're a professional and therefore it's much more likely that you'll be able to dispose of him rather than the other way around?"

"Yes, I keep thinking the same thing. But look at what happened today. This was the second time he's tried to have me killed. After the first attempt I thought I'd make sure he wouldn't try again. I guess I thought wrong. If it weren't for the pure chance that you were here, Brezhnerov, the big man, would killed me. But that's something else that's been puzzling me: how come you happened to arrive here just in time to stop Brezhnerov? What are you even doing in the States? I thought you were retired."

"Cotterell was having me followed, for reasons I still don't understand; but yesterday I had a little chat with the man who was tailing me. He told me that Cotterell intended to kill you this morning. I recognized your name, of course, but I had to call in a bunch of favors to find out where you lived. I guess I got here just in time.

"Anyway, to get back to you; what job did you pull for Cotterell? I don't remember any assassinations in the past couple of months."

This was it: the moment he had been waiting for ever since the explosion. Everything had pointed to Harris. It had to be Harris. There was no one else. But would Harris now condemn himself with his own words? He hoped that Harris had not noticed how nervous he was.

"It wasn't supposed to be obvious," Harris said. "Do you remember the Gatwick bombing a few weeks ago?"

So it *was* Harris. And, behind him, Cotterell. The were no pieces missing now. The puzzle was complete.

Kelton swallowed the lump in his throat and asked in as normal a voice as he could muster, "Yes, I remember. Some bigwig in the British Secret Service was killed, wasn't he?"

"Yes, that's the one. Well, that was the job that Cotterell paid me for."

"But what connection could there possibly be between a wealthy American businessman and a British spy?"

"That's the funny thing about the whole business. There was no connection at all. The man who was killed was head of one of their spy agencies. But he wasn't the target."

Kelton heard himself ask the question as if from a very great distance. "But then who was the target? He was the one that the papers made all the fuss about."

"True, but his presence was simply a coincidence. No, the real targets were a woman and her four-year-old daughter. Their names were Catherine and Elizabeth Kent. I never could understand why Cotterell wanted them dead."

Kelton turned away, and covered his sudden desire to throw up by hurrying to the kitchen and dousing his face under running water.

When he returned a couple of minutes later his face was grim but he was once more in control of his emotions. He sat down. Harris looked at him speculatively, but Kelton just told him to continue with his story.

"I never could figure out for sure who the Kents were," said Harris, "or what relationship they had to Vincent Cotterell. Cotterell claimed that the woman had been blackmailing him for years. I checked out the place where they lived, and they sure got a pile of money from somewhere. No one seemed to know how the Kents had come by their money — I asked around — so maybe Cotterell's blackmail story was true. I don't know. But he sure wanted them dead. Paid five million dollars, up front, the biggest contract I ever had. And he was very concerned that it look like an accident so that no one would suspect it was a job. I think I did that pretty well.

"I called a newspaper and gave them the story that the ILF was responsible, and everyone seemed to buy it, a least for a while. The Brits seem to have finally figured out that the ILF had nothing to do with it, but I was careful not to leave any clues and I don't think I'm in any danger of being caught. Shackleton being there was just icing on the cake; everyone naturally assumed he was the target. It all worked out very nicely."

Kelton said, with the greatest effort he had ever made to speak normally, "Yes, it's all worked out very nicely; except that your client is now trying to kill you."

"True. And as I said, this is the second time he's tried. The first time was a couple of weeks ago, in the middle of the night. I killed one man and sent a second back to Cotterell with a message that he'd better not try again, otherwise the news that he was behind the Gatwick bombing would come out.

"I don't understand why he'd want to risk that by coming back for me a second time. Maybe he thought I was bluffing, but I'm not. If anything happens to me, I've left strict orders for a computer file to be sent to the FBI. It doesn't make sense."

"You think he might come back for you a third time?"

"I'm not going to give the bastard the opportunity."

Kelton indicated Harris's wound.

"I know," agreed Harris. "I can't do much like this. Any idea how long it's likely to be before I'm functional again?"

Kelton shrugged. "Hard to say. I'm not a doctor. I'd guess it'll be fairly painful for a few days; but if you manage to stay off it and give it some rest I'd think you should be back to normal in a week or so. Maybe in the meantime we could get you out of the area, into a motel or something, while we plan what we're going to do about Cotterell."

"Yes, at the very least I need to get out of this house and hole up somewhere safe for a while. But what do you mean: 'we'? Why are you involved?"

"I'm beginning to wonder if he doesn't aim to go after me next. Otherwise why has he been having me followed?"

"I guess that's a possibility. But have you ever done a job for him?"

"For Vincent Cotterell? No. But I did one a long time back for his brother Carl. Back when I was just getting started in the business Carl needed a DEA agent killed and I did it for him. Maybe his brother found out about it and he's trying to remove all associations between the Cotterell name and the deaths for which they've been responsible. I really don't know. Nor do I care. But I'm worried enough that I think it would be in both our interests to see an end to Vincent Cotterell, and the sooner the better."

"I'd be glad of the help, of course, especially in this condition. So what happens now?"

"We leave. There's no telling when more of his hired thugs might show up. You direct me, and I'll pack your things. My car is at the end of the track. I'll bring it here and we'll load you into it. We'll be gone in an hour. Another hour and we can be in another state. We'll find somewhere to hole up. And then we can decide exactly what we're going to do about Vincent Cotterell."

An hour later, a dark blue Oldsmobile pulled out of a half-hidden track a couple of miles outside the village of Torrington, Vermont. The vehicle, which contained a driver and a single passenger, turned on to the road and headed west.

Chapter 31
Wednesday, December 12
Outside Dixon Mills, Chautauqua County, Western New York

Three mornings later, in a Holiday Inn two hundred miles from Torrington, one of the two guests who had registered in the early hours of the morning two days earlier entered the lobby and picked up a copy of the local newspaper to read with his breakfast of danish, orange juice and tea.

Kelton had nearly finished eating when his eyes lit upon a short story in one of the inner sections of the newspaper. The headline read: *Fire guts Vt. residence — two bodies found.* Underneath, the story ran:

> *Torrington, VT – Fire ripped through an isolated house just outside this sleepy Vermont town in the small hours of the morning. The house was beyond saving by the time firefighters arrived at the scene, although they managed to stop the spread of the fire to the surrounding forest.*
>
> *The cause of the fire is unknown, although fire chief Charles Mason stated that he suspected arson. No bodies were found in the house, and the owner of the house, Mr. George Templeton, who appeared to be away at the time of the blaze, has yet to be found and notified of the loss.*

The story took a bizarre and gruesome twist with the discovery by firefighters of two bodies in the forest near the house. Firefighter First Class Randy Smith says that both bodies appeared to exhibit bullet wounds, possibly fatal. Police chief Paul Gibbons would not comment on Mr. Smith's statement, but did say that they hoped that Mr. Templeton would be located quickly as the fire had raised questions that the police desired to have answered as quickly as possible. He declined to elaborate further.

Kelton folded the newspaper and returned with it to Harris's room.

Harris was just coming out of the bathroom, walking with the aid of a cane.

"Look at this." Kelton opened the newspaper at the story and handed it to Harris.

Harris scanned the story and asked, "I wonder if Cotterell thinks that's the end of it?"

Kelton shook his head. "No. Look; it says that there were no bodies found in the house. Whether or not Cotterell's men found the bodies in the forest before they set the fire, you can be sure they'll have identified them by now. And notice there is no mention of the Range Rover Brezhnerov arrived in. Cotterell must have had it removed before the fire was set. No, he knows you're lying low somewhere. All he's done is destroy your base of operations.

"Do you feel up to spending another day in the car? I'm not comfortable here. We need to put more distance between us and Vermont. A man as rich as Cotterell probably has extremely sensitive ears."

"I'm not used to running, Kelton," objected Harris.

"Neither am I. But only a fool doesn't know when to make a tactical withdrawal. Don't worry, Cotterell's already dead. It's just that he doesn't know it yet, that's all."

———————

Reflexive Action

Vincent Cotterell had flown into Denver International late last night. The PlanetAir board meeting that had just started would occupy him for the rest of the working day. Once the meeting was over, Cotterell would escape the city, flying the short distance to Vail, where his luxury condominium and some of the finest skiing in the world awaited.

Only a couple of blocks from the Cotterell Building, Harris and Kelton were ensconced, as they had been for several days, in a downtown condominium rented out by the week to wealthy executives visiting the city on business.

Harris looked at his watch. It was shortly after 9 a.m. The board meeting should be under way by now. He looked across the room at Kelton, a query on his face. Kelton consulted his own watch, returned Harris's look, and nodded. Harris lifted the telephone and dialed a local number.

"Cotterell Industries." A pleasant female with the relatively featureless Colorado accent answered the telephone.

"I'd like to leave a message for Mr. Vincent Cotterell," said Harris.

"I'm sorry, sir, but Mr. Cotterell is not available through this number."

"My name is George Harris, and I kill people. This is not a joke." Harris paused a moment to let his words sink in. "You will inform Mr. Cotterell that I called, and that I expect to see him at 10 a.m. sharp, tomorrow morning. That's Friday, the twenty first. Tell him I will meet him in his office on the thirtieth floor where we met once before. And tell him I shall be unarmed. Did you get all that?"

"Sir, I don't think...."

"Just give him the message."

Harris put the phone down.

It was eleven o'clock when Kelton strode into the Cotterell Building. He was dressed immaculately and carried an attaché case, an expensive out-of-town attorney on his way to an important meeting. Without hesitating, he walked past the building directory and made straight for the elevators.

He stepped out on the seventh floor, looking quickly up and down the corridor. There was no one in sight. He walked purposefully toward the southwest corner of the building.

He stopped when he reached the corner. Embedded in the wall was a large, metal door with a push bar. A sign warned: "Fire Exit — Alarm will sound if door is opened." Nearby, in the ceiling, were a sprinkler and a smoke detector.

He looked around to make sure no one was watching, then, withdrawing an aerosol can from his case, he leant against the door. Instantly, a warning bell sounded. The bell continued to sound as he let the door close once more.

Raising his arm high in the air, he sprayed the contents of the aerosol can towards the ceiling. Seconds later a new, more urgent alarm joined the first. Unlike the door alarm, which sounded only locally and caused a light to flash in the control room in the basement, the fire alarm sounded loudly throughout the entire building. At the downtown fire station half a dozen blocks away, a bell rang and, a few seconds later, the building's address raced across a computer screen.

In the basement of the Cotterell Building, a security guard swore and angrily slammed down a copy of the latest best-selling paperback thriller. He glowered at a pair of panels on which red lights were shining. The seventh floor this time, and the security alarm had preceded the fire bell by a few seconds. It was the eighth time that something similar had happened this past week — always a different floor, sometimes one alarm, sometimes both. It was getting beyond a joke.

In a plush room on the thirtieth floor, the PlanetAir board of directors was listening to a presentation by the senior Vice President of the company, who was arguing that PlanetAir would be wise to make a hefty donation in support of a proposed new runway at the Denver airport.

The ringing of the fire alarm broke through the tedium of the presentation and a series of frowns and puzzled looks crossed the table. The directors began to get up as a secretary knocked inaudibly on the door and then walked into the room. As she had suspected, the directors — all of them male — were flustered and confused. She and her colleagues would have a good laugh about that over lunch today.

The secretary had to shout to make herself heard. "I'm terribly sorry. There's a problem with the fire alarm system in the building. This has happened at least once every day this week. I'm sure there's no fire, but we have to evacuate the building all the same."

Down on the seventh floor, a well-dressed professional stood waiting for an elevator as people sauntered out of their offices, grumbling.

"Come on, let's use the stairs. We'll be here all day if we wait for the elevator," said one as he looked at the slow-moving lights.

"Yeah. I guess you're not supposed to use the thing when there's a fire anyway," someone replied.

"If there is a fire, I guess that makes sense," the first said. "But this must be the sixth or seventh time this has happened this week. And each time I lose half an hour's work. I think I'll just take an early lunch today. I'm telling you, pretty soon the owners of the building are going to have a lawsuit slapped on them because of lost productivity. Maybe I'll even do it myself."

Someone else in the group laughed.

They passed out of earshot, and Kelton turned and followed them in the direction of the stairs.

On the thirtieth floor, Vincent Cotterell was shouting into a telephone, his temper ragged

"What do you mean, you can't find the damned fault? Whose responsibility is it anyway to fix the alarms? You just listen to me. I own this stinking building, and I'm ordering you to fix the problem once and for all. We're lucky we haven't been sued. And get the damned noise shut off."

He slammed the telephone down and glared at the directors. "Damned fools," he said to no one in particular.

The alarm stopped, and for a moment there was silence. Outside, on the streets, the first fire engines were arriving, their sirens blaring; but the noise was all but inaudible inside the well-engineered quiet of the modern office building.

It had been a long day for Vincent Cotterell, and he was tired.

PlanetAir was teetering on the brink of financial ruin. Of questionable viability when he had bought it, recent escalating oil prices had pushed the company to the brink of insolvency.

Most of the directors had arrived for today's meeting interested in only one item on the agenda: what company might be persuaded to buy the ailing airline? They had been astonished by Cotterell's dogmatic intransigence that the airline could be turned around.

Cotterell, of course, could hardly explain the real reason for his reluctance to sell the airline: if he lost control of the airline, he would also lost control of the lucrative newly-widened Golden Pipeline. So he had had to argue, from the shaky ground of financial statements and debatable projections, that the airline was merely in temporary crisis and that it would be foolhardy to try to sell it unless and until the situation continued to deteriorate.

In the final vote, a compromise motion had passed. The company would, for at least the next thirty days, attempt to remain solvent. In the meantime, although it would publicly be made clear that the airline was not for sale, advances would be made to possible suitors regarding the possibility of a merger or a buyout at some unspecified date in the future.

Thirty days, Cotterell thought, would be enough. In that time he should be able to orchestrate a scheme whereby PlanetAir would be swallowed by one of his other concerns. By this mechanism, he could remove those members of the board who had voted against him today and gain even tighter control of the airline. The thought occurred to him that perhaps it was time to liquidate a portion of his oil holdings, before the market dropped. With the profits he could begin to construct a new transportation conglomerate with Planet-Air at the center.

He walked into his office, part of his mind wondering whether such an idea was really viable, the rest of it thinking how glad he was that the day was over and he could begin to relax and look forward to Vail.

There was a small stack of papers on the desk. By itself, off to one side, was one other sheet. He crossed to the desk and read: "Urgent — Mr. Cotterell" handwritten across the top of the sheet in large red letters. He picked it up and read the message. Then he re-read it.

"Damn!" The expletive escaped his lips as he felt for the chair and sat down. He swore a second time.

What could Harris want? And, more to the point, how could he possibly be so stupid as to demand to meet Cotterell? It made no sense. Surely Harris could not believe that his threats to expose the link between Cotterell and the Gatwick bombing still carried any weight? Although Cotterell doubted that Harris understood *why* exposure was no longer a threat, surely he must understand that Cotterell was no longer intimidated by the possibility.

Was the man such a fool as to come voluntarily to the spider's den? No, Cotterell could not believe that. Harris was nobody's fool. There had to be something protecting Harris that Cotterell did not know about. But what could that be?

Harris was a dangerous man. Cotterell had sent a total of four men out against him now, including Victor Brezhnerov.

Only one of the four had returned; one was missing, and the most recent two had been found only last week, after he had angrily ordered Harris's house burned to the ground. It had been obvious that Harris had killed Brezhnerov and his driver and, further, had escaped the arson committed against his house. Subsequent enquiries in the area had now made it clear that Harris had gone to ground, and it was unlikely that he would be found until such time as he wanted to be found. So why was he now demanding a meeting with Cotterell?

And then there was that other matter, with the other killer, Kelton.

Kelton had dropped out of sight after ignominiously ridding himself of his tail more than a week before. Where was he now? He had not returned to his house in England. He had not been seen in any major airport. So what was he doing? Did he know that his daughter was dead? Had he put two and two together? Was it possible that somehow he had managed to link Cotterell to the death of his family? But if so, how? Was it even possible that there was not one but two professional assassins who had set their sights on Cotterell?

The sound of the fire alarm burst in on Cotterell's thoughts.

"Shit! Not again," he thought wearily. "What the hell is wrong with that thing?" He looked at his watch. Five fifteen. He picked up the phone. It was time to start firing people.

Kelton entered the building at a quarter to five. He was dressed as he had been earlier in the day, with the addition of a light overcoat draped over his arm. He nodded to the concierge as he rushed past.

Kelton made a point of looking at his watch, a man obviously late for a meeting. In his hand he swung an attaché case, larger than most, but not so large as to attract attention. He hurried to the elevators, and plunged into a waiting car. He stabbed at a button for a floor roughly half way up the building.

For the next half hour he made his way up and down, mixing with office workers leaving for the day, biding his time until the building would be empty enough.

It was nearly quarter past five when he decided that it was time. He was on the twenty fifth floor, and began to work his way towards the south-west corner of the building. As on every other floor, the corridor ended abruptly in a security door with a warning attached. He cast a quick look around, withdrew his can of chlorofluorocarbon and sprayed it at the nearby sprinkler and fire detector. As soon as the fire alarm sounded, he pushed the bar open and walked through the door.

The fire alarm sounded throughout the building, accompanied on the twenty-fifth floor by the sound of the security bell. Kelton listened through the clamor for the sound of security doors opening on other floors. He heard a few doors bang farther down the building, as the heavy doors were opened and then slammed closed behind people entering the concrete stairwell. There were no such sounds above him.

He leaned against the stairwell wall and waited. After about five minutes the alarms stopped. Then he walked quietly up the stairs until he reached the twenty-ninth floor.

The steps here, as on all the floors, were interrupted to create a small, bare landing. He put on his overcoat and sat down, leaning against the metal of the security door. Across from where he sat was a single bare 60-watt bulb glowing inside a painted metal cage. Next to the bulb, painted in red and black garishly against the off-white of the stairwell wall was the number "29" in digits a foot high.

He placed his case on the floor beside him and spun the combination locks. He removed his FN-Browning High Power and slipped it into his pocket. The only other contents of the case were a paperback novel, which he also removed, a small box of matches, and a large sealed plastic bag which almost filled the remainder of the case. The bag was filled with a glutinous red liquid; from one corner extended a short length of whitish, pliable string-like material. He extracted the box of matches and placed that in his pocket as well. There was a vague smell of hydrocarbon products in the air as he closed the case once more.

He crossed the tiny landing and sat directly underneath the light. He tried to make himself comfortable against the hard concrete of the floor and wall, without success; then, giving it up as a bad job, he opened the paperback and began to read.

Chapter 32
Friday, December 21
Denver, Colorado

George Harris entered the Cotterell Building at 9:50 a.m.

Under his arm he carried a small, softsided black case, which bulged slightly with the bulk of its contents. Outside, light snow was falling. The forecast was for a blizzard.

Once inside the building he removed his hat and brushed off into a trash can the thin covering of snow that had accumulated during the short walk from the rented downtown condominium. Carrying the hat in one hand and the case in the other, he walked through the lobby towards the elevators. He pressed a button and waited for a car to arrive.

There was a ping and, a few seconds later, doors opened and two people came out of an elevator. They barely noticed Harris as they passed, absorbed in their conversation. He entered the vacant car and pressed the button marked "29."

He went through the same procedure as on his last visit to the building, changing elevators on the twenty-ninth floor before arriving on the thirtieth. As he stepped out on the thirtieth floor, he called out, "I'm unarmed. No need to manhandle me."

The guards were ready and waiting, one on each side, ready to grab at him if he made any kind of a suspicious movement;

324

and, as last time, about ten feet to his left was a third guard standing against the opposite wall, a gun in his hands and pointed directly at Harris's torso.

Harris raised his hands slightly. "I have an appointment to see Mr. Cotterell at ten. I have this hat and some papers in here." He dangled the case in the air. "It's not locked."

"I'll take those," said the guard immediately to his left, taking the items from Harris's grasp.

The guard rifled the papers in the case while Harris was forced to lean against the wall. Hands patted him down, more carefully than last time but with no more success. Harris stepped away from the wall, the wire around his right ankle still undetected.

He was handed his case, and one of the guards told him to follow as he set off toward Cotterell's office.

They walked down the same corridors as before, but now Harris paid no attention to the doors as he passed; he merely kept his eyes on the guard ahead and followed dutifully in his footsteps.

They stopped outside Cotterell's office. The guard rapped on the door. "Mr. Harris is here to see you, sir. He seems to be clean."

"Send him in," came a voice, rendered distant by the intervening door. The guard opened the door and stood to one side, allowing Harris into the room. Then he withdrew, closing the door and leaving Harris and Cotterell alone.

The man behind the desk did not rise, nor did he smile. Harris found it difficult to see Cotterell's face clearly; the entire wall which he was facing was white, the snow falling outside making the window almost shine with its brightness. By contrast, the man's face was dark, almost a silhouette against the winter storm gathering outside.

"Take a seat, Mr. Harris," said Cotterell, indicating the chair on the opposite side of the desk, in front of Harris.

"Thank you."

"It's a cold morning, Mr. Harris. Would you like some coffee?" asked Cotterell, a slight smile playing around his face.

"Yes, thank you."

Cotterell leaned forward and pressed a button on an intercom on the desk. "Please send in some coffee for Mr. Harris."

Cotterell turned slightly to look out the window, so that Harris saw him almost in profile. "Looks like a real storm coming in."

"So I heard on the weather forecast this morning. There's supposed to be six inches by the end of the day."

"I wouldn't be surprised if there was rather more than that," said Cotterell. "Ah, here's the coffee."

A man walked into the room with a tray. He left it on the desk and then left, without saying a word.

Harris helped himself to the coffee, aware that Cotterell was watching him closely. He drank slowly. He was not going to be the first to speak.

He was nearly halfway through the coffee when Cotterell could not contain himself any longer.

"What do you want, Mr. Harris? By my count, you are responsible for the death of at least three of my employees, including someone whom I regard almost as a friend. Yet you have the temerity to send me a threatening message and demand a meeting. Do you take me for a fool, Mr. Harris?"

Harris remained silent and looked thoughtful, as if he were pondering the question. Cotterell's patience snapped. His hand, which had been hidden under the desk since Harris had entered the room, now appeared. In it was a pistol; he pointed it at Harris.

"Let's stop screwing around," said Cotterell, his taut anger clearly audible in his voice. "Unless you give me a good reason not to do so in the next five seconds, I'm going to kill you."

Harris appeared unperturbed. He slowly replaced the coffee cup on the tray, then leaned back in his chair. "Here, in your office?" he asked.

"You have two seconds," said Cotterell.

"It would be a grave mistake to kill me," said Harris, looking Cotterell in the eye.

Cotterell's hand tensed on the pistol, but he did not pull the trigger.

"Why?" he asked.

"As I told you before, if I'm killed, a message detailing your connection to the Gatwick bombing will be sent to the FBI. You may be rich, Cotterell, but even you can't buy the FBI."

Cotterell smiled, and his hold on the gun relaxed. "Your naïveté astonishes me, Mr. Harris. One does not try to buy the FBI. As my brother demonstrated on two occasions, it is enough simply to buy the jury.

"But tell me about this message. I trust that it is in the hands of someone whom you can trust?"

"Yes." Harris did not elaborate.

Wordlessly, Cotterell opened a drawer and withdrew a folder. He opened the folder, and flicked through the exposed sheets of paper with his left hand, his right hand still holding the gun. He found what he was looking for.

"Ah, yes, here we are," said Cotterell. "You prefer for communication between yourself and clients such as myself to be made through computer electronic mail; a very advanced method of communication, and I applaud you for your use of the technology. Unfortunately, however, like all technologies, it is not without its flaws."

A frown flitted briefly across Harris's face. Cotterell was too calm, too much in charge. He had something up his sleeve. But what? To hide his anxiety, he drained his coffee.

"What exactly do you mean?"

"According to my notes here, your account is tied to a computer in Switzerland; an especially secure computer run by a company that prides itself on providing unbreakable security and privacy for its account holders."

"Yes, the Secure Computing Corporation."

"Exactly so. It seems that you sent a message from your account to the manager approximately one month ago giving full details of our agreement, along with instructions that the information was to be recorded and held secure until such time as your account should become delinquent, at which time the file was to be sent immediately to the FBI."

Harris sat forward, too quickly. If there had been any coffee left in the cup, it would have spilt. He set it down. "I don't understand. How did you...?" As he spoke, his hand reflexively ran over his right ankle, feeling the comfort of the hidden length of lethal wire. Five seconds, that was all he needed: five seconds to expose the garotte and unwrap it from his ankle.

"How did I persuade the management of the Secure Computing Corporation let me have access to your file? Simple, Mr. Harris: I *own* the Secure Computing Corporation. Within hours of your instructions being sent, the file in question was printed and then deleted."

Cotterell closed the folder in front of him with a flourish. "The only extant copy is here," — he tapped the folder, then leaned forward and eyed Harris carefully — "so, you see, there really is no reason for me not to finish this here and now. I have nothing to fear from you at all. As soon as you are dead, I shall burn this file. Do you have any last words?"

"I do. Just one word."

Cotterell raised an interrogative eyebrow.

"Kelton."

There was a long silence, at the end of which Harris rose from the chair and asked, "May I use your rest room?"

"What do you mean: Kelton?"

"You may have rendered me no threat to you, but the bigger threat from Kelton still remains. And if you kill me you will be signing your own death warrant, because I'm the only man who can stop him. Now, may I use your rest room?" Harris gestured to his left, in the direction of the door to the bathroom.

Cotterell was trying to make sense of what Harris had said. What did Harris know about Kelton? And what did he mean when he said that he was the only person who could stop him from killing Cotterell? "What are you talking about?"

"The restroom, please?"

Cotterell smiled. "Of course. But only after you've removed the wire from your ankle. I am not the fool you take me for, Mr. Harris. Unfortunately for you, I'm afraid it's a lesson learned too late." He pointed the gun steadily at Harris. "Now," he snapped. "The wire. Slowly, if you please."

Harris bent down and peeled down his sock. Underneath, a length of wire was wrapped three times around his ankle, the ends attached to loops of flexible plastic large enough for him to put his wrists through. He slowly unwrapped the weapon.

"Drop it on the desk, if you please."

He dropped the garotte, hatred at Cotterell flaring in his eyes, then turned and stalked away toward the bathroom.

Harris closed the door behind him and urinated into the toilet. He flushed it and walked quickly out through the door opposite the one through which he had entered the bathroom.

The bedroom was just as he had described it during the planning sessions with Kelton. There was the door. And, he saw with relief, directly over the foot of the bed, was the one thing he had not been sure about: a sprinkler head.

He crossed the room in half a dozen strides and leaned against the security door. An alarm not far away began to ring. He leant against the partway-open door just long enough to see a hand appear from the other side of the door and grab it. Then he turned and sprinted back the way he had come.

He ran through the bathroom and slowed to a walk as he returned to Cotterell's office. Not more than five seconds had passed since the alarm had begun to ring.

As he appeared in the doorway a more urgent sound, the fire alarm bell, joined the security bell. Cotterell was standing beside the desk, the pistol one hand and Harris's garotte in the other. He turned and looked worriedly at the bathroom door.

329

It had evidently occurred to him that through that door lay a possible escape route for George Harris. His countenance cleared visibly when he saw Harris.

"What's that noise? Is there a fire?" asked Harris.

"No, come back here and sit down," said Cotterell, waving his gun and pocketing the wire. "It's only a malfunction with the alarm system; it's been happening several times a day. Forget it."

While Harris sat down, Cotterell dialed the telephone, thrusting violently at the digits. He barked into the instrument, "This is Vincent Cotterell. Switch that damned noise off. And if it happens one more time while I'm in the building, I'll fire the whole damn lot of you." He slammed the phone down so hard that Harris wondered if it would ever work again.

Cotterell remained standing, counting under his breath until the noise ceased. Then he sat down in his seat, paused for a moment to gather his wits, and looked once more across the desk at Harris.

"Now, what exactly were you saying about someone called Kelton? I'm not sure I recognize the name."

Kelton was stiff, sore and tired. It had been a long night, propped against a hard metal door, sitting on cold, equally hard, concrete, with the glare of an unshaded light on him all night.

But at last it was morning. He tried to drum up some sort of interest in the paperback thriller, but it contained too many inaccuracies and wild impossibilities to make a good read. He alternated between reading and trying to doze, until finally his watch told him it was ten o'clock. Time to move.

Stiffly, he arose and gathered his belongings. Then he climbed the single flight of stairs until he was standing in front of the security door on the top floor of the building, the red and black "30" painted on the wall behind him.

He placed his case on the floor beside him. The pistol he held in one hand, leaving the other free. He checked that the aerosol can, uncapped, was easily accessible in one pocket and the matches were in the other. He stretched himself several times to try to help his circulation. It was cold out here, and he would have to move quickly when his time came.

He waited, but not for long. With no warning, the door in front of him was suddenly thrust open a distance of about a foot. Somewhere in the distance on the far side of the door, an alarm bell began to ring. He grabbed the door. Immediately, whoever had opened it let go: he could feel the force of the spring as the door tried to close itself. He held on firmly, and then, grabbing the case, he quickly entered the room. The door closed behind him.

He stood still for a moment, getting his bearings.

He was in a bedroom. There was only one other entrance to the room, a door in the wall opposite that was wide open and through which he could see Harris's back as he rushed into the room beyond. Glancing up at the ceiling, he smiled at the sight of the sprinkler unit.

He tossed the case and pistol on the bed. Then, climbing on to the bed, he withdrew the can of chlorofluorocarbon and sprayed it directly into the fire detector. Moments later, the fire alarm sounded.

He jumped down to the floor, retrieved his pistol, and opened the attaché case.

Kelton took the bag filled with red jelly from the case and, walking almost on tiptoe, he moved across the bedroom and through the bathroom until his head was only inches from the narrow opening into the room beyond left by the almost-closed door. Silently, he placed the bag and the matches on the ground. Crouching, he pressed his left hand against the door, ready to throw it open in an instant. In his right hand he still held his pistol; he flexed his fingers, waiting for the moment.

The sound of the alarm suddenly ceased; in the silence that followed, it was easy to overhear the conversation in the room beyond.

Harris was speaking. "Don't play games with me. We both know who Kelton is, and unless you're a much greater fool than I take you for, you know he's trying to kill you."

In the office, Cotterell frowned, wondering how much Harris knew and, more importantly, how he had come to know it. Could Harris be bluffing? Perhaps. But he obviously knew *something*.

He continued playing dumb. "Kelton? Kelton? Is the name supposed to mean something? I really don't think I recognize it."

"That's not what I hear. According to my information, you were having him followed until he gave your man the slip."

How the hell had Harris found that out?

Cotterell tried to brazen it out. "Mr. Harris, a lot of things go on in this organization under my name. Some of them I know about and some I don't. Now, who exactly is this Mr. Kelton?"

"He kills people for a living, Mr. Cotterell."

"And you're saying he wants to kill me?" Cotterell managed a good facsimile of a laugh. "If anything, I would have thought you were a more likely target."

Harris frowned, puzzled at the odd statement. "Huh? How do you arrive at that conclusion?"

On the other side of the bathroom door, Kelton had heard enough. Another few moments and Cotterell would tell the whole story. Harris would realize that he had been responsible for the death of Kelton's family. Another second after that and all the pieces of the puzzle would fall into place in Harris's mind. Not that Kelton couldn't just open the door and kill them both, but Harris was for later. He had to see Harris's face when Harris knew he was going to die.

He sprang forward.

A sudden movement caught Cotterell's eye. Involuntarily, he turned, just in time to see a figure raising a pistol in a two-handed grip. As Cotterell watched, immobile with surprise, the alignment of the pistol shifted slightly, until he was looking directly down the length of the barrel. It was the last thing he saw. The head that housed the brain of Vincent Cotterell ceased to be a complete whole, its top ripped off by a chunk of speeding lead.

Kelton waited no more than a fraction of a second after firing the shot; just long to enough to be sure that no second shot was needed.

He bent down, picked up the bag and matches and tossed them to Harris, who was now standing by the chair in which he had been seated just a moment before. Harris caught them and placed the bag on the desk, pulling the string that extended from one corner towards him. Then he struck one of the matches. The match sputtered into flame; Harris applied it to the string.

The fuse caught and began to hiss. He looked at it for perhaps a second to make sure that it had taken, then shouted, "OK, let's go."

Kelton turned and began to run back into the bathroom, closely followed by Harris. The two rushed through the bedroom and Kelton, in the lead, leaned against the fire door. Without stopping, they both hurried through. The security alarm began to ring in the distance. They began to descend the concrete steps.

The door to Cotterell's office was thrown open as a security guard rushed in, his gun unholstered. He was halfway to the desk when he halted abruptly, aghast at the sight of the body of his former employer stretched out on the floor on his back, head incomplete and scattered about the floor in pieces, exactly as it he had seen it on the security monitor.

The guard's eyes alighted on the desk in the center of the room and focused on the red object lying in the middle of the desk. The white string had turned dark along its entire length.

The flame passed through the wall of the bag and came in contact with the soft jelly-like substance inside.

The explosion wracked the room, and flaming jelly spewed out in all directions. The floor buckled, and the first pieces of flaming, white hot jelly came into contact with the Styrofoam acoustic tiles of the ceiling of the floor below.

A moment later the fire alarm sounded and the sprinkler system came into operation. But as water spewed out on to the flames that were beginning to take hold, in places it touched the flaming jelly. Immediately, dark black smoke spewed forth from these places, small pieces of burning jelly spitting out over enormous distances, landing on as-yet unlit surfaces that now burst into flame and fueled the conflagration.

Kelton and Harris were among the first to leave the building, even though they had to descend thirty flights of stairs: almost no one else in the building had yet realized that this time the alarms were for real; after so many false alarms, no one gave a moment's thought to the possibility that a fire was actually burning out of control.

The two men rushed out the building and on to the sidewalk, part of a small but rapidly growing crowd of people leaving the building. There was, as yet, no sign of the fire department; but the smoke was now visible from the street, even through the thickly falling snow. The two men made their way to the edge of the crowd and slipped around a corner.

They were cold. Kelton's thin overcoat was no protection against a Denver snowstorm, and Harris's coat was now no more than charred remains on the thirtieth floor of the building behind them. Harris hailed a cab and ordered the driver to take them to the Sixteenth Street downtown mall. Less than ten minutes later, the two men were once more out on the streets, this time insulated against the increasingly miserable cold by expensive overcoats.

The two walked side by side, hands in pockets, in the direction of the condominium. As they approached it, they heard the sound of sirens. Twice they stopped and watched as, first a fire engine, then an ambulance, raced past with lights flashing and sirens blaring. The snow, falling even harder now, hid both the building and the billowing clouds of black smoke entirely from their view.

Back at the condominium, Kelton turned on the radio to the local all-news station. Harris turned on the television with the volume turned down. While they waited for the news to break, Kelton brewed a pot of coffee.

The first news came fifteen minutes later. Across the bottom of the television screen scrolled a banner that announced: "A large fire has taken hold in a downtown Denver building. Detailed news to follow at 11:30." The two men smiled at one another.

Kelton went to the telephone, and returned a couple of minutes later.

"Bad news, I'm afraid. The airport is still open, but less than ten percent of flights are leaving. They say that the situation will only get worse. They expect they'll have to close down completely within the hour."

"Damn! Do they have any idea when it will reopen?"

"They didn't say. But the weather is supposed to stay like this for at least the next twenty-four hours. I guess we're stuck here at least until late tomorrow."

"Great. Just great." Harris paused for a moment, giving him time to think. "I don't suppose it will make any difference. It would have been nice to split up and get clean away today. But, on the other hand, this way we get a chance to celebrate."

"Good idea," agreed Kelton. "I'll get the phone book and we'll have dinner at the best restaurant in town. And there's another good thing about being stuck here: this way we can easily keep track of the local news reports." He disappeared in search of the phone book, and Harris returned his attention to the TV screen.

He had not seen the look on Kelton's face.

It was five minutes to midnight.

The two assassins had celebrated at a swank restaurant four blocks from the condominium, not daring to venture farther afield because of the treacherous weather. Having demolished one bottle of champagne during the meal, they had bought a second bottle before leaving the restaurant, and had halted briefly at an all-night liquor store before concluding their unsteady journey back to the condominium.

Now they sat in the condominium, Harris on the couch, Kelton in the armchair, finishing the second bottle of champagne. They were both relaxed, talking about their respective careers, each assuring the other that he was the best there had ever been. In the background, light music played on the radio.

"Your glass is empty," observed Kelton, "and that was the last of the champagne. Let me go mix something up; I'll be back in a couple of minutes."

Harris, humming along with the tune playing on the radio and waving his empty glass in his right hand as if it were a conductor's baton, smiled vaguely and nodded his head, grunting his assent to this excellent suggestion.

Kelton went past Harris into the kitchen, and halted in front of the sink. The time had come. While Harris had been drinking all evening, Kelton had almost stopped drinking after the first two glasses of champagne. The first two glasses already in him, Harris had not noticed and had assumed all evening that Kelton was in a similar happy, heady mood to his own.

Kelton ran cold water into the plugged sink, and threw two full trays of ice cubes into the water. He thrust his face into the water and held it there for fifteen ice-cold seconds. When he surfaced, his head felt clear. He toweled his face dry. He was ready.

He left the kitchen, and silently climbed the stairs to the bedrooms. He returned half a minute later, a gun in his hand, a silencer screwed on the end of the barrel. He slowly walked down the stairs and, keeping the gun hidden from

Harris's view, walked across the room to the stereo cabinet, bent down, and abruptly switched off the music.

Kelton straightened himself. Harris was immobile, his hand at the end of a conductor's swing, clutching his empty glass, a surprised look on his face.

Kelton brought the pistol into view and, keeping it carefully aimed at Harris, sat down in the armchair that he had previously occupied. As he did so, Harris's face ran through a series of expressions in almost comical sequence: intoxicated happiness, surprise, query, surprise, query, realization, shock and, finally, query again.

"Huh? What are you doing?" Harris finally asked.

"It's time we talked, Mr. Harris," said Kelton, his tone as icy as the water into which he had so recently plunged his face.

"Huh? What about? I don't get it...."

"No, you never did, did you? You never understood what any of this was about, did you? Tell me, didn't you ever wonder about Catherine and Elizabeth Kent? Why did Cotterell really want them dead? Didn't you ever stop to ask yourself that question? Surely you didn't believe that ridiculous story about blackmail?"

Harris was confused, his mind working slowly and uncertainly. He tried to gather his thoughts. When he spoke, it was slowly, as he concentrated on getting his tongue around the words.

"I don't know why Cotterell wanted them dead. It always seemed strange to me that he was willing to pay so much to get rid of two people no one had ever heard of. I even broke into their house once, but Brezhnerov stopped me before I could do much searching. My best guess was that the man in the house, Paul Kent, I think he was called, anyway, I assumed he must have crossed Cotterell at some time and this was Cotterell's revenge for whatever Kent had done. But I don't understand. Why are you pointing that gun at me?"

Kelton ignored the question. "You see," he said, "you *can* work things out if you try. Now, let's see how much more you can put together. There really isn't much to it, and you have all the pieces. Think back to earlier today, to just before I killed Cotterell. What was the last thing he said to you? Do you remember?"

"I remember. It was something about how you wanted to kill me as much as he did. Even at the time it didn't make sense, but everything happened too quickly, and I'd forgotten it till now. But why? What have I ever done to you?"

"Just one more question. How did Cotterell become head of the family business?"

"Everyone knows that. His brother was killed by a sniper...." Harris's voice trailed off. The pieces had suddenly tumbled into place.

Kelton said, "You see, it wasn't so hard, was it?"

Harris was mute.

"I retired five years ago because I found someone with whom I wanted to spend the rest of my life. I created a new identity for myself and we were married. We had a child, a girl...."

Kelton's hand began to tremble as he spoke. Seeing the movement of Kelton's hand, Harris half rose out of his chair, twisting sharply to one side as he moved.

The sound of the muffled shot was buried beneath Harris's scream: "No!"

The shot was not clean. Kelton had been aiming for Harris's head, but the bullet struck his clavicle, creating a hole from which blood gushed. Harris's shout became a strangled cry and then a dull moan as he slipped towards the floor, a sudden sharp pain filling his consciousness as the lifeblood gushed out of him on to the carpet.

Kelton stood up and looked down at Harris, and aimed the gun for the final shot. Then he shook his head, and tossed the gun aside. Now that Harris was dying, Kelton could keep Paul Kent at bay no longer.

A tear rolled down a cheek. "Catherine and Elizabeth," he said, his voice breaking. "I love you. Please forgive me. I'm sorry. I'm so sorry. If only...."

Harris saw the gun lying on the floor. He tried to stretch for it, but it was too far away. A mist descended, and the gun receded into the distance. He knew only that he was lying on the floor, looking up at the man who had shot him.

The man buried his face in his hand with a moan. He was saying something, but the words were indistinct, and in any case nothing he could say was important any more. The man seemed to be somehow moving further away, becoming less important with each passing moment. A wave of intense fatigue washed over Harris. He closed his eyes.

For a while, the only sound in the room came from Paul Kent's sobs. When he finally took his hands away from his face and looked down, George Harris was dead.

Kent turned away, revolted by the sight of the man responsible for the death of his wife and child. He took his coat from the closet and draped it over his arm.

Then he crossed to the telephone and dialed a transatlantic number.

Five thousand miles away, Patricia Worthington, just finishing her breakfast, wondered who could be calling so early on a Saturday morning. She swallowed the last of her toast and picked up the phone.

A man's voice said, "Good morning, Dr. Worthington."

"Mr. Kent? Is that you?"

She had heard nothing from him since the day she had told him that Elizabeth was dead. Several times since then she had wondered what had become of him. She had even gone by the Kent house, but it was locked up and it was obvious that no one was living there. Mr. Kent had not even put in an appearance at Elizabeth's brief, hospital-arranged funeral. Why was he calling her now, after nearly two weeks of silence?

A knot tightened in her stomach as an impossible idea came to her. Was he still in America? The last newspapers articles on the Gatwick bombing had speculated that it might have been the work of an American. No. It couldn't be.

"Dr. Worthington, you once told me that you hoped that the person responsible for what happened at Gatwick would be caught and killed."

The knot tightened further. Perhaps it wasn't so impossible.

"Two people were responsible. I wanted to tell you that both of them have been found, and both are now dead. Thank you for everything you did. We will never meet again."

The line went dead. Slowly, a smile creased her face.

Stopping only to put on his coat, Paul Kent walked out of the condominium and into the night.

Colophon

The main body of the text of this book was typeset with the plain TEX digital typesetting system created by Donald Knuth. The typefaces used are from the Latin Modern family, set at 12/13·5. The paper stock used for the body of the book and for the cover depends on the particular printer that created the book you are holding.

The text editors VEDIT PLUS and Emacs were used to create the original text.

The cover was created with the Scribus desktop publishing system, in conjunction with the POV-Ray and Inkscape programs.

Computer processing for this edition of *Reflexive Action* was performed on an AMD 64-bit dual-core system running the Mandriva 2006 64-bit distribution of the GNU/Linux operating system.